FIREWALL

ANDREW WATTS

FIREWALL

Severn River Publishing
www.SevernRiverBooks.com

ISBN: 978-1-64875-111-0 (Paperback)
ISBN: 978-1-64875-112-7 (Hardback)
ISBN: 979-8-50715-176-9 (Hardback)

ALSO BY ANDREW WATTS

The Firewall Spies

Firewall

Agent of Influence

A Future Spy

Tournament of Shadows

The War Planners Series

The War Planners

The War Stage

Pawns of the Pacific

The Elephant Game

Overwhelming Force

Global Strike

Max Fend Series

Glidepath

The Oshkosh Connection

Air Race

To find out more about Andrew Watts and his books, visit

severnriverbooks.com/authors/andrew-watts

PART I

"Artificial intelligence is the future, not only for Russia but for all humankind . . . Whoever becomes the leader in this sphere will become the ruler of the world."

– Vladimir Putin, 2017

1

Seattle, Washington

Colt McShane sat at the rear of the Westin conference hall, looking at his phone. "Damn. Cell signal here sucks."

His coworker looked at him. "Yeah, well, this is the biggest tech conference in North America. Between all the smart-watches and tablets and phones and computers, the network juice is getting sucked out of the air."

"You know I'm just a money guy, but I don't think that's how it works. Technically inaccurate description aside, however, I think you're right," said Colt. His friend chuckled. Both worked for a New York investment bank. They were at the conference to evaluate companies in attendance, network with clients, and size up potential new investments.

But Colt had an additional mission, one his colleague knew nothing about.

Colt said, "Hey, I think I'm going to skip this next one. I might try to catch a few innings of Yankees/Red Sox at the hotel bar. Can you let me know if I miss anything?"

"You're going to miss Jeff Kim? He's the main event. Just

connect your phone to the conference WIFI and check the score."

"No way. One of these techies will have my credit card and social media password inside of five minutes."

"You're paranoid."

"I'm cautious."

"People here aren't hackers. They're engineers and marketing nerds."

A woman in the row ahead of them turned at the comment.

"Sorry. Not you." Colt's coworker held up his hands. He turned back to Colt, lowering his voice. "Stay for Jeff Kim. He's the main event. Besides, they're part of our portfolio." Colt's company was handling the next fundraising round for Pax AI, Jeff Kim's company.

The lights in the conference hall dimmed and the crowd noise fell to a hush. Colt checked his watch and whispered, "All right, I'll stay for a few minutes."

In truth, Colt's cell signal was good enough to check the score, and he was only slightly paranoid about the WIFI being used as a medium to hack into his phone. The CIA had assured him that with the software they had installed, he was protected against such attacks.

But he didn't want to be late for the meeting with his agent.

Colt watched as the CEO of the hottest artificial intelligence company in the world walked onto the stage. The audience of several thousand clapped approval, and Jeff Kim gave a wave. He was in his mid-thirties, Korean-American, and notoriously introverted. He rarely conducted interviews, but that had been changing lately. His company was about to get a jolt of funding and begin a rapid expansion. CEOs like him had to go on media tours like politicians, jazzing everyone up before taking their money.

The event host began speaking. "Ladies and gentlemen, our next guest really needs no introduction. In my preparation for this interview, I found the phrases most often used to describe him are 'genius,' 'revolutionary,' and 'master of innovation.' Last year he was shortlisted for *Time* magazine's man of the year. He's often compared to Steve Jobs, Elon Musk, and even Albert Einstein. Jeff Kim, welcome." The audience clapped again.

The interview went on for twenty minutes. It was standard fare. Background. Leadership lessons.

There was one unexpected moment when a protester ran into the auditorium, shouting and holding up signs. "AI is our destiny! Trinity is the truth! Jeff Kim, release your code! The end is coming!"

The man was tackled by security and dragged into the hallway. People's shock at the disruption turned into snickering after the man was subdued. The host on stage shook his head and apologized before continuing.

The rest of the interview went smoothly. Questions about what the future might look like as AI became more sophisticated. Jeff Kim dropping hints at new breakthroughs. The audience ate it up, and the session ended with a standing ovation and thunderous applause that filled the convention hall. Colt remained seated, pulling out the phone that had just buzzed in his pocket. His coworker looked down at him, Colt's face lit by the screen.

"I thought you weren't getting a signal?"

"Must have squeaked through." Colt shrugged. "Hey, I got to run. I'll try to catch you later."

Colt could still hear the clapping as he pushed through

the swinging door in the back of the room. He walked at a brisk pace, picking up his phone to double-check the message.

Marisha Stepanova, senior lieutenant of the Russian Foreign Intelligence Service (SVR), had just arrived at his hotel.

2

Outside the conference hall, Colt passed a group of police officers questioning the handcuffed protester who had burst into the auditorium. He rode the escalator down to the first floor of the Seattle Westin, scanning the vast hotel bar area. Comfortable couches and spacious lounge chairs under thirty-foot ceilings. Waiters in suits carrying expensive cocktails and appetizers. Patrons happy to wind down after a busy day of conference lectures and business meetings. In the center of the room stood a horseshoe-shaped bar with brightly backlit liquor shelves. A handful of TVs, each tuned to a different sporting event.

Most of the people sipping drinks were conference attendees. Engineers, marketers, and salesmen hawking their newest product or service. Some were bloggers or industry journalists trying to get the scoop on the Next Big Thing. Many at the bar were in town to do business with one of the city's thriving corporations. Creative ad agencies, suppliers, and manufacturers came to Seattle daily from around the world. Tech and commerce had transformed the city seemingly overnight.

But scattered among the jungle of programmers and branding experts, AI engineers and venture capitalists, was an altogether different species.

The spy.

Colt knew that within this room, more than a few intelligence officers from around the world were present. They would be posing as other jungle animals. Salesmen or journalists or marketers or . . . *investment bankers*. Any cover legend that could help them blend into the wilderness of tech and allow them to creep up on unsuspecting prey.

Colt sat down at the bar, scanning the room for anything or anyone out of place. He searched for his agent's face among the crowd, knowing she shouldn't be here but checking just to be sure. This meeting was too important, the conference too well-attended, to risk being seen together.

As one of the CIA's elite non-official cover operatives, Colt McShane had been ushered away from any official US government business as soon as he finished his training at The Farm a decade earlier. Since then, Colt had been operating almost completely alone. Reporting only to his CIA handler, Ed Wilcox, now the agency's station chief in Vancouver.

Everyone else who had graduated from Colt's CIA training class had gone on to become operations officers in the Clandestine Service. These men and women lived and worked in US embassies and consulates overseas. They held official government covers like Agricultural Advisor or Economic Attaché. The blander the better. If they got caught spying, countries like Russia or China would usually expel them back to the United States, who would repay the favor by expelling a proportionate number of "diplomats." The rules of the game were clear, and in a way, gentlemanly.

But non-official cover operatives like Colt had no such protections.

If he was identified by a foreign intelligence service, there were no rules. So it was crucially important he not get caught. His cover had to be airtight, and he had spent years working in the world of corporate finance, carefully cultivating a cover legend with minimal agency contact, choosing the time, location, and manner of his agent debriefs with painstaking attention to detail. Meetings like tonight were the test to how well that cover held.

Colt motioned to the bartender, who nodded in his direction.

"What can I get you?"

"Actually, my wife was here earlier and put my tab on the wrong room number. Redhead. White coat. She said she ordered a glass of the Malbec."

"Sure, she was just here a few minutes ago."

"She asked me to double-check that it was on the right room; would you mind?"

The bartender walked over to the stack of bills and flipped through the first few until he found the right one.

"Here you go."

Colt checked the room number and memorized it. He also saw the faint underline below it, his agent's signal that she was not under duress. The old-fashioned technique served as a double verification outside their normal means of communication.

"Okay. That's the right room. Sorry about that." Colt slipped the man a tip and headed toward the elevator.

Three minutes later, he was looking out his room's panoramic window on the sixteenth floor. The hotel was constructed of two identical towers, positioned about one hundred yards from each other. From his vantage point, Colt could see into the rooms in the opposite tower. It was getting dark, and the contrast made it possible to make out individual details.

He withdrew a magnifying camera lens from his travel bag and attached it to his phone, which he had set up on a small tripod near the front of his desk. Then he removed a grease pencil and ruler, making a series of markings directly in front of him on the glass window. He silently counted up from the ground floor and over until he had marked the room number he had memorized at the bar. Colt positioned the camera and set up the encrypted chat on his computer.

On his phone screen, the zoomed-in image of Marisha Stepanova appeared. Marisha, one of the CIA's most valuable assets inside Russian intelligence, had been recruited several years ago when she was a junior SVR officer stationed in Vancouver. Wilcox and the CIA quickly determined they needed a special way to collect information from her on a regular basis while protecting her from Russian counterintelligence. Colt, with his non-official cover, had been made her handler.

Now Marisha sat at her own desk, looking out her window into the dark chasm between their two hotel towers. As she began typing, Colt noticed two small bottles of wine resting on her desk, one of them empty. Hitting the minibar early tonight. She liked to drink. He would need to monitor that.

Marisha: Good evening.

Colt typed on his laptop, which had been modified by CIA technical security experts to protect against electronic surveillance.

Colt: Good to speak with you.

Marisha: Same.

On the video, Colt saw Marisha peering at his silhouette in the hotel tower across from her.

Marisha: Five.

Five was her challenge. As was their custom, Colt

subtracted three from her challenge number, then flashed his desk light on and off twice. This signaled that everything was copacetic on his end. He had video.

Marisha didn't like Colt using his cellphone to view her, seeing it as a security risk. But over time, he had convinced her it was actually the opposite. Another level of verification that she was the source of communication, and not under duress. The video was not recorded, to ensure no one in the US government other than Colt would know her true identity. To those who held a high enough security clearance to read Colt's intelligence reports, Marisha was known only by the cryptonym SANDSTONE.

In some locales, Colt was able to meet with his Russian agent in person. But high-risk areas such as this Seattle tech conference were brimming with foreign intelligence agents and surveillance teams.

Their comms procedure in high-risk areas was to use an encrypted text messaging app. The history of their texts would be deleted instantly from the app and their phones, and the encryption was so good even the NSA had trouble penetrating it. Theoretically, this technique allowed both parties to plausibly deny taking part in the meeting and hide the evidence. In reality, it wasn't that simple. There were many ways they could be caught. But every layer of concealment helped. And it kept them from being seen together, which would be the end of both of their careers . . . and maybe more.

During these debriefs, Colt bombarded her with questions pre-written by Langley analysts, every answer transmitting back to Langley in real time via encrypted satellite communication. He tried not to think about whether any foreign intelligence services had cracked this encryption, or the social media app that the NSA swore by. You could drive yourself crazy worrying about all the technological obstacles to spy craft these days.

They communicated every few months, and only in specific time windows. It wasn't good to rely on the encrypted apps for daily communication. Counterintelligence could catch you that way. At least once per year, Colt made sure they met in person, where he would order room service and wine and dine her. That was the way he liked to meet with his agents. Keep them happy. Keep them talking.

Marisha's role as an SVR officer stationed in the Russian consulate in Houston, Texas, came with elevated risk. She—along with a handful of other Russian intelligence officers in Houston—were assigned to run agents in the North American tech hubs. Marisha was an incredibly valuable agent for the CIA, a treasure trove of information. The Russians had teams from SVR counterintelligence—Line KR—whose sole job it was to uncover moles like her. It was a treacherous game.

Colt typed away, his eyes darting to his phone screen so he could see her face, gauging her mental and emotional state of mind as she typed her responses. Marisha informed him of the updated names of every Russian diplomat, military attaché, and intelligence officer stationed in the Houston consulate with her. She provided Colt with details on their latest assignments, their comings and goings in the US, drinking habits, gambling habits, who was sleeping with whom, and who wanted to be sleeping with someone else. Of special interest were the operational activities of her SVR superior, a man by the name of Petrov. He was the SVR's senior man in the Houston consulate, and head of all Russian economic espionage operations in North America. Petrov had been spending a lot of time in West Coast cities lately—San Francisco, San Diego, Seattle, and Vancouver. But Marisha didn't know what he was working on.

Colt: Is it normal for him to keep operational details to himself?

Marisha: No. Normally we brief everything together.

Colt: When did this pattern begin?

Marisha: A few weeks ago. He brings one of his low-level men with him. Agapov. A man who is more for security. Or for wet work, if there is any.

Colt: I understand. What do you think they are doing?

Marisha: I don't know. I am sorry.

Colt: It's okay. Thank you, this is helpful.

Colt didn't like the sound of Petrov keeping information from SANDSTONE. It was possible that he was recruiting new agents and would assign them to subordinate SVR officers one at a time. But it could also be something else . . .

Colt: Do you think he is behaving this way because he suspects something with you?

He watched the video of Marisha. She paused, taking a breath before typing her response.

Marisha: I don't think so. But we must watch this and be careful.

Colt updated her on communications procedures for their next meeting. He also gave her a refresher on extraction procedures should they need to make her disappear from her Russian friends forever. He asked a series of questions about contact with possible counterintelligence personnel. She quickly answered no to each one.

Then they moved on to the big agenda item.

Several months ago, the SVR had struck gold. The Russians—like other intelligence agencies all over the world—were attempting to develop penetrations inside artificial intelligence companies. Pax AI was one of their main targets, and the Russians had identified a top scientist at the company by the name of Kozlov. Russian by birth, he was now a naturalized US citizen of several years, though his parents and siblings still lived in their home country.

The SVR used his Russian family to recruit him. Promises and threats were made. The threats worked best. Scared of what might happen if he didn't obey, Kozlov quickly became a compliant agent, helping to plant SVR malware on the Pax AI computer network and describing some of Pax AI's most hush-hush technological breakthroughs to Marisha Stepanova, his new SVR handler. They met at tech conferences and out-of-town corporate events. Kozlov traveled for work almost every week, and her travel destinations soon matched his.

Colt's superiors were very concerned with this development.

Aside from capturing the minds of tech enthusiasts around the world and having a CEO with a cult-like following, Pax AI was quietly involved in cutting-edge projects with the US government. Special-access programs that were classified at the highest level, with occasional supervision from secretive federal research agencies like the Intelligence Advanced Research Projects Activity and Defense Advanced Research Projects Agency (IARPA and DARPA).

But Kozlov's recruitment, while horrifying, might be turned into something useful, if the CIA could pull it off.

Tonight, members of a joint FBI-CIA counterintelligence team were planning to meet with Kozlov, in hopes they could turn him into a source. Colt's handler, Ed Wilcox, was several blocks from Colt's current location, supervising the Kozlov meeting. Colt had worked carefully with Marisha on this. No one wanted her to get burned. Kozlov would have no idea Marisha knew anything about it. And the CIA wouldn't tell him.

By the end of the night, if everything went well, Kozlov

would begin acting as a double agent. He would still spy on his American company for Russian intelligence, but everything he passed on would be screened and manipulated by the CIA.

Pax AI's security was state of the art, however. And for all of Kozlov and the SVR's efforts, actually stealing the technology had, so far, not been possible.

Marisha: There is a new development. A security breach we have been able to take advantage of. Kozlov was able to bring us Pax AI's weather-prediction algorithm. Very advanced. Our scientists confirmed it was legitimate.

Colt: How was he able to access that data?

Marisha: Pax AI has four levels in its San Francisco headquarters. Each floor of the building is progressively more secure. With Kozlov's access, Russian cyber operations specialists have been able to see data stored on servers from the first three levels of the Pax AI headquarters building. But the top floor has a physical barrier and very sophisticated firewall. These new files, including the weather-prediction algorithm, could only have come from the fourth floor.

Colt: So how did Kozlov get them?

Marisha: We think someone has transferred data from the fourth floor and moved it onto a server on the third level.

Colt: Someone? Not Kozlov?

Marisha: Correct. Not Kozlov.

Colt: Who?

Marisha: We don't know.

Colt: How were they able to do that?

Marisha: Our cyber team was unable to determine the method.

Colt: Why would someone else be removing data from level four and taking it to level three?

Marisha: The same reason we were trying to do it. To obtain Pax AI information.

Colt sat back in his chair, letting out a slow breath. The

Russians had stumbled onto another organization's espionage operation inside Pax AI. Wilcox was going to flip out.

Colt: Can you describe the security breach?

Marisha: Our cyber team found it while exploring the third-floor network. Each floor's network has a separate firewall. Kozlov works on the third floor. We gave him a device to take to work. When he logs into his computer, our device is able to do the rest. From there, we can get the data onto our drive, and he can walk out the front door without being discovered.

Colt: So he is at the mercy of whoever is doing this? You guys don't know what information you are getting, or when?

Marisha: Correct. So far there have only been three data dumps. Two were less significant. The last was the weather algorithm.

Colt: Why would they store it on the third floor? Why wouldn't the person who stole it from the fourth floor just transfer it out themselves?

Marisha: It is possible they have a multi-person team. One person with fourth floor access to remove the data. And then a courier transports it out. If the internal transfer is less risky, it would protect the identity of the higher-level person.

Colt checked his watch. Wilcox's surprise meeting with Kozlov should now be taking place in a hotel three blocks away. Colt would need to head over there soon and meet with Wilcox in person. Marisha had scheduled a meet with Kozlov later tonight, their normal agent-handler rendezvous. It would also serve as a test of Kozlov's viability as a CIA-controlled double agent. Would Kozlov tell Marisha that the Americans had approached him? Or would he keep quiet and serve his new master?

Colt: Do you have any concerns about tonight?

Marisha: Of course I do. But I trust you will make sure it will not be traced to me. Kozlov is scared for his family. If your team provides him with reassurance about his family and his future, that should work well.

Colt: You are sure that he won't report this to your superior?

Marisha: He doesn't have a direct line. And as long as you don't demand he do anything different, he should continue to report information to me.

Marisha was smart. She knew what Colt and the CIA would do without having to be told. Wilcox wanted to recruit Kozlov and keep him sending information to the SVR, allowing the CIA to modify the Russian intelligence stream.

But because this operation was on US turf, FBI counterintelligence would likely take the lead tonight. Colt would find out from Wilcox momentarily what the plan was going forward. The CIA's priority was to protect Marisha and keep the intelligence stream flowing. Whatever happened, she had handed them quite a victory.

Colt: You know what to do if you see any sign of Kozlov trying to contact someone else in the Russian government?

Marisha: Yes. I will contact you. Then I will live in a wonderful American farm town for the rest of my life, just like you have promised.

Colt: Okay. It is very important we watch for signs. Thank you once again. This is exceptional work. I need to go. I'll check back in at our scheduled time, after your rendezvous.

Marisha: Goodbye

Colt finished typing and looked at the zoomed-in video feed on his phone. Marisha's face was somber as she closed her phone and keyboard. Colt sighed. Wilcox had talked to him about this—the great dilemma of the case officer. When the risk to one's agent must be weighed with the value of future gains. Everything was a measurement of pros and cons, with human lives on the line and terrible consequences for those agents who were discovered.

Colt turned off the video and made sure the digital record had been sent to Langley before double-checking the program had deleted all stored data.

Then he sent a text to Wilcox, who replied seconds later.

Ed: It's going well. Come on over.

Colt looked back out into the darkness between the two hotel towers. He could still see Marisha, now sitting on her bed, legs crossed. Her face lit by the soft blue glow of her phone, the rest of the hotel room dark. A minibar bottle of wine in one hand. Colt worried for her. The risk she was taking was enormous.

Colt knew she liked the money the CIA paid her. But greed wasn't her motivation. Marisha wanted freedom and knew it would take money to get there. One night, during a wine-heavy in-person meeting, she told him that the thought of retiring in her forties and living out her days in a quiet village, away from the danger and hypocrisy of her SVR life, was what kept her going. He hoped she would reach that goal.

Colt knew she was not without flaw. Like many informants, Marisha was probably more flawed than good, but he saw flecks of character in her secret mission. She could have made money in other ways, used her training to avoid the long reach of any Russian black bag men who might come after her if she went AWOL. But she chose to do this. Colt admired her bravery in the face of a government that was merciless to its enemies.

The Moscow Rules were the legendary rules CIA officers had developed while running covert operations in Moscow during the Cold War. Back then, fifty thousand KGB agents made it their mission to stop a few dozen American CIA case officers. Both countries raced to develop technological capabilities that would strengthen their nation's grip on power and make the other obsolete. Was today much different? China had dramatically increased its participation in the game. But other than that? The agency names had changed. The technology had changed. But the game itself hadn't. And certainly not the stakes.

Colt wiped down the grease pencil marks on his window, threw his computer and phone in his travel bag, strapped the bag over his shoulder, and headed out the door. He took the elevator down to the ground floor, walked past the crowded bar area and out the revolving doors. The Seattle streets awaited him, alive with the sounds of traffic and pedestrians. The smells of international street food and gourmet coffee shops filled his nostrils.

The walk to Wilcox's hotel took several minutes, and he had time to think over what he had just learned from Marisha. Russian intelligence had stumbled upon another espionage operation aimed at stealing from the most secure floor of the Pax AI headquarters.

One question kept popping into his mind: whose operation had the Russians found?

3

Colt reached Wilcox's hotel and headed up to his room on the seventh floor, knocking twice. Wilcox opened the door and offered Colt a seat at a small round table. His computer was open on the desk, the video image of a man in his late forties or early fifties on the screen.

"Is that him?"

Wilcox nodded. "It just wrapped up. Everything with SANDSTONE go well?" Wilcox had served as Colt's sole handler—the only CIA officer Colt had face-to-face contact with—for the past eight years. Four years ago, he had been made the CIA's Vancouver station chief. The city had turned into ground zero for the CIA's counter-espionage work in the tech sector.

"It was very productive," Colt replied, running Wilcox through everything he had just learned from Marisha. Wilcox responded with his trademark eyebrow raises. More of a unibrow, really, but that was what made it special.

"Kozlov is a remarkable pickup," said Wilcox, stroking his beard. "I'll ask Langley to give SANDSTONE a bonus."

"She'll like that," Colt said, looking at the video screen.

Kozlov was sitting in the hotel loveseat near the window, his arms folded across his chest. "The Kozlov meeting go all right? He looks like he's in deep thought."

Wilcox nodded. "It went surprisingly well, actually."

"FBI led it?"

"Yes. A veteran agent out of the San Francisco office. Ron Rinaldi. Don't tell him I said this, but he's very good. He and a few others are part of our interagency tech counterintelligence program."

"Cool," Colt replied. "The video kind of sucks, though."

Wilcox looked at the screen, narrowing his eyes. "It's the FBI's. Secure wireless."

"Really? I thought they had the big budgets. Woulda thought their surveillance equipment would be higher resolution than this."

"Maybe the lens got smudged or something."

"Yeah, maybe. Never underestimate a human being's ability to screw up technology."

"It's good enough for government work. Kozlov signed on, so we're in business. That's all that matters. I was just happy I got to observe from down the hall."

"He's on this floor?"

Wilcox nodded. "Old boy here is four rooms down. Don't stray on your way out."

Colt frowned. The proximity was a little too close for comfort. That was unlike Wilcox, but Colt knew this operation had a lot of moving pieces. "What's the plan with running Kozlov?"

"The FBI has agreed to let us continue to run him, at least for a while. DOJ and the DNI both recognize the importance of protecting your agent. And based on what Marisha just told you, we'll need to keep Kozlov in place so we can identify what other organization is stealing from Pax AI."

"Did he mention anything about that?"

"No. They didn't get into the details of his operation with the Russians. It was mostly just a recruitment."

Colt nodded. "Okay. Pretty crazy how they stumbled onto another op, though. And to think we wouldn't have found it without the SVR. Did you ever think the Russians would be doing counter-espionage for us?"

Wilcox frowned. "We'll see."

"You don't believe SANDSTONE?"

"I don't know yet. We'll proceed with caution. But we sure as hell need to follow the trail. The FBI will schedule us to meet with Kozlov again tomorrow. I'll join this time. The meeting Kozlov has with SANDSTONE tonight will give him a chance to screw up. You'll need to speak with your agent as soon as it's finished and find out if Kozlov has divulged our contact so we can determine if he's trustworthy."

"Understood. He'll probably be pissing himself."

"Probably. But if there's another operation inside Pax AI, we don't have the luxury of time. The programs they work on are too sensitive."

Colt checked his watch. "SANDSTONE is scheduled to meet with Kozlov in two hours."

Wilcox studied Colt's face. "How much do you trust her?"

"SANDSTONE?" Colt shrugged. "She's always provided us with reliable intel. Including things that the SVR wouldn't want out."

"But . . ."

"But . . . she is SVR," Colt said. The implication was obvious. The SVR was unlikely to use one of their case officers in a long-term disinformation play like this, but it wasn't impossible.

"Yes. She is." Wilcox sighed.

Two hundred yards away from Kozlov's hotel room, a McMillan TAC-50 sniper rifle was being aimed at its target. The shooter lay in the prone position on a sturdy dining room table that had been moved to a far wall, positioned fifteen feet back from an open window. One boot made contact with the wall to help brace him for the power of the recoil.

They had chosen to execute this shot from the furnished model on an unoccupied floor of luxury condos. Construction was still going on in and outside the building. The loud noise would mask the sound of the mechanical clink of the suppressed fifty-caliber rifle fire. There were few personnel in the building, and no one within two floors of the assassination team. The suppressor would also mask the muzzle flash to anyone but the most direct viewers from the hotel across the street.

His spotter stood behind him, looking through a scope. A third team member stood behind both, ready to clean up and help with their quick escape when the job was done.

The sniper breathed slowly, readying himself for the shot. The spotter's phone lit up with a text notification. After reading it, the spotter gave the shooter a thumbs up.

One final breath, bracing himself for the kick, and then his finger pressed the trigger.

The powerful subsonic fifty-caliber rifle fired with a mechanical clink that shook the room. The round traveled the two-football-field distance across the street, penetrating the high-rise glass of Kozlov's hotel room and slamming into his chest.

4

"What the hell was that?" Wilcox said, hearing the noise.

For a brief moment, Colt's brain couldn't understand what his eyes were telling it. He had been watching the screen with Kozlov's surveillance feed. One second, he was sitting quietly in the loveseat. The next second, the chair had flipped over and dark red blood surrounded a gaping hole in the wall. Kozlov's body was on the floor, ripped to shreds at the torso, his lifeless head now pressed into the chair at an impossible angle.

"Ed . . ." Colt said.

"I see it," Wilcox answered. They were both standing now. Colt's heart was thumping, his mind spooling after the shock of seeing a man decimated in front of him.

Colt heard people shouting and running down the hallway outside their hotel door. Wilcox headed that way, opening the door. Colt followed, looking out.

There were four people. Three men and a woman, handguns drawn.

"FBI?" Colt asked.

They were outside the hotel room four doors down, looking like they were about to kick it open.

Wilcox shouted, "Rinaldi! No."

One of the men holding a pistol snapped up, meeting Wilcox's eyes. He nodded understanding and said to the others, "We need to treat this like an active shooter situation."

Colt saw at least two of the FBI agents look at him, which he didn't like. He would worry about his cover later.

Wilcox turned to Colt, alarm in his eyes.

Colt said, "SANDSTONE."

Wilcox nodded. "Yes. Tell her to wave off. Bring her in if you think you need to. But go now."

Colt nodded and headed to the stairway, bursting through the door. He hustled all the way down to the parking garage and began jogging on the city sidewalk, heading to his hotel. No time for a surveillance detection route; he needed to warn his agent.

He slowed to a brisk walk as he reached the Westin, his mind still racing through the images of violence he had just witnessed. Colt waded through the busy sidewalk of tech workers and businesspeople headed home from work as he entered the hotel's sliding doors.

Colt walked through the lobby, the bar area ahead of him. Here he had a choice to make. He could go left and take the south tower elevator, heading straight to SANDSTONE's room. That would be the quickest way to warn her. Or he could go right, taking the north tower elevator and going to his own room, contacting her through their encrypted messenger.

His head was clearing, his survival instincts kicking in. He needed to slow down. Be deliberate. Be disciplined. Quick reactions without thinking through the scenario were a surefire way to get someone killed.

Colt headed over to the bar, sitting at an empty cushioned chair, scanning the area for possible surveillance. A waiter came over and asked him if he wanted a drink, and Colt ordered an ice water. The thought that Marisha could be in harm's way was excruciating. But he forced himself to be patient.

Was it possible for Kozlov to be killed and Marisha to remain clear of suspicion from Russian counterintelligence? Yes. Was it possible she was being watched this moment, to see if anyone came to her after Kozlov was killed? Yes. But if that was the case, would they have known she was communicating with Colt an hour ago? He didn't know the answer to that.

Colt took a sip of water, removed his cellphone from his pocket, and accessed the encrypted messenger app. He sent an emergency message to SANDSTONE, a series of letters and digits from the communications procedure they had both memorized. To anyone observing, it would look like gibberish. But to both of them, it was a clear message: *Emergency. Contact me ASAP.*

She would take the message seriously when she saw it. But they weren't due to check in until later tonight, so Colt couldn't predict when she would see it. He would wait here for a few moments, checking for anything out of the ordinary, and then go to his room to see if he could glimpse Marisha. If she didn't contact him in the next hour, he would knock on her door.

On the TVs above the bar, Colt half-watched SportsCenter replays of the day's games, all the while using his peripheral vision to scan the room and occasionally taking quick, nonchalant glances at areas of interest. Two Asian men sitting alone wearing headphones in the corner, not speaking and not drinking. A white woman with her phone set on the table, angled so that its camera could have captured the bar area.

One of the waiters glancing over in Colt's direction twice in the last thirty seconds. All these people were almost certainly civilians. But that's exactly what surveillance would want to look like as they monitored him.

Colt thought about what Wilcox had asked before Kozlov was killed. Did he trust SANDSTONE?

Was it possible that Marisha had been setting him up? Had the SVR been using her to feed the CIA false information this whole time? Of course, that was possible. But was it likely? Marisha had once tried to sleep with Colt during one of their in-person meetings. It had been a long night of debriefing over wine and gourmet food, alone in a fancy hotel room. Colt had politely declined and chalked up the incident to a combination of genuine attraction, loneliness, and alcohol. But was it possible she had been working him? Was Marisha another Anna Chapman, the Russian sleeper agent who was arrested for seducing Americans as part of a Russian espionage operation? The Russians definitely used honeytraps as a way to ensnare potential assets. But Marisha was an SVR case officer, working an official Russian diplomatic cover. It was doubtful that someone of her status would use sex to recruit him. It was beneath her.

Besides, if that was the case, why have him meet with her today if they were going to kill Kozlov?

Maybe the Russians didn't kill him. Or maybe they didn't know about Marisha's work for the Americans. But then how did they know to kill Kozlov today? Too many questions. The answers would have to wait. For now, he needed to stick to his plan to protect his agent and assume she was still loyal.

Colt's visual scan froze on a group sitting in the hotel restaurant fifty feet away. He blinked. A brunette woman in a black dress twirled a lock of her hair. Dark features. Full lips.

Ava Klein.

A wave of emotions flooded through him and he knew he should look away. Ava was laughing, covering her mouth, her eyes glowing. She tenderly touched the shoulder of the man next to her, and Colt realized he recognized him. It was Jeff Kim.

Bzz. Bzz. Colt's phone pulled him back to the present. He looked down.

A message notification.

He could find out what Ava was doing here later. That was a personal interest. He needed to focus on the problem at hand. He . . .

When he looked up, Ava was staring at him.

Colt turned away. A reflexive action. As interested as he was, he didn't have time for this. He needed to walk out of this room right now without drawing any further attention to himself. He stood and began to walk, sneaking a sideways glance back at her table.

She was gone.

No. Not gone.

Walking through the hotel lobby, toward the bar area.

Toward him.

They were looking at each other now. An elated smile on her face. Colt's feet cemented to the floor. Heads at the bar turned as she walked by, eyes both coveting and envious, following the stunning brunette.

Bzz. Bzz. Colt's phone notified him he'd just received another message.

It was SANDSTONE, texting him back. Or Wilcox, alerting him to some new bit of information. Either one of them could be communicating any number of crucially important things Colt needed to know right now.

"Colt?" Ava's face was a mix of disbelief and pleasure. "Oh my God. It *is* you. I can't believe it."

As they embraced, he felt her bosom press against his chest and the warmth of her body beneath her dress. An intoxicating whiff of her perfume filled his nostrils.

He smiled. "It's so good to see you."

"What are you doing here?" she asked, looking incredulous.

"I'm attending the tech conference. You?"

"Me too. Who are you with?"

"I work in finance. Phillips and Jefferies Investment Bank, out of New York."

"Oh, you're kidding. You guys are working with my company. I'm with Pax AI." She was slowly shaking her head. "Colt, it's really good to see you." They both stood there, not knowing what to say. Memories of young love flashed through his mind. Long walks on Israeli beaches and sweaty nights in Tel Aviv hotels. And the abrupt, painful end that he hadn't thought about in nearly a decade.

Colt felt his phone vibrate again. He said, "Hey, I'm really sorry, I don't mean to be rude. I actually need to go take a call for work. But we should catch up."

Ava's face flashed disappointment, her lips parting slightly, but then she recovered. "Of course."

His phone buzzed in his hand.

Colt said, "I'm really sorry. It's pretty important . . ."

"No problem at all. My email is easy. Ava@pax.ai. Definitely get in touch." Her eyes sparkled.

"I will." Colt held her gaze for a moment and then turned away, cursing himself as he headed toward the north tower elevators. He took the elevator up to his floor.

When the doors opened, Marisha Stepanova was waiting for him.

5

"What are you doing here?" Colt tried not to curse at her. If they were spotted together, both of them were screwed.

"You told me it was an emergency," she said.

They walked quickly to his room, and he ushered her inside, deadbolting the door behind them. They stood near the door while they spoke.

Marisha looked frightened. "I checked in with one of my contacts. There are police and ambulances everywhere at Kozlov's hotel. What happened?"

"He's dead."

Her eyes were full of fear, but not surprise. "How?"

"I think it was a sniper. He was shot through the hotel window. I saw it happen."

She shut her eyes for a moment, turning away. When she looked back, she whispered, "If it was from my side, then they are watching us right now."

"Marisha, we can stop now. We can get you somewhere safe."

"Defect."

Colt nodded. "What do you want to do?"

She shook her head. "If the SVR knew, I would already be dead. They wouldn't risk letting me get away." She gritted her teeth. "The next few minutes will tell us, I think."

"What do you want to do?"

"I will go back. But I don't know if I will continue with you." A new expression now. A hint of anger. "Someone told the person who fired the shot where to find Kozlov. We need to think about who it was." She put her hand on the door.

"Marisha, wait. When will we meet again?"

"Don't contact me. If I decide to continue, I will reach out."

She walked out the door, and it closed behind her with a metallic clack.

Colt's phone vibrated, displaying an incoming call from Wilcox. He connected his CIA-issued wireless earpiece and swiped to answer.

"Hello?"

Wilcox said, "You in your room?"

"Yes."

"Good. Stay there for now."

"What the hell happened?"

"Nobody knows. This thing is an effing mess. You talk to your friend?"

"Yeah. My friend's going dark."

Wilcox said, "Okay. Probably for the best."

"Yeah."

"Listen, it's probably smart for you to get back home soon. Like, tonight. We'll reach out in a day or two for a debrief." Colt would need to come up with an excuse to give to his company about why he had to return to New York, but that wouldn't be difficult.

"Understood."

"Hey, one more thing. Some weird shit is being reported on the news. No idea if it's true, but you should check it out."

The call ended and Colt turned on the TV, switching the station to the local news. Outside the hotel, he could now hear numerous police sirens in the distance.

A few minutes later he saw the news story Wilcox had been referring to. By that time, Colt had finished scheduling his red-eye flight back to New York City.

The chyron of BREAKING NEWS in big red and white letters at the bottom of the screen was subtitled with:

CONSPIRACY GROUP TRINITY CLAIMS RESPONSIBILITY FOR SHOOTING OF AI SCIENTIST IN SEATTLE

6

New York
One week later

Colt sat at his desk combing through spreadsheets and financial reports, trying to get work done before his much-anticipated morning meeting. Phillips and Jefferies Investment Bank's office space took up two full floors, high up in the clouds of One World Trade Center. The work he did for the privately owned investment bank could be grueling. Eighty-hour weeks. Cutthroat competition, both inside and outside the firm.

"Colt, you catch the Knicks game last night?"

Colt looked up from his computer. One of his coworkers was walking by, carrying a laptop from one meeting to another. "Yeah, nice game."

The coworker shook his head. "You didn't watch it. They lost, man."

Colt winced. "You got me. I was up late working. Going through Pax AI's quarterly report."

"You're a machine, buddy. A machine. But that's why they put you on the Pax AI job."

Colt noticed just a hint of resentment in his coworker's demeanor. Everyone wanted to be on the Pax AI assignment. Colt nodded and his coworker walked into the meeting room, the door closing behind him. If the guy only knew. Colt's reassignment had nothing to do with his work ethic.

The only person at the firm who knew of Colt's attachment to the US government was the company's founder and CEO. After the CIA decided to place Colt on the non-official cover track, he had been sent to business school where he graduated near the top of his class. He then spent six months in a corporate internship, meeting with his handler on weekends to finish his training as an intelligence officer. Only then was he sent to his current job, where he began operational work for the CIA.

The CEO's arrangement with the agency wasn't unique. Throughout the world, there were others like him. People of power who shielded their nation's intelligence operatives, seeing it as their patriotic contribution, or a stroke to their ego. The arrangement allowed the CIA to guide Colt's work portfolio. His work travel often included corporate visits in foreign nations where he would perform financial analyses.

Colt was good at his job. The investment bank regularly used Colt's financial analyses to make major investment decisions. Pension funds and college endowment portfolio managers often hired Colt's firm to evaluate companies they wanted to invest in. Colt would tour business headquarters and meet CFOs by day, and then recruit potential agents over drinks at night. His occupation gave the CIA wide access to a variety of foreign corporations and investors.

A calendar notification slid onto Colt's computer screen,

reminding him it was time to leave. As if he hadn't been thinking about this meeting every minute since he left Seattle one week ago.

He snapped his laptop shut and walked down the hall, waving goodbye to the smiling secretary and taking the elevator six floors down. Same building, lower cloud layer. The elevator waiting area was empty other than a clean-shaven Wilcox, waiting with his hands in his pockets.

"You lost the beard?"

"It was time for a change." Wilcox turned and began walking. "Come on, this way."

Colt followed his handler as they headed toward a conference room on the left. From the hallway, Colt could see the room's spectacular view of the river, fifty-two floors up.

"How'd you get this meeting space?"

Wilcox shot him a look as they entered the room. "FBI, man."

"Ah, yes, the FBI and their New York field office connections," said a man in a blue suit standing at the far end of the table. He had a sly grin. FBI. Colt recognized him as the man he'd seen in Kozlov's hotel hallway, holding a pistol and telling the others not to enter the room. The FBI agent said, "The floor is empty for another week. Then Goldman or somebody is moving in. I was told not to leave any scratches."

Wilcox said, "Colt, this is Special Agent Ron Rinaldi, FBI."

Rinaldi walked over and they shook hands.

Wilcox said, "We've been working together to stand up the National Technology Counterintelligence Unit. That's the interagency task force that was working the Kozlov case. I've been asked to serve as the supervisor for the NTCU."

"You're leaving Vancouver?" Colt asked.

"I'll still be in Vancouver, for now. That's the federal

government for you. Why give someone one job when they can have two for the same salary?"

Rinaldi smirked.

They each sat down, and Wilcox began speaking. "The FBI is investigating Kozlov's murder."

Colt looked at Rinaldi, feeling uncomfortable. It was extremely rare for Wilcox and Colt to meet while anyone else was present. "How much can I say here?"

Wilcox said, "You can say anything. The room has been swept and I've read Agent Rinaldi in on your program. Please speak freely."

"Is he read in on SANDSTONE?" Colt asked.

Wilcox nodded. "Yes. Has she made contact since the incident?"

Colt shook his head. "Not a peep. Do you have surveillance on her?"

Agent Rinaldi said, "Ed asked us not to."

Wilcox said, "I didn't want any possible Russian countersurveillance to detect us. That would put her at risk."

"Well, I'd say we're past that point," said Colt, feeling guilty and angry that his agent had been put in this spot. "The news says this group Trinity has claimed responsibility. I've been reading up on them and it seems . . . far-fetched. Maybe a lone-wolf inspiration, but the group seems nuts. What do you know?"

Agent Rinaldi said, "The local TV news station got a call shortly after the crime scene went active. Our analysts have been over the recording. The voice is computerized, the phone call untraceable. Simple message: Trinity claims responsibility for killing the Pax AI scientist Nicholai Kozlov. They will continue to fight for humanity's AI future, or something to that effect. I'll show you the exact quote if you want."

"You buy it?" Colt asked.

Rinaldi said, “We’re investigating all possibilities.”

Colt looked at Wilcox. “What do you want me to do about SANDSTONE?”

“Just hang tight for now. Let us know if she contacts you.”

Colt could see the look in both men’s eyes. They had arrived at the part of the conversation they’d come here for. Wilcox by himself could have told all this to Colt or sent him a covert message. Something was up. Based on the new assignment from his investment bank job, Colt thought he had a clue.

Colt said, “So my firm booked me on a flight to San Francisco tomorrow. And I’ve got a meeting with my boss later today. You have anything to do with that, Wilcox?”

He nodded. “Given the circumstances surrounding Kozlov’s death and the information he provided, the ITCU decided we need better eyes inside Pax AI.”

“I can’t spy on an American company inside the US, Ed.”

Wilcox and Rinaldi exchanged glances. Rinaldi said, “We looked at a variety of candidates and decided you were our best option. We’ve gotten all the approvals. Technically you’re on loan to the Department of Justice.”

Colt raised his eyebrows. “Seriously?”

“Yes.”

He bit his lip. “Kozlov was killed seven days ago.”

Wilcox said, “Correct.”

“And my agent has gone dark.”

Wilcox nodded slowly. “I understand why you’re concerned.”

Colt clasped his fingers together. “I would think you would be just as concerned, Ed. If someone knew about Kozlov, then they easily could have known about SANDSTONE. And if they knew about SANDSTONE . . .”

Wilcox finished for him. “Then they might know about

you. We've game-planned out every scenario, Colt. But the risks don't outweigh the rewards here. If your cover is intact, then security isn't an issue."

"And if it's not?"

"Honestly? Then Langley is willing to have you outed, if that's the price. This operation is vital to national security." Wilcox's eyes were steel. "Your cover is expendable."

Colt took a deep breath. "I knew this was what you were going to say as soon as I saw that San Francisco itinerary."

Rinaldi said, "You'll be in good hands. We've got an excellent support team. Ed and I will be there, too, helping you out."

"So more people are going to know about me?" Colt turned to Wilcox. "Sounds like you're pretty much resigned to the non-official cover being burned."

"Not necessarily. It's a very small group. The people in this room and two others. That's it."

Colt sighed. "There's a complication. I know someone at Pax AI. A woman I had a prior relationship with. It was in my after-action report."

Wilcox said, "We read it."

"And that's not a liability?"

"Quite the contrary."

"Ah. I see."

Agent Rinaldi leaned forward on the desk. "Listen, Colt. Pax AI is working on some extremely sensitive stuff, including several top-secret government projects. And thanks to Kozlov and your agent, we now know that someone is stealing those secrets. That could be catastrophic."

Colt said, "Don't you have government inspectors who can do this officially? I mean, you are running government programs with Pax AI. You must have an oversight capability. Why do you need me?"

Agent Rinaldi sniffed. "There are government scientists who periodically visit their Mountain Research Facility. And we do have federal inspectors who can turn Pax AI upside down. With a normal company, we might take this route. Hell, the FBI is at the Pax AI headquarters right now, taking official statements on Kozlov's death. But I can tell you, in all my time doing counterintelligence, none of that official investigation stuff will work if we're dealing with a pro."

Colt sat back in his chair. He knew Rinaldi was right. Men like him were trained not to get caught. And if there was any sign of a hunter, the rabbits would go underground.

Rinaldi said, "It's better to make this a mole hunt than a cyber forensics investigation anyway."

"Why?" Colt asked.

Rinaldi said, "Frankly, I'm not overly confident our investigators would know what to look for. We're talking about cutting-edge technology. Do you know how slow the FBI was to understand cybercrime in the early 2000s? I worked with a guy who was there, in one of the FBI's first meetings with a group of white hat hackers. These were the good guys—experts who were trying to help. Trying to warn us what was going on under our noses. So, the FBI sat in a meeting with them for two hours while they talked about all the security vulnerabilities to our nation's infrastructure. Vulnerabilities to personal computers. To banks. Everything. This was back when the internet was really taking off, right around the dot-com boom. Our guys sat there listening quietly, and then they left. My buddy told me one of the hackers made a comment on the way out. He was surprised we weren't talking more. Asking more questions or giving feedback based on what we were already doing to prevent these security issues. They assumed it was because we wanted to keep it classified."

Colt said, "But it wasn't."

Agent Rinaldi shook his head. "It was because the FBI agents in that meeting had no friggin clue what the hell these hackers were talking about. Our government has always been remarkably sluggish in understanding new technology, and any investigation into Pax AI will be limited by that lack of ability."

"I'm no AI specialist," Colt said. "My expertise is in corporate finance and business viability assessments. If you have government projects at their Mountain Research Facility, don't you have agreements that you can leverage . . ."

Rinaldi shook his head. "There's a lot of separation of church and state in those agreements. We wouldn't be able to see all their hidden rooms and business secrets without getting FISA warrants that, admittedly, we probably wouldn't get. FISA courts have tightened up a lot recently. Especially when dealing with the tech companies."

Wilcox sat back in his chair, looking at Colt. "The real need isn't technical. We need good old-fashioned human intelligence. We need to get inside their minds. Understand what they are thinking. What motivates them. What decisions we think they'll make. We need you to embed yourself into the Pax AI executive inner circle. That's the only way we're going to be able to provide good intelligence assessments as to what comes next. There is a tremendous amount of pressure from above to let Pax AI operate full speed ahead. Any investigation we do needs to be . . . how do I say this?"

Rinaldi said, "Frictionless."

"Yes. Exactly," said Wilcox. "Two reasons. One, Washington thinks Pax AI's well-being is tied to America's. Both economically and technologically. They have consistently led the industry in AI breakthroughs. As they monetize this capability, Pax AI could earn enormous amounts of money. No one wants to hurt America's best chance at winning the future AI economy."

"And the second reason?"

"National security. Pax AI has a very big contract with the Pentagon. If we shut this company down, we end up setting back American AI progress in defense and intelligence. Switching horses will guarantee we lose progress, and likely the race. We need to investigate them to protect our national security. But we also need to continue to allow them to make forward progress to help national security. Ironic, isn't it?"

Colt said, "Ed, this is very different than my normal operations. Why do you think I'll be able to help?"

"We'll be with you. We'll back you up. Pax AI is going to do what they have to for the FBI's investigation into Kozlov's death. It will be surface-level compliance, overseen by their team of lawyers and their security head. But for their *investors*, whom you represent, they'll go the extra mile. You'll get an inside look at what's going on there. The projects. The employees. Corporate secrets. Personal secrets. It will be similar to your other operations, just with a mole hunt wrapped up in the middle. And with your prior existing relationship with Ava Klein . . . well, that's a much quicker avenue for establishing trust."

Colt looked at Wilcox. "What about my other work for you?"

Wilcox said, "This takes priority. Everything else will be shifted over to other case officers. We'll discuss that offline."

Colt shifted in his seat. "What if whoever killed Kozlov discovers what I'm up to?"

Wilcox and Rinaldi exchanged a look. Wilcox said, "Your mission has been deemed to be of the highest priority." Translation: *we're willing to take that risk.*

Colt smirked. "Great."

Agent Rinaldi said, “We’ll be there for—”

“I know. Backup.” Colt looked out the window at the Hudson River below. “One thing you should know about the Ava Klein part. Our relationship was close. But it ended rather abruptly.”

Wilcox said, “You’ll figure it out.”

7

Haifa, Israel
10 years earlier

"I got number one?" Lieutenant Colt McShane, United States Navy, was sitting in his commanding officer's stateroom aboard the USS *Cole*, looking down at the paper copy of his annual fitness report. The Navy's official evaluation of his military performance.

The captain of the ship sat behind his desk, sipping coffee and watching Colt's reaction. "Don't be surprised. You earned it."

"Sir, I mean, I appreciate it. It's just . . ." Colt looked up, uneasy.

"Say what's on your mind," replied the captain.

"This is going to screw over some of the other junior officers. Sullivan, in particular. This is his last fitrep on this set of orders, and . . ."

"NAV." The captain referred to Colt by his Navy job designation as navigator aboard the USS *Cole*, a US Navy Arleigh-Burke-class destroyer. "I don't play the games that some of these other commanding officers play. I give my early promotes to the best performers, period. Now you are the best junior officer on this ship. And frankly, it ain't close. You are a technical expert at every facet of your profession. You're a respected leader. Hell, your chief tells me the men would run through a brick wall for you if you asked them. And you're an exceptionally hard worker. But more importantly, you show excellent judgment, oftentimes when there isn't a clear answer."

Colt's face reddened. "Thank you, sir."

"I want to make sure the US Navy knows that you, Lieutenant McShane, are my number one ranked junior officer."

Colt was still thinking of his fellow junior officers. This would help his career, but it might hurt theirs. He decided to try once more. "Sir, I still have another fitrep before I'm scheduled to rotate to my next tour."

The captain said, "Then if you keep up your performance, you'll get ranked number one twice in a row. It's the right thing to do."

Colt said, "Yes, sir. Thank you, sir."

"Do you want to be a CO?"

Colt didn't hesitate. "Absolutely, sir."

"Do you want to make flag?"

Colt shifted his eyes down to the floor. "Sir, I'm too junior. It's probably silly to think about things like that . . ."

"It's not silly to plan your career. Moments like these are when you should discuss it. Do you want to make admiral someday? Is that a career goal?"

Colt met his captain's stare. "I would like to go as far as I can go in the Navy, sir."

The captain smiled. "Good. This is going to keep you on that path. You keep performing at this high level, and good things will come, Colt. Now, get the hell out of my stateroom and go take some hard-earned liberty. Bravo Zulu." *Good Job.*

Colt stood. "Aye, sir." They shook hands and Colt left, walking down the passageway, still stunned at his high marks.

He went to his stateroom, changed out of his uniform and into civilian clothes. Then he grabbed his backpack and hustled to the gangway. He showed his military ID to the sailor on duty, walked down the gangway, then stopped and stood at attention while facing the flag before continuing onto the pier.

Colt felt elated as he stepped onto the pavement in Haifa, Israel, the sun on his face and a feeling of freedom in every breath. He wore khaki cargo shorts, a polo shirt, and sneakers that were worn from running on the ship's treadmill. He gripped the straps of his backpack and looked through wrap-around sunglasses as his "swim buddy," newly married Lieutenant Mick Feyman, made his way down the gangplank.

"How'd your fitrep debrief go? You get an EP?" Mick asked.

"It went well," Colt replied.

"Ah. You got an EP. I knew you would. Attaboy. That's going to be two in a row. Shit hot, man."

"Let's just get out of here. I don't want to think about the Navy for a few days," Colt said.

"Sounds good to me, man," Mick said, grinning widely. He wore an almost identical outfit. The joke was that even in civilian clothes, sailors wore a uniform. "God it feels good to be off that stinking ship."

The two men walked down the pier, passing the line of ship's company waiting for buses to prepaid tours and hotels. Colt and Mick headed several blocks further into the city before hailing a cab.

"The Ritz-Carlton, Tel Aviv," said Mick as they slipped into the back seat.

The cab driver gave him a look, then held up five fingers, saying something in Hebrew.

Mick began fishing around in his wallet for cash, but the cab driver, seeing that he had enough, mumbled something and began driving. They drove south along the flat highway, catching glimpses of beach over low grass-covered sand dunes. Colt and Mick exchanged amused glances at the Israeli rap music playing on the taxi's radio. Mick was texting on his phone, laughing every few minutes. Colt was in a euphoric state after being let off the ship following weeks of sea duty. Stress melting away. A couple days of freedom.

Mick's wife greeted them at the hotel drop-off, jumping up and down in her sundress as her new husband got out of the car. Colt paid the driver as the newlyweds greeted each other for the first time in several months. They said their goodbyes and, to Colt's amusement, were off to their hotel room swiftly. He doubted he would see Mick again until it was time to go back to the ship. That was fine by him, he thought, admiring the view of the marina behind the hotel.

Colt checked in and headed up to his own room, flopping down on a comfortable queen mattress, letting his backpack of folded clothes and toiletries fall to the floor. He let out a deep breath. It had been a long time since he'd had this much space to himself. He got up and walked over to the sliding door, opening it. A tiny patio area with two chairs overlooked the marina below. He could hear the sounds of live music and clinking silverware from the restaurants in the square.

It was a beautiful day. Warm sun. Gulls swooping by. A light breeze. Paradise.

Colt had fewer than three days to enjoy it, and he planned to savor every grain of beach sand, every note of music, and every morsel of local food. A few brief days of rest and relaxation before going back to his sleepless job as the navigator aboard a US Navy destroyer.

He hadn't slept more than four hours a night for the past week and had been up all last night prepping the charts with his relief, who had just arrived on the ship.

Maybe he would just rest his eyes for a moment, he thought, lying back down on the bed. The soft pillow cushioned the back of his head as his eyes shut.

Colt awoke to darkness. Refreshed and ravenous, he hopped out of bed and walked out onto his balcony barefoot, making sure the paradise below hadn't disappeared during his slumber. To his relief, the promenade remained alive with music and laughter. The outdoor bar and restaurant area were packed with patrons eating and drinking, dancing and laughing.

Colt checked his watch. Best get down there quickly. Navy port calls were, like the story of Cinderella, a timed event. One had to cram in as much fun as possible before they transformed into a pumpkin.

He took a hot shower—God it felt good—then threw on his "fancy" outfit. The slightly less wrinkled polo shirt that didn't yet have sweat stains.

Colt walked out the door, patting his front pocket to check for his hotel key and slapping his rear pocket to check for his wallet. The elevator numbers couldn't count down fast enough on his descent. Then he was in the lobby, the sweet scent of fresh flowers in the air as he walked through the hotel and out the back exit.

Outside, the nearby docks were teeming with the nightlife of wealthy boat owners. Gleaming charter fishing boats were empty and dark. Exotic powerboats, small yachts, and multimillion-dollar sailboats, their lines clinking against masts as they took light rolls, were lit up and filled with well-dressed partygoers.

A catered party was being held on one of the larger vessels, complete with waiters in summer tuxes who carried trays of food and booze. A stunning brunette about twenty years old caught his eye as she leaned on the yacht's golden rail. She wore a blush-pink evening gown and held a glass of bubbling champagne, occasionally sipping it as she stared out toward the promenade. Colt turned to look where she was gazing and saw a music stage just behind him, which looked like it was being set up for a small band. When Colt turned back toward the yacht, he and the girl made eye contact. Colt's heart skipped a beat and he looked away instinctively as he continued walking. When he looked back, she had turned to speak to other partygoers on the yacht.

Colt moved on, feeling like he had just seen into another world. To his right, in the square next to the Ritz-Carlton, a few restaurants had outdoor seating with umbrellas over the tables. Lively patrons drank and chatted loudly as the band began playing music in the center of the square.

He decided to try the nearest restaurant. Its large windows provided a great open-air atmosphere. Colt took a seat at the bar stool nearest the courtyard. He ordered a beer and asked the bartender for a menu. Everything looked good, and he ordered an appetizer and an entree.

Colt sipped a cold beer and enjoyed the music coming from the stage. Soon a waitress brought him a plate of hummus with grilled bread and olives. He was about to order another drink when voices from just outside the restaurant caught his attention.

Colt looked up and saw the girl from the yacht, hands on

hips, standing on the red brick walkway. She held her chin up as a well-dressed man of about fifty lectured her in a sharp tone, his pointer finger jutting out. A middle-aged woman stood next to the man, looking uncomfortable. By their body language, Colt guessed the girl was their daughter.

The argument was in the rear corner of the square, out of view of nearly everyone in the restaurant but Colt.

Colt saw a single tear stream down the girl's cheek, rolling over her full lips. She remained silent but the father wasn't letting up. The mother tugged at the father's arm for him to calm down. The argument was loud enough for Colt to hear that they were speaking Hebrew, but the noise of the band ensured that no one in the restaurant took notice. No one but him.

Finally, the man Colt presumed was the father turned and walked away. The mother wiped away a tear on her daughter's cheek and gave her a sympathetic look before following her husband. The girl's eyes were emotionless as her parents departed.

Whether the girl in the pink dress sensed that Colt was watching her, he wasn't sure. But for the second time that night, his heart skipped a beat as her gaze rested squarely on him. This time he was only about fifteen feet away, sitting at the bar.

For a moment, they stared at each other. Then she wiped away the final tear streaking down her cheek and began walking toward him. Colt was a deer in headlights, unable to move a muscle as an eighteen-wheeler raced straight at him.

She slowed at the low barrier that separated the bar-restaurant area from the square, holding fistfuls of her dress as she gracefully raised one perfect leg at a time over the barrier until she stood only a few feet from Colt.

He blinked once, then moved to the empty seat to his

right, holding out his hand and offering her his bar stool. She sat down, not saying anything. Colt felt like he was witnessing a unicorn run through a forest. He didn't want to say anything to spook it.

Her face was flushed from the earlier confrontation with her father, but she held her chin high as she studied the liquor bottles stacked above the bar.

Colt had trouble keeping his eyes off her. Long, dark hair that flowed down to her waist. Full lips. Voluptuous figure. She was clearly still pissed at whatever her father had said. She clenched her jaw, nostrils flaring. He could practically feel the anger radiating off her.

"Everything okay?" Colt asked.

She snapped her piercing hazel eyes away from the liquor bottles, taking him in.

On the stage, the band had just finished their performance and the ambient noise level descended. The crowd in the courtyard had grown in size, and now all the standing tables had patrons, most several drinks in.

"My name is Colt." He held out his hand like an idiot.

She tilted her head. "What do you want?" She spoke in thinly accented English.

Colt could feel his heart beating. "Uh . . . nothing?"

She turned back to the bar.

Colt said, "I just . . . over there. You looked upset. I just . . . wanted to see if there was anything I could do to help."

She turned back and studied him for a moment longer. Then the bartender came over and they conversed in Hebrew. The bartender flipped down a shot glass in front of her and poured until the clear liquor dribbled over the top. She lifted the shot glass to her lips and swallowed it down in one gulp, then placed the glass back down on the table and said something else in Hebrew. The bartender nodded and refilled her glass, then he walked away.

"You are American?" she asked, facing him.

"Yes," Colt said. "Please excuse my intrusion, but I noticed you looked a bit upset over there. May I ask what you were arguing about?"

She sipped the liquor this time. "I got into a school. A master's program."

"Isn't that a good thing? What school?"

"Juilliard."

Colt raised his eyebrows. "That sounds like great news. Congratulations."

"I can't go," she said, taking another sip of liquor.

"Why not?"

She looked at him. "You saw my father's reaction. He has forbidden it."

Colt said, "Do you need his permission?"

She looked at him sideways, seeming to see him for the first time. Another sip of liquor from her shot glass. She said, "Music has always been my passion. I play piano. And I sing. I have always wanted to perform on a big stage, to play at the highest level. But it is, in the words of my father, not a serious endeavor."

"He doesn't like music?"

"He believes very much in science and mathematics. Not so much in art. I am angry tonight." She sighed. "But tomorrow, I will move on. I won't disappoint my family."

Colt took a gulp of beer. He noticed several men down the bar casting glances in their direction. Probably checking out the statuesque brunette in the pink dress, wondering why she was talking to the wrinkly-shirted American tourist. He realized they were the band members who had just finished their set.

She looked up at him. "Have you ever played an instrument?"

Colt's cognitive function became inhibited by her spectacular décolletage. He forced his eyes up and managed to say, "I play a little piano."

She raised one eyebrow. "If I told you to play something now, could you do it?"

"Maybe."

"What would you play?"

"Gershwin probably . . . well, definitely." His eyes danced along the floor. "I only know one song, and to be honest I would probably embarrass myself if I tried playing it."

She looked forward over the bar, taking another sip of her drink. "I like Gershwin." Sadness in her voice.

Colt looked at the empty music stage and then back at the girl. He looked around the restaurant until he saw someone who appeared to be the manager counting receipts in a hallway near the kitchen. "I'll be right back."

She gave him a confused look as he left.

Colt walked up to the restaurant manager and made his pitch. The manager listened carefully until Colt was finished and then snapped his fingers for the bartender to come over.

"My boss doesn't speak English," said the bartender. "What do you need?"

Colt, feeling more foolish by the moment, thumbed back toward the bar. "You see the girl in the pink dress?"

The bartender smiled. "Everyone sees her, I think."

Colt said, "She's a world-class pianist, and she can sing. Tell your manager I'll pay five hundred dollars if he'll let her go up on that stage and perform."

The bartender raised his eyebrows and translated to his boss, who listened and looked over at the girl. Then he replied to the bartender.

The bartender said, "He asks how he knows she is any good? This is a very nice area. He can't just let anyone play."

Colt said, "She's incredible. She is well known in the United States."

The bartender translated. The manager looked at her again, frowning and shaking his head as he said something in Hebrew.

"He says he can't."

Colt turned back to look at her. Her cheeks were still red from tears. "One thousand dollars."

The manager said something and the bartender translated. "He says if you pay two thousand, he will let her play for one hour. But if she is not good, he will pull her from the stage."

Colt felt the same adrenaline he did at a poker table when moving a large stack of chips into the pot, or on the bridge of his destroyer, when going out on a limb with a decision that could get him fired if he got it wrong. "You take a credit card?"

The manager didn't wait for the bartender to translate before he smiled. "Yes."

A few moments later and two thousand dollars further in debt, Colt sat back down at his bar stool next to the beautiful Israeli girl whose name he still didn't know. "Well, I have good news."

Her smile was melting him. "And what is your news?"

"I've arranged for you to perform tonight. One last hurrah before you go live the life of the obedient daughter."

She narrowed her eyes. "What are you talking about?"

Colt told her he'd arranged for her to play on the stage, leaving out the part about his monetary contribution.

She gasped. "I can't."

"Why not?"

"I can't just go up and play." But her eyes said something else. A glimmer of excitement.

Colt said, "It's already been arranged."

Something changed at that moment. Her sadness melted away. The tone in her voice was different. "That was very thoughtful."

"You're welcome. I think you can go talk to that man over there to figure out when to go up." He pointed at the manager.

She kept her eyes on Colt. "I would be nervous to go up there on my own." She finished her drink and shifted in her seat, her figure prominently displayed under the tight dress.

"Oh. I thought that was what you wanted. Maybe I misunderstood."

"No, you are right. But I think I need help. You said you played piano . . ."

Colt glanced over at the expensive Yamaha keyboard in the center of the stage, the bravery he'd felt moments earlier beginning to fade.

She must have seen his hesitation, as she moved in close, her lips near his left ear as she whispered, "What do you say? We can perform together." Hot breath against his neck. The dizzying scent of her perfume.

What was going on? He was just trying to do something nice. He desperately tried to think of a way out.

"I'm sorry, I can't. I'm underdressed. And you. You're beautiful."

She flashed a radiant smile. Her eyes snapped to the bartender, and she barked something in Hebrew. He answered but she cut him off and then addressed the manager. The manager's body language at first appeared strong, but Colt watched this delicate girl transform into a commanding presence, verbally beating them both into submission. When she was finished, she pointed her thumb at the two men and said,

"The bartender has a waiter's outfit you can wear in the back room. That will do."

Colt looked at the manager, who shrugged.

"I haven't played anything in years . . ."

"What happened to Gershwin?" She winked.

"This is crazy. Look, I was just trying to do something nice. I still don't even know your name."

"Ava."

He took a deep breath. "Ava, I may have oversold my playing ability . . ."

"What's yours?"

"My name? Colt."

"Like the horse?"

"I guess so, yes. Look, I can't . . ."

The bartender placed a hot plate of steak and roasted potatoes in front of Colt. "Does he want another beer?" Colt noticed the bartender asked Ava, who was apparently in charge now.

Ava answered, "No, he doesn't. Get us two more shots of this, please." She held up her shot glass.

Colt frowned. "What is that?"

"Don't worry about it. Just drink it." She plucked one of his roasted potatoes and popped it into her mouth. "Look, you were trying to cheer me up. This is how you can do that. So, go up there with me. Be brave." Amusement in her eyes.

Colt felt his heart pounding.

Ava, seeing his hesitation, sighed and once again leaned in close, her hand resting on his leg this time. For balance. "Colt, do you find me attractive?"

She was gorgeous, and she knew it. "Moderately."

She started to laugh, and then regained her composure. "Would you like to take me out? Would that be of interest to you?"

"I probably would have said yes a few minutes ago, but honestly, I'm a little afraid of you now."

Her face was still. "Consider this a test. If you go up on stage with me, then I will let you take me out to dinner."

Medusa's song to a sailor far from home. Colt looked over at the empty stage. A small crowd sat in chairs just in front of it. Was it public speaking that people feared more than death? This had to be the same thing. Colt screamed a prolonged curse word in his head.

The bartender placed two filled shot glasses in front of them. Ava picked them up, handing one to Colt.

She said, "Well, what will it be?"

Ten minutes later Colt wore a ridiculous waiter's tux, complete with bow tie, while he sat behind a three-thousand-dollar professional keyboard. There must have been at least fifty people gathered in front of the stage now. Another two hundred more watched from their seats in windowless restaurants and cafés that surrounded the square. Ava leaned over the piano, turning a music book to the proper page.

"We'll start with this." She flipped through pages. "Then here. And then here. If there is any problem, we'll improvise."

Colt looked over the sheet music. It was beyond anything he'd done before, and a wave of panic set in.

Ava watched his face.

"How long do I have to study this?" he asked.

She began laughing. The crowd continued to gather in front of them, waiting for the performance to begin. And Ava was near tears, laughing, gesturing for Colt to . . . get up?

Colt looked at her like she'd lost her mind, and he began

to wonder if he had completely misjudged her. He was, perhaps, dealing with a crazy person.

She finally got control of herself, closed the sheet music book in front of Colt, and took him by the shoulder, helping him up.

Ava said, “Okay. My fun is over. You passed. Well done, chivalrous knight. Now go sit down over there.” She pointed toward an empty seat off the stage.

“You don’t need me to play?” Colt had no idea what was going on anymore.

She shook her head with a mischievous grin. “I just wanted to see how dedicated you were. And perhaps to see how you would look in this bow tie.” She flipped her fingers through the tie. “Now, if you please.”

She held out her hand, gesturing for Colt to leave the stage, which he quickly did, still bewildered. When he looked back, Ava’s expression was confident and professional as she took her seat at the piano.

Colt sat down in one of the audience chairs set up in the square, still wondering what the hell had just happened. On the stage, Ava had closed the music book and repositioned the microphone to be near her at the piano.

When she began playing, the crowd near the stage went quiet. Colt could immediately tell she was gifted. At first, there was still a lot of chatter from the restaurants surrounding the square.

Then she began singing.

Her voice mixed with the notes she played, and the result was extraordinary. Colt got chills as she hit certain octaves. And as the performance went on, the surrounding bar and restaurant patrons fell silent, entranced by her music.

Ava played and sang for almost an hour, mixing renditions of slow popular songs that Colt recognized with others he assumed were traditional Israeli tunes. All the while, she radiated energy and charisma. This girl who had been taking shots of liquor and toying with him moments ago was now performing music at a world-class level.

By the end of her performance everyone was hushed, and the crowd in the square had swelled to several hundred. People in the marina had wandered over to listen, each spectator hanging on Ava's every note.

The last song was slow, and some in the crowd wiped away tears. It was in Hebrew, and although Colt couldn't understand the words, it was one of the most beautiful things he had ever heard.

It was a surreal experience. Colt was half a world away from home and only hours into a port call on a Navy deployment. Lightheaded from the alcohol. A warm sea breeze in his face. And completely entranced by this ravishing woman who every so often glanced his way, smiling as she played.

When she finally finished, the crowd roared with applause. People stood, clapping for a full minute. Colt heard some whistling approval and the manager of the nearest restaurant seemed to be begging Ava to continue. But she declined and eventually the crowd dispersed.

It was after midnight when she and Colt sat down at the bar again.

"I see you gave the waiter back his clothes," she said. She didn't smile, but Colt could see the amusement in her eyes.

"Ava, you were *really* good. Really."

"Thank you." She bowed her head.

"And please, no more tricks about getting me up on a stage."

She shrugged. "No promises." She looked up at the clock above the bar and clicked her tongue. "I must go home now."

Colt didn't want to break the spell but had to ask. "May I see you again?"

She walked up to him and leaned in, giving him a gentle kiss on the cheek. "Tomorrow night. Here. Sunset. And thank you."

Then she turned and walked away, her footsteps echoing on the brick square. Colt watched her enter the backseat of a black Mercedes taxi.

He swallowed the last of his drink and paid his tab. The bartender gave him a knowing look. "You got hit by something, I think?"

Colt nodded and walked away, seeing Ava's cab pull away and disappear down the road before he walked to his hotel.

As promised, Ava met Colt at the bar the next evening. He arrived an hour before sunset to make sure he wouldn't miss her. She appeared wearing a sundress and a smile and handed him a black motorbike helmet without saying anything. She just kept a straight face and nodded for him to follow. She walked him to a motor scooter parked in front of the hotel and gestured for him to get on behind her. Colt held on to her waist as she drove them north.

They parked the scooter near Ga'ash Beach and hiked to a secluded patch of shoreline. Sheer cliffs of sand formed a private enclave behind them. The recent sunset painted the clouds above the Mediterranean in reddish-orange light.

Ava placed a large blue and white beach towel down on the sand, setting a basket atop it. She began taking food out of the basket, along with a bottle of wine.

"I brought the corkscrew but forgot the glasses," she said, shaking her head.

Colt twisted out the cork and took a swig. Then he handed her the bottle, saying, “Problem solved.” She nodded approvingly and did the same.

They ate with their hands. Spiced chicken and vegetables kept warm in tin foil. A delectable eggplant spread. Fresh flatbread that she used to soak up the leftovers. Every mouthful seemed better than the last.

“This is delicious. Did you make it?”

Ava smiled. “My mother made most of it. I helped.”

“That was nice of her.”

Ava shrugged. “I told her I have a date. She is hoping that I will impress a nice Jewish boy and marry him.”

Colt looked confused. “I am not Jewish.”

“I guessed as much. But she doesn’t know that. And no one is perfect.” Ava took another swig of wine, her eyes daring Colt to say something to the contrary.

Colt smiled and said, “So, about last night. Your singing and piano were really great. Have you done that a lot? Performed in front of people?”

Ava laughed. “Not really.”

“But that’s what you want to do? Perhaps you should try again with your parents?”

She sighed, looking out over the sea. “My father will never let me.”

“I mean, I don’t want to get in the middle of anything, but you are old enough to make your own decisions, right? I mean . . . well, how old are you?” Colt felt his cheeks redden, not sure if he was allowed to ask that.

She looked at him innocently. “Sixteen. Why?”

Colt’s eyes widened.

Ava burst out laughing. “I’m sorry. That’s not funny. Twenty-two. I’m twenty-two. I graduated college last year. Oh my God, your face. That was mean of me.”

"I don't think I can take any more of your jokes."

She took another swig from the bottle and handed it back to him. He followed suit, then said, "Well, you were really good. That's all."

She looked at him, deadly serious, and for a moment Colt thought he'd said something wrong. Then she leaned over and kissed him before sitting back down.

They sat in silence for a while, enjoying the scenery. Eventually, she turned to him and said, "Why are you here? In Israel, I mean."

"I'm in the Navy. My ship is in Haifa."

"How long will you be here?"

"A few days. We're not really supposed to tell people our schedule."

"Loose lips sink ships," she said.

He smiled. "Yes, exactly. How do you know that phrase?"

"Why wouldn't I?"

"I guess . . . I just thought since you lived here . . . that's, like, an English phrase."

"I went to high school in the US."

"Really?"

"Yes. I was born in the US."

"No kidding. Well, I guess I'm presumptuous."

"Yes, you are. We're both American. My parents didn't name me after a horse, though."

They both laughed.

Colt said, "Then I guess the question is, what are *you* doing here?"

Ava said, "My mother and father are divorced. She lives in Tel Aviv, near her family. My father works in New York." She stared out toward the Mediterranean Sea. The last remnants of sun had sunk below the horizon. "So, if you are in the Navy, I won't see you again."

Colt said, "Again, I'm not supposed to say . . . but . . . I think there is a good chance I might be in town again a few more times over the next couple of months."

She didn't react at first. She just took another bite of the food, then turned to face him, licking her fingers clean of spices. Then she leaned over, grabbed him by the back of the neck, and kissed him, deeper this time. His pulse raced and his mind blurred as he tried to keep calm.

She pulled away as suddenly as she began. Then she stood and lifted off her sundress, revealing a dark one-piece bathing suit underneath.

"Come on, let's go for a swim." That mischievous look again.

"I, uh, didn't think I needed a bathing suit."

"Then don't wear one."

"And I think you're supposed to wait forty minutes after eating . . ."

She rolled her eyes and began jogging into the calm surf. Colt stood, stripped down to his boxers, and followed. They were each stealing glances at the other. He marveled at her body as she dove in.

Dusk turned into night, and they spent the rest of the evening swimming in the cool saltwater. Talking about life and their interests. And feeling the tension build between them.

Colt learned she was from a wealthy family. Her parents married young and divorced when Ava was a toddler. Her father was some type of investor and lived primarily in New York, although he traveled often. Ava went to a boarding school in Connecticut until she was eighteen. She graduated from the London School of Economics last spring, and was taking a year off before either getting a master's degree or a job. She'd deferred acceptance from several of the top MBA programs in the US and UK.

"And Julliard. No big deal."

She looked down. "I had to apply there without my father's knowledge. I just told him last night. That was why he was so mad. Ironic that they paid for me to take all those music lessons and don't want me to do anything with it."

Colt shrugged in the moonlight, the water lapping at his neck. "People get ideas of what's important. It's instinctive, I think. We just do things like we're programmed that way. Whether we think about the end-state or not. Whether we think about our overall happiness or not."

"Is that why you went into the Navy? Pre-programmed?"

"Not at all. I'm following my passion."

They were half-standing, half-treading water. She moved closer to him. "And what passion is that?"

"You see, for the past five years, I've been searching the world for mermaids."

"Find any?" Her seductive eyes gazed at him from just above the waterline, her face illuminated by pale moonlight.

"Only one so far."

She spat out a stream of seawater at his chest. "Tell me the truth."

Colt leaned back, floating. "Okay. Someday I want my own ship."

"So you are going to buy a boat?"

Colt shook his head. "No, I mean I want to command a US Navy warship. I've wanted to do that since I was a kid. That's my goal."

Ava said, "Impressive. To those with great gifts come great expectations. That's what my father would say."

Colt said, "What about you?"

She swam closer to him. "I'm a mermaid, looking for a Navy boy." She pushed him away playfully with her foot, which he took, pulling her in close. He felt dizzy, his heart pounding faster as he stared into her eyes, the blue moonlight on her perfect skin.

Their kiss was wet and passionate. Bodies pressed together. Hands caressing. Ava wrapped her legs around his waist as he held her, buoyed by the sea. She leaned back and smoothed strands of wet hair off her face.

A large wave splashed saltwater on their faces. They laughed as he regained his balance. She rested her hands on his bare chest and turned to look up and down the shore. It was dark, no one in sight.

Ava looked back up into his eyes and said, "Let's take this to the beach."

Colt and Ava continued to see each other for the next few months, his ship making several more port calls in Haifa. Their passionate young love grew stronger with every meeting.

She took him on tours of beautiful Israeli sights. Historical destinations, beaches, and restaurants she wanted to share with him. With Colt's encouragement, Ava scheduled two more musical performances. Small events, both of which Colt attended. He could tell she enjoyed it immensely and was blown away by her talent. They also spent a good deal of time in his hotel room, exploring each other and falling in love.

After one of their nightly sessions, they lay together on his hotel balcony, looking out at the stars over the water. She wore a thin satin nightgown as she sat on his lap, sipping a bottle of water.

"I don't want you to leave," she whispered.

They could both feel it. Their time together was coming to an end. This was the last of his port stops in Haifa, and she needed to make a career decision about what she would do next.

"I have another night," he said.

"I want more."

"You could stay with me. Find a job or MBA program in the US. I'll be back there in a month or so."

"You don't even know what you'll be doing. You said they will probably transfer you somewhere else. Maybe on the other side of the world. Or you could go right back out to sea. And what would I do? Lounge around your apartment?"

He gave her a kiss. "That doesn't sound so bad."

She didn't kiss him back, instead splashing a few drops from her water bottle onto his face. "I am being serious." She sighed. "I will need to decide on a master's program. Or a job that sufficiently—"

"Satisfies your parents' expectations?"

"Something like that, yes. One that satisfies my own."

Colt said, "Okay."

"I will need to grow up."

"Okay."

"Stop saying that."

"I just want to keep seeing you."

"Maybe you could quit your Navy job and lounge around in my apartment?"

Colt laughed. She didn't. "Oh, you're serious?" he asked.

"See? You are just as programmed as I am."

They didn't say anything for a moment.

Colt said softly, "Why are you really upset?"

"Because I feel like it's all out of our control."

"I mean it, Ava. I want to be with you."

She turned to look up at him, then reached for his chin

and kissed him. "You're only saying that because I'm here in your lap. In a few months, American girls will be clawing at you, I'm sure."

He sighed. "I know what I want. Let's figure out how to make it work."

"Okay." She rested her head on his chest, and they both looked out at the starry night sky over the Mediterranean Sea.

The next morning, they ordered room service breakfast. Colt sipped coffee while looking out over the beach. He could hear the diesel motors in the marina mix with the cry of the seagulls and the clanging of sailboat masts as they rocked in the waves.

Ava had just come out of the shower and was wearing the white hotel bathrobe while drying off her hair. When she was done, she walked over to him, biting her lip.

"What's wrong?"

"I've decided something."

"What?"

"You should meet my parents."

Colt raised both eyebrows. His coffee cup froze halfway to his lips. "Are you sure?"

She nodded, lips pressed tightly together. "My father is in town again. He is meeting my mother and me for lunch today."

"I thought they were divorced."

"They're weird, I told you," Ava said. She raised her chin, which Colt had learned meant she had made up her mind. "I thought about what you said last night. If you are really serious about being with me in America, then I want you to—I *need* you to—meet them and make a good impression. I know the timing is not ideal, but you're leaving and . . . this is the best we can do."

He shifted in his seat. "If that's what you want. Okay. Of course I'll go."

Her head bobbed. "Good. Good." She walked over to him, loosening the cloth belt on her bathrobe and allowing it to open a bit, her face softening. "And if you need any more convincing . . ."

Colt let out a breath, staring at the sliver of exposed skin between her breasts.

"I will do *whatever* you say."

Ava smiled, tightened her robe, and twirled around to finish getting ready, casting him a devilish glance as she went. "No convincing needed, then. Good. I'll call my mother and set it up. What time do you have to be back at your boat?"

"Ship," he corrected.

She rolled her eyes. "*Ship*. What time?"

He looked at his watch. "I need to check in with someone on the ship this morning. So I'll need to go to Haifa first. I don't think the timing will work for me to come back to Tel Aviv."

"That is okay. My mother lives north of here. We can meet somewhere close to your boat." She winked.

Colt knew something was wrong as soon as he arrived at the pier. There were extra security personnel at the gate and around the ship.

His friend was on duty just beyond the metal detector lines. Colt walked over to him. "Hey, Mick, what's up with all this?"

Mick leaned in close, speaking in a hush. "They just upped

the Force Protection Condition. Some sort of terrorist threat. My division chief just told me. Rumor is we might be leaving early."

Colt was worried. "Seriously?"

"Yup. XO says liberty is canceled. They're calling everyone back early. The captain is looking for you. He asked you to see him as soon as you get on board."

Colt cursed himself and headed aboard the ship. Ten minutes later he stood before the ship's captain and was given orders to prep for an early departure. It took them an hour to go through everything, during which Colt kept checking his watch.

When they were finished, Colt tried to make a phone call on the bridge wing, but there wasn't a cellphone signal. He dialed Ava's number, but it wouldn't connect. He tried again a few more times but the call never went through. He sent her a text, but it kept showing up on his display as "error, message not sent." A feeling of dread grew in the pit of his stomach.

She was going to think he stood her up.

Colt went to his stateroom and logged into his computer to send her an email. He cursed himself that they didn't make any plans beyond lunch today. God, he hoped this didn't screw up his chances. He had really fallen for her.

Over the next two hours, as the crew finished returning to the ship and set sea and anchor detail, he kept trying to call Ava but couldn't reach her. Soon the tugs came alongside, and by noon his ship had left the pier.

Colt was on the bridge, looking toward the city of Haifa when it happened.

Gray-black smoke, rising up from several miles inland.

"What the hell is that?"

Commotion in the pilothouse. Sailors pointing and shouting.

The captain and officer of the deck glanced at the smoke in the distance while keeping their focus on the ship's course and speed. Reports from the tactical action officer began streaming in. They had received intelligence updates from Sixth Fleet that a bomb had gone off in a marketplace in Haifa.

The journey home was heart-wrenching. Colt kept telling himself that Ava was fine. For weeks, while his ship transited west through the Mediterranean and across the Atlantic, he didn't hear a word from her.

Then, a few days before pulling into their home port of Norfolk, Colt finally received an email. She let him know she was okay, that he shouldn't worry.

And that she didn't think they should see each other anymore.

His response was immediate, filled with emotion and questions.

Ava responded, but each time her replies were delayed. Cordial and concise, ignoring many of his questions and only providing short, unsatisfying answers to the rest.

She was fine, she said. She wasn't hurt. She had enjoyed their time together very much but decided she wasn't going to come to the United States. When he suggested he could take leave and visit her in Israel, she told him that wouldn't be a good idea. She didn't respond to his apology for not showing up to lunch with her parents. Or to his questions about how close they were to the terrorist attack that day. And she wouldn't say where she was going to live next.

Their relationship was over.

Colt's homecoming was bittersweet. His ship pulled into

Naval Station Norfolk to a sea of cheering friends and families. Colt's parents had come to meet him when he walked off the gangplank and they embraced. But all he could think of was Ava.

Two months after he returned from deployment, Colt was selected—again—as the number one lieutenant on his fitness report, the coveted spot that would guarantee early promotion and a promising career. He was on track to fulfill his dream of one day becoming a ship captain.

But he felt empty. Having tasted pleasure and love so sweet, only to have it ripped away without explanation. Colt questioned everything and found himself immensely dissatisfied with where his life was headed. He needed change.

Colt met with the captain of his ship and turned in his letter of resignation. He was done with the Navy. The captain tried to change his mind, but nothing the senior officer said had any real effect.

A few weeks later, Colt walked off his ship for the last time and headed to a Virginia Beach bar to meet with a few of his fellow Navy friends. They had a few laughs and a few beers, toasting Colt's farewell to Navy life. At the end of the evening, Colt and Mick were the last two in the bar. Mick, newly married, had also decided to get out of the Navy after his initial five years of service were complete, although he was a few months ahead of Colt in the process.

"How are the job interviews going?" Colt asked.

"It's like a full-time job, finding a job. Nobody ever told me it would be this much work. Nobody understands what we did, unless they were military themselves, and even then it can be hard to translate if they're from a different community." Mick took a swig of beer. "Do you know what type of job you will look for?"

Colt looked out the window. A brunette girl walked by,

reminding him of Ava. He sighed. "I don't know, man. I've done a few online applications but haven't scheduled any interviews yet. To be honest, I'm thinking about traveling a bit before I do."

"Where to?"

Colt looked at his friend. "Maybe to Israel."

Mick made a face. "To chase that girl you told me about? Dude. I mean, no offense. But if she's not returning your emails . . . I don't want to say take the hint or anything, but . . . take the hint."

"I told you what happened, though."

"Yeah, I know. But house guests and desperate ex-boyfriends start to stink after a while."

"But . . ."

"Dude. You gotta find something for yourself. Something exciting that can take your mind off her."

Colt finished his beer. "Yeah, you're probably right."

"So, what jobs excite you the most?"

He sighed. "I don't know. I guess I was thinking about law enforcement or something like that. Maybe apply to the FBI. That'd be pretty cool. That would be kind of like the military, right? But none of these shitty deployments."

Mick nodded. "That would be cool. You know, I just ran into an old buddy at a government job fair who was hiring. Looking for the kind of guys with Top Secret clearances. You have your TS/SCI, right?"

"Yeah."

"You were near the top of your class in college, right? You've had significant experience in foreign countries. You speak any foreign languages?"

"Poorly."

His friend laughed. "Seriously. Let me send your resume to my friend. He's looking for a specific type of person. I've seen you in action. You're smart, good with people, and can think on your feet. I think you might be a good fit."

Colt narrowed his eyes. "Who does your friend recruit for?"

"The CIA."

"What's his name?"

"Ed."

PART II

"... spies will never leave Silicon Valley. As the region's global clout grows, so will its magnet-like attraction for the world's spooks. As one former US intelligence official put it, spies are pulled toward the Bay Area 'like moths to the light.' And the region will help define the struggle for global preeminence—especially between the United States and China—for decades to come."

– Zach Dorfman, writing for Politico, 2018

8

Present Day

Colt sat in the business-class window seat of a Boeing 767, sipping a ginger ale as the aircraft taxied toward the runway. Bouncing his knee, he thought about Ava, and his task at hand.

He wondered what he would find in the elite world of Silicon Valley executives and power brokers. He thought about how he would handle spending time near Ava again. He was going to have to lie to her. Even more daunting, it was possible he might need to recruit her as an informant. That prospect made Colt ponder the fate of his last agent. How would Colt react if Ava's life was on the line? What had happened to Marisha?

The aircraft took off down the runway, and Colt felt the familiar flutter in his chest as he began heading west at hundreds of miles per hour.

Colt's flight landed in San Francisco. He was met in the baggage area by a driver wearing a tie and holding a sign with Colt's last name. The driver led him to a clean Mercedes sedan and dropped him off at The Four Seasons Hotel. Colt tried to pay for the ride but was rebuked.

"Courtesy of Pax AI, sir."

The hotel receptionist gave him a similar greeting, informing him that his room had been upgraded courtesy of his host. Pax AI was trying to butter him up prior to his multi-week inspection, he knew. Many of the companies Colt evaluated provided similar attention. He had seen it all. In some countries, cash bribes or late-night visits from escorts were not uncommon. Colt's reputation as a man of integrity was sterling, however, and his New York firm paid top dollar to keep it that way. The CIA also monitored his finances . . . and probably his "social" activity.

Colt thanked the receptionist and headed up to his room. It was spacious and opulent and had a great view of the city. But he didn't spend time on the view. Within minutes he was out the door, conducting a surveillance detection route he'd planned the previous night. Certain he was in the clear, he headed to the address Wilcox had sent him, south of the Market District.

The safehouse was a single-story auto repair shop with a closed sign in the window. The outer walls were brick, painted periwinkle blue. The windows were protected by wrought iron bars, and a smattering of graffiti garnished the chained front entrance. Entering through a side door in the alley next to the shop, Colt counted three security cameras. Wilcox had informed him the only personnel with knowledge of the safehouse were members of the National Technology Counterintelligence Unit. And the only personnel allowed in right now were Special Agent Rinaldi, Wilcox, and two others he was about to meet.

Colt was greeted by Rinaldi, who opened the side door and showed him the entrance procedure: a numbered code, and approval by someone inside. Only Rinaldi and Wilcox could enter by themselves. The special agent then showed Colt into the field operations area inside the building. The place was kept tidy. Sparse furniture. A stocked fridge, a stove, and a microwave. A few back rooms, one a bathroom and one that stored some IT servers. The main room had several computers with government classified stickers on them, and some electronics equipment he didn't recognize. The small safehouse gave him the impression that the NTCU team both lived and worked here.

A woman who looked to be in her late fifties sat at a foldout table in the center of the room, scribbling on a notepad. She wore reading glasses and a light sweater. She had black skin and close-cropped gray hair, and when she looked up, Colt saw eyes that captured everything. She placed her pen down and stood.

"You must be Colt." The woman stuck out her hand. Her grip was firm, and she looked him right in the eye as they shook. "I'm Jennifer Sims."

Agent Rinaldi said, "Special Agent Sims works with me. FBI counterintelligence. She's been at the Bureau long enough that I need to remind her to stop referring to the Russians as Soviets."

Sims cast him a look. "Was that a shot at my age?"

"Only complimenting your experience, Ms. Sims."

"Hmph," she said, then turned back to Colt. "Sometimes I need to remind Special Agent Rinaldi that he's no spring chicken himself."

Rinaldi shook his head, looking at Colt with a half-smile.

"You see what I'm dealing with? In all seriousness, Jennifer is a true pro and we're lucky to have her."

Sims seemed satisfied with the compliment.

Colt looked between the two of them and did his best to sound respectful. "Good to meet you. I'll do my best to soak up everything I can."

Rinaldi said, "Take a seat and we'll give you the lay of the land. You already know Wilcox. He's in the server room in the back, making a call. Only room out of earshot, unfortunately. He'll join us when he's off the phone." Rinaldi looked up at one of the security cameras. "Oh, and I see we have our junior CIA officer here."

Colt detected frustration in Rinaldi's voice as he looked up at the screen.

"Be nice," said Sims. "She'll get there."

Colt realized he knew her face. "Is that Heather Weng?"

"It is," Rinaldi said, pressing the button that unlocked the outer door.

A moment later a woman in her thirties appeared in the room wearing jeans and a backpack. She gave a wide smile when she saw Colt.

"Well, well . . . Colt McShane lives." Weng punched him lightly in the arm. "So much for failing out of The Farm."

Colt shook her extended hand, smiling. "Yeah. Sorry about that. It's good to see you again."

She smirked. "It's not personal, just business, right? But I'll still treat you as an inferior washout, if that's cool?"

"If that makes you feel better," Colt said, a thin smile on his lips. He remembered Heather Weng's spicy sense of humor. Weng had been in Colt's class at the junior officer training program when they had entered the CIA. On a military base near Williamsburg, Virginia, the training course was like boot camp for spies.

Their time at The Farm was years ago. Colt didn't remember their conversations, but he remembered his impression of her. She was a cool chick. Smart, no-nonsense, and incredibly competent. He had instantly liked her.

When Colt was selected for the non-official-cover program, his classmates were told he had washed out of the junior officer training course. Most of them went on to become operations officers in the CIA's clandestine service.

Rinaldi said, "I'm very happy you have a new friend, Heather. Maybe he can help you finish your intelligence assessment reports on time?"

"Almost finished with the Hawkinson one."

Rinaldi scoffed and said, "See, Jennifer? Millennials. Even their spies are lazy."

Weng turned to Colt. "Rinaldi acts like a superior and condescending G-man, but don't let him fool you. He's really a teddy bear who loves working with the Agency."

Sims chuckled.

Rinaldi rolled his eyes, then connected his laptop to a monitor on the table. "Let's get this briefing underway."

An image of Kozlov appeared on the monitor, and the trio's banter gave way to an atmosphere of quiet professionalism.

Sims said, "From what Kozlov told us before he was killed, someone is removing Pax AI's most advanced IP from the high-security data servers on the fourth floor of their headquarters. And whoever had that capability was likely on a small list of people with the company's highest security clearance. Pax AI employees who were cleared both to the fourth floor and to their Mountain Research Facility."

Weng turned to Colt. "Their headquarters building is located a few miles away from here in San Francisco. There are four floors, each with progressively more security as you go up. The top level is restricted to only a handful of their top scientists and executives. The projects stored there are what every intelligence organization and competitor business on the planet is trying to get eyes on."

Colt nodded. He knew some of this already, but it didn't hurt to hear everything they had to say.

"Do you have a list of suspects? People you think might be our mole?"

Sims said, "We do. But until we get you inside Pax AI, it's only an educated guess."

Colt said, "But just to be clear, you now have multiple access points to the company, right? The FBI is investigating Kozlov's death, and government research agencies are involved in projects at their Mountain Research Facility?"

"We are not revealing the fourth-floor leak to anyone at Pax AI," Wilcox said, entering from the back room. "Excuse my tardiness, ladies and gentlemen." He looked at Colt. "Welcome back to the West Coast."

Colt nodded.

Wilcox took a seat. "Special Agent Rinaldi and I have decided we do not want to disrupt the normal patterns of life at Pax AI. While the FBI has interviewed their personnel about the events surrounding Kozlov's death, Pax AI employees shall not be treated like suspects. At least not publicly."

"You don't want to spook anyone," Colt said.

"Precisely. It is very likely that multiple intelligence services are attempting to embed themselves in the company. If Trinity—or any group covertly operating inside Pax AI—discovers we are onto them, it will inhibit our ability to catch them in the act."

Rinaldi said, "Let's go over the key players. Colt, based on what Kozlov told us, these are the people we think were most likely to have been removing data from the Pax AI fourth floor." The screen changed to an image of a man in a white research coat.

Sims said, "This is Luke Pace. Their chief scientist."

Rinaldi said, "He and Kozlov worked closely together, and they were on the same shift at the Mountain Research Facility. Both had access to the fourth-floor projects and the Mountain Research projects. Only a dozen others had that type of security clearance."

Colt raised his eyebrows. "Only a dozen? Companies like this normally have large teams working on top projects."

Weng clicked her pen. "Pax AI's top projects are *extremely* secretive. A lot of the development programs at top tech companies have security measures that rival the intelligence community." She paused. "Stop me if you already know all this."

Colt nodded politely, "I'm familiar. Much of my work involves such corporations."

"Not like Pax AI," said Wilcox. "They're on another level."

Colt said, "I've only read a little about The Facility. That's what they call it, right?"

Weng nodded. "The Pax AI Mountain Research Facility is where they conduct their shielded AI experimentation."

"Shielded?" Colt asked.

Weng continued, "A remote research center in the forest about an hour's helicopter ride to the northeast. Researchers have to live and work there in multiweek shifts. No outside contact when they're running their experiments. They seal off any electronic signals going in or out of the facility. Both for safety and security reasons."

Colt said, "Sounds like overkill."

Rinaldi nodded. "Think of the R&D at Pax AI like Skunkworks during the Cold War. The programs they are developing . . . it's cutting-edge stuff. Pax AI is consistently ahead of the pack."

"How are they doing that?"

Rinaldi said, "Honestly, no one knows. But they've consistently beat competition to the punch in reaching new milestones in artificial general intelligence, AI-neural interfaces, and quantum technology."

Weng leaned forward in her seat. "I mean . . . we know how they're staying ahead, right? It's Jeff Kim. Their CEO is the thread that connects all these things. He's a mathematical genius, and he's got a particular knack for everything AI."

Rinaldi said, "The point is, Pax AI is the crown jewel in a technological arms race that the entire world is invested in. Where foreign spy services once trolled Washington and London, now they are casing agents on the streets of San Francisco, Seattle, and Vancouver. China and Russia, mostly, but others too." Rinaldi paused, seeing Colt nodding. "Sorry. I keep forgetting you aren't exactly new to this."

Colt waved his hand. "No, it's all right. Broadly I'm familiar. But I haven't spent much time in San Francisco, or any with Pax AI until recently. It would be great to get a lay of the land."

Weng said, "You and I can grab lunch after this, and I'll show you some of the fishing ponds."

"Fishing ponds?" Colt replied.

Sims said, "Where the Russian and Chinese agents recruit people. This area is flush with so many potential agents coming in and out that we joke it's like they're keeping the place stocked with fish."

Rinaldi pointed to the screen at the head of the table. "Let's continue. Gerry Nader, the chief technology officer."

The image changed to a man in a business suit.

"He also has access to the Pax AI fourth floor and The Facility. He turned down offers two to three times his current salary from much bigger companies because he wanted to work there. Nader rose through the ranks of Silicon Valley, hopping from company to company. There's a lot of speculation that he's gunning for Jeff Kim's CEO spot."

Colt said, "Do we think either Pace or Nader have connections to this Trinity organization?"

The two FBI agents shifted in their seats at the word "Trinity." Weng looked at them.

Rinaldi said, "You are assuming that Trinity exists . . ."

"You don't think it does?" Colt asked.

Rinaldi looked at Sims, who said, "I've been working in the FBI's counterintelligence division for a long time. We've been hearing rumors about this Trinity network for years. But it's like Bigfoot and UFOs."

"It's all over the internet. Whether it's rubbish or not, Trinity's following is very real. And growing. There are social media groups full of people worshiping it like some sort of cult," Colt huffed, shaking his head.

Sims said, "The evidence suggests Trinity is nothing but a conspiracy. But . . ."

She looked at Rinaldi, who tapped on his keyboard. The screen changed to a view of city buildings. "Seattle FBI captured an image fragment of the shooter. Take a look."

Colt didn't recognize the building, but a map next to the image showed the location as just across from Kozlov's hotel.

The image zoomed in to a masked man lying in the prone position on a long wooden table. He was fifteen to twenty feet deep inside the room, which concealed him from anything but a direct line of sight. The man wore all black and was looking through the scope of a high-powered rifle. Even with the spotty image quality, Colt could see the weapon was enormous.

"Fifty-caliber?"

"Yes," said Rinaldi. "ATF just got back the forensics. Subsonic round, with a suppressor. There was construction going on in the building where the shot was taken, which likely helped to mask the sound."

Another man stood behind the shooter, elbows out, looking through his own scope.

"How'd you get the photo?"

"This was taken from a cellphone. Someone in Kozlov's hotel took a picture while looking outside their window. They happened to get a still frame just before the shot was fired. So far this is the only image of the shooter."

"Is that a tattoo?" Colt pointed at the screen. The sniper's forearm was exposed from the wrist to the elbow, revealing an ink pattern.

Rinaldi said, "Good eye. We think it's this." The screen changed to show an up-close tattoo of a burning cross wrapped in barbed wire. Rinaldi translated the Cyrillic lettering on the cross. "It reads, 'Faith in God, not in communism.'"

"That doesn't sound so bad," Weng said.

Colt said, "It's a Russian gang tattoo, I believe."

Rinaldi and Sims looked impressed.

Sims nodded. "He's right. This guy's probably been in a Russian prison. Which doesn't mean he's working for the Russians. Could be just a hired gun. But our investigators have spent days studying every security camera and cellphone data point surrounding this location, and this is the only evidence that's turned up."

Wilcox said, "Meaning, these guys are good at what they do."

Rinaldi nodded. "A lot of people could have made this shot. Not a lot of people could have evaded detection so well."

Colt said, "So this makes you think the Trinity claim of responsibility is . . . what? A distraction?"

"We're still investigating. It's just too early to say," Rinaldi replied.

Sims added, "To play devil's advocate, let's say Trinity really is more powerful and well-organized than we thought. Or maybe there are just a few Trinity followers who have deep pockets and criminal connections? They could be taking certain actions and claiming responsibility under the name Trinity."

Weng said, "Almost like a self-fulfilling prophecy. A self-fulfilling conspiracy theory group. You tell people there is a group that wants to use violence to harm AI tech companies, and the crazies come running to join in the fun. Before you know it, that's what's happening. It's not unlike Islamic extremist lone-wolf terrorism. All you need is to seed the idea for it to come true."

Colt cursed. "How do you fight that?"

Uneasy looks from around the table.

Colt folded his arms. "Okay. Is it possible that someone who follows Trinity is stealing information from the fourth floor? Could that be the stolen data Kozlov stumbled onto?"

Wilcox removed his glasses, rubbing the lens clean with his shirt sleeve. "We don't know. But I think we should treat it as a real possibility until we have more certainty."

Weng said, "That's why we need you on the inside."

"What about Ava Klein?" Colt asked. "Is she on the list of potential suspects?"

The screen switched to a professional photo of her. Sims said, "As the head of marketing, Ava is less privy to the research and development side of the house. While she is included in fourth-floor meetings with the Pax AI leadership team, she doesn't have access to the Mountain Research Facility. So according to Kozlov, that rules her out."

Rinaldi tapped on his computer and the screen shifted to a middle-aged man in khakis and a polo shirt.

"This is their head of security, Sean Miller. Formerly with the Defense Intelligence Agency. Retired about eight years ago and cashed in bigtime. He's got access to everything, but one would hope with his background that his loyalty is indisputable."

Colt frowned. "Is there any way he knows about this fourth-floor data leak?"

Wilcox shook his head. "Unlikely. I've had closed-door conversations with him, and he's been very honest with me. I didn't show our cards, but I think he told me everything he knows. I think they are completely unaware they have a mole. Trust me, he's looking for them."

The screen changed to show several magazine covers, each with Jeff Kim in various proper poses.

Weng recited his bio. "Jeff Kim. Second-generation Korean-American. Ultra-successful entrepreneur. He left college early to start his first company, which he sold for more than eight figures. He's driven. Intense. Introverted. You never know what he's thinking, but when he speaks, it's usually to say something brilliant. He has a following on social media that rivals Taylor Swift."

"Is that good?" Rinaldi said.

Wilcox cleared his throat. "Go on."

Weng said, "Jeff Kim's profile in *Vanity Fair* was revealing. In an interview, he said something to the effect that he harbored deep worry about mankind's future . . . with his gifts come great responsibility, and he feels the burden of being the one who might unleash AGI upon the world. He actually told the interviewer he thinks he'll either be mankind's savior, or our destroyer. He doesn't think there will be an in-between."

Colt narrowed his eyes. "Sounds like he thinks highly of himself. That's good, though. We can use that. But is he really a person of interest here?"

Wilcox shook his head. "For obvious reasons, it's highly unlikely that he is stealing his own data from the headquarters. He's in charge of the company. He has good financing and government support, and has great talent working for him. He just needs to execute, and he'll be at the forefront of the next major tech revolution. Why would he sabotage himself?"

Colt said, "Exactly."

Rinaldi argued, "But that doesn't mean he couldn't have been involved in Kozlov's murder. We don't know that Kozlov's death is related to the data breach."

Colt raised his finger. "That raises a question. You said you don't want to disrupt patterns of life at Pax AI. You haven't informed their head of security about the data breach. Does that mean you are going to continue to let whoever is doing this steal information?"

Everyone looked at Wilcox. "Tomorrow, when you get there, they will give you a desk and a computer on their network. You'll help us install surveillance software to make sure we can monitor for any further data theft."

"Without their knowledge?"

Rinaldi said, "We have a warrant."

Colt looked at Wilcox to check that he approved. His face said he did. "Okay."

Wilcox said, "I think we can be reasonably confident Jeff Kim is not the source of the data theft. And again, we need to catch whoever that operative is. But we don't want to piss off Jeff Kim. He's a national treasure. Hurting our relationship with him hurts our national security. Understood?"

Colt nodded. "Understood."

Rinaldi said, "We have three major questions to answer. Question one, who is the mole inside Pax AI, and who are they working for? Question two, who killed Kozlov?"

Colt said, "And the third question?"

Weng leaned forward in her chair. "Whoever eliminated Kozlov wouldn't have taken that risk if he'd already passed on everything he knew. There must be something more. Something he hasn't told us . . . or something he didn't know he should tell us. Maybe he didn't understand its importance. So . . . what did Kozlov see that was so important he had to be killed?"

9

An hour later, Weng and Colt walked along the streets of Chinatown.

"This is the Dragon's Gate," said Weng. "It's a famous tourist spot." A Chinese-style faded green roof sat atop stone pillars. Small orange serpents rested above the gate. It reminded Colt of a Chinese temple or ancient building.

They turned to walk up a very steep street—Colt was finding that every street was a climb here. They passed gift shops selling traditional Chinese dresses, statues, and trinkets. A cable car bell rang a few blocks away.

"The financial district is down there." Weng pointed down the hill, people and cars everywhere. Some of the buildings had Chinese architecture, their rooftops curved upward. On one street Colt saw beautiful murals painted on brick walls. One with Bruce Lee, his body flexed in a kung-fu stance. Another mural extending nearly one hundred feet along a city block depicted a red and purple dragon with a golden tiger's head. And many of the restaurants and shops were titled with both English and traditional Chinese lettering.

They walked for several blocks, and Weng filled him in on

street names and notable buildings. A lot of them were three- and four-story buildings with residences atop ground-level shops. Fire escapes zig-zagged along the street-side exteriors.

Colt tried to categorize the faces of people on the street. To keep aware of any eyes that might be watching from the windows, but there were so many it was nearly impossible.

He said, “This place must be a nightmare for street work.”

Weng said, “It is. But we know a few places where the sharks like to feed.” She nodded toward a Chinese restaurant to their right. “Let’s get a bite to eat.”

They entered and Colt felt like he was no longer in the US. Elaborate decorations of red and gold adorned a polished wooden wall. Dark metal statues of ancient Chinese-style animals rested between tables. Tasteful paintings of Chinese landscapes hung on the wall. Colt was one of the only white people in the place.

The waitress showed them to a seat near the front of the restaurant. She offered them two menus, but Weng said something to her in Mandarin and the waitress hesitated before taking them back. Weng said something else and the woman replied in a conciliatory tone, departing with a slight bow.

“She was gonna give us the fake menu. Hmph.”

Colt frowned. “Fake menu?”

“They give it to all the white people. The tourists who come in here. All good Chinese restaurants have two sets of menus. One for people who can read Chinese and know what to order and one for people like you.”

“Good to know.”

“So are we going to get a different menu?”

Weng shook her head. “Nah. I know what to get here.”

Soon the waitress was back, bringing tea, followed a few minutes later by Peking duck, a dough-like bread, and green onions. It wasn't a ton of food, but it was excellent. And they weren't really there to eat anyway.

Weng's eyes were on her food when she whispered, "The guy across the street, about half a block down, sitting by himself under the pink umbrella."

Colt glanced in that direction. A line of umbrellaed tables stood outside another Chinese restaurant. "I see him."

Weng said, "His name is Liu. MSS."

"Chinese intelligence hangs out in Chinatown? Isn't that a bit obvious?"

Weng turned to Colt. "There are a lot of benefits. Easier concealment for him and any ethnic-Chinese agents he is running. His countersurveillance blends in as well. And to be honest, I think he likes the food."

They stopped talking as the waitress came by with the bill. Weng paid and thanked her in Chinese. Colt followed Weng out the front door and headed left down the sidewalk, in the opposite direction from where Liu was sitting.

After walking around the corner, Weng continued their discussion. "I've been tracking him for the past year. He usually eats there a few times a week. I figured we might get lucky."

"Does he meet agents there?"

"Not that we've seen. He's very careful. Liu is officially a science and technology advisor to the Chinese consulate here in town. We know he is actually a twenty-year veteran of Chinese intelligence. He runs a network of agents in the Bay Area, most of them students or Chinese citizens with temporary visas. China sends so many people here for school or work that there is no shortage of informants. Their agents usually don't even think of themselves as working for the MSS. They're just students, and sometimes a government man might come around, asking them questions about the latest tech research, and they know to pass information along when asked."

Colt knew what Weng said was true. He had seen evidence of it during his own clandestine operations.

"Anyone at Pax AI?"

She shook her head. "We haven't found a connection yet, but that's concerning because Pax AI must be a target."

Colt said, "So you think the MSS has someone inside Pax AI, and we just don't know who."

Weng signaled for a cab, and a luxury SUV pulled up. A strange radar-looking contraption sat on top. When Weng saw him looking at it, she said, "Driverless cars. Looks like this particular unit is still in testing, but some taxi companies in the city are already fully automated."

Inside the car, Weng told the test driver where to go, and he typed in the location on a central control unit. Then the test driver sat behind the wheel, not touching anything as they began moving through the hilly streets.

"Check out over here," Weng said, her voice low.

Colt turned to see a gentlemen's club as they drove by.

"It's owned by a guy with connections to the Russian mob. The GRU has an officer we've identified who goes there a lot. We think he sometimes picks off low-hanging fruit in there. Cyber-security managers. Programmers at big firms who are involved in government contracts. They have a few girls on the payroll at several clubs in the area."

Colt saw a sign for the Civic Center, and Weng leaned forward in the car, saying, "You can let us out here."

The car stopped on a city street painted red in the center lanes. Wide brick sidewalks emptied into a large brick plaza. Some people stood in line for food trucks while others ate their lunch on stone steps surrounding fountains in the center of the plaza.

They grabbed iced coffees from a nearby coffee shop and continued walking. Weng pointed to a few buildings, listing off several venture capital firms.

"This is where the SVR does its work."

"What do you mean?"

"The SVR's strategy is to recruit agents from the executive ranks of these venture capital firms. I'm not sure you can even call it recruiting, really. More like making deals. Finding partners. Not all of these firms play ball. But it only takes a few. The VCs know they're making a deal with the devil. But they have teams of lawyers making sure they don't get caught. This one here is Sheryl Hawkinson's firm."

"Hawkinson? As in Guy Hawkinson? The CEO of that private security contractor?"

Weng nodded. "Lots of rumors about her, none of them proven. Wilcox won't let us go near her, though. Too risky, he said. Her family contributes to half the politicians in the state, including one senator on the intelligence committee."

"Wonderful," Colt said. "Where is the SVR running this out of?"

"The Russian consulate in Houston, we think. Petrov is the *rezident* there. He's also the number two SVR officer stationed inside the continental US. He's made half a dozen trips to San Francisco just this year. Rinaldi is pretty sure this VC recruiting thing is his op."

Colt's instincts tingled. "I know who Petrov is. He oversaw my agent. The one who disappeared after Seattle."

Weng said, "So you must already be familiar with this program."

Colt shook his head. "No. First time I've heard about it."

They traded a look of concern.

Colt checked his watch. "I should get back to my hotel. I need to prep for tomorrow. I'm still playing catch-up on Pax

AI. I need to know the numbers by heart when I meet their executive team. Don't want to get in there and look suspicious."

Weng ordered them another car ride, which came in less than a minute. As they were driving away, they passed a grassy park. Pedestrians walked along a paved path, many accompanied by dogs. Trees were scattered throughout the gentle slope of the lawn.

Under the shade of one of those trees, a woman sat on a park bench, speaking to a man in a business suit who was sipping an iced drink. The woman looked very familiar.

Colt craned his neck to keep his eyes on her as they drove by.

"What is it?" Weng asked.

He didn't answer for a moment, mentally replaying what he'd seen. Then Colt leaned over to Weng and whispered, "You say it's the SVR that operates in this area?"

She nodded. "What did you see?"

"I can't be sure, but I think I just saw my missing agent."

10

Colt awoke at four the next morning, his body still adjusting to the Pacific Time Zone. He threw on workout clothes and hit the hotel gym for an hour, listening to music while his mind turned over the same few questions plaguing his team.

Who was the mole inside Pax AI, stealing secrets from their most secure area? Who killed Kozlov, one of Pax AI's lead scientists, and why?

Had Colt really spotted his agent yesterday? Marisha Stepanova, known only by her SANDSTONE cryptonym in the CIA's classified intelligence reports, was one of the highest-placed Russian intelligence agents America had scored in years. She had gone dark after Kozlov was murdered. Colt would have done the same. As the one who had provided Kozlov's name to the Americans, she needed to protect herself. If the Russians had killed Kozlov, they very likely knew she was a traitor. If she was really here, operating in San Francisco, SANDSTONE may have felt comfortable enough to continue her work with the SVR. She hadn't fled.

Or it could mean she hadn't been truthful when supplying information to the CIA. Perhaps she had been in on Kozlov's murder? Weng said Petrov, Marisha's SVR direct superior, was in charge of recruiting San Francisco-based venture capital executives as Russian agents. If so, why hadn't Marisha ever informed Colt of the operation? Had she not been aware? If Colt really had spotted her here yesterday, that seemed unlikely.

Colt finished on the treadmill and grabbed a towel and bottled water, heading up to his room. Once there, he ordered a light breakfast, showered, shaved, and dressed in his business attire. Breakfast came and he read the *Wall Street Journal* digital edition while he ate.

He arrived at Pax AI's headquarters at nine a.m.

Colt got out of the host company car and thanked the driver, who once again wouldn't accept a tip. The headquarters building was at least thirty years old, by the look of it, and the exterior wasn't flashy. Four floors. Gray paint on the walls. Decorative black shutters surrounded the windows, all of which had shades drawn. Next to the headquarters was a two-story elevated structure with an orange windsock. Their company helipad. Impressive.

Colt noticed a lot of CCTV cameras. Dark half-orbs like robotic eyes, taking everything in. Colt wondered if anyone was watching him as he headed toward the main entrance.

He passed an armed security guard who watched Colt enter through a revolving front door. The interior of the building had a more vibrant feel. Sleek hardwood floors, splashes of bright color on the walls, modern architectural design. A woman with purple hair sat at the front desk. Two more security guards stood at a desk behind her.

The front desk woman greeted Colt with a smile and took his name, then began typing a message to someone on her computer.

She looked up and spoke with a cheery tone. "Gerry says he will be right down."

One of the security guards walked up and said, "Sir, if you would come over here, we'll get your badge. Arms out, please. He'll take your bag."

Colt handed his briefcase to the second security guard as the first waved a metal detector wand around his outstretched arms and legs. They rifled through his bag and then handed it back before printing out a plastic ID card and attaching it to a lanyard.

"Please wear this around your neck at all times. You'll need the chip to access your office and computer."

Colt thanked them and then stood by a cluster of empty chairs in the waiting area, studying his surroundings. Wide floating stairs led to the four floors above. The sweet smell of baked goods and coffee filled the air. He heard what sounded like an espresso machine whirring from an internal café around the corner. Several employees were laid out on beanbag chairs and couches, wireless headphones plugging their ears as they typed away on stickered laptops.

"Colt McShane?" A tall man wearing khakis and a white button-down shirt called out as he walked down the stairs.

The man walked over and stuck out his hand.

"Gerry Nader, chief technology officer here at Pax AI," the man said, giving Colt a million-dollar smile.

"Good to meet you," Colt said.

"Come on, let me show you around." He gestured for Colt to follow him. They walked around the corner and up to the café. "Would you like anything? One thing we pride ourselves on here is great coffee."

A barista smiled from behind the counter. Both men ordered lattes and made small talk as they waited for their drinks, sharing personal history and business contacts. Playing the game of "oh, do you know so-and-so?" The typical first conversation Colt encountered when starting an investor evaluation.

They discussed Colt's plans for the next few weeks regarding financial analysis, and Nader provided recommendations on how to spend his free time in the city. Then the lattes arrived, and Nader continued their walk around the first floor. Colt saw a man wearing a visitor badge with the words *Special Agent* preceding his name.

"Is he with the FBI?" Colt asked after they walked out of earshot.

Nader nodded somberly. "Yes. By now you must have heard about the death of one of our AI researchers."

"I did. I'm so sorry. Any word on what happened?"

Nader shook his head. "Well, these crazy Trinity people have taken credit for it. You saw the extra security at the front desk. Our head of security is doing a complete evaluation and we'll be getting much stronger on that front."

Colt said, "How is everyone holding up?"

"It's been a mess, to be quite honest. Security is the main issue. And the HR issues that go along with it. We've asked most of our rank-and-file scientists and engineers to move into temporary housing so we can provide better security. Essentially, we bought up a floor of suites at a luxury hotel in Palo Alto. A logistical nightmare with all the families. Some of our employees quit, citing safety concerns. Others didn't want to deal with the hassle. The executives all have personal bodyguards staying with us now."

"Oh my. I didn't even think of that. So, you think what happened to Kozlov . . . something like that could happen again?"

Nader shrugged. "Personally, no, I don't think so. I think it was probably some deranged lunatic. A tragedy certainly, but our head of security is working closely with the FBI and they tell us we are all very safe. Still, we must be cautious."

"Must be hard on all the employees."

"It will be. It's an enormous amount of work . . . and it's quite challenging for a company like ours to replace personnel at that talent level . . ." Nader's face reddened as he realized that wasn't what Colt meant. "But obviously everyone feels just awful. Kozlov was a very nice man. It's just such a shame. These conspiracy theories have gotten completely out of hand. Anyway, you saw the FBI agent. They're wrapping up the last of the interviews with us. Such a tragedy."

They reached the wide stairway, which was right next to an elevator. Nader said, "Hope you don't mind, I'm trying to get my steps in." He held up his smartwatch and they walked up to the second level.

The entire second floor was a combination of open office desks and glass-walled huddle rooms. Colt looked into one of the meeting rooms as they passed. Engineers and scientists gathered around a long whiteboard. They were young, most in their twenties and thirties. One was pointing at the board and speaking as another scribbled down a complex formula.

"This is where the sausage gets made," Nader said. "These are some of the smartest people on the planet." He turned to Colt. "How familiar are you with our work?"

"I've read all of the pre-reading your firm prepared. Artificial intelligence is a fascinating field. But I'm sure everything I know would be miniscule compared to the people who work here."

Nader said, "No problem. We've set up a crash course tour for you this week. And Jeff has said to give you whatever you need, so just say the word."

"Thanks."

Nader stopped outside one of the glass-walled offices. "Here's you. You can put your bag down inside if you like."

It was a simple office. A bamboo standing desk with a push-button control on the side. A computer and a few office supplies. Colt placed his leather travel bag on the desk.

"Now we'll head up to the third floor and say hi to Jeff real quick."

As they walked up another flight of stairs, Colt caught a glimpse of the fourth floor. The stairway led to a door with what looked like a fingerprint and eye scanner. An armed guard sat on a chair outside it, looking back at Colt. Beyond him, the glass walls were opaque.

"Looks like a higher level of security up there?"

Nader said, "That's where our development team works. Only a handful of our one hundred and fifty employees are allowed up to the fourth floor. We also hold some of our lead team meetings there, when the meeting covers those programs."

"I assume I'll be able to check it out?"

Nader gave an awkward grin. "We'll have to check with Jeff on that."

So much for whatever you need.

The third floor had less open floor workspace, and the offices were larger. Some of them had transparent glass while others were opaque. Colt watched as a glass office wall transformed from opaque to clear as someone walked out the door.

Colt nodded toward it. "That's a cool party trick."

Nader said, "Yeah, all the glass on the third and fourth floors has a polarization mechanism so we can make meetings visually private. Seems high tech at first, but you get used to it."

Kim's corner office was transparent, and Colt saw the

famed CEO kneeling on a yoga mat, his eyes closed, hands on his knees.

Nader said, "It looks like he's meditating. He's really into that. But I think he'll be done soon." Nader tapped the touch screen outside Jeff Kim's office, swiping to check the CEO's schedule. "Yeah, he's only got two more minutes of this."

They waited in silence, which Colt found weird. As the clock hit the top of the hour, Nader tapped on the glass door and Jeff Kim's eyes opened. He gestured for them to enter and stood to greet Colt.

"Mr. Kim, thank you for having me," Colt said.

Kim said, "Absolutely. Given that one of our senior researchers passed away unexpectedly, I understand the perceived risk among our investors. It is only prudent to have a trusted third party conduct a financial prospective analysis."

Nader remained quiet while Kim spoke, assuming a deferential posture a few feet to the side. Colt had the distinct impression that Jeff Kim's employees worshiped the ground he walked on.

Colt said, "I appreciate your honest perspective."

"Of course." Kim turned to his CTO. "You'll show Mr. McShane around today?"

"We have a few days of presentations showing him everything about our company."

"Including the fourth floor, I hope?" Colt said.

Nader shot him a look, but Colt didn't blink. He was, as far as they were concerned, there on behalf of investors. It was expected that Colt would want to get his eyes on all aspects of Pax AI's business, especially their most tightly kept secrets.

Kim gave a thin smile, his voice soft. "I'm sure we can figure something out. We'll just need to take security precautions." He looked at Nader. "Let's make sure Colt gets a tour of the fourth floor soon. He should have full visibility."

"Will do, Jeff."

A dull knock on the glass door behind them caused Colt to turn. Two men stood at the door, one holding a tablet computer with a stylus.

"Does Jeff have a moment?"

Nader said, "Guys, we're in a meeting."

Colt said, "I don't mind."

"Thank you." Kim walked over to the door.

Nader said, "You will have to excuse my engineers. These two are working on our new language algorithm we just announced."

The room went silent as Kim held the tablet, his eyes scanning the screen.

"What is this?" he asked, pointing at the tablet. Colt snuck a peek, but to him it just looked like random streams of text and numbers. "This isn't right."

One of the engineers said, "We double-checked it."

"Then you got it wrong twice." Kim walked over to a dry erase board near his desk. "Look, I'll write it out."

Colt watched as Kim began scribbling what looked like multi-line calculus equations on the board. He handed the tablet back to one of the engineers with his free hand while using the other to finish the math. "See? Take a look at the second page of code. Line 32. Then look at this. If you release it like that, you'll still have grammar induction errors in the linguistic model."

The two engineers looked at the board and then back at the tablet, understanding dawning on them.

One of them said, "Oh shit. He's right. We missed that." He looked up. "Sorry, Jeff, we'll get it fixed."

"Take a picture of this, please." Kim gestured to his white board, and the engineer holding the tablet took a picture.

Kim's voice was patient as he said, "Please take your time and get it right."

The two men nodded and walked out of the office. As they left, Colt heard the second engineer whisper, "How the hell did he catch that?"

After they left, Kim turned back to Colt. "Do you know why you are here?"

"Given the stage in your company's development, and the amount of financing that could be injected into your balance sheet by the investors I represent, I am here to provide a risk assessment."

Kim said, "That pretty much sums it up. And it's part of our job to wine and dine you in hopes that it improves your evaluation."

Colt gave a polite laugh.

"In all seriousness, if you need anything, let me know. This is very important to us."

"Thank you," said Colt.

Kim inclined his head to Nader, who said, "Thanks, Jeff."

Nader and Colt departed, heading down the hall as Kim's door slid shut. With his peripheral vision, Colt could see Kim standing behind the glass door.

He was still watching them when the glass walls of his office became opaque.

11

Colt followed Nader into a third-floor conference room, thinking about Kim's ability to pick out flaws in the AI language algorithm just by glancing at his engineer's tablet. He realized that some of these people were scary smart. That level of brainpower was off the charts. Even if Kim had something to hide, would a man like that make a mistake?

Nader gestured for Colt to sit down. "We'll spend the morning in here. We have a few short presentations, followed by lunch at a nice place downtown, and then we'll be back here in the afternoon to let you pore over financials."

Colt smiled. "Sounds like fun."

A short, bearded man entered the room carrying a laptop, a pen tucked above his left ear.

"Colt, this is Luke Pace."

Pace nodded without saying hello, then sat down and began furiously typing on his computer.

Nader said, "Despite his manners, he's an exceptionally talented chief scientist, and unfortunately he's all we can afford at the moment."

Pace snorted. After a few more seconds of typing, he

slapped the laptop shut and made brief eye contact with Colt. "Sorry, I was just finishing something up. Lots to do."

"No problem at all. A pleasure to meet you," Colt said.

"Cold-pressed coffee?" Nader asked. "Cold latte? It's the good stuff. La Colombe. We keep them chilled in this mini-fridge if you want any. For hot coffee, you'll need to go back down the stairs."

"I'm good." Colt held up his still-full cup from downstairs. These people wanted for naught.

Nader gave Pace a look. "Ready when you are."

"Oh, I'm presenting, aren't I?" Pace said, re-opening his computer. He tapped a few keys and the projection screen on the conference table lit up.

A video began playing, the narrator's voice a middle-aged woman with a British accent.

"What is learning?" said the narrator.

On the screen, a toddler walked on a flat lawn, blurred green trees and water in the background.

"What is intelligence?"

The video showed high school students at their desks, taking a test.

"What is our goal, when we train machines to learn and become more intelligent?"

Now the video showed Pax AI employees animatedly talking to each other in front of white boards or typing on their computers while sitting in beanbag chairs. The video cut to images of robot hands manipulating dinner plates.

"At Pax AI, we believe that machine learning needs to be done in a way that is safe and beneficial for all mankind."

Now the robot hand was solving a Rubik's Cube. A smiling researcher observed, the Pax AI logo emblazoned on his white lab coat.

"As our technology progresses, so does learning. What once took

our species years to learn can now be completed in seconds. At Pax AI, we can run thousands of simulations simultaneously, teaching our machines faster than ever."

Now the video showed four-legged robots hiking up rocky terrain, assisting miners in what looked like a third-world country. A graphic of a climbing stock chart overlayed the screen.

"*Using reinforcement learning, our AI programs develop increasingly complex strategies for solving problems. Using multi-agent game play to allow our bots to interact with each other, we've been able to improve our AI system's ability to learn. Reinforcement learning is the same way that human beings have become generally intelligent. But that took countless generations and a lot of time. Computers are not bound by the same speed limitations. A generation of learning, in a simulation, can take a nanosecond.*"

Colt watched as video game competitions pitting human teams against Pax AI teams flashed on the screen. Then a separate video showed red and blue bot-on-bot simulations.

The video went on for another ten minutes, showing the separate projects the company was working on, AI programs that could learn to anticipate and fulfill human requests. Ordering groceries when running low or scheduling a meeting after being introduced to a new client.

"What is that?" Colt asked.

The last part of the video showed a woman putting on headgear as scientists helped her.

Pace paused the video. "One of our projects has a cranial-mounted device that enables a neural interface."

Colt looked at Nader, who translated. "It's a type of headgear that allows primate animals and human beings to control machinery without physical inputs."

Colt snorted. "You're kidding, right?"

Pace said, "I'm surprised you haven't read about it. Our competitors are working on similar devices."

He unpaused the video, and the narrator began speaking again.

"With our market-leading prediction algorithms, Pax AI's goal is to safely introduce our AI systems to an increasingly complex set of environments and—"

Nader smirked at Colt. "Sorry, I think our engineers are writing this copy."

"With increased computing power, AI-augmented code development, and breakthroughs in AI techniques, we hope to bring about the first real artificial general intelligence to the world, improving lives through science."

Nader and Pace both looked at Colt when the video was over, a sense of pride in their eyes.

"It's very impressive," said Colt. "And we can really do all those things?"

Pace nodded. "Oh yes."

"What was that simulation with the red and blue bots? In that video game thing?" Colt asked.

Pace's eyes lit up. "That's one of my favorites. We trained two different AI teams to play children's games in 3D environments. Games like tag, capture the flag, hide-and-seek. So, the AI teams are each comprised of separate agents."

"Agents?" Colt asked.

Nader said, "Think of each agent like its own unique machine."

Pace nodded. "So the AI agents, or teams, work together, communicating and learning as we make the games increasingly more complex."

Pace typed on his computer and the display screen changed to a YouTube video with Pax AI branding. It showed little red and blue human-shaped characters moving around blocks and walls, tagging each other and capturing digital flags.

"The agents on the same team actually talk to each other in their own language. We ran thousands of simulations, and over time, they get better and better at overcoming the opposing team. It's incredible what they've learned to do."

The video showed one team moving the blocks around to form barriers, while the other team used blocks to break through one of the barriers and capture the opposition's flag.

Pace said, "Each of the agents has its own combination of neural networks. Some are for vision sensing. Others are for . . . well, thinking and learning. You fast-forward these thousands of simulations and the bots learn new strategies and tactics. Each team overcomes the other and introduces new obstacles until there is no more progress."

Colt said, "What does that mean, no more progress?"

Nader said, "Until one team of bots has a strategic advantage over the other."

Colt said, "Sounds like business. Or war . . ."

"Ha. Yeah, exactly." Pace smiled.

Nader shifted in his seat. "Well, not *war*. Learning. Improvement, optimization."

Colt said, "And . . . that cranial neural interface . . . are you guys actually able to link up machines with people's brains?"

Pace said, "One of our competitors actually had a chimpanzee control a computer with its mind. Neural interface control would be huge in the medical field. Disabled people being able to use an appendage they could control without physical input."

Nader said, "It would be incredibly lucrative."

Colt was incredulous. "How far along is this? Are your results public?"

The two men looked at each other. "We have a way to go. And nothing is public yet."

Nader looked at his watch. "How about we take this conversation to lunch? I'm famished."

The three men headed down the stairs and out the front door, each of the executives shuffling away their own set of engineers and scientists who were eager to speak with them about ongoing work.

A white electric SUV was waiting for them outside. It sped them off into the heart of downtown, dropping them outside an upscale restaurant on California Street. A waiter showed them to a corner table covered by a white cloth and decorated with fresh flowers. The restaurant served mostly Chinese-inspired cuisine, but Colt refrained from telling them he'd had similar food the day before. And this place was much higher-end. Soon Colt was drinking hibiscus iced tea with mint and looking at a menu that didn't have any prices. If you had to ask . . .

"I'll order for us if you don't have any objections. They do it family-style here," said Nader. He ordered in Mandarin.

"You know Chinese?" Colt asked after the waiter left.

Nader shrugged. "I took it at Stanford, and then did an internship in Shanghai for a few months after graduation. The way China's tech is booming, it's been quite helpful."

Interesting. Colt didn't remember seeing that detail anywhere in Nader's file. He would have to ask Weng what she knew about his time in Shanghai.

Soon the waiter brought them a circular wooden box of dumplings and sauce. Colt used chopsticks to hold his while biting into it. An explosion of tasty broth, pork, ginger, and spices filled his mouth.

"Oh my God, this is incredible. Do you guys always eat this well?"

Pace didn't respond. He was thumb-typing on his phone.

Nader laughed. "We're very lucky to have some nice restaurants nearby. I must admit that as our company has taken off, my diet has improved. My weight, not so much."

Colt said, "I did examine your overhead on the plane ride over. Pay and benefits for AI engineers is very competitive."

Nader said, "It's a bit embarrassing what some of these AI companies will throw at you nowadays. Disgusting sums. But that's all going to change."

Colt looked at him sideways. "Are you saying companies will no longer pay top dollar for AI engineers?"

Pace shook his head, looking up from his phone. "No, he means people won't be paid so differently. AI will completely upend our economy in the next ten years."

Colt said, "What do you mean by that?"

Nader sipped his drink. "One of the realities our world will have to confront is that more and more jobs will go by the wayside. And not just blue-collar jobs, either. Bots will replace almost all of us. But here's the thing: how long does it take the average person to learn a new job? Six months? A year? Five years to really gain mastery? AI will learn much, much faster. Doctors, accountants, lawyers . . . they'll all be replaced. Or augmented, and we'll need fewer humans in those roles."

"So . . . you're saying we're all going to be out of work?"

Pace looked up, now interested. "Those who keep working are all going to be working different types of jobs. Ones that demand emotional intelligence or a deep human understanding to do well. But technology keeps evolving at a faster rate. Up until our era, the rate of change was manageable. But with AI . . . *now* you can write some code that displaces *millions* of jobs within a few days' time. As machines begin writing their own code, they will displace jobs even faster . . . hell, they can *invent whole new industries* within nanoseconds. Human beings can't keep up. It's like that *I Love Lucy* skit with the chocolate factory production line. People weren't meant to work around the clock like they do today. Getting emails all night long. Eyeballs in their phones. Screens and computers pummeling information in and sucking data and money out. But machines can always go faster. Human beings can't."

Nader threw up his hand. "Nice going, Luke, there goes our funding. You've converted another one."

Colt smiled, but he had to admit, he felt a little chilled by Pace's doomsday view. "So, Luke, I thought you were excited about the future of AI?"

Pace sighed. "Oh, I am. I don't mean to scare you. For most people, the pressure and the demand of daily work will finally cease. Make no mistake, however, universal basic income *will* be required. The old days of everyone pulling their weight and getting money in exchange for value creation will be gone. People simply cannot keep up with the pace of change. And in a world where humans are surrounded by immortal, all-knowing, *thinking* machines, why would one person ever make more money than another?"

Colt offered what he hoped was the right answer. "You are suggesting they wouldn't?"

Pace pointed his finger at Colt. "Bingo. We are ten to twenty years away from living in a world where wage inequality will start to go away."

Nader snickered.

Colt said, "You don't agree?"

Nader glared at Pace. "I had hoped to shelter you from Pace's doomsday scenario."

Pace looked like he realized he'd gone too far. "Sorry. Maybe I am a bit pessimistic. I have a lot of work back at the office."

A few moments later, they left the restaurant, passing

through a crowd of tourists. Colt scanned the faces in the crowd, trying to maintain good street awareness even in an impossibly crowded environment.

Colt saw her coming.

Marisha Stepanova approached him from the east, masked by the crowd. She wore a beige waterfall coat over a white tee, skinny jeans torn at the knees, and dark sunglasses, and was carrying a Starbucks cup in her left hand.

With her right hand, she executed the brush pass.

She slipped a thin phone into Colt's right pants pocket as she walked by. He forced himself not to react.

"After you," said Nader, holding open the SUV's door for him.

"Thanks," Colt replied, and ducked as he entered the back seat. When he was inside the car, he glanced out the back window.

SANDSTONE was gone.

Colt waited until they were moving and both men were distracted, checking their emails on their own devices. Then he removed the phone Marisha had slipped into his pocket and tapped to illuminate the screen.

It was unlocked, but required him to set a password, which he did. On the home screen, he saw two messages awaiting him.

M: Cease all previous communications methods. Check this device daily.

He texted a reply.

C: Okay.

He was about to stuff the phone in his pocket when he saw the three flickering dots that signified the other party was typing a response. It came a moment later.

M: I will know more about the leak soon.

12

"She'll know more about the leak soon?" Wilcox repeated. It was just after eight p.m. local time. The other team members were gathered around the central table in the counterintelligence unit safehouse.

"That's what she wrote." Colt nodded.

Weng tapped her pen on a notepad. "And no other information?"

"Just the part about comms being compromised. She wants me to use the phone she provided for all further communication."

Weng said, "If she's going to get the identity of the Pax AI mole, does that mean it is more likely another Russian intelligence source?"

Colt frowned. "Wouldn't she already have known about it?"

Weng shrugged. "I don't know. Could be a parallel operation. GRU not wanting to share with the SVR? I mean, how else would SANDSTONE ascertain the identity of a mole in Pax AI unless she had access to information there? And if

Kozlov is now dead . . . doesn't that imply the Russians have another agent inside?"

Rinaldi said, "A logical deduction."

Wilcox shook his head. "I don't know if we can trust her at this point."

Sims said, "At least she's back in contact. Have you messaged her yet?"

"Not yet. I wanted to update you guys first and go over next steps. I agree with Wilcox. I could be getting played."

Rinaldi said, "We can get some of the crypto guys to take a look at the phone. You want to give it to me? Where is it now?"

Wilcox sighed. "We should never allow one of our agents to dictate what *covcom* we use. It's very possible that a GRU cyber espionage unit is using that device to monitor everything you do. If it's within fifty feet of you, they'll know your location, listen to your conversations."

Colt said, "I know, Ed. I have it in a storage locker across town. I'll obviously never take it to Pax AI or to any meetings."

Weng opened a stick of chewing gum and popped it into her mouth. "We can set up countersurveillance on the drop box. That way you don't get rolled up during your daily comm checks."

Rinaldi said, "You'll keep us updated on everything she sends you?"

"I will."

"We should go over any responses, too." Wilcox frowned. "I just don't like this. It would be better to set up a face-to-face, so you know it's her."

Colt said, "I imagine she's under intense scrutiny after Kozlov's death. Or she's been loyal to the SVR this entire time . . ."

Wilcox rubbed his hands together. "Bottom line, we need more confidence in the information she provides. She wants you to use that phone to communicate. Fine. But what else can we do to mitigate the risk?"

Colt said, "I have a technique that I've used in the past with this agent, when we were in high-population-density areas. We can set up a meeting but be in different buildings, across the street from each other, windows facing, so we can see that neither party has a gun to their head. I can tell her I want to do that again. We can still use her phone but set up cameras to verify the accuracy of communications."

Rinaldi said, "I can help with surveillance. What's the name of the storage facility? I'll send a team there now to watch it."

Colt gave him the name and Rinaldi turned to Wilcox, who nodded. "Please set it up."

Weng slapped Colt on the shoulder. "How did the rest of your first day of school go, honey?"

Colt walked over to the fridge and grabbed a bottled water, then sat back down. He took them through every detail of his first day at Pax AI. The morning briefs, the lunch conversations. After lunch, he'd spent the rest of the day being shown around by several different teams, learning more about their projects and future plans.

"Still no fourth-floor access?" Wilcox asked.

"Kim implied it's coming," Colt reassured him.

Rinaldi said, "So you think Pace is discontent?"

Colt said, "If anyone I've met there thus far is sympathetic to Trinity, it's him. He was reciting the same concerns I've read about in news articles about Trinity. Pace is worried the race to develop artificial general intelligence is dangerous. 'Playing with fire,' he said. He seemed particularly worried about their work at The Facility."

Weng was still chewing gum. "Makes sense. Pax AI's Mountain Research Facility is the Area 51 of AI development. A lot of highly classified government contracts are underway there. In all the Trinity conspiracy chatrooms, The Facility is ground zero for their impending AI doomsday scenario."

Colt said, "What kind of projects are they working on there?"

Sims said, "Both IARPA and DARPA have a few. You can use the computer in our back room to access the Congressional summary on those programs. But it's pretty sparse on details. Most of the programs are codeword-level programs that even we aren't cleared for."

"And Pax AI researchers are?"

"Only a few," said Wilcox. "And trust me, they are all being closely monitored."

Colt said, "How is that not a security risk?"

Wilcox clasped his fingers. "It's a technology arms race. Think of it like the Manhattan Project. The US government needs the best scientists in the world working on its behalf, or we'll lose. And a lot of the best AI engineering talent comes from foreign nations. The same thing happened during the nuclear arms race. A lot of our scientists were under suspicion for being sympathetic to our enemies. Today we have an additional level of risk due to our partnerships with private companies like Pax AI."

Colt knew he was right.

Rinaldi said, "I'll put more surveillance on Pace. We'll have our cyber team go through everything he's ever typed. If he's involved in Trinity, we'll know about it."

"What about Nader's Chinese connections?" asked Colt.

Rinaldi turned around the laptop he had open on the table. "His post-college internship in Shanghai was in his file, but plenty of business executives have spent time in China, especially in Silicon Valley. But check this out . . ."

The group leaned in to see what Rinaldi was pointing to on the screen.

Weng hummed. "Very interesting. Gotta love my boy Liu and his MSS college recruiting program."

Colt said, "So Liu was recruiting agents at Stanford while Nader was getting his degree there."

Rinaldi nodded. "Yup. And then he gets an internship there. It's circumstantial, but it's something. Keep your eyes open, Colt."

Colt arrived at the Pax AI office early the next morning. Many of the engineers were already there, working on their computer or conducting tests with robotics in labs. As Colt walked to his office, he again saw meeting rooms packed with diverse groups of scientists, working through complex formulas and graphs they had drawn on white boards.

Colt sat in his black leather swivel chair, the glass walls allowing him to see into several of the adjacent spaces. The company CFO appeared at nine a.m. They met for an hour, going through financial data and projections.

After he left, Colt headed down to the break area to grab a cup of coffee. Gerry Nader was there, speaking with two of his subordinates. Colt overheard him saying something about the control problem. The two employees left, and Colt found himself stirring his coffee, alone with Nader only a few feet away.

"Sorry about Pace at lunch yesterday."

"What for?"

"Oh, he can be a bit of a downer when it comes to conversations on our future. A brilliant mind, but definitely a pessimist."

Colt thought that was putting it mildly. "Don't be silly. I hadn't given it a spare thought."

Nader said, "So is there anything you need?"

Colt smiled. "Just hoping for that fourth-floor tour."

Nader said, "I'm told it's coming. I'll see if I can push the powers that be a little harder."

Someone called to Nader from down the hall.

"Gotta run. I'm already late for my ten a.m."

Colt headed back to his office and continued going through company documents. As much as he was there for the counterintelligence investigation, Colt still needed to perform his duties for his cover job, providing a thorough financial evaluation on Pax AI for deep-pocketed investors. He spent the rest of the morning going through the company's quarterly reports. He ate lunch at his desk and was taken through various projects by Pax AI employees in the afternoon: autonomous navigation, conversational interfaces, ambient computing, and productivity gains from big data synthesis.

There was even one on agriculture, led by Luke Pace.

Pace showed him a video of a farm near Fresno, California. "We have automated a lot of the process. Solar-charged quad-copter drones monitor the fields. We use deep learning programs to evaluate what issues our crops are facing. Whether it be pests, irrigation, fungi . . . whatever . . . the drones provide imagery, our AI analyzes the images, evaluates the problem, and sends out a command to fix it. In most cases, that still requires some human intervention. But our team is working on automated robotic solutions to nearly every issue we face. This can increase crop yields and lower costs dramatically."

Colt nodded. "Fascinating."

Pace said, "And you can see how the same AI programs, using deep learning to evaluate and learn from large data sets and automated responses, could be applied to many other areas. Take health care. Automated, online diagnosis and prescriptions. Boom. Patient time is reduced, quality and costs all improve. Take computer programming. Our new language algorithms can write code as good as most mid-level coders. We can now tell the AI what our objective is, start writing the code, and they will finish hours of work in mere seconds. We no longer need human coders to slog away through lines and lines of code. Instead, human coders become more like proofreaders or editors, double-checking for errors and quality issues. And the AI will learn from that work too."

"Rapid continuous improvement."

"Exactly."

Colt decided to dig. "It sounds like these programs can replace just about everything. What's left for us?" He saw that same flash of fear that had been in Pace's eyes at lunch yesterday. "I'm sorry. I wasn't trying to say anything controversial . . ."

"Not at all," Pace said. "To be honest, you hit the nail on the head. It *will* be a scary transition for people. Until now, technology advanced at a manageable rate. This evolution will be much bigger, faster, and more impactful. Anyone who tells you they know how we will all come out of it is lying, whether they know they are or not."

A movement outside the glass office door caught Colt's eye. A man with a crew cut cracked open the door. "Mr. McShane?"

"Hello?"

The man said, "Your schedule says that you're free after this meeting. Would you mind coming to see me?"

Colt glanced at Pace, who snorted. "God, Sean, you're scaring the guy. Colt, this is Sean Miller, our head of security."

Miller frowned. "Mr. McShane, I'm told you need a security briefing to get fourth-floor access. I have time if you do."

Colt glanced at Pace, who looked impressed as he said, "Welcome to the club." Pace turned to Miller. "Just make sure to go easy on the rectal probe, Sean."

Miller glared at Pace. "My office is down the hall on the right. Just come on down when you're finished."

"Sure thing," said Colt.

Pace's meeting soon adjourned, and Colt was at the security head's office within minutes.

"Please have a seat."

Colt took the chair across from Miller's desk, noticing several pictures on the wall. Miller in military fatigues decades earlier. Miller in khakis and a dark polo, standing next to a tent in the desert. Miller wearing aviator sunglasses, a rifle slung over his shoulder, with what looked like the mountains of Afghanistan in the background.

"You served in the military?" Colt asked as he sat.

"Among other things," Miller answered, studying Colt. "Listen, Mr. Kim asked me to provide you with a comprehensive security brief, which I'll do. He also asked me to prep you for visiting some of our highest security areas."

"Excellent."

Miller hummed disapproval. "Yes, well. I advised against it, but ours is not to reason why."

Miller began speaking about the security procedures in place within the company, and then asked Colt a series of questions, reminding him of a security clearance check for the federal government. Probing for any gambling, drug, alcohol, or debt problems. Asking about foreign travel. Colt gave him all the right answers, and the interview wound down.

"That about wraps it up. We've done our external background check already. I'll reset the access on your badge."

"Glad to know I passed," Colt said. "Mr. Miller, I hope you don't mind . . . I have a question for you. As you know, my goal here is to evaluate the long-term profitability of this company. In my experience, tech companies must fiercely protect their intellectual property. May I ask what Pax AI is doing to prevent cyber theft and industrial espionage?"

Miller didn't look happy to be on the receiving end of any questions. "I can assure you that Pax AI is practicing good cyber hygiene. We are segmenting critical networks, backing up all our data, and using the latest anti-viral software. I also have a team of defensive cyber security personnel working for me in house."

"Can you talk to me about how you segment Pax AI's critical networks?"

Miller scoffed. "No. Not really."

Colt frowned. "Mr. Miller, I'm sorry, but Mr. Kim assured me I would be granted any help needed to evaluate the company and conduct a robust analysis for our investors."

Miller said, "Oh really?"

Colt didn't respond as they stared at each other.

Miller sighed. "Fine. Here's my segmentation metaphor. Imagine that Pax AI's data is all stored on a very large ship. You were a Navy man, right?"

Colt nodded. "I see your background check was thorough."

"It was." Miller continued, "So, let us say that our Pax AI ship is sailing in the North Atlantic and comes into contact with an iceberg. It develops a severe gash in the hull. Now, because we have segmentation of our secure data, the internal compartments of our ship would instantly be sealed off. This will stop catastrophic flooding. In the world of cyber-theft, the moment we are alerted to a penetration, the system shuts off each compartment. This minimizes how much they can steal, or how much damage they can do."

Colt said, "And what if you are not alerted?"

Miller's eyes were steel. "We have some of the best cyber security experts in the world on our payroll. Trust me, we'll know."

"I can't help but think of the Titanic, that's all."

Miller said, "As an additional security measure, much of our most important technology is stored at the Mountain Research Facility. I work with our CTO and chief scientist to make sure the company migrates its most vital IP to that location each calendar quarter."

"And The Facility is more capable of defending against a cyber-theft?"

Miller nodded. "Certainly. It's among the most secure data storage centers in the world. We have multiple physical and electronic barriers that would prevent cyberattack. The Facility's remote location, and our robust security procedures on site, make it as impenetrable as the Pentagon."

"Impressive," Colt said, wondering how many times the Pentagon had been hacked over the years.

"We keep research teams at The Facility very small. Only a dozen or so at a time, including government scientists. There is more human security outside The Facility's walls than personnel who are allowed to enter. Researchers who go there have to abide by very strict procedures. They are kept isolated inside. Oftentimes this is a week or more. The assignment isn't for everyone."

"You're kidding? Why?"

"There can be no electronic transmission in or out of The Facility. The work there is very sensitive. I'm afraid that's all I can tell you."

"Fascinating," Colt said. "Has Pax AI had any cyberattacks?"

Miller snorted. "Of course. Weekly, if not daily. This company is one of the most valuable tech resources in the world, and everyone knows it. We're a ripe target. But like I said, our protection is top-notch, so the frequency of unsuccessful attempts shouldn't concern you."

"What about cyber ransom?"

Miller said, "Ransomware gangs don't normally go for corporate targets. Too dangerous. Much easier to hack into a few rich people's computers and get them to pay. It's industrial espionage you need to worry about. Our security precautions are so great that it would take someone inside our organization to really do damage."

"Industrial espionage. As in, spies?"

"Yes."

"And do you think there are actually spies within your organization?"

"We do everything we can to prevent it. But we've terminated employees and decided against hiring certain personnel, because red flags came up. Even if they aren't spies per se, they might be negligent in their handling of classified information. Or worse, intentionally providing information to third-party professionals. Either corporate contractors . . . usually ex-intelligence operatives . . . or current intelligence operatives from foreign services. The Chinese are our biggest threat there."

Miller looked toward his office entrance, and Colt turned around to see Jeff Kim enter.

"Good morning, Jeff."

"Good morning. I just came to see how things were going. I'm told that you are ready to see the good stuff."

Colt said, "I'm eager to, yes."

Miller chimed in. "Sir, I would still like to conduct a polygraph and . . ."

"A polygraph?" Colt asked.

Kim waved off the comment. "Not necessary. Our investors

sent him here. I think we can be reasonably confident Colt isn't going to steal our secrets. He's being paid to see them."

Miller looked annoyed.

Kim said, "Colt, please forgive the inconvenience, but with the loss of Mr. Kozlov, we're being extra careful. And as you know, we are on the leading edge of some incredible discoveries in the field of AI. You understand that we need to follow proper safety and security protocol before we give you the full tour, right?"

"Yes, of course."

"Thanks for your understanding."

Miller looked satisfied.

Kim said, "Oh, one more thing, Colt. We're having an off-site social event at my home tonight." He shrugged. "It's my birthday. Not the best timing, but things like this help boost morale. Anyway, please know you're invited."

"Thank you very much, I would enjoy that."

"Oh, and Colt? Ava Klein will be there. I understand you two know each other." Kim's eyes locked onto Colt's.

"Yes, we do. It will be good to see her again."

Kim bowed and left.

13

Colt saw the signal as he approached his hotel. A green paper square in the corner of a drugstore half a block down the road. Colt headed up to his room and locked his computer in the safe, affixing a clear strand of fishing wire across the doorline with a drop of adhesive.

He changed into running clothes and headed out of the hotel, donning his wireless headphones as he began running along the city sidewalks. Two blocks down he got Wilcox's call.

"I'm in the café to your left. There's a garden area around the side. Last table, by the side exit."

"Okay," was all Colt said in response. He tapped his earpiece to hang up the call and ran one block past the café before doubling back at a four-way stoplight. He scanned for anyone who might be following him as he made his reversal and did a full loop around the block before reaching the café's entrance.

Satisfied he was in the black, Colt strode in, ordering a bottled mineral water and paying with his phone. He took in all the patrons in the place—only a handful. Two new moms, each with a stroller, sipping sugary iced drinks. A teenager wearing a denim top, eyes buried in her phone.

And a white guy in his early sixties sitting across from a diminutive Asian woman, both wearing tasteful yet not too expensive business attire, while they sipped black coffee. Wilcox and Weng.

Colt said, "I only have a few minutes. I need to get ready. I have a dinner party to attend."

"With whom?" Wilcox asked.

"I like parties," said Weng.

"Jeff Kim invited me to his home. He's having a birthday party tonight."

Wilcox frowned. "Does it strike you as odd that they are throwing a party right now? While the FBI is speaking to them about the death of one of their employees?"

Weng waved away the comment. "His mom probably wasn't thinking it would be a problem when she was banging Kim's father all those years ago, you know what I'm saying?"

"Delightful," said Wilcox.

Colt said, "Of course it strikes me as odd. But I'm not the one throwing the party. And to be honest, everyone I've met at Pax AI thus far strikes me as odd. But Ava is going to be there."

"Speaking of banging . . ." Weng raised her coffee cup before taking a sip.

"Where's she been the past couple of days?" Wilcox asked.

Colt said, "On a business trip."

"You'll need to start building the relationship," Wilcox said.

Weng started to say something, but Wilcox glared at her.

"I understand why I'm assigned here," Colt said. He paused. "Why'd you signal me?"

Wilcox said, "A few updates. We looked into Nader. You were right to be suspicious. There were at least two instances of him and Liu being in the same social gathering while Nader was in college. We were able to refurbish an archived social media photo of someone else who was at the event. It showed them speaking to each other. Still circumstantial."

Colt nodded. "Okay. So, if he's working for the Chinese . . ."

Weng said, "Hold your horses on that one. We stepped up our surveillance on him since yesterday. This morning he met with Sheryl Hawkinson."

Wilcox said, "You know Hawkinson Venture Partners, right?"

Colt turned to Weng. "That's the firm you were telling me about."

She nodded. "It's one of the top VCs in the Bay Area. It was owned by Sheryl Hawkinson's father, who passed away years ago. She and her brother inherited a fortune while they were in their twenties. Sheryl now runs the VC firm. Her brother Guy opened a private security business with contracts all over the world. The Hawkinsons have very strong political connections. Their uncle is Senator Hawkinson of Wyoming. And their political action committee funds some of the biggest names in Congress."

"Why does it matter that Nader met with her?" asked Colt.

Weng leaned forward, careful to speak in a low volume. "Sheryl Hawkinson has been on the FBI counterintelligence division's radar for some time. She's done business with some very controversial clients. So has her brother, for that matter. Some were either connected to the Kremlin, or . . . well, I'm from Jersey, and I think the saying there is that they knew a guy, who knew a guy . . . if you catch my meaning."

"WTF. So Nader is talking to *both* Chinese and Russian operatives?"

Wilcox said, "The Hawkinsons are complicated. It's not quite as simple as saying they're working with Russian state actors. As far as we can tell, they have no desire to further Russian interests. Her brother's company, the defense contractor, has been known to work with the CIA overseas."

Weng said, "You can see why we are careful when dealing with anything Hawkinson. They have serious political connections, and it might not look good for us if we draw attention to them."

Colt frowned. "So . . . the FBI isn't looking into this?"

Wilcox said, "I've been working with Rinaldi on tech counterintelligence for the past three years. There are few things I'm sure of anymore, but this is one: no one in law enforcement wants to go anywhere near the Hawkinsons. Trust me. But if the chief technology officer at Pax AI is providing classified information to her . . ."

Weng finished, "That changes the equation. The stuff they are working on at Pax AI is too important to overlook."

Colt said, "So what does she want with Nader, then?"

Wilcox sipped his coffee. "Sheryl Hawkinson has been angling for a stake in Pax AI for years. To date, Jeff Kim has always held her at bay. But controversy like Kozlov's murder and negative public perception from Trinity followers could impact that. Is it possible Hawkinson is involved in passing secrets from Nader to Russian intelligence? Maybe. But it's even more likely that Hawkinson is playing a different game: trying to maneuver herself to get equity in the company. Or steal Nader away to a competitor she has an interest in."

"What do you want me to do?"

"Keep your eyes and ears open for anything to do with her and Nader. But steer clear of her for now. It's not worth the political flames."

"Will do," said Colt, standing up to leave.

Weng winked. "And good luck with Ava."

14

The Pax AI driving service dropped Colt off at the gravel roundabout entrance to the property. Jeff Kim was the proud owner of a half-acre home in Palo Alto, and it must have cost a fortune: terra-cotta roof tiles, reinforced concrete walls, rich wood panels on the inner ceilings, recessed lighting, spacious open floor plan. The lawn was better manicured than a professional golf course. Smooth egg-shaped stones of various sizes were scattered throughout the grass. A long two-lane swimming pool, its water a captivating dark blue, ran across the backyard. Tall trees surrounded the property, providing privacy.

Several dozen partygoers mingled on the lawn, most wearing expensive clothes and jewelry. The valets must have parked more Ferraris than were on display at the local dealer.

Colt spotted several security personnel among the guests and caterers. Some he recognized from Pax AI, but others must have been brought in for some of the guests.

People were spread out in the backyard, scattered around tall tables holding drinks and food. Colt saw Nader, Pace, and some of their employees gathered in a cluster, drinking and talking among themselves. Colt joined them, taking a glass of champagne from a passing server.

Pace's face was red like he'd been at it for a few hours already. When Colt approached, Pace said, "What say you, Mr. Money?"

Nader looked at Pace disapprovingly. "Come on, Luke."

"I'm sorry? I must have missed the question," Colt replied.

Pace shook off Nader's hand on his shoulder. "We were just discussing whether or not we deserve all of this."

He held up his hands, looking around the multimillion-dollar home's palatial grounds. A server passed by with crackers covered with cream cheese and caviar.

Colt laughed. "I'm not sure I'm qualified to answer that."

"Ah, a cop-out."

Nader said, "All right, I'll bite. Yes, we deserve it. The people at this party are some of the smartest, hardest-working people in the world. We create value. We deserve to get paid for it. It's the natural way of things."

Pace scoffed.

Colt sipped his champagne. "You disagree?"

Nader rolled his eyes. "Of course he does, he's a communist at heart." Pace and some of the others laughed.

"Communists can't afford my car," said Pace.

Eyes turned at the sound of clapping and a few cheers near the back of the lawn. Jeff Kim had come out from a structure near the back of the property.

"What's that little house?"

"That's his meditation room," said Pace. "Kim is really big on meditation. He uses that room as his personal office sometimes, too. Nobody goes in there except for him. He's rather weird about it."

A small group surrounded him. People Colt didn't recognize.

"Who are they?" he asked.

"The upper crust," Pace said. "Those are other CEOs and VCs from the valley. They've come to pay their respects like Mafia dons. Boss man's turning forty."

Colt smiled. "I should have brought a present."

"Nah, he hates that stuff. Just look around his house. It's amazing, but you'll find it is pretty spartan."

Pace left the group and headed toward the bar. The server looked miffed as Pace took the bottle of bourbon and poured himself a glass with ice.

Nader shook his head. "Please excuse him. He gets a little wild at these events. Great researcher, but you'll find a lot of our best engineers don't have the social graces you and I do. Probably a product of not being normal human beings." Nader smiled, turning to look behind himself. "I'll be right back. I'm going to go suck up to the boss for a bit." The engineers left with him, following like schoolchildren.

Colt raised his glass in farewell. Pace rejoined him, bourbon glass in hand. His words were a bit slurred. "Hey, just so you know . . . I'm not trying to be a jerk about all of this or anything, but it's hard to voice an opinion on ethics without sounding like you are bashing the company."

"What do you mean?"

"I mean, there are different loyalty factions inside Pax AI. Maybe inside the whole tech world. Definitely among us AI types. People like Nader think people like us are special. I hate using this term, but sort of like a *master race*. That when AI blows up, we deserve to be the winners. We deserve to be the aristocracy that rules over everyone else."

Pace spoke with conviction, like he thought this description of the future was an obvious possibility.

He went on. "Others say we should share utopia equally with everyone. A progressive outlook, if you will. But even the more open and progressive employees recognize there is serious danger in sharing too much of their AI code too soon." His eyebrows rose to emphasize his point.

"What about you? Where do you stand?" Colt asked.

"I think there's real truth to the warning. If this AGI thing blows up and it goes sideways, that's it. Game over, man."

"Like robots taking over the world?" Colt smiled. "Isn't that just science fiction?"

Pace's face darkened. "You have any idea how many of us tech executives have fortified oh-shit bunkers up in the California wilderness? You'd be shocked. I mean . . . let's be honest, people like me can afford it. But *still* . . . it takes a lot of extra time and effort to buy that shit."

Colt looked at Pace with renewed interest. His personality was very different than Colt would have thought. Much more introspective.

"You were Kozlov's boss, right?"

Pace took another sip of bourbon. "I was."

"How is your team handling the Trinity stuff? Are they worried about their own personal safety?"

"Well, half of my team is living in a hotel with security guards walking the hallways." He snorted, then took another drink of liquor. He looked toward Jeff Kim, surrounded by fawning executives and high-rolling VCs. "Sometimes I don't know what the hell we're doing. You gotta be careful who you say that around, of course."

"What do you mean?"

Pace nodded to the far portion of the lawn. "See that guy?"

Standing there alone, holding a glass of ice water, was Sean Miller, the head of security. He was scanning the crowd, seemingly uninterested in small talk.

"Yes, I met him earlier."

"Careful what you say around him."

"You don't feel like you can speak freely around your head of security?" Colt asked.

"I mean, the guy is like the thought police. Part of his job is to make sure we don't leak trade secrets to competitors. See all those VCs Jeff is schmoozing with? Any one of them would love to take a big wet bite out of this company. Jeff knows it too. That's why he invites them here. He's smart. Keep your enemies closer, you know?" Pace sighed and took another sip of his drink.

"I'm not sure I follow. What's this got to do with Miller? Why don't you feel comfortable speaking freely around him?"

Pace tilted his head toward Colt. He was getting drunk. "Because, man. He's the thought police. If he thinks you aren't loyal to the company, he puts you on his list. And you *don't* want to be on his list." Pace's eyes shot over to Colt. "Some people say Kozlov was on that list . . ."

Colt kept his eyes on his glass, not wanting to alarm Pace. Keep him talking. His reply was casual, almost uninterested. "Really? Huh."

Pace continued. "Miller monitors everything going on at Pax AI. I mean everything. I helped design one of the algorithms he uses to scan our email. Hell, he even reads transcripts of our lead team meetings, which are supposed to be only for a handful of us C-suite types."

"Isn't that just part of his job?"

"Of course. Sure." Pace seemed to catch himself and held up his hands. "Look, it's not that I don't like him. It's just . . . well, he wouldn't have been my first hire. Just a little bit of a questionable background is all."

"How so?"

Pace leaned in, lowering his voice. "Well, Jeff once told me that Miller worked for federal law enforcement for years. They aren't exactly known for their moral compass."

Colt kept his face friendly, fighting off his annoyance and amusement at the comment. "But a lot of people in Miller's security role have that type of background, don't they? Doesn't that make him better at his job?"

Colt could see Miller looking in their direction. So was Nader, for that matter.

Pace was oblivious. He took another sip of his drink, his words getting a bit more slurred. "I guess. But I heard he worked for a cyber security firm that supposedly did some shady business with the Chinese government."

"Really?"

"It's what I heard."

Colt made a mental note to have Rinaldi look into it.

One of the servers walked by and Pace accidentally bumped into him, spilling liquor on his shirt. "Ah, shit."

"Oh, sir, I'm so sorry. Please let me clean that up for you."

"It's all right. I'll get it." He excused himself and departed.

Colt scanned the crowd. He was about to head over toward Nader when he spotted Ava standing on the second-floor balcony.

She was looking down at him, a Mona Lisa smile on her lips. Ava wore a form-fitting white dress and light makeup that accentuated her eyes.

Colt raised his glass in greeting. She raised hers back, then turned and left his view. She appeared a moment later, walking out onto the lawn, her movements graceful. The wealthy businessmen and women clinking glasses and chatting parted like the Red Sea, and soon Ava was standing next to Jeff Kim.

He squeezed her shoulder, another gesture of affection. Not the normal employer-employee relationship. Colt found himself both curious and slightly jealous, unable to take his eyes off her. Soon she was laughing and smiling and drinking from a flute of champagne as the group continued speaking around her. Ava whispered something into Kim's ear, their bodies an inch too close to be anything other than what it was.

Colt averted his eyes, annoyed with himself for not seeing this sooner. He wondered if Wilcox and Rinaldi had missed it. Or maybe they knew, and didn't tell Colt?

A jazz band set up on the far portion of the lawn. They began playing low bass guitar, saxophone, and piano. Colt grabbed another drink, letting the music soothe him as he took in the setting. He realized these were the future kings and queens of the world. Their parties had the best food, the best alcohol. Their clothes and cars and homes were exotic and expensive. Their work was something only they could really understand, but it would eventually control the rest of the world. In the distance, past Jeff Kim's futuristic meditation room, the sun had set in spectacular fashion, a fiery red and orange cloud layer high above them illuminating the California mountains.

Nader spotted Colt standing alone and called him to join his group. Colt walked over. He recognized the woman next to Nader as an actress. A star on a popular TV series. Before long, Colt learned she was dating one of the Pax AI executives, a man at least ten years her senior. A few other minor celebrities were also in attendance. Kings and queens.

Colt felt a tap on his shoulder and looked to see one of the security guards. "Excuse me, sir, but Mr. Kim asked if you would join him?"

Colt excused himself from Nader's circle and headed over to Kim, his eyes on Ava as he approached. Kim made introductions. Two CEOs of tech companies Colt recognized and a philanthropist. A few venture capitalists.

"Ava, I believe you already know Colt."

Ava offered her hand. "Yes, we're old friends. It's good to see you again."

Colt shook her hand, forcing a smile. "You too." Her eyes pierced his own.

Colt remained silent while the group chatted together about the state of the tech industry. They voiced concern about new federal regulations that might be imposed, and bemoaned growing competition.

"It's just getting awful. Stealing your competitor's idea used to be so much more chivalrous!" said one of the CEOs. Most were laughing, although Jeff Kim didn't crack a smile. He remained mostly silent, taking everything in.

Ava stood at his side, charming everyone in their circle. Her comments were humorous at moments, insightful at others. She spoke of business, government, and technology, and seemed to have mastered all subjects.

The music paused and the guitarist spoke into the microphone. "And now, ladies and gentlemen, we have a special guest who will be delivering a surprise birthday performance."

Heads turned to see Ava walking to the performance stage in her tight white dress. The pianist stood and Ava took his seat. She adjusted the microphone and spoke in a low tone without looking up. "Happy birthday, Jeff."

When Ava began playing, a familiar hush fell over the crowd. Colt found himself transported to the first time they met, when she had played piano and sung in a hotel courtyard on the shores of Tel Aviv.

But she didn't sing this time. Just piano. Still, her music was slow and beautiful. Judging by the crowd's reaction, it was the first time she'd played for them.

"Oh my God," Colt heard one of the Pax AI employees say.

"She's amazing," another agreed.

As she played, Ava looked up at Kim. She gave him a captivating, radiant smile.

Then she said, "And I have one more song to play, if that's okay."

The crowd cheered approval.

When Colt heard the first notes of "Rhapsody in Blue," he almost broke out into laughter. She glanced in Colt's direction, if only for a moment, to make sure he got the joke.

Gershwin. She had remembered.

It was a tough song to play well, and Ava displayed her incredible talent as it reached its peak, becoming lost in the music. When she finished, she stood and took a bow as the crowd erupted in applause. Some whistled. Others raised their glasses. She didn't look at Colt as she walked back toward Kim, leaning up and kissing him on the cheek when she reached him. Colt felt a pang of longing as he watched her, thinking about what might have been.

"Are they together?" Colt asked Nader, now standing next to him.

"Ava and Jeff?" He shrugged. "I don't think so. Not officially anyway. We all kind of look the other way on that one. Everyone knows not to ask questions."

"Anyone have a problem with it? HR-wise, I mean?"

Nader arched an eyebrow. "No one's going to challenge the king in his court." Colt could hear a trace of annoyance in his tone. Nader was ambitious, and envious of Jeff Kim. Colt had met many men like Nader. Lifelong climbers. Executives with a singular focus on career ascension, seeing their peers and subordinates as footsteps and handgrips for the journey. Colt didn't trust men like Nader, but he knew enough never to show it.

"Look at this guy," Nader said.

Pace was making his way onto the stage, his drink sloshing from his glass.

Nader shook his head. "Here we go." He tapped one of the Pax AI employees on the shoulder and said, "Can you help me get him off the stage?"

The other man snickered, and they headed over to rein in Pace's drunken show.

When they left, Colt felt a tap on his shoulder. "Did you like my song?"

Colt turned to see Ava standing behind him, alone under an olive tree. Its branches were lit with strings of tiny golden lights.

She held out her champagne flute and they clinked glasses. She watched him as she sipped.

"Your music is just as wonderful as I remember. And yes, I liked your Gershwin."

She smiled. "I was hoping you would remember."

"I will never forget. No singing this time, though?"

For a brief moment, Ava's face flashed a distant despair. "Not in a long time. But hopefully this was still enjoyable."

Colt said, "You were great. Did your employer appreciate it?"

Ava tilted her head, apparently detecting something in his delivery. She appraised him before responding, "You need not worry."

"I know you well enough not to worry. You can take care of yourself," Colt said.

She stared at him a moment, her eyes twinkling. "I missed you."

"Me too."

"I'm no one's property, you know," Ava said.

"I know."

She sipped her champagne.

Colt said, "Want to go somewhere we can be alone? Catch up?"

Ava's mouth opened, and she gave a little laugh. Her chin jutted upward. "That sounds dangerous. When?"

"Now."

"You're being serious?"

He didn't blink.

"You are being serious." She finished her drink and placed it down on the tall table nearby. "All right. Let's go."

They turned and began walking toward the house. Party attendees stole glances at her as they walked. Colt felt both nervous and enthralled.

This was sheer madness. A ludicrous fantasy. Despite what he felt, he knew he wasn't really getting a second chance. He wasn't rekindling a cherished relationship. He was doing what Wilcox wanted him to do. He was recruiting an agent.

As they walked, Colt looked up to see Jeff Kim on the balcony above them, speaking intently with a serious-looking woman.

Ava followed Colt's gaze. "That's Sheryl Hawkinson. You know her?"

"I've heard the name," Colt said, mentally cataloguing the sighting for his report. "How is she involved with Jeff?"

"They've had a few private meetings recently. To be honest, I don't know what was discussed. Jeff's like that sometimes. Nader thinks she wants to be cut in to the next equity round. You know anything about that?"

"I'm in appraisals. Different part of the house."

"Ah, I see. Well, Sheryl can be vicious. So be careful if you ever interact with her."

"I'll remember that."

Colt saw Kim and Sheryl looking down in his direction.

Ava waved and they both smiled, and then their walk took them under the balcony and out of sight.

"Let me run to the bathroom. I'll meet you out front," Ava said, then strode off. She turned to look back, smiling when she caught him watching her. Her dark eyes were still full of passion and playfulness, just the way he remembered.

An awful ringing sound caused him to snap his head toward the stage. Luke Pace had apparently escaped from Nader's compatriots and was now wrestling the microphone away from one of the performers. Colt could see Kim and Sheryl, now back down on the lawn, the former looking annoyed at Pace's drunken display.

Pace said, "Excuse me. Excuse me, ladies and gentlemen. I'd like to propose a toast." He raised his glass. "To the man who's made such a difference in all our lives. Who has helped us to conquer the algorithms again and again . . ."

The crowd was laughing and playing along. Many faces looked at Jeff Kim.

But Colt saw something different in Pace's expression. Something in his tone. Pain.

Pace continued, ". . . A lot of people don't realize what sacrifice this job demands. Your family, your time . . . the money doesn't matter so much if it takes those things . . ."

The laughter was dying down now as other people began to see what Colt saw. Pace's face, while red from inebriation, was solemn.

". . . And it can even take your life. So, let's all raise our glasses to our fallen brother-in-arms. To Kozlov! The sacrificial lamb!" Pace raised his drink above his head and then downed it.

The lawn was dead quiet now. Colt saw a mix of reactions. Some followed the toast, raising their glasses. Others frowned.

Kim whispered something to the nearest security guard, who strode up to Pace.

"I'm all right . . . all right . . . I'm going . . ." Pace turned over the microphone and fought off the security guard's arm as he headed through the crowd toward the exit. A few seconds later the music picked up and so did the crowd noise.

"Quite a display," came a woman's voice.

Colt turned to see Sheryl Hawkinson standing next to him. She appraised him, saying, "You're the one from the investment bank? I'm Sheryl Hawkinson."

"Colt McShane," he said, and they shook hands.

"A world of opportunity out here," Sheryl said. "If you pick the right investments."

"AI is a great investment."

Sheryl said, "It's going to transform the world. If it doesn't destroy it first."

"Well let's hope that doesn't happen."

Sheryl scoffed. "Hope is not a strategy." She walked away without saying goodbye.

Colt felt a hand on his shoulder.

"Are you ready?" He turned to see Ava again.

"Yes, let's go."

"You okay? What were you talking to Sheryl about?"

"Nothing. Just an introduction. She's a little different."

"I warned you."

They walked out the front entrance of the home onto a circular gravel drive. Ava spoke to the valet and a black SUV drove up. As she got in, Colt saw Pace swaying near the front steps, alone.

"Ava, please give me one moment."

She nodded and Colt walked over to Pace.

"Hey, you all right? What was that in there?" Colt asked him.

Pace turned to Colt, trying to focus on his face. "Hey. You know I know something *they* don't want you to find out. *You* need to be careful." He swayed as he spoke.

Colt narrowed his eyes. "What do you mean?"

Pace shook his head. "It didn't happen like they say it did. He was *killed*."

"Who? Kozlov?"

Pace nodded.

"I know. I'm sorry. It's tragic. The FBI is investigating—"

Pace waved his hand. "No. No. They're looking in the *wrong* place. He was *killed somewhere else.*"

Colt frowned. "What are you talking about?"

Pace leaned in, his eyes wide, his breath smelling of liquor. "He died in *The Facility* . . ."

Colt stood watching Pace, not knowing what to say. Pace just looked down at the ground, breathing, then spitting into the gravel. Probably getting ready to be sick soon.

"Luke! There you are!" Gerry Nader came out the front door and onto the driveway. He placed his arm around Pace.

Nader looked at Colt. "I'm really sorry. We're not usually like this. I'm afraid he's had way too much to drink. Let me get him a ride home." Nader began walking Pace inside.

As Colt watched them walk through the front entrance, Nader glanced back at him, a worried look in his eye.

Ava called from inside the car, "You coming, sailor?"

Colt walked over to the vehicle and hopped inside, a list of questions spiraling through his mind.

15

Ava wore a bemused look as she stared at Colt in the back of the SUV.

Colt was still turning over the wave of information he had just learned.

"What's on your mind?" Ava said.

"Just taking it all in."

Her face softened. "It's a different world out here."

"It is."

"Do you like sushi?"

"Love it."

She leaned toward the driver and gave him the name of a restaurant. He nodded and tapped in something on the navigational screen.

Ava sat back in her seat and said, "So, how have you been?"

The effect of her gaze was part truth serum, part aphrodisiac. Through the fog of emotion, Colt forced himself to stick to the script. He gave her standard, rehearsed answers. A summary of his last ten years that carefully left out his work for the CIA.

"What about you?" Colt asked. "The last I heard you were thinking of shunning your father's instructions and heading off to Julliard."

Ava's expression changed.

"What's wrong?" he asked.

"My father passed away."

"I'm so sorry. I didn't mean to . . ."

She shook her head. "No, it's no problem. It was a long time ago. Right after we last spoke, actually."

"What happened?" Colt had actually read the file on her parents, but he couldn't admit that or say anything to indicate he had been studying her government file. Ava's parents had been the victims of a terrorist attack. His feelings of sympathy were very real.

Ava said, "An accident. I don't really want to talk about it, if that's okay." She paused, and then said, "I ended up moving to the US, living with my aunt in New York while I got my MBA at Columbia." Ava ran through her work and living history, all of which matched what Colt had memorized on the plane ride to San Francisco.

"You must have done very well to land at Pax AI. I imagine quite a few people wanted this job."

Ava looked humble. "I consider myself very lucky."

"Somehow I doubt it was luck," Colt said.

The car came to a stop and Colt opened his door, stepping out onto the sidewalk before he reached back and helped Ava out of the vehicle. Her hand was soft to the touch, and he caught a glimpse of her smooth thigh between the high slit of her dress.

Ava thanked the driver and the car departed. She looped her arm through Colt's elbow, and they walked down the city street. They sat in an outdoor eating section of the restaurant beneath a leafy green tree. Red cushioned seats and plenty of space between tables gave them comfort and privacy.

A waitress arrived and they each ordered cocktails. Ava got a vodka soda with lime. Colt ordered an Old Fashioned.

They reminisced, laughing with the memories, delighting at how much fun they both had that summer. The more they drank, and the longer they spoke, the more Colt felt at ease.

Ava described her current lifestyle, and her role at Pax AI. "It's incredibly busy and stressful at times. At other moments, it's like this." She gestured to their incredible food and surroundings.

Her face had a few more lines than he remembered, and he could see them more clearly in this light. But she was as radiant as ever, and the way she spoke while looking him in the eye showed she really cared about him and what he had to say. He smiled to himself inwardly. It was the same way he tried to speak to agents. Making them feel special. But with Ava, it was sincere.

"So it's all a dream job? Nothing left to be desired?" Colt said.

Ava stroked the droplets of condensation on the outside of her water glass. "I don't know. I shouldn't say anything negative to you."

Colt gave her a gentle look. "Consider me off-duty."

"Promise?"

He nodded.

"I don't know. Sometimes it feels like we are doing all this extraordinary work, making advances that are mind-blowing. But . . . maybe we haven't thought about the implications."

"A lot of technology companies probably feel that way, though, right? I remember my mom telling me I was like a zombie in front of our TV when I was growing up. That was when you could only get an hour of cartoons per day. Compare that to now."

She wrinkled her nose. "The attention economy is certainly part of it."

"The attention economy?"

"Yes. The idea that time is our most valuable resource. Now it is being chopped up and parceled out for money. It's like we're being turned into cogs in a massive wheel. All the while, the wheel is spinning faster and faster."

"And we have no control over it."

Ava said, "Right. But that's actually something I think Pax AI can help with. I'm optimistic we can achieve another level of artificial intelligence. One where technology begins to give us our time back. I want to be bored again." She winked.

"You're referring to artificial general intelligence."

"Yes."

"So if you are optimistic about that . . . then what's the problem?"

Ava looked guarded. "Just, some of the areas AI gets into. It gets a little creepy. To the point that I worry about how much control humans will have over their lives in the future."

Colt raised his eyebrows. "Well, that's a scary thought. Care to expand on that?"

She laughed. "No. Not really. Not right now."

Their drinks came and they both took a sip.

Colt said, "Do you miss performing? Making music, I mean?"

"Very much so."

"Ever think about giving this all up and pursuing it?"

Ava looked a little sad. "Those days are over for me, I'm afraid. But even with art and music, technology has changed everything. You know what some of my independent musician friends spend most of their time on now? Digital marketing. A small fraction of their time goes to making the music, and most of their time to promoting themselves. It makes me sick thinking of that. I would hate nothing more than self-promotion. 'Look at me. Look at how great I am.' This is the world we've created. Chasing clicks and likes. Blah. Vomit."

"I can see why they hired you for marketing at Pax AI."

She laughed. "Hey! You said you were off-duty. But I outsource a lot of that type of work. And I have no trouble promoting my company anyway. It's the self-promotion that I dislike. That's not how I was raised."

"What do you spend most of your time doing? At Pax AI, I mean."

"Strategy and communications. A lot of the outward-facing work the CEO normally does, but because Jeff is so intensely focused on his engineering work, he delegates everything he can to me. I won't lie, it's very exciting. Sometimes I think I'm one of the few people he really trusts."

Their sushi came and they ate, both of them raving about how good it was. After a few minutes of eating, Colt said, "I should tell you I'm sorry."

She kept eating, her eyes on her food.

He continued. ". . . About how things ended, I mean."

Ava placed her chopsticks down and met his gaze. "Me too. I think of you often." Her eyes were soft. "Sometimes I think if things had just unfolded differently . . ."

Colt wanted to ask her what she meant by that. Ask her why she had stopped communicating with him. Instead, he just said, "Maybe in another lifetime . . ."

They stared at each other for a few heartbeats, and then Ava shook her head, her cheeks flushed.

Colt said, "I think we may need another drink after this."

"You might be right. I know a place."

They finished eating and got their check. Ava ordered them another car and soon they were riding along winding streets through the city hills. It was after midnight when they arrived at a rooftop bar called Twenty-Five Lusk. A view of the San Francisco skyline was off to their left as they enjoyed a cocktail. Ava and Colt shared a seat, her leg resting against Colt's own on a tightly spaced sofa, just one of the signals of the tipsy conversation growing more intimate. The brush of his fingertips against her bare shoulder. Her squeezing his knee to emphasize a laugh.

She said, "How have you found your time here?"

"It's very interesting. My work usually takes me to more consumer-focused companies. Building the world's next great razor blades or something like that. It's incredible to see Pax AI's technology. About how much your company could change the world."

She laughed.

"What's so funny?"

"*Change the world* . . . it's kind of an inside joke at Pax AI. Everyone who interviews for a job with us says they want to change the world. It's cliché."

"May I ask why you made the decision to give up music? Why you went into business?"

She sighed. "I guess my father's spirit still haunts me. His dying wish that I become a doctor, lawyer, or business executive. The successful Jewish son he never had."

"I'm sorry about your father."

"So am I." They went silent for a while. She dug an ice cube out of her cocktail with her spoon and began crunching it between her teeth.

Colt decided to steer the conversation back to Pax AI. He told Ava about the orientation Nader had given him, and how interesting he thought Pax AI's portfolio was. Then he said, "But to be honest, I'm most excited about the things I haven't yet been approved to see. Your fourth-floor projects, for example. Or the infamous Mountain Research Facility."

Her face darkened a bit.

"What's wrong?"

"Nothing. It's just, I want to be proud of what I do. And like I said, some of those more advanced programs are a little bit creepy."

Colt nodded, trying to convey empathy. And trying not to hint at how interested he was. *So, she wasn't proud of what went on at The Facility? Why not?* This was the type of thing he could work with. If she was worried about the ethics of Pax AI's more secretive programs, Colt could exploit that. It was the type of motivation that drove his most committed agents. Money and sex and power be damned. Get an agent who was a true believer, and they'd run through a brick wall for the cause.

Colt said, "Well, I'd sure like to see those programs. I think I'll have to, for my work. It's just hard with the red tape right now. All of the security concerns."

Ava said, "Well, if it makes you feel better, I'm not even cleared to go to The Facility anymore. I probably could go if I pushed, but they've limited it to so few people now. And after Kozlov . . . everything is just so strict. Still . . . perhaps I could help. Maybe say something on your behalf, if it's really important to your work?"

"That would be much appreciated," Colt said.

Ava placed her drink down on the table. "It's getting late."

"I'm ready when you are."

Ava was looking at him, her face close. She wrapped her hand around the back of his neck, pulled him in gently, and they kissed.

When they stopped, she whispered, "Let's go."

Colt stood, ears ringing, head buzzing as she led him by the hand through the crowded bar and into the elevator. The elevator was soon packed and they were standing in the corner, her body pressed against his, her arm outstretched, their fingers intertwined. He could feel her breathing. Then the elevator reached the ground floor and they walked out to the curb, neither making eye contact but both knowing what they wanted next.

The others who had been on the elevator were also on the sidewalk, waiting for rides. Ava had her phone to her ear, calling for their car.

Colt's phone buzzed in his pants pocket and he glanced at the screen to check.

Weng: CIP

Shorthand for *check in please*.

Ava waved for Colt to follow as she walked down the curb, a white SUV pulling up with a strange humming noise, its LED headlights blinding everyone on the sidewalk.

"What is that thing on top?" Colt asked.

"It's a LiDAR. Light detection and ranging."

"Oh. I know those. I worked on a project with a company that had autonomous driving . . . where the hell is the driver?"

Ava laughed. "It's an autonomous vehicle. They have them all over the place here. Have you not been to San Francisco lately?"

"No, now that you mention it. Do I need to have a will filled out? Or maybe a priest standing by for last rites?"

Once both were in the back seat and the doors were closed, Ava tapped on her phone and the car began moving. Colt was amazed by the car driving them, and equally amazed with the kiss they had shared on the rooftop bar.

Colt was also thinking about Weng's message. She was

supposed to check the phone SANDSTONE had provided. If SANDSTONE was reaching out, her message could be time-sensitive.

Colt snapped out of that thought as Ava leaned back into the leather seat, her fingertips stroking his palm. They were both buzzing from too many cocktails. Her eyes forward, chest pressing tight against her white dress as she breathed.

He knew what he wanted. But down that path lay danger. Didn't the Moscow Rules say not to fall in love with your agent? Colt was pretty sure that rule wasn't supposed to mean love in the literal sense. But the Moscow Rules also didn't cover the scenario of an intelligence officer already being in love with his agent prior to recruitment.

The autonomous-driving SUV came to a stop on a steep street. Ava climbed over Colt, straddling him for a moment with a smile before stepping out onto the sidewalk. Colt laughed and followed, standing by the car door. The block was lined with expensive-looking attached city homes.

Ava stood there on the sidewalk, looking up at him, biting her lower lip. "Did you want to come up?"

Colt had one hand still resting on the open car door. "We probably shouldn't. Not with Jeff . . . not with my job."

Her eyes flashed surprise, then hurt. Then back to her original softness. But Colt knew the spell had been broken.

"Maybe in another life," she said.

Then she turned and walked up the steps.

Colt watched her enter the home and close the door without looking back. He pictured her standing there, alone behind the door, angry or sad. Then the sound of the deadbolt locking snapped him out of it, and he re-entered the vehicle. There was a touchpad in the center console that was pretty easy to use, and Colt was able to get the car to take him to his hotel. He made a call on his encrypted CIA phone while they drove.

Heather Weng answered.

"You get a message?" Colt asked.

"Yup. Just now. SANDSTONE wants to meet."

16

Jeff Kim awoke at dawn, rays of sun coming in through the skylight twenty feet above his bed. He rose and stretched, putting on a pair of designer fleece athletic pants and a comfortable hoodie. As he walked through the halls of his spacious home, he inserted a wireless headphone into his right ear and said, "Call assistant."

Kim was quickly connected to his team of virtual assistants who had for the past three hours been preparing for his daily call.

"Good morning, Mr. Kim," said the head assistant. He was based in London and handled most of the communication with Kim. Two others were based in Mumbai and did most of the research and production of assets. Creating reports, looking up company data, and sending requests for information to anyone not on the call. A fourth assistant was local, handling any appointments and communication in the United States—dinner and travel, mostly. After each call, the head assistant would go over the call notes with the team and make sure all of Jeff Kim's instructions were adhered to.

Kim listened to their updates as he walked out the back

door and onto the now-empty lawn. The catering company had removed everything from the previous night. One of Kim's butlers was laying a white cloth over the poolside table. Seeing him, the man handed Kim a bottled water. He thanked the servant with a nod, and walked barefoot onto the grass, heading toward his meditation room as the team filled his ear with company updates from around the world.

Every few seconds, Kim would interrupt the assistant. He made quick decisions with the information he was given, parsing out tasks and asking follow-up questions. The assistants would send emails to dozens of Kim's employees, contractors, and partners after the call.

There was only one sacrosanct rule, they knew. Do not, under any circumstances, waste Jeff Kim's time. His mind was a priceless resource.

Kim reached the far side of his back lawn and entered the meditation room. He closed the door behind him and began pacing while he listened.

After a few more exchanges, he bid his team of assistants goodbye and set the earpiece on a tray table on the single desk in the room. He pressed a button on the wall and the mechanical shutter covering the large vertical panel window shifted and shuffled out of view, revealing the mountains in the distance.

Kim sat on the yoga mat in the center of the room and checked his smartwatch. One minute to spare. He folded his legs underneath him and placed his hands comfortably on his thighs. He gave a voice command, and music emanated from speakers in the floor and ceiling.

He closed his eyes, focusing on his breathing. In . . . and out. Focus. Concentration. In . . . and out. The music soothed him. The steady breathing lowered his heartrate, calming his mind. The session lasted forty-five minutes, after which his watch vibrated once on his wrist, and he immediately heard a knock on his door. Everything timed to perfection.

A brunette woman in black yoga pants and a Nike workout top entered. One of several personal trainers. She greeted him and then began to gently place his body into different stretching positions, moving each limb to its limit and through a full range of motion for the next fifteen minutes. They barely spoke, other than her commands. That was the way he preferred it to be. Efficient. Clean. Professional.

While the stretching went on, Kim's mind raced, thinking through problems and strategies.

"We're all finished, Mr. Kim," the woman said.

"Thank you."

"Would you like me to send in your masseuse this morning?"

"Not today, thank you."

"Very well, have a good day."

She left, and the housekeeper, who had been waiting outside, knocked on the door.

"Enter."

She peeked her head around the pale wooden door. "Where would you like your breakfast, sir?"

"By the pool, please."

"Yes, Mr. Kim."

He waited for her to leave, then headed into his walk-in shower, tucked away behind a wall in the meditation room. Another skylight here, towering above. Rays of bright sun cast onto the glossy wooden shower area. Multiple side- and top-mounted nozzles sprayed hot water onto his body, with a waterfall shower above, sunlight shining through the droplets as they made their way down. Kim toweled off and changed into a clean pair of clothes, which had been laid out by his housekeeper early that morning.

Moments later he sat at the table by the pool, breakfast now laid out over the tablecloth. A French press coffee pot, fresh granola and yogurt, fresh fruit, toast, and eggs. Fresh-squeezed orange juice rested in a small glass with ice.

"I'm sorry I'm late," Ava said, walking out from his home and onto the lawn, her hair still damp from a recent shower.

Kim rose from his seat, pulling out a chair for her.

"Thank you."

"Coffee?"

"Yes, please," Ava said, and Kim poured her a cup.

"You left early last night."

Ava sipped her coffee. "Jeff."

He scraped food onto his plate and took a bite. "I was surprised. That's all."

Ava shot him a look. "Please don't worry about it."

"Ava, I understand you had a relationship with him in the past. But the man is here to evaluate our company. His opinion will have an enormous impact on how billions of dollars of financing flow."

"Yes, but that's not why you are concerned." Her lips were pressed together.

Kim placed his fork down on his plate and wiped his mouth with his napkin. "I respect your decision to not change the nature of our relationship."

"Then relax. This is a big moment for you and for our company. That's where our focus needs to be."

"I agree."

Ava said, "And anything else is a distraction."

Kim said, "Did you hear about Pace?"

"I heard he toasted Kozlov and was talking too freely."

Kim nodded. "Sheryl Hawkinson was there."

"I saw."

"I think she smells blood in the water."

"What did she say?"

"She has heard rumors."

"Of?"

Kim's gaze shifted into the distance. "She told me there is a broker who has reached out to her. This broker represents Trinity—the same group that took responsibility for Kozlov's murder. Trinity claims to have obtained some of our intellectual property, and they are now shopping around for buyers."

Ava covered her mouth. "Do you think she's telling the truth?"

"I don't know. But people I distrust often tell me the truth, if it suits them." He looked at Ava, who didn't blink.

Ava said, "What did they take?"

"They are trying to sell our weather-prediction algorithm."

"That's worth billions." Ava clenched her fists on the table. "If it's true, how did it happen? Have we checked—"

Kim poured himself some coffee. "Miller audited our system after Kozlov's death."

"You told me he didn't find anything suspicious."

"He looked again, last night, after I spoke with Sheryl and I told Miller what to look for. There was evidence of a fourth-floor data breach. Someone was able to steal parts of our weather-prediction algorithm."

"Oh shit . . ."

Kim flexed his jaw, breathing out of his nose. "Sometimes it feels like the whole world is against us. Everyone trying to either get their hands on our IP or destroy us before we're even off the ground. I just don't know who I can trust anymore."

Ava's hand gripped his forearm. Her skin felt smooth to the touch. "You have me."

"Someone inside our company has betrayed us," he said.

"Who do you think it is?"

"I'm working on it. But I suspect Kozlov was somehow involved."

She removed her hand. "Has Miller told the FBI yet? About the data breach?"

Kim shook his head. "I asked him not to. We'll investigate it ourselves."

Ava looked surprised. "Is that allowed? I mean . . . legally, are we not obligated to inform the authorities?"

Kim looked her in the eyes. "Authorities? The world is changing, Ava. We are at the end of an era. Governments will be too slow to adapt. The days of rendering to Caesar are coming to an end."

"You're going to keep this from the US government? Won't that jeopardize our DOD contracts at The Facility?"

"It's a short-term risk," Kim said. "But everything is a risk. We are weeks away from getting funding approved that will give us a significant advantage. Our investors are spooked after the Kozlov incident, and we need to reassure them."

Ava said, "I understand our investors want more information on the fourth-floor projects. We could allow Colt McShane access. He's been asking for it."

"Do you trust him?"

"Yes."

Kim nodded. "Then I'll allow it. But we must do more. Our investors waver, and our competitors attack us, not because we're being secretive. It's because they do not respect us."

"What do you want to do?"

"We need to make a bold statement. A show of strength. A product announcement and demonstration. It is time for us to reveal some of our secrets."

17

Colt woke up early, downing two Advil with a glass of water, an attempt to stave off his blossoming headache. He ran for thirty minutes on one of the treadmills in the hotel gym, followed by calisthenics, doing his best to sweat out the previous night's alcohol intake.

He showered, shaved, and ate a granola bar during the taxi ride across town. The car dropped him off several blocks away from his true destination. He conducted a thirty-minute SDR before heading to the tech counterintelligence team's clandestine operations center. On the way, he opened his mobile phone and accessed the scrambler app that would protect him from electronic surveillance. The app made him appear on the move, blocks away from his actual location, using distant cellphone towers until he was finished with his clandestine movement.

As he approached the tech counterintelligence unit's safehouse, Weng saw him on the security cameras and beeped him in. Only she and Jennifer Sims were there on a Saturday morning.

"Morning, Romeo," Heather Weng said as he entered.

"Enjoy your evening of sushi and cocktails?" Sims smiled from her seat, removing a teabag from her cup.

"I did, actually," Colt said. "Where's the SANDSTONE message?"

Weng pulled out her phone from the back pocket of her jeans, turning the screen for Colt to see. "I took a photo of the text with my phone before I placed it back in the vault."

M: Meet Sunday @ 8:30 a.m. in SF. You send location.

Colt said, "We add three hours onto all of our communicated times. The meet will be Sunday at 11:30 a.m."

Weng nodded, unsurprised. It was a common procedure in clandestine operations, meant to throw off any adversaries who might intercept the message.

Sims said, "I'll let Rinaldi and Wilcox know. They have a few meeting spots picked out."

Colt shook his head. "I'll select something."

Weng said, "Ed is growing more concerned that SANDSTONE could be a dangle. They want me to go with you in case something goes wrong."

"She's not a dangle."

"A triple-agent, then."

Colt nodded. "She's not a triple-agent. And Ed should know better than to suggest it. Besides, the SVR isn't going to use one of their US-based officers like that. It would be too obvious. And if SANDSTONE were really loyal to the Russians, why would the Russians feed us Kozlov? It doesn't make sense that they would kill off a source as valuable as him."

"That was my argument. The Kozlov angle. I said that to Wilcox," said Weng.

"What'd he say?"

"That Russians sometimes do weird things."

Colt scowled. "That answer seems woefully inadequate. What's the concern here? That I'm walking into a trap?"

Weng nodded. "Maybe. Or that SANDSTONE is just continuing to provide us with disinformation."

Sims said, "Maybe Kozlov wasn't working out, so the Russians decided the Seattle job was a way to dump him while convincing you SANDSTONE is loyal to us?"

Colt bounced his knee, thinking it through. "What's the first question a case officer asks a prospective agent?"

Weng said, "You ask him if he knows of any penetrations in your service."

Colt nodded.

Weng said, "So . . . SANDSTONE has given up other SVR officers. Is that what you're implying?"

Colt played coy. "You'll have to ask Ed. But all I know is if she's been lying this whole time, she's got a lot of help, and deserves an Academy Award."

Weng smirked. "I'm sure you've had women lie to you before without knowing it."

Sims said, "Now, now, Heather."

Weng said, "All kidding aside, SVR officers are carefully tested for their allegiance to the cause before they are placed in the field. And they decided to send SANDSTONE to the US —that's the big leagues. Which means she is one of their most skilled officers, and they vetted her more thoroughly than others. We have to assume there is at least the possibility she's actually loyal to the SVR."

Colt shook his head. "I'm telling you, the intelligence she's been giving us has been quite good."

Weng said, "The SVR has been known to create quite good chicken feed."

Weng was suggesting SANDSTONE could have been

providing the Americans with real intelligence, but that it wasn't all that damaging to the Russian Federation. And the delivery of that information had been okayed by Marisha's SVR superiors, meant to establish her bona fides to the Americans.

Colt said, "I'll concede that anything is possible. But my instincts tell me she's not a triple-agent. SANDSTONE is rare, but genuine."

Weng said, "Well, it won't hurt for you to have me at the meeting for backup."

"Just make sure to get black before you show up."

Weng arched one eyebrow. "If I can run agents in denied areas in China, I think it's safe to say I won't screw up your op."

"Fair enough." Colt didn't mind Weng's questions. It was healthy to be skeptical, and she made good points.

Weng said, "Now, you got a few minutes to debrief us on last night?"

"Yes, ma'am." Colt grabbed a bottled water out of the fridge and began to tell them everything he had seen and heard the previous evening. He shared Pace's comments about Kozlov, which Weng discounted as the ravings of a drunk, but promised to inform the team; Sheryl Hawkinson's conversation with Jeff Kim and her introduction to Colt, which they both found intriguing; and his evening alone with Ava Klein, with enough detail that Weng looked skeptical.

"That's it? You just left her hanging by the door? No under-the-covers agent handling?"

Colt gave her a look. "Moscow Rules. Don't fall in love with your agent."

Weng said, "What ever happened to James Bond rules? Don't be boring, I need this. I live vicariously through you while trapped in here."

Sims just shook her head, smiling.

Colt saw a text message notification pop up on his phone. He read the message and whistled.

Weng said, "What's up?"

Colt smiled and stood to leave. "Looks like Pax AI just granted me fourth-floor access. Effective immediately."

"Wilcox will be happy." She narrowed her eyes as she looked at his screen. "Can I see your phone for a minute?"

Colt handed it to her. "Sure."

Weng said, "You're using an out-of-date scrambler security app." She was referring to the CIA-recommended app on his phone that helped keep him clear of electronic surveillance. "Who told you to use this one?"

"Ed. A while ago."

She frowned. "He should know better. He should have had you upgrade it to this one." She showed him her phone and pointed to an icon on the screen. May I?"

"Be my guest."

Weng brought his phone over to one of the classified CIA computers and connected it, downloading the app and setting it up for use. "It's the same procedure, just without the security flaws."

Colt didn't like the thought that he'd been using an out-of-date technique for something so vital to spy craft nowadays. "Thanks. I guess Wilcox and I don't get to meet that often, so . . ."

She waved away the comment, changing the subject. "When will you actually get inside their fourth floor?"

"I'll go today. Now."

Sims said, "He should take the box."

Weng nodded, rising and heading toward the back room. "Wilcox was supposed to train you on it, but I can give you a quick rundown." She came back with a black leather wallet. "For all your years of dedicated loyalty, the CIA's Office of

Technical Service presents you with this unmarked, empty black wallet."

Colt examined the wallet.

Weng said, "You'll need to put your ID and some cash in there to make it look legit. It'll pass a metal detector and airport scanner. We've reviewed the security procedures at Pax AI and are ninety percent confident you should be able to get it onto the fourth floor. But . . . if a security guard starts taking the wallet apart, you might be in trouble."

Colt raised his eyebrows. "Do I have to do anything to activate it?"

"No. It's got GPS and knows its location. Forty-eight hours of battery life. And it is pre-programmed to go emission dark during any security scan windows. When you go through security, it'll look just like a wallet to their scanners. Once you're on the fourth floor, it will turn on and start doing its thing. Oh, and don't lose it. Thing costs more than a Ferrari, not to mention it's got some tech that China and Russia would love to get their hands on."

Colt looked at the wallet and then back at Weng. "I think I heard you say ninety percent confident?"

She winked. "Relax, you'll be fine. Maybe pick up some flowers for your future agent on the way? Or some really sexy lingerie?"

"Those techniques worked for you before?"

"As a woman? Or as a case officer making a recruitment?"

"Both."

Sims said, "You can't go wrong getting a woman flowers."

Weng cocked her head, thinking. "Honestly, the best way to impress me is to feed me. I love to eat. And I'm much more of a sweatpants kind of girl. You know, now that you mention it, those two things may be related."

Colt laughed and bid the two women farewell.

He took the Muni bus to the stop nearest the Pax AI headquarters building. When he arrived, he flashed his badge to the woman behind the front desk and nodded to the security guards, who watched him go through the ground-floor metal detectors before proceeding further. So far so good with the wallet.

He had expected the Pax AI office to be empty since it was a weekend. But as he walked up the stairs, he heard voices echoing from above and saw what looked like the entire leadership team making their way through the fourth-floor security entrance. The security guard took each person's ID, running them through biometric scanners, and then the sliding glass door whooshed open as they entered one at a time. By the time Colt arrived at the top, Ava, Nader, Pace, and a few others had all gone in without seeing him. Jeff Kim was the only one still waiting.

Kim spotted Colt and smiled. "Well, that was quick. When did you get access, one hour ago?"

"I couldn't wait until Monday." Colt grinned.

Kim nodded like he understood, regained his ID from the security guard, and then walked forward into the open doorway. The fourth-floor doors slid shut behind him, and the security guard gestured for Colt to come forward.

"First time up here?" he asked.

"Yes, sir."

"Thumbprint here. We'll scan your right eye for next time. And I'll need your ID. Any phones or electronic devices must stay out here with me." The security man raised one eyebrow. "And if you forget anything, this doorway leads to a body scan machine that will help you remember."

Colt handed the man his phone, praying that the CIA's techs knew what they were doing with the James Bond wallet in his back pocket.

The guard nodded for Colt to proceed, and he walked forward into the chamber. The door closed behind him, and he heard a voice say, "Hands above your head during the scan, please," followed by the sound of a rapid mechanical sliding motion from above. Then the door in front of Colt opened with a whoosh to reveal another guard waiting behind a standing desk, beckoning Colt forward.

"First time up here?" the second guard asked. Colt got the impression the ID check was nothing more than lip service. These men knew exactly who was allowed up here. It was a small, exclusive club.

"Yup."

"Okay, we got you at computer station number six, down there on the right. You can use your fingerprint to unlock it. Let me know if you want any help. We close shop at sixteen-hundred today."

"Okay, thank you," Colt said, and began walking along the main walkway toward his assigned desk. The fourth floor was another open office design. Very spartan. No personal effects on any of the desks. And only a single conference room toward the center of the floor surrounded by floor-to-ceiling glass panels, the type that went opaque at the touch of a button. Right now it was still clear, and Colt counted eight Pax AI executives inside. They were talking animatedly to one another, but the room was soundproof so Colt couldn't hear a thing.

He found it interesting they were holding this meeting on a weekend, the night after a raucous party. His instincts told him something was up.

Colt arrived at his cubicle and sat down. He unlocked the computer with the fingerprint scanner and went to work. He wondered if the device sewn into his black wallet was already humming away, sending out electronic feelers to probe the servers on this floor.

The operating interface on the assigned computer was easy to navigate. Colt had gone through their less-confidential program folders in his downstairs office and found it to be similar in organization. But the information here was much more robust. Now Colt could see all the different Pax AI programs of interest. Language generation. Automated navigation. Robotics. Colt took his time, reexamining Pax AI project summaries, progress reports, and financial projections. Up here, almost everything was visible.

There were still some programs with abridged summaries. Hints of the Mountain Research Facility projects that were classified beyond even this level. But the information he could see was still very helpful.

Colt's New York financial analysis firm had prepared pages of data on Pax AI and its competitors. The company's team of business researchers were in many ways just like the CIA's own analysts. Both had given Colt requirements lists. Information they wanted him to obtain. Colt had done his homework, studying the prep material and putting most of the competitor facts and figures to memory before he arrived.

Looking at Pax AI's program summaries here, he saw a substantial difference between competitor benchmarks. On almost all fronts, Pax AI was leading the competition by a wide margin, beating them on cost, performance, and schedule. It was almost too good to be true. If this information was all accurate, it left Colt with two questions: One, how was Pax AI able to consistently achieve these superhuman results? And two, how soon could his investors send their checks? If this rate of technological progress kept up, Pax AI was going to become one of the most valuable companies in the world.

Colt continued his analysis for the next hour, mentally

taking notes and identifying more research requests to send to his team back in New York. He was just about to take a break when he heard commotion coming from the conference room.

The Pax AI executive meeting had adjourned. Colt could see the group emptying out of the room, heading toward the exit doors and down the stairs, each of them looking confident and serious.

Luke Pace halted at Colt's desk, looking nervous. His eyes darted toward the floor as he spoke quietly. "Hey, uh . . . I'm sorry about anything I might have said last night. Too much to drink, you know. I was really out of it. Please disregard whatever I said. Okay?" His eyes met Colt's gaze, pleading.

Pace *had* been very drunk. Colt wondered if he even remembered what he'd said. Colt certainly did. *Kozlov wasn't killed in the hotel.* That wasn't the kind of thing you got confused about no matter how much you had to drink. But it was also dead wrong. Through the video surveillance feed, Colt had seen the blood spatter on the wall. From several rooms away, Colt had heard the smack of the fifty-caliber round embedding itself in the wall, only nanoseconds after breaking through glass and flesh.

So then why did the look on Pace's face bother him so much?

Because Pace wasn't being truthful.

Colt nodded, looking sympathetic. "Sure, man. No problem." He smiled. "To be honest, you were pretty tipsy and I'm not sure I understood everything you said."

"Yeah, well . . . sorry." Pace left looking uncomfortable.

Next out of the conference room came Ava, her high heels echoing on the floor, her stride both feminine and elegant. Her features striking. Was it possible she'd grown more beautiful over the years?

"Here on a Saturday? You're quite driven," Ava said, stopping at his desk, her tone and face unreadable.

Colt shrugged. "I guess. How are you? You okay?"

"You mean after last night?" she said softly.

Colt nodded slowly.

Ava bit her lip. "I probably had a little too much to drink."

"That seems to be a theme around here," Colt said.

Ava looked confused.

"Never mind," he said.

Ava turned to check that no one was behind her before saying, "Well, anyway, I'm sorry. I don't know what came over . . ."

"Don't apologize."

She looked self-conscious. "Thank you for being gracious."

Jeff Kim exited the conference room and began walking toward them.

Colt stood as Kim arrived. An old military habit, standing for the commanding officer.

"Has she told you the news?" Kim asked, looking between them.

Ava said, "Not yet."

Colt frowned in confusion.

Kim said, "We're going on a business trip. Wheels up in two hours. Would you like to come with us? I have something to say, and I think our investors will be very interested."

18

One hour later Colt was back in the tech counterintelligence unit's office, knee bouncing under the table, checking his watch. Weng, Rinaldi, and Sims had also rushed to be here. After Kim's invitation, Colt had raced back to his hotel, texting Wilcox from the taxi before frantically packing for the trip.

When they all sat, Wilcox said, "Thanks, everyone, for coming on short notice. We have a few moving pieces and it's best to get us all in here to sort it out."

"I've only got a few minutes," Colt stated.

"We'll move fast," Wilcox said. He looked around the table. "McShane was granted fourth-floor access. Today he entered the space with one of our surveillance devices. Heather?"

Weng shook her head, looking at her laptop. "Bottom line, we didn't get what we needed. I spoke with the techs. They say the device activated. But the data was limited, and we weren't able to upload our program in the appropriate servers."

"Did the techs tell you why it didn't work?" Colt asked.

Weng said, "They have a few theories. It might be that Pax AI segments data based on who logged in to the system. So, if one of their top scientists was working on a program, those drives might be unlocked. But if it's just you, they only let you see what they want you to see."

"The project summaries and projections I reviewed today were something they have kept internal. It was way more than they've shared before."

Sims said, "You were almost certainly looking at genuine company secrets. But your electronic surveillance device wasn't able to gain access to their entire network."

Weng nodded. "Right. They let you see some stuff. But if you knew where to go, you would have gotten stonewalled if you tried to access some of their data. It's not project summaries and slideshows we need to see. Our cyber operators need access to the data farms that house their algorithms and sensitive research."

Wilcox said, "So how do we get that?"

"Our techs are consulting with NSA experts. But they told me there may be a vulnerability window created when Pax AI runs one of their sophisticated AI programs at the Mountain Research Facility. That would open the right valves, so to speak. Then our surveillance software will be able to look inside."

Colt turned to Wilcox. "The demo."

Wilcox nodded. "That's going to be our best bet. Please tell the group what Kim told you."

Colt filled them in on Kim's invite to Canada. "He called it a major announcement. To be followed by a more public demonstration next week. They're going to use technology that is held at the Mountain Research Facility."

"I thought The Facility was a closed system. Don't they shut it off from all communication to the outside world?" asked Rinaldi.

Colt said, "I asked the same thing. Ava told me when they run controlled demonstrations, Pax AI has the capability to securely transmit and receive data between The Facility and the fourth floor of the Pax AI HQ."

"How?"

Colt shook his head in amazement. "A proprietary quantum communication system. From the headquarters, they can beam it to the outside world. Ava said they developed the technique so Pax AI could demonstrate their AI capabilities while simultaneously protecting their IP."

Rinaldi hummed in admiration. "So they run all their AI programs behind a secure wall."

Colt nodded. "They use this system to protect all of the AI programs that haven't been released as open source. No one can hack it."

Weng said, "Unless we have our surveillance device on the fourth floor while one of their controlled demonstrations is running . . ."

Knowing looks from around the table. A plan was forming.

"Why Banff?" Wilcox asked.

Weng was typing on her laptop. "There's a summit for tech CEOs being held in Banff, Alberta, this weekend."

"Correct," Colt said.

Weng glanced up from her laptop. "Guess who is moderating?"

"Who?" Wilcox asked.

"*Sheryl Hawkinson*. Apparently she's one of the event sponsors."

Wilcox and Rinaldi exchanged looks.

Colt said, "Maybe that's why she was talking to Kim at the party last night?"

"Must have been," said Sims. "But I'm surprised he accepted. She's known as an activist investor. Rumor has it that Kim has been avoiding her attempts to take a piece of his company for years."

Colt said, "They're planning to use this conference as the platform for the announcement. Just so you know, I gave my New York employer a heads up, and they told me there's already media buzz about it. Whatever Kim's going to say, it will make the news."

Wilcox turned to Colt. "When's your meeting with SANDSTONE?"

Colt shook his head. "It's supposed to be tomorrow. That's one of the things I needed to run by you. What's the priority? Should I go on this trip and reschedule with SANDSTONE? Or call the Pax AI folks back and tell them I can't make it?"

Wilcox said, "I don't want you missing this trip. It smells like a prime recruitment opportunity."

"My thought too. I'll contact SANDSTONE and postpone. If the SVR suspects her, it will put some more distance between us anyway."

Wilcox said, "No. Weng will meet with your agent."

Colt looked at Weng, and then back at Wilcox. "Ed . . . SANDSTONE will freak out. I'm surprised she's even willing to meet after Seattle."

Weng said, "Colt, I can handle it."

Colt looked at her. "I know you can. But the idea of sending someone in my stead, without letting her know . . . it's not smart."

"So we'll let her know," said Wilcox.

Colt let out a breath. "It's clumsy. What if SANDSTONE goes dark again? She's already taking a huge risk meeting with me. I'm the only American intelligence officer she's communicated with in the past two and a half years."

"You can't be in two places at once. And you're the only one who got an invite to the Pax AI jet. Both are operational requirements."

Colt ran his hand through his hair, looking at the ground

as he thought through their options. "Why can't we just put off the meet with SANDSTONE?"

Wilcox said, "She's based out of the Houston consulate. If the SVR is concerned with her loyalty, which they tend to be after one's agent is killed by a fifty-caliber sniper round, then any change to her travel itinerary will look suspicious. If she's made plans to meet with you tomorrow, it's very likely she's taken extensive precautions to ensure she isn't tracked. And given the circumstances, she might not have plans to be back here anytime soon."

Colt knew he was right.

Wilcox said, "We can't afford to wait on this. Weng, despite her extensive personality defects, is a very competent intelligence officer."

"Thank you," said Weng.

"She can do this. Please send SANDSTONE a prep message so she doesn't react negatively. That's my decision."

Colt nodded in acceptance, then turned to Weng. "I'll walk you through our comms procedures when we're done." He said to Wilcox, "Anything else before I leave?"

"Yes, actually." Wilcox turned to Rinaldi, who cleared his throat.

"This morning we got a lead on the shooters in Seattle. The FBI found new video evidence about a mile from the crime scene that night. We now think there are three of them, working as a team."

"Do we have any names?"

Rinaldi said, "Negative. But we traced them to a safehouse. FBI SWAT raided it this morning. Guess where it was?"

Colt shrugged. "Where?"

"Palo Alto."

"They're here in the Bay Area? Shit. You think they're planning to hit Pax AI again?"

"We don't know. But it's very possible," Rinaldi said. "There's something else. The agents on the raid found something in the house. A symbol carved into the hardwood floor of the living room."

Wilcox leaned forward over the table. "It was one of those Trinity symbols. I wasn't convinced before—I'm still not, not completely—but we need to consider that these guys might be fanatics after all."

Special Agent Sims turned her laptop around so everyone could see the images on her screen. "It's called the *Triquetra*. A three-sided knot interlaced. It's been used by several groups throughout history, including the Celtic Nations."

"Ah, yes, the Celtics. Great basketball team," said Weng. "Have we considered that these people might be from Boston?"

Wilcox shot her a look, and she went quiet.

Sims continued, "Some Christians adopted it to symbolize the Holy Trinity in the nineteenth century, and it's been seen in pop culture on several TV shows. Now it seems these AI-worshipers have hijacked it. It's all over their message boards. T-shirt sales of it are through the roof."

"Why?" Colt asked.

Sims shrugged. "Have you read much about the Trinity AI conspiracy group? I recommend you don't spend too much time doing so, but if you did, you would discover it's essentially a choose-your-own-adventure conspiracy game. An alternate reality, where participants find clues in real-world events, then use them to solve supposed mysteries."

"It's madness is what it is," said Rinaldi.

Sims said, "When the followers of Trinity mostly agree that one thing is connected to another, it becomes part of their tapestry. It becomes canon if one of the higher-ups in their organization approves it."

"They have ranks?"

"Sort of. It's a hodgepodge. Some groups are well organized. Others aren't. All of this to say . . . the Trinity symbol's semi-religious connection, and the supposed heritage of the group coming from the Manhattan Project . . ."

Colt did a double take. "Wait, what?"

Weng was shaking her head. "It's bullshit . . . don't even bother . . ."

Wilcox held up his hand. "I agree. Let's not spend any more time on this."

Rinaldi said, "What matters here is there may be a small team of professional assassins who are inspired by this group. The Trinity symbol was carved into the floor of their safehouse by a large knife. Forensics said the carving was a few days old, but there were signs that the crew had left only this morning."

Colt looked around the table. "But, hold on. That hit on Kozlov was very well executed. Do we really think followers of Trinity are doing this? Not a foreign intelligence service?"

Rinaldi said, "The truth is, we just don't know. In all likelihood, Kozlov was killed by these men." He pointed to his computer screen, which showed the FBI image of three obscured silhouettes walking on the Seattle street. "But let's think about it. Who had the most to gain from his death?"

Weng said, "We know from our sources that China is actively working to steal information from Pax AI. With his access and a little time, Kozlov could have helped us find out who was stealing Pax AI's technology. An operation that sophisticated is likely Chinese. Maybe Russian. Let's say the MSS found out Kozlov was pulling from China's covert cache of files inside Pax AI every week and handing it to the SVR. China would have wanted to put an end to that. Maybe eliminate the competition while they are at it. I just don't buy that it was Trinity. Everything I've read on them points to a disaggregated cluster of amateur hackers and conspiracy websites. Running an agent inside the hottest AI company in the world is varsity stuff. Trinity is JV at best. Maybe a freshman squad."

Colt said, "There was a lot of underestimating Al Qaeda before 2001."

Weng shrugged. "Maybe, but Al Qaeda was training to kill people. So far this Trinity stuff doesn't delve too far into violence. And as for Russia, they were benefiting from Kozlov, so it's unlikely they did it."

Sims said, "Unless the Russians discovered Kozlov was meeting with US agents?"

Colt said, "I think it is very likely that whoever planned this knew he was meeting with US agents. The timing is too coincidental to conclude otherwise. Which further suggests a professional service commissioned the killers."

Rinaldi said, "That's almost worse. State actors like Russia and China know the rules of the game. There's been a lot of press comparing the race for AI supremacy to the Cold War and the nuclear arms race. In either era, assassinating someone on US soil is a huge escalation. Think about what it would mean for such an act to have been approved by their leadership. Whatever they are going after must be immensely valuable."

Wilcox looked around the table. "Ladies and gentlemen, we're running out of time. After the raid, Rinaldi and I were on a call with DNI. Both of our bosses were on the call, as were theirs. This is going to make the president's daily briefing tomorrow. There is an enormous amount of interest in our counterintelligence operation at Pax AI. The US government has some covert programs running in the Pax AI Mountain Research Facility that are considered vital to national security. But our government experts—in the DOD, the intel community, and their scientists—have low confidence they know about everything Pax AI is working on. We think Pax AI is keeping secrets. People are afraid of what they don't know. One person has been killed already, increasing those suspicions. And we now know that foreign intelligence has, at least once, penetrated the corporation. The White House is afraid this situation will explode."

Colt said, "Where do we go from here?"

Wilcox's face was flushed. "For now? Stay the course. But *expedite*. We want to make this clean. Collect the information we need, protect our existing sources, and quietly unearth any industrial espionage operations at Pax AI. Our cyber team needs access to the Pax AI fourth-floor data without anyone made aware. If we can do that, we can insert a tracking program, and we will know who's behind the breach. I'm getting pressure to show results from this op soon, otherwise we'll need to take a riskier approach. We may have to shut the company down or bring in Jeff Kim. Either way could hurt US interests. Trust me, that's not the way we want this to go."

Colt said, "Let me work on Ava some more . . . I should be able to ascertain how helpful she'll be if I spend a little more time with her this weekend." Colt felt Weng's foot under the table at that comment, but he ignored it. "Can you at least give me until next week?"

Wilcox said, "Do your best. No guarantees."

Colt looked at his watch again. "I need to get to the airport. Weng, let's discuss the comms procedures for SANDSTONE."

She nodded and began walking to the back room where they would have some privacy.

The others got up to leave. Before Wilcox walked out the door, he turned and said, "Colt, just be sure to watch your back. Whoever they work for, the team that killed Kozlov is still active."

19

A few hours later, Colt and Ava sat facing each other on Pax AI's chartered jet, both busy working. Ava used a stylus to make notes on her tablet. Colt typed on his laptop. The bright sun peeked through the windows, lighting up her face.

Jeff Kim sat further up the cabin, speaking with Nader about the reveal. Pace remained behind, something about manning the controls during the show. A handful of other assistants were also present.

The jet landed in Calgary, where they were whisked by luxury cars to the Fairmont Banff Springs. The majestic hotel looked like a modern castle, surrounded by pine forest. A wall of Canadian Rocky Mountains covered the horizon, and a turquoise river cut through the valley just north of the hotel. The property was something out of a luxury catalogue. Magnificent golf courses spanning the landscape. Expansive heated indoor swimming pools with ultra-high ceilings. Marble columns reminding Colt of ancient Rome, and stunning architecture all around.

"You travel to places like this often?" he asked Ava when they stepped into the lobby.

Ava said, "Travel is one of the perks of the job."

The hotel manager showed Kim and his assistants to Kim's suite as soon as they arrived.

Nader walked over to Colt and Ava, saying, "Colt, you'll have to excuse us this afternoon. We need to go over a few things internally before Jeff's presentation. We got you a room —on us, of course. You're welcome to stay the night and head back with Ava tomorrow or return with us tonight. Up to you."

Colt looked at Ava. "I didn't realize you weren't all going back together. You're not traveling back with them?"

Ava said, "No, actually, I'm taking advantage of that travel perk for a night. My aunt loves this place. We vacationed here once, and I thought it might be nice to fly her out for a quick visit."

Colt remembered that Ava lived with her aunt in New York after her parents died. They were undoubtedly close.

Colt said, "Well, I wouldn't want to intrude . . ."

Ava waved her hand. "Nonsense, don't be silly. She would be happy for you to join us. We can fly back together tomorrow evening."

"If you're sure . . ."

Nader said, "Okay. I'll let our admin know to make the arrangements. Ava, we'll see you in Jeff's room for prep."

She nodded and Nader disappeared.

Ava said, "Jeff doesn't speak for a few hours. If I were you, I would enjoy yourself until then. Promise me you won't work the whole time."

"I'll find something to do."

After dropping his bag off in his room, Colt went for a stroll in downtown Banff, wanting to get familiar with his surroundings. The town was very pleasant. Chic restaurants, rustic bars, and decorative storefronts. Colt kept an eye out for possible surveillance as he walked.

In the movies, spies always knew exactly who the bad guys were. But in the real world of covert operations, identifying surveillance was exponentially more difficult. It was about assigning probabilities to a list of unknown possible watchers. It was the kind of thing that could make you paranoid.

As he walked, Colt spotted several people who might have been surveillance.

A young couple across the street sitting at a café. Probably just honeymooners. But the woman was watching him through her sunglasses and Colt saw her whisper something to her partner. They remained seated as he passed.

A clean-shaven man with dark curly hair, wearing a black leather smoking jacket. The man kept pace with Colt, but always remained one block behind and across the street. His clothing was European-style. Maybe a tourist on vacation . . . or maybe not? Colt ducked into a store, and then lost him in a reversal.

An older man with rimmed glasses was reading a hardcover book on a park bench. The man wore tiny white headphones and held his phone up in front of his face like he was conducting a video call. It would have been easy for the man to take video of Colt as he walked by, if he wanted to.

Modern technology was making clandestine operations more and more challenging.

Colt mentally documented each of these unknown subjects while walking through the town streets. After half an hour, he headed back to the Fairmont for lunch, again marveling at its beauty.

He walked into a small sitting area, his footsteps echoing on the hardwood floors. There was a small bar surrounded by antique wooden tables with a few patrons eating lunch. Colt sat down at the bar and ordered a soup and salad.

A petite woman who looked to be in her late seventies was attempting to sit at the unusually tall bar stool next to Colt. She huffed and placed her purse on the bar surface before trying again, looking embarrassed.

She saw Colt watching and smiled at him. "Perhaps this is a sign I'm getting too old to attend bar."

Colt said, "These stools are oddly tall, aren't they? How about a table?"

"Oh, you may be right. But I hate to eat alone."

Colt looked across the empty ballroom area adjacent to the bar. Some of the tech CEO conference attendees were starting to funnel into the presentation hall. He checked his watch. He should have fifteen or twenty minutes before it began. Ava would be finishing up with prep soon, but he had time.

"Well how about I join you?" Colt asked.

"Oh, don't be silly," the woman said.

"It's no trouble. I could use the company."

Colt signaled the waiter that they were moving to a window seat. Tall panoramic windows offered a clear view of the mountains.

When the waitress came over, the woman squinted at the menu, then looked at Colt's plate. "Is the soup good?" she asked.

"It's life-changing."

"Quite an endorsement. I'll have the soup. And a glass of beer."

Colt smiled. "A woman after my own heart. I'll take a beer too, please."

The waitress smiled.

"My name is Samantha."

"I'm Colt."

"It's nice to meet you, Colt."

The beers and her soup arrived, and they spoke for a while. She was from New York. Had worked as a journalist there for many years but was retired now.

"Is this your first time in Banff?"

"It is," Colt said.

From their table, Colt watched as more business executives and press arrived. He recognized some of the faces in the crowd. Most notable was Sheryl Hawkinson, flanked by two security guards. Interesting that she saw the need for that.

While Colt used their vantage point for reconnaissance gathering, Samantha spoke of her late husband, who had been a banker. "I would have loved for him to see this. It's such a romantic place. Do you have anyone special here?"

Colt reddened and let out a small laugh but didn't answer.

"Oh, it looks like you do. Good for you, dear."

Colt turned at the sound of laughter coming from the small banquet hall across the way. Ava was there, surrounded by fawning business executives. She was the only woman in the group, and her wide smile and charm were clearly stealing the show.

Samantha saw Colt looking and said, "Is that her?"

Again, he let out a small laugh. "You're quite the detective, Samantha."

"At my age, darling, there's no reason to hold back." Her eyes twinkled. "Are you two going to get married?" Colt noticed a slight accent when she said the word *married*.

He twisted his head, feeling like he needed to brace himself for this stranger's questions. "Unfortunately, I think that ship has sailed."

"Why is that?"

Colt said, "We were together a long time ago. I think circumstances have changed."

"But you still have feelings for her?"

Colt laughed. "Samantha, you are an excellent interrogator."

"You didn't answer my question." She raised her eyebrows.

"I know." He finished the last sip of his beer.

Ava spotted Colt from across the way and her eyes lit up. She excused herself from the group of businessmen and began walking quickly toward him with a big grin.

Ava reached their table. She looked unusually happy, her gaze going back and forth between Samantha and him. Somewhere in his mind, Colt's instincts twitched.

"Well, well!" she said. "Isn't this a pleasant surprise. How did you two find each other?"

Colt's eyes narrowed. He turned to look at Samantha, whose expression was one of triumph and amusement. Colt felt the blood draining from his face as he tried to recall every word uttered in the last sixty seconds.

"Aunt Samantha, it's so good to see you."

"You too, dear! Thank you again for inviting me."

"And how did the two of you meet?" Ava asked.

"Oh, this nice young man just offered to keep me company. I'm afraid we didn't even know our connection."

Ava said, "Would you like to come to the presentation?"

"Oh no, I don't think so. I have made a spa appointment this afternoon and I intend to keep it."

Ava said, "Okay, well, Colt and I have to go now. Do you mind if he joins us for dinner? The reservations are late. Eight p.m."

Samantha stood. "That sounds lovely. Well, Colt, it was very nice speaking with you. I hear the restaurant we're going to eat at tonight is very good. You two should go do some sort of vigorous activity beforehand. Work up an appetite for dinner." Her eyes held a mischievous glimmer.

Colt attempted to speak but his vocal cords were failing.

Ava said, "We need to get into the conference hall before my boss begins speaking. But I'd love to go on a hike later. Are you interested, Colt?"

"Oh, I'm sure he is." Samantha raised one eyebrow.

20

The conference hall was small compared to the one in Seattle Colt had attended a few weeks ago, but the guests were a more exclusive bunch. A select group of executives and their respective business entourages. A handful of journalists, each well known in Silicon Valley and Wall Street. King makers and king slayers of the media world. Altogether, Colt estimated maybe one hundred and fifty people were in attendance.

He and Ava sat in one of the back rows, all the way to the edge, just like he preferred. He liked to be able to make a quick getaway, if needed. Ava did too, apparently. The lights in the room dimmed. Jeff Kim and Sheryl Hawkinson were both sitting on stage. Colt kept switching his gaze between the stage and the large projector screen on his side of the auditorium, which displayed the close-up video of the speakers.

Sheryl Hawkinson gave a cordial opening statement, thanking everyone for coming, especially Jeff Kim, who, she noted, had declined and then reinvited himself. There was modest laughter at that.

"But in the world of business, one must always be nimble," Sheryl said. This was the first time Colt had seen much of her.

Listening now, he found her to be, like many he had met in this world, very sharp and a bit arrogant.

"Ladies and gentlemen, Mr. Jeff Kim," she said, finishing her introduction.

When the clapping died down, Kim said, "Thank you." His voice was calm and cool. The interview began with the normal softball questions discussing Kim's upbringing and motivation. Then they got to the good stuff.

Sheryl said, "We have an interesting topic today. On our guest list this weekend are the heads of some of the top tech companies in the world. We intend to ask everyone this next question, but I think it will be particularly interesting to hear your answer, given your expertise in the field. How long do you think it will be until we develop an AGI—artificial general intelligence—or what some people call a superintelligence?"

Kim cocked his head. "Well, Sheryl, I think it is important to agree on the definition and language. When I say AGI, I mean an AI program able to comprehend and learn any task a typical human being can learn. And if that is the standard, then I think we will develop an AGI within the next ten years."

"You really think we're getting that close?"

He held up a finger. "Forecasting a technological leap is how people like me get laughed at on YouTube. So, my prediction must stay in this room, okay?"

The crowd laughed.

Kim said, "But it is funny you mention predictions . . . I have a surprise for you today, if you are willing to participate in a small experiment."

Sheryl looked delighted. "Absolutely."

He held out a hand to the audience. "And to all of you out there, are you willing to be observers in our experiment?"

The audience cheered.

Kim said, "Excellent. I will tell my lawyers that I have

signed NDAs." More laughter. Kim looked to the side of the stage, where Nader was standing with a tablet computer in hand. "Are we ready, Mr. Nader? Yes. Okay. Let us begin."

Colt watched as the large projector screens on each side of the stage went black.

Kim said, "Sheryl, you asked me to predict the future . . ."

The screens began streaming text from top to bottom.

Sheryl, you asked me to predict the future.

"As you know, my company—Pax AI—is making rapid advances in the field of artificial intelligence."

As Kim spoke, the screen continued transcribing everything he said in real time.

Sheryl quipped, "Which is a good thing, considering you placed AI in the name of the company."

Kim smiled. "Very true."

The audience laughed again.

The side screens continued to populate with the transcribed dialogue. Colt noticed that the line of text was precipitated by the name of the speaker, in real time.

Colt overheard someone sitting in the row ahead of him. "Impressive software."

The person's companion replied, "Yeah, not bad. Plenty of competition for voice-to-text, though. What's up with the coloring?"

Colt saw what he meant. On the screen filled with streaming text, the lines first appeared yellow, then turned green a split second later.

Colt turned to Ava for an explanation. She just smiled.

The person ahead of Colt said, "Must be part of Jeff Kim's experiment." A woman turned around, casting them a mean look for talking too loud.

On the stage, Sheryl looked at the screens filled with their transcribed conversation and asked, "So what is our experiment?"

Jeff Kim looked out at the audience. "More of a new product demonstration, really. But I ask for your patience. Let us wait a little longer and see if the audience can figure it out. You asked me when I think we will have an AGI. Regardless of the timing—whether it's minutes or months or years—I believe the system that first makes that leap will then grow exponentially in its capability. A true AGI will race past the threshold of what Bostrom termed a *superintelligence*. This explosion of artificial intelligence will be swift. If we are not careful, it could be unexpected. And an AI that begins this journey will make the most gifted human intellects look like insects by comparison."

Colt felt the room go quiet. He realized the majority of people around him were hanging on every word.

"That's a little frightening," said Sheryl.

Kim nodded. "Yes, but it's also exciting."

"But how *risky* is it? Some of your peers see significant danger in the creation of an artificial superintelligence. And there is a growing divide among society as to how to handle the development of AI. I know you are well aware of the group known as Trinity."

Colt could see Kim's veneer crack a little. "Unfortunately, we at Pax AI are well aware of such groups. We have watched with growing concern as more and more people have begun subscribing to some of the more radical beliefs of the Trinity movement. And, as many of you know, the FBI believes that one of our own scientists was killed by a deranged follower."

The room went quiet.

Sheryl said, "If you would like to move on . . ."

Kim raised his hand. "No. In the past, I would have thought to ignore this type of thing, thinking it was human nature. It will die out. Move on, don't give them any more airtime, so to speak. But I think we have learned it's important we do not ignore such conspiracies, as they can metastasize into something perilous."

Sheryl turned to the audience. "For those who are unfamiliar, Trinity's main belief is that a superintelligent being will be created by mankind, and that this is our unavoidable destiny. Followers of Trinity believe this superintelligence will be . . ." She hesitated.

Jeff Kim cut in. "It's hard to even say it, isn't it?"

". . . will be our ruler," Sheryl finished.

"I think you mean to say the word *God*, not ruler. Believers in Trinity think that artificial general intelligence will bring about the end of mankind. And that for anyone left, the chosen ones, the newly created superintelligence will be their God. And . . . they *welcome* this. Because, of course, anyone who follows Trinity considers themselves one of the chosen ones." Kim sounded very frustrated. "If it sounds crazy, that's because it *is* crazy."

Sheryl was respectfully subdued. "Jeff, I wonder if I might ask . . . do you think the closer we get to developing an AGI, the more scared and desperate people will become?"

"I understand that," said Kim. "People want control over their lives. And the rate of technological change is outpacing our ability to adapt. It is important for us to discuss all aspects of these changes, not ignore them. But look, we need to be honest about this. Trinity is a cult. A small group of individuals seeded the idea on message boards and social media, and now it seems to have taken over the lives of hundreds of thousands of impressionable people. And make no mistake, Trinity's teachings are dangerous. We at Pax AI are very aware of the growing threat posed by the Trinity cult. It is our view that

Trinity encourages irresponsible behavior that could do real harm."

"Go on."

"Trinity has radicalized many of its followers. Trust me, I understand how the idea of exponential growth in machine learning, of computers advancing beyond human capability, is extremely frightening. It is natural for human beings to look for ways to explain the unknown, and to deal with their fears. This Trinity group is just another way of doing that. But one of Trinity's tenets is the notion that humanity is unworthy of controlling itself. That when an AGI is developed, we should place a collar around our necks and hand over a leash to the machine. Excuse the dramatic description. Another belief of theirs is that all artificial intelligence technology should be shared with everyone around the world as soon as it is developed, regardless of how dangerous it may be. I vehemently disagree with these ideas."

"I think we can all appreciate the desire for freedom. But regarding the sharing of technology, some would argue what you and other tech companies are developing is so powerful, it needs more transparency. More shared control."

"I disagree that transparency equals shared control. And during development—"

Sheryl said, "Critics argue that corporations shouldn't be the ones in charge of a technology that will have so much impact on our lives."

Kim raised his head. "I am trying to lead my company in a way that ensures our technology is developed safely and used responsibly. At Pax AI, we want to create a better world for everyone. But I will be honest, developing artificial intelligence is dangerous. Like any new technology, there are ways it can be used that, if our algorithms fell into the wrong hands . . ."

He looked out at the audience, a dramatic pause that drew everyone in.

"Well, I don't need to scare anyone. I founded my company because I think it is crucial to bring about AGI the *right* way. We at Pax AI prioritize safety and security above all else. We are on the precipice of a giant leap in machine learning. I honestly want this next stage to make the world a better place. Think about all the good we can do. The problems we can solve. Inequality. Hunger. Health care. Disease. The leap to artificial general intelligence will make the invention of computers and the internet look minuscule by comparison. AI is already changing the world at a rapid clip. We now have AI programs that have literally saved lives by correcting erroneous medical diagnoses. And our weather-prediction algorithm is rapidly outpacing what was once thought to be the limit of meteorological foresight."

The interviewer said, "And that saves lives too . . ."

"Indeed, it does. Not to mention the economic benefit. We are focused on bringing about these changes for good. So it's important that we keep our intellectual property secure so that no malicious actors use it to harm others, before safety controls are in place."

Colt's ears perked up as some of the spectators nearby began whispering to each other. People in the crowd were noticing something unusual. Colt looked up at the dialogue transcription but couldn't tell what people were responding to. The colors looked different. And the text had grown. It was showing paragraphs now instead of just sentences. He noticed that the first half of the text was in green, and the second half was in yellow as the dialogue first appeared on the screen. The text seemed to be converting to green after being displayed for a longer period of time.

On the stage Kim was saying, "Our AI, combined with

some pretty innovative developments we've made in quantum computing, can now predict a hurricane's track more than five days out with unheard-of precision. We can alert people in the path of a tornado fifteen minutes before the funnel has even *formed*."

"That's incredible . . ."

". . . and we can even predict the progression of forest fires. With enough wind data, topological profiles, and real-time satellite imagery, our AI can eliminate surprises and help prevent the devastation that has become all too common."

Some in the audience clapped, but others were murmuring even louder, talking and pointing at the screens.

"Unreal . . ." someone said.

"This has got to be a trick . . ." added someone else. The audience was filled with so much chatter now that Colt could barely hear the interview.

He frowned, trying to understand what they were seeing.

"Holy shit." He looked at the screen of transcribed dialogue. He had finally made the connection, understood what people were so excited about.

"Did you figure it out?" said Ava, eyes twinkling.

"Ava, this is incredible . . ."

On stage, Jeff Kim stood. "Okay, well, it sounds like our experiment has worked."

Sheryl said, "Can you let me in on the surprise now?"

Nader walked on stage and handed Kim his tablet computer. The screens switched back to a live video image of the stage.

"Ninety-eight percent at a one-minute interval. Not bad at all," Kim said to a scattering of claps and whistles from the more astute audience members.

"What does that mean?" asked Sheryl.

Kim had shaken off the unease from the conversation about Trinity and now looked triumphant.

"During our conversation, we were testing one of our most advanced AI models. We combined a language-prediction algorithm with some other predictive seed data and our real-time voice data. The audience was able to witness the experiment as we spoke. The text of our transcribed conversation had two colors, yellow and green. Green, when it was in real time."

"And yellow?"

"Yellow was the prediction of what we would say next. About halfway through our conversation, we began projecting out the next words each of us would say. Similar to the way an AI language algorithm predicts what you might want to type."

"Very impressive," Sheryl said.

"Yes," said Kim. "And also, much more advanced than anything that's been developed before. I'm happy to report that our AI was ninety-eight percent accurate at predicting the exact words of our conversation. *One minute into the future.*"

Sheryl's mouth dropped open, and the audience again fell silent. After a moment, she said, "You . . . predicted what we would say one minute into the future?"

"That's right. In real time. Ninety-eight percent accuracy. We recorded everything, and we'll make it available for peer review."

The audience erupted in conversation. Some people got up from their seats, leaving to make phone calls. Colt heard at least one person talking to his stockbroker, trying to find out how to invest in Pax AI.

Sheryl said, "Jeff, this is incredible. Can you . . . I assume there are limitations. You can't just do this with any conversation?"

"You are correct, I'm afraid. We had to feed a lot of data

into our computers. Information on both of us. Past interviews we have done. Papers we have written. Public record conversations. The more data, the better the accuracy, of course. All this information is fed into our most powerful quantum computer, which augments some of our analysis. This was about the limit of our capability right now. But we are making progress each day."

"I'm just trying to wrap my mind around this. I mean, the implications are huge."

"Yes. Which brings me back to your original set of questions on the future of AI. The more we can develop our AI systems to predict the future, to learn, and to react accordingly, the closer we get to achieving our goal. AGI can create more value for humanity than any invention that has come before it. But as I mentioned in our discussion, we've got to bring it online in a safe manner. It is so crucial that we get this right."

"Well, I think that's a great place to end our interview. Jeff Kim, thank you."

"Oh, one more thing . . ." said Kim. "We'll be conducting a live experiment in San Francisco next week. We wanted to show some of our partners here first, so they can help us get the word out. But we plan to conduct a public demonstration that will be live-streamed with a variety of subjects. It will be fun to see what this baby is really capable of."

The audience rose to their feet, clapping.

Colt's mind turned over the new information. Kim had mentioned the use of their quantum computer. Pace had stayed home to man the controls. This program used communication between The Facility and the fourth floor at Pax AI. And they were going to run it again next week, at a set time.

Colt needed to tell Wilcox.

This was their way in.

21

Jeff Kim, Nader, and Ava were busy making the rounds following the demonstration. People were enthralled with the AI breakthrough. Most of the business executives and journalists in attendance wanted a word or a photo with Kim. Everyone wanted a piece of what they had just witnessed, anything they could bring back and use to their advantage.

The Pax AI team had made their intended splash. Phillips and Jefferies, Colt's New York investment firm, was already sending him requests for more information on Pax AI's new language-prediction program. Their phone had been ringing off the hook with high-net-worth clients trying to get in on the gold rush. The emails Colt received contained both more work requirements and gentle suggestions that he hurry up so his firm could start slicing and dicing the company a little sooner.

Ninety minutes later, he and Ava stood at the hotel entrance as Kim, Nader, and their entourage departed in a luxury SUV motorcade, headed to the private jet that would take them back to California.

Ava turned to Colt as they left. "Quick hike before dinner?"

Colt smiled. "Wouldn't want to go against Aunt Samantha's suggestion."

They changed into appropriate exercise clothing and were soon heading toward Bow River's bright turquoise water. Colt could hear nearby waterfalls as they walked along a paved path, passing the thick whitewater of the falls and continuing over a pedestrian bridge near downtown Banff.

On the north side of the river, Ava led them down a more secluded gravel pathway called Hoodoos trail. They were shaded by tall evergreens and a wall of rock. Colt breathed in clean mountain air, a light sheen of sweat forming on his chest and forehead. Birds of prey soared above the riverbed, looking for their next meal.

"I hope my aunt didn't question you too much."

"She is a very nice woman." Colt was breathing heavily, partly from the elevation, but also because Ava moved at a remarkable pace. He noticed her calf muscles bunching while she walked. He didn't remember her being so athletic.

"Sorry for her inquisition," Ava said. "She has always been protective of me. She took care of me after they passed."

Colt said, "She's on your mother's side or . . ."

"Father's."

They stopped at a flat, open riverbank. Smooth stones crunched under their hiking boots. Colt picked one up and skipped it in the blue river.

"The demonstration today was incredible," he said.

Ava glanced at him. "Thanks. I have to admit, it went better than expected." She picked up a stone and threw it into the river, skipping it like Colt had.

"Will the public event next week be much different?"

"I think they'll have a few more variations to show how it can perform in different scenarios. Different types of people.

Different amounts of information on each participant prior to running the program."

"Where was Pace during all of this?"

Ava said, "He was on the fourth floor. They turned the conference room into a control center, relaying data from the Mountain Research Facility. It protects our network from hacking, but still allows us to show off what we can do."

"Any chance I could be there next time? On the fourth floor?"

Ava gave him an apologetic look. "I'm sorry, but I don't think they'll let you. Miller was adamant about security. Jeff has already signed off on the small group. I'll tell you about it, though." She winked.

"You'll be there?"

She nodded.

Colt skipped another rock. "The other night you mentioned you were a little creeped out by some of the technology you guys are developing. Was this language-prediction program part of that?"

Ava made a face, showing her discomfort. "I don't know. This one is interesting. But it does have the potential for misuse. We'll need to be very careful making sure it is safe before we release it."

Colt said, "How could it be misused?"

"How can predicting the future be misused?"

"It just predicts what someone will say next, right? How harmful could that be?"

"Well, it depends who is talking. Can you predict what a CEO or a world leader is going to say, far in advance? How long before language prediction turns into thought and opinion prediction? Because we've done the research. Those are very similar. The brain functionality is nearly identical. So you could see a scenario where one can make decisions to sell stock or pull out of a trade agreement or . . ."

"Go to war?" Colt offered.

Ava pursed her lips. "Yes, I suppose so. And there are much more personal scenarios too. It could end marriages or get people kicked out of school or fired from their jobs. All for future predictions, not for actual events. Maybe for scenarios that were kept private in the past. That's the other thing this AI program takes away—privacy of thought. If it really can predict, with accuracy, what people will say or do . . . who's to say that some authoritarian government couldn't use it as a way to determine loyalty and go around—"

"Ava." Colt was stunned to hear her voicing these concerns.

"Sorry."

"This really bothers you, doesn't it?"

She nodded. "It's just not something I can talk to people about. Voicing concerns over the ethics or morality of our technology is akin to professional suicide. I mean . . . this is what makes our company money. This technological progress is why we exist. And if we don't do it, someone else will . . ."

"But Pax AI is way ahead of the competition. I've seen the files."

Ava raised an eyebrow. "Interesting how far ahead, isn't it?"

Colt narrowed his eyes. "What do you mean?"

"Nothing. I'm sorry. Please don't tell anyone about this conversation. Seriously. These are things I've been struggling with, but I do like my job and the company and I do think we can do good things. I just worry, that's all. But that's normal, right?"

"Sure," said Colt. "I promise I'll always keep our conversations just between us."

Ava took his hand, then reached up and kissed him on the

cheek. "Thanks." She turned toward the path. "Come on, let's finish this trail loop so we can make it back in time for dinner."

They continued walking, reaching a bend in the trail that gave Colt a clear view up the river. For a brief moment, he caught sight of a lone male figure standing on the pedestrian bridge a few hundred yards away. It was hard to tell at that range, but Colt was pretty sure he recognized him as the clean-shaven man with the dark curly hair he had observed earlier. The man had his black leather smoking jacket slung over his shoulder. He had been half-hidden behind a pine tree on the south side of the bridge, but he had moved when Colt and Ava began walking to keep a clear line of sight on them.

Colt recognized what the man was doing. He was surveillance.

22

The rest of their hike was uneventful. Colt didn't tell Ava about the man on the bridge, and he was gone when they returned to cross it. At the hotel, they split up to shower and get dressed before meeting Ava's aunt in the lobby. They went to the bar for drinks. The women ordered white wine and Colt ordered his usual Old Fashioned. He watched the bartender garnish it with an orange peel while Samantha peppered him with questions on his business.

"And after the Navy, you joined up with this firm?"

"That's correct," Colt said. "I met some of their recruiters at a job fair when I was in business school. The company had a veterans program, which helped a lot."

"I'm familiar with Phillips and Jefferies. It's a very good company. And it's very impressive that you were able to land a job there." Samantha looked at Ava.

Actually, Aunt Samantha, I spent about eighteen months training with the CIA. But I can't go into that because I'm trying to recruit your niece to be an agent so she can spy on her coworkers.

"Thank you," Colt said.

The dinner was excellent, although Samantha's continued interrogation got more embarrassing as the night went on.

"And you've never been married? A handsome man like you?" She looked at her niece again. "Seems like a waste if you ask me, eh, Ava?"

Ava was shaking her head. "Colt, I'm so sorry. We Jewish women aren't known for our subtlety when it comes to matchmaking."

Samantha said, "Hmph. I'm only trying to help. You weren't interested in any of the boys I tried to set you up with in New York."

Ava shot her a look.

"I'll take it as a compliment," Colt said. He could tell that Ava appreciated his playing along.

After dinner they went to a wine bar in downtown Banff where they ordered dessert and continued talking, drinking, and laughing.

When her aunt was in the bathroom, Ava said, "She's impressed. You've passed all of her tests."

"I didn't know I was being evaluated."

Ava looked skeptical. "Yes, you did."

Colt said, "Listen, I was thinking about what you said to me. About wanting to be proud of what you are working on. About feeling like some of the things Pax AI is working on are less than ethical. There's something I need to ask you. The other night, when we left the party, Luke Pace said something to me . . ."

"Luke was rather drunk."

Colt made a face. "I don't know. I don't think this was the alcohol speaking."

"What did he say?" Ava looked worried.

"That Kozlov died in The Facility."

Her face went rigid. "What?"

"He said that the FBI was investigating the death in the wrong place. That Kozlov didn't die in the hotel like everyone thought. He said Kozlov died in The Facility. Do you have any idea what he was talking about?"

Ava shook her head, looking confused. "No idea. But . . . that's not what happened."

"I know."

This part would be delicate, Colt knew. "But that's a really weird thing to say, right?"

"Yes. Very."

Colt paused, and then said, "You know as part of my work, I have been introduced to someone whose job it is to make sure that dangerous technology doesn't fall into the wrong hands. We're friends, and I've consulted with him in the past whenever I have questions about...legal issues."

She didn't respond.

Colt said, "You told me that some of the things you work on creep you out. We both know how powerful Pax AI's technology is. Are you at all concerned that there might be something going on here that isn't . . ."

"Legitimate?" Ava said.

He shrugged. "Yeah."

Ava's eyes went to the floor, dancing nervously. "I don't know. Sometimes, maybe."

Colt said, "This friend of mine, he's very discreet. Maybe we should just meet with him and get his opinion about Pace's comment. It would ease my conscience. He might have questions, though. Would you come with me? You don't have to say anything if you don't want to."

"Colt, I don't feel right about that. I wasn't there when Pace made that comment, and I don't know what he was talking about. Maybe he was just drunk. You can tell your friend about what Pace said if it makes you feel better. I don't need to be there."

"Then where do your concerns stem from?"

Ava said, "There has been a lot more secrecy around some of the work lately, that's all. I'm more uneasy about the lack of visibility I have with some of The Facility projects."

Colt nodded. "Everyone has told me how powerful this technology is. How much it will change the world. There must be people who want to steal Pax AI's intellectual property. You don't worry about Kozlov's death being related to that."

"Of course I do. We are all worried about it, we just don't talk about it. It's driving me crazy pretending everything is normal. But we have a world-class security department working round the clock to protect our secrets. I'm much less involved in the development side of the business. They keep everything that goes on at The Facility very hush-hush." She was visibly upset.

Colt said, "You told me you could get access to The Facility if you pushed for it. Maybe you could get both of us a tour of the place? Use me as an excuse. I've requested it for my work, but Miller is stalling, I think."

Ava's mouth opened, but she didn't speak. She studied Colt for a moment. The only noise was the chattering and music from the bar.

"What do you want me to say?" she said.

"Say you will help me."

"Why do you need me?"

"Something feels off. And I need someone I can trust."

The structure of the sales pitch was familiar. Building trust. Fueling her fears. Massaging her concerns. Enticing her to act. But their prior relationship made this difficult.

Ava's dark eyes stared back at him. "It's just . . . it's a lot to process. I'm not sure how I feel about this. Or about you asking."

He was about to respond when Ava's eyes fixed on her aunt, who was walking through the sitting area of the wine bar. Samantha saw them sitting close and talking, her expression that of a satisfied matchmaker. Colt smiled and took a swig of his drink, trying to wash away the odd mix of guilt and defeat that had come over him.

Their night wound down after the wine bar with a slow walk back to the hotel. Samantha hugged them both and said she needed to get a good night's sleep to catch her early flight. Then Ava and Colt shared the elevator in silence.

Ava's floor came first. She said goodnight and then stood there, looking at Colt as she held the elevator door so it wouldn't close. He could sense the internal struggle going on before she spoke.

"I'll get us into The Facility. I'll speak with Jeff. I know how to convince him. But I won't speak to your friend. I don't feel comfortable with that."

Colt gave her an almost imperceptible nod. "Okay."

She removed her hand and stepped back, and the elevator door closed.

23

The next day, Heather Weng stood in a grove of redwood trees in Golden Gate Park. She'd been waiting for forty minutes before a brunette woman of about forty approached.

SANDSTONE wore yoga pants, a flowing canopy wrap sweatshirt, and sunglasses. Weng's first thought was that Marisha Stepanova looked like a rich housewife. Her second thought was that she looked pissed off.

She cursed in Russian and then said, "Why the hell isn't Colt here?"

Weng started to answer, but Marisha stormed past her. Weng rolled her eyes and began following the Russian intelligence officer up an incline, deeper into the shady grove of giant trees.

"He had something he couldn't miss. He asked me to apologize."

"When will he be back?"

"Tonight, or maybe tomorrow."

"I must see him."

"I can help you with whatever you need. We wanted to make sure . . ."

Marisha stopped walking and turned, her eyes blazing. "You meeting me like this is poor tradecraft. For the past three years, you have protected me by only using Colt. I don't know you."

Weng could see how afraid she was. This was about more than just Colt's absence. "Marisha . . . may I call you that?"

She shrugged. "That's fine."

"I've known Colt for a long time. I learned about you only one week ago. I do the same type of work you do. And like you, I'm very good at my job. I will not take risks. I will not make mistakes that could put you in danger. Now if you think it's time for us to take more drastic measures to protect you, we can have that discussion. Is that the situation?"

"I don't know," said Marisha. She was pacing next to the trunk of a huge redwood.

In the distance, Weng could hear the sounds of the park. People talking. Dogs barking. Helicopters and jumbo jets. Ambulance sirens. The air brakes from municipal transportation buses. But here, in this small, wooded area in the heart of a technology-driven city, two spies stood in solitude.

Weng said, "Is there anything urgent you need me to pass on?"

Marisha sulked. "Yes."

Weng waited.

Marisha removed her cellphone from her flowing sweatshirt pocket and swiped to unlock it. She scrolled through it until she found what she was searching for, then held the screen for Weng to see.

"I don't speak Russian," Weng said. Marisha's phone showed an image of a typed letter, about one paragraph long.

Marisha said, "My superior at the SVR has been traveling to San Francisco for an operation that, until recently, I was not part of. He has just brought me into that operation. This is an invitation."

"An invitation?" Weng removed her phone and opened the camera app. "May I?"

Marisha nodded and Weng took a picture. This method of copying it would be more secure than asking Marisha to electronically send it somewhere. "An invitation for what?"

Marisha said, "A private sale event. The SVR is going to purchase Pax AI's language-prediction algorithm."

Weng looked up at Marisha before looking down at her picture, examining the quality. "Who is the seller?" Studying the letter, she noticed a familiar symbol on the bottom of the page.

Marisha said, "Trinity."

After the meeting, Weng walked north along the beach. She called Wilcox on the way, using her CIA-issued phone.

"Just met with her," Weng said. "The SVR has been contacted by Trinity. SANDSTONE said they have an agent who received a paper note inviting them to a private sale. Trinity claims to have the language-prediction technology that Pax AI just announced. The same AI tech they are going to publicly demonstrate in San Francisco this Friday."

Wilcox said, "Do we know when or how they are making the transaction?"

"No. This was just an invitation. I have a photo of a photo of the original. I'll show you soon."

Wilcox said, "Who was the SVR agent who received this invitation?"

"SANDSTONE didn't know. She's going to try and get that name."

"Are they inside Pax AI?"

"I don't know, Ed." Weng went quiet as she passed a few beach walkers. Then she said, "SANDSTONE says the SVR thinks they can identify the Trinity mole. Their agent is trying to confirm who is stealing the technology from Pax AI. But SANDSTONE wants Colt at the next meeting."

"Not a problem. Did you set something up?"

"We agreed Colt would reach out."

"Okay. Colt arrives today. I'll let him know. Get back here so we can take a look at that note."

"Will do."

Three hundred feet above the beach, a small quadcopter drone followed Weng's path to the north. The buzzing of the rotors was drowned out by the noise of the surf. But the directional microphone on its undercarriage, augmented by sophisticated computer programs, was able to cancel out the background noise and record her side of the phone conversation.

To the Chinese Ministry of State Security, Heather Weng was a known CIA intelligence officer. Her presence in the San Francisco Bay Area had been noted by MSS facial recognition programs. The Chinese intelligence service's cyber operations division had hacked into San Francisco's CCTV cameras four years ago, and MSS AI programs now sifted through millions of faces there each day. The MSS mostly used this information to track anti-Chinese dissidents who traveled in the city. But that same cyber division also knew that Heather Weng, until recently, had been stationed in the Vancouver area, most likely under the leadership of the CIA's head of station there, Ed Wilcox.

Weng's presence in the city was interesting enough that the MSS approved a small surveillance team to monitor her activities. The quadcopter drone had been launched from the Golden Gate Park. It transmitted the recorded conversation back to the MSS-owned minivan, which, if inspected, would show several custom-installed antennas. The data was received and evaluated by an analyst inside the van, who realized its importance right away. He downloaded the file from the drone to his computer and sent it to his superiors in an encrypted email. He then wiped all evidence of the recording from the drone.

In the Consulate General of the People's Republic of China in San Francisco, Liu Xing, the MSS's top spy in the city, sat at his desk. He had been reading through emails from Beijing while eating lunch when the knock at his door came. One of his operations officers came in, excited.

"Sir, please check your email. You need to listen to something," the man said.

Liu did so. At first, he struggled with the quality of the recording. But after his second time hearing the conversation, he understood the significance.

"Trinity?" Liu said.

The operations officer nodded.

"Our reports on Trinity do not support this capability."

"Correct, sir."

"It could be that the Russians are playing games with the CIA," Liu said.

"What do you want me to do?" his subordinate asked.

Liu stood, looking out his window at the San Francisco skyline. He took a moment to think about what he had just heard. Pax AI was one of their primary economic espionage targets. The company's AI advances were mind-boggling, and Beijing was obsessed with catching up to them. Liu had personally worked on developing penetration agents at the company, but it had been difficult.

Liu said, "The SVR runs its West Coast agents out of their Houston consulate now, correct?"

The Russian consulate in San Francisco had been shut down in 2017 by the US State Department. A tit-for-tat measure taken after the Russians ordered more than seven hundred US diplomats expelled from their country, a response to American sanctions following Russian interference in the 2016 presidential election.

"Yes, sir. Houston."

Liu said, "Find out who the *rezident* is in Houston. Tell him that I would like a word with him in private. And if possible, make sure no one else in his organization knows about it."

"What will you do?"

Liu said, "If this Trinity group is really selling Pax AI technology, we want a seat at the table."

"But why would the Russians . . . ah. I see."

Liu smiled as his subordinate made the connection. "Yes. The SVR will help us because we can offer what they value most. The name of a traitor."

24

Colt didn't know what she said to Jeff Kim, but Ava had come through. Facility access was approved, much earlier than expected. Kim was even taking time out of his busy schedule to go with them.

A Mercedes SUV dropped the three of them off at the private helipad section of San Francisco International Airport. Colt hadn't flown on a helicopter since he was in the Navy, and that had been just a few times strapped in the back of a barren cabin, barely able to hear anything over the engine noise.

This was a whole different experience. Pax AI's helicopter had plush leather seats, prepped lunches, and beverages on ice, and soundproofed cabin walls allowed them to have a conversation while they flew.

They took off, heading over the bay. Out the window, Colt had an amazing view of the city. The Golden Gate Bridge. Alcatraz. Soon they were over wine country, the hilly vineyards of Sonoma and Napa below.

Jeff Kim was reading something on a tablet computer while munching on a turkey wrap, oblivious to the stunning views. Ava saw Colt's expression and smiled. But her face held a hint of fatigue. She didn't like lying, Colt knew.

He asked, "How long is the flight out there?"

Kim looked up from the tablet. "About an hour. Miller provided your security brief?"

Colt nodded. "No cellphones, no communication in or out while we're inside. I can't believe your employees do multi-week shifts like that. Do you ever stay there that long, Jeff?"

Kim shook his head. "I'm afraid I could never get away for that amount of time." He held up the tablet. "The company would go up in flames. I would love to, though. I would like to get more hands-on with our experiments. But I only get in to see The Facility during the changeover between crews. We have three of them. Each one spends a few weeks inside The Facility, then a month or so working out of our San Francisco office. I go over the results with the team on the fourth floor where I can look at the recordings and data. But we don't run any of the live experiments unless The Facility is locked down."

Colt said, "Why is that?"

Kim said, "You will see."

Ava pointed. "Here we are."

Colt looked out his window. The helicopter zoomed a few hundred feet over dark green pines. A freshly paved road sliced through the forest below. He saw a perpendicular cutout in the trees ahead and a double ring of razor wire fence, about twenty feet between them. The two lines of razor wire formed a perimeter, which intersected the road at a manned security gate. Their helicopter flew overhead, and Colt counted four armed guards and two off-road vehicles.

"Those guys look like they are wearing military uniforms."

Kim said, "Yes, the US Air Force guards that outer perimeter gate. That was in our contract with the Department of Defense. The internal security is privately run." Colt wanted to ask more but thought better of it.

He could see the buildings now. Four octagonal structures rose out of the ground like futuristic pillboxes. They were identical in size and shape, about fifty feet tall. A skinny shaft with a door. The top looked like a single-level room on an elevated platform. He couldn't tell if the material they were constructed from was metal or stone. Maybe some type of alloy? These buildings were built into the forest. Trees surrounded them, providing shade. A two-hundred-foot water tower stood behind the buildings. About fifty yards away, where the road ended, another larger structure was carved into the base of a mountain.

"Wow," Colt said. "This must have cost a fortune."

"It did." Kim laughed. "Which is one reason we need another round of funding."

The helicopter landed on a ground-level helipad, one of the lone areas that had been cut out of the dense forest. Next to the helipad was another security station, though these guards didn't wear military uniforms.

One of them approached the helicopter from the side. He opened the cabin door and escorted them out of the rotor arc. Soon after, the helicopter rose up, its rotor wash scattering dirt and debris. Then its nose dipped, and it began climbing, turning to depart toward the south.

As the echoes of the aircraft faded, Colt was struck by the silence. They were truly in the middle of nowhere, an evergreen forest in all directions.

"Come on, this way," Kim said. They headed toward the structure embedded into the mountain base. As they approached, Colt got a better look at the construction. Sharp-angled and gray, with dark metallic blue panels lining the top third of the single level and forming a honeycomb pattern. He estimated this building to be about two hundred feet in length.

"It's huge," Colt said.

"You can only see about one-third of it. The rest is built into the mountain. The solar panels provide enough energy for emergency power, but there are wind turbines and a massive battery supply surrounding this mountain."

"What are those other buildings? The ones back there in the woods?"

"External laboratories," said Luke Pace. He wore a white lab coat and had been standing by The Facility's main entrance. "We use them to segment some of the work, and conduct experiments that we want to transmit back to headquarters. At least, that's how it is supposed to work."

Kim said, "How are things looking?"

"Horrible. Can you give me six more months?"

"Two days."

Pace glowered. "We'll do our best."

Ava said, "Hello, Luke."

"Hi, Ava. Can you explain to Jeff that performing miracles is not a sustainable business practice?"

"Why don't you show us in?" Kim said. "I'm sure you and I can discuss your concerns in private. Without bothering Mr. McShane, who represents our investors."

Pace let out a sigh. "Sorry. Sure." He turned and placed his hand on a biometric reader. The double glass doors slid open and Pace led them into a cavernous hallway.

They walked through the hall, its smooth stone walls broken up by metal doors with triangular windows. Through the windows Colt could see into the various rooms. Some were filled with metal piping and computer servers. Others with bright white panels that reminded Colt of a NASA laboratory or a microchip factory. One of the rooms had a pair of workers inside. They wore what looked like spacesuit outfits, which Pace said was to protect their computers from particulate impurities.

The group reached one of the research rooms and Pace opened the door with another biometric scanner. Inside, Kim sat down at one of the computer terminals. In front of them, a long horizontal pane of glass spanned the room, revealing a cavernous purplish-glowing space beyond.

"What is it?"

"*That* is our quantum computer," said Kim. "When we run our simulations, it allows our AI programs to conduct massive calculations. It can evaluate permutations we would never be able to with a legacy device, given the computing power required."

The machine was like no computer Colt had ever seen. It looked like two massive upside-down cathedral organs, their bronze pipes combining. Shining gold discs sliced through hundreds of tiny metallic cylinders. Layers of purple light reflected off the dark walls surrounding it. Near the ceiling, a thin white cloud layer hung in the air.

Ava said, "Beautiful, isn't it?"

Colt turned back to face them. "It's like a work of art."

Pace said, "It's worth more than any piece of art. Maybe more than all of the art, if it gets us where we're trying to go."

"What's with the purple color?" Colt asked.

"Hydrogen gas. The space is filled with it," Pace said.

Kim turned to face Colt. "All right, Mr. McShane. Welcome to The Facility. It's time we show you what we're doing here."

Kim said, "When I first began Pax AI, I had one goal in mind. You know the saying 'all roads lead to Rome?' Well, it is my belief that in tech, all our innovation, eventually, will lead to mankind's one final invention."

"Artificial general intelligence," Colt said.

Kim pointed at him. "Bingo." He gestured to a large rectangular monitor near the side of the room. Kim typed a few keystrokes and the monitor illuminated, showing a group of scientists, each wearing a white lab coat, gathered in this very room.

"Who are they?" Colt asked. He recognized Kozlov's face in the center of the group, but didn't want to make that known.

Kim looked at Colt. "This is video footage of our AGI team. The scientist sitting down in the center of the group is Mr. Kozlov." His voice sounded melancholy when he said Kozlov's name.

As the video played, Colt saw the scientists growing more animated as they gathered around Kozlov's computer monitor.

"What are they watching?" Colt asked.

Kim typed in a few keystrokes and the point of view shifted. A new angle of the smiling scientists, their eyes wide with excitement. A number in the bottom left of the screen was rapidly increasing.

"What is that number?"

"Keep watching."

The number was ticking up furiously now. 0.005%. 0.01%. 0.1%. Finally it hit 1.00% and everyone cheered. A red "simulation paused" caption appeared over the number.

"What happened?" Colt asked.

Kim said, "What you just witnessed was our AGI team reaching a major milestone. They went further than anyone's ever come to achieving AGI."

Neither Kim nor Pace looked happy. Colt said, "But why aren't you celebrating?"

Kim said, "Because now that Kozlov is dead, we can't replicate the experiment. The best progress humanity has ever made, in the most important scientific breakthrough, is now lost."

Colt and Ava both looked dumbstruck.

Colt spoke first. "Why can't you repeat it?"

Kim said, "It has to do with how we were able to reach that milestone. Do you see that room over there?"

Colt looked to his left, toward a white door that resembled a submarine hatch. "Yes."

"Beyond that door is one of our research rooms. It houses another of our most advanced programs—a neural interface. AI-augmentation in humans. Our capability is very advanced. And importantly, it is proprietary technology."

Colt narrowed his eyes. "AI-augmentation? You mean like . . . like *cyborgs*?" He looked at Ava, who seemed less surprised, but was still listening intently.

Kim chuckled. "Not exactly like cyborgs, no. Think of it more like how people use their mobile phones to access information or make calculations. But we've created a much more direct interface."

Pace leaned forward. "*Much* more direct."

Colt looked back at the monitor showing Kozlov's achievement. He squinted, looking more closely at the man's head. It was hard to see details on the video, but Kozlov looked to be wearing a thin winter cap. The headgear had two wires running out of the back that connected somewhere on his computer's undercarriage.

Pace nodded. "He's wearing one of our lighter models there. It allows him about fifty percent of what the new heavy system can do."

"And that actually works?" Colt said.

Kim said, "It depends on the user. But yes, we've achieved substantial neural-computer interfacing. Some users are much more adept at using it than others. The more testing we've done, the more we realize it's like playing an instrument or performing an athletic feat. Some people are naturally more talented at manipulating the neural interface. Kozlov was the best."

Pace said, "And that program was a key part of how we were able to make such good progress in our AGI program."

Colt said, "How?"

"It's complicated," said Kim. "But it has to do with monitoring multiple systems and making tweaks in real time. You would be amazed at what we're capable of when we don't have to use these clumsy things." He held up his hands.

Colt frowned, looking at the screen again. "How long after this was taken did Kozlov turn up dead?"

Pace shifted his weight and glanced at Kim, who didn't blink. "Six days."

Colt opened his mouth. "And the FBI knows all about this?"

Kim said, "We answered all their questions truthfully. The FBI knows that Kozlov was closely involved in an important project here. The investigators don't know the exact nature of the project, but we are working closely with our government sponsors in IARPA and other agencies."

Pace said, "Some of our Facility projects cannot be shared, due to nondisclosure agreements with the government. We had to get special approval for you just to be here."

Colt wasn't sure whether to be amused or depressed by that bureaucratic circle. "Glad we could make it work." He turned to the monitor. "That number at the bottom of the screen. What is that?"

Kim said, "The PNR score."

"PNR?"

"Point of no return," said Pace. "It's something we came up with recently. Jeff wanted all our most relevant metrics to be distilled into a single number. It measures variables in the AI system, and determines how close the AI is to achieving . . ." His voice trailed off as he looked at Kim. Pace was uncomfortable with this, Colt could see.

Kim said, "A superintelligence explosion. The number is our best guess at the probability that the AI system would achieve its superintelligence explosion. That one-percent score was magnitudes higher than we've ever gotten before."

Colt felt a chill run down his spine. These guys were playing with fire. "That sounds pretty dangerous. Given what happened to Kozlov, how is your security?"

Kim said, "It's top-notch. We know how valuable our technology is, so we have planned for every situation. That's why you saw teams of armed personnel on the road outside. And any environmental disruption that compromises the integrity of the internal laboratory will initiate a shutdown sequence."

"Has the security system ever been triggered?"

Pace said, "Yes, a few times, due to an environmental phenomenon. Bad windstorm threw some trees and debris into our wind farm on the other side of the mountain. A large animal—we think maybe a grizzly—went through a security fence. Oh, and once due to a forest fire on the southern quadrant."

Kim said, "But some of the environmental triggers have to do with quantum computing. We need to reduce noise."

"Noise?"

"Instability. The research laboratory cannot have any interference when we're running our quantum computer. And everything is interrelated. The efficiency of our quantum computer requires a very stable environment. The capability of our AGI relies upon the efficiency of the quantum computer, integrated with our neural network. This machine . . ." Kim thumbed at the window toward the ethereal purple glow of the quantum computer. ". . . really is like a world-class musical instrument. We need to finely tune the machine and get musicians who are capable of playing it . . . both of which are very difficult to do."

"And Kozlov was one of your musicians?"

Kim nodded. "He was our absolute best."

"And now he's gone," Colt said sympathetically.

"Now he's gone," Kim echoed.

Colt said, "So can anyone else help you achieve AGI? Do you have another musician, so to speak?"

Pace said, "We have a few in training, but no one else really came close . . ."

"So your progress there . . . is it lost?"

Kim gave a frustrated sigh. "Replicating that success will be challenging. We're focusing on other AI programs that are ready now. Like the language-prediction program we've just announced. And some government projects here at The Facility are also quite promising."

The door opened and two men in white lab coats appeared. "Mr. Kim, we're ready for the language prediction test run. We're in lab nine."

Kim checked his watch, then turned to Pace. "We need to move on."

Pace nodded, then addressed Colt and Ava. "I've asked one of my techs to finish your tour while Jeff and I are working. He'll bring you back to the entrance in one hour so we can catch our flight back."

25

Their tour guide's name was Paul Devlin. He was an engineer, and one of Pace's program managers. Colt immediately showered him with questions as they walked through the halls of The Facility, many of which he avoided. They toured a few of the other labs, avoiding the one where Kim and Pace were running their preparatory test for this week.

"What's in here?" Ava asked. "I don't remember this lab being used the last time I was here."

"This is a new program." He checked his pockets. "Where did that list go. I had a list of AI programs I was supposed to take you to. I can't remember if this one was on there."

Ava held her hand up to the biometric scanner. It glowed green and the door unlocked with a beep. "I guess we're allowed in."

The engineer stopped searching for his list and shrugged. "Well, that works too, I guess."

Several researchers were working in the dark interior. As Ava and Colt walked inside, he felt eyes snapping to them, following them along the floor. He got the impression people here didn't get many visitors.

"Sorry about all of the stares," the engineer said.

Colt said, "It's okay. With my looks, you get used to it." Ava rolled her eyes but smiled.

"In here." The engineer gestured to a centrally located conference room, glass walls on all four sides. Like the offices in the Pax AI headquarters building, the walls went opaque as they entered.

The engineer sat at the head of the table and typed on a wireless keyboard. The video screen on the wall began to show footage of people looking at their phones.

"Where are you running this?"

"South Africa. We ran into issues with some of our testing methodology in the US and Europe. The safety and privacy laws were too strict. But our team in Africa has been doing really cutting-edge stuff." The engineer spoke with enthusiasm. "This is one of the more unique programs we've worked on. What you are seeing here are time-lapse images and short diary videos from subjects involved in the test."

Ava said, "What's the stimulus?"

The engineer said, "Their phones. This particular AI program is embedded on their phones and selects what they are served. The AI essentially created an overlay of the actual apps. Everything appears normal to the subjects in the test. But the AI chooses everything they see on their social media feeds, every news article on their news apps, videos they are recommended on streaming video apps. It curates all of the content the subject consumes on their most frequently used apps."

Colt glanced at Ava, wondering if she was getting creeped out yet.

She said, "What are the numbers?"

"On the right side of the screen you see a few different values that our AI program has assigned to each person."

"Values?" Ava said.

"Yup. Each of these values indicates what our program perceives to be that individual's opinion on a given subject. It represents what they believe to be true."

Colt tried not to let his disturbed feeling seep into his voice. "What kind of opinions? Like, what topics are you monitoring?"

"It could be anything. Social beliefs. Political views. Favorite sports team. What they like to eat. Whether they want to attend a four-year college. All sorts of things. These are time-lapse cameras. It's a six-month test for each participant."

The timestamp was progressing weeks at a time, and the numbers were changing dramatically.

"The numbers are changing," Ava said.

The engineer's eyes lit up. "That's right."

Colt spoke softly, fearing he already knew the answer. "Why are the numbers changing?"

"Because we're programming them."

Ava said, "Reprogramming." Now she looked very uncomfortable.

Colt and Ava were both glued to the video.

Colt shook his head. "That's not possible."

The engineer said, "A few years ago, it was impossible. Today, it's hard, but it's very possible."

Colt narrowed his eyes. His voice dropped an octave as he thought through the implications. "This was a government project?"

"Yes. The Intelligence Advanced Research Project Agency, I believe. Or maybe this one was DARPA and the other one was . . . sorry, I'll need to check."

"There's another project like this?" Ava asked.

The engineer said, "Sure. Much of the AI work we are

doing for the US government is around deepfakes and propaganda. Detection, mostly."

Ava said, "I was aware of that. But this isn't detection . . ."

The engineer seemed to pick up on her uneasiness for the first time. "Er . . . well . . . that is . . . our charter also has studied both offensive and defensive capabilities, on behalf of the defense and intelligence agencies."

The door changed from opaque to clear and opened. Jeff Kim walked in, flanked by Luke Pace, who looked horrified.

He turned to face the engineer who had been giving them a tour. "What are you guys doing in here?"

The engineer said, "They asked to . . . I mean, her hand unlocked . . ."

Pace said, "You may leave. We'll finish this."

The engineer scurried out of the room, red-faced.

When the door closed, Ava looked at Kim. "Why didn't I know about this?"

He said, "These are highly classified projects. Very few people in our organization know they exist, and I prefer to keep it that way."

"Even me?" Ava said.

Kim said, "We need to do this work, Ava. I understand why you might not be okay with it."

"And you are?" Ava turned to Pace. "What about you? I know you've voiced ethical concerns within our company before. How do you feel about these tests, manipulating people's opinions?"

Kim's lips tightened. "If we didn't, then someone else would. Pax AI *must* be at the forefront of this innovation. Think about what this could do if it ended up in the wrong hands."

Ava said, "If all guns are outlawed, only criminals will have guns?"

"Something like that, yes," Kim said.

Pace was looking down at the floor.

Colt said, "How does it work?"

Pace said, "We've meshed together several of our best AI programs. The deep-learning AI monitors millions of social media accounts. They detect what people are looking at, what articles they click on, how long they spend reading an article or watching a video. They track where each individual goes and match it up with various other bits of information to create a values profile. We cross-reference different surveys and activity patterns to determine what the subject believes. Another AI program introduces stimuli and measures the impact. Taken together, each person's online behavior can be studied and mapped out. The more data we get, the better we become at learning how to influence opinions."

Colt folded his arms across his chest. "How is this different than what advertisers and social media companies have been doing for the past decade? Political campaigns do this all the time. It's very hard to sway opinion. Marketers spend billions trying to get people to pick one brand over another."

Kim nodded. "You're right. But you just named two organizations. Social media companies and political campaigns. Social media companies have much of the same capability we do. They have the data and can control a lot of the stimuli. They even use AI. But they normally don't try to change opinion. Instead, they make money selling to advertisers who try to do that. But the advertisers are half blind with one hand tied behind their back since they don't have all of the data or control most of the stimuli."

Pace said, "Our program fully integrates into a person's devices. We have all the capability of a social media company, but not just on the social media apps. We're controlling everything the subject is served, with the goal of shifting opinion."

Kim said, "Think of it this way. A political campaign advertiser can serve you a paid ad and take up about ten percent of your feed. Maybe fifty percent of your advertising. But they can't control the organic social media exposure, or the recommendations from the streaming video apps. They can't control what news articles you are served and recommended. Our AI program does all of that. And here is the important part: our AI measures how different stimuli change opinions after exposure, and learns what to show them next, with our ultimate behavioral change goal as a target."

Colt said, "This is like a mind-control algorithm. You can really change people's opinions? Your engineer mentioned something about deepfakes?"

Kim gave Pace a look.

Pace said, "The DOD has us incorporating some deepfake stimuli into the tests."

Colt played dumb. "What are those?"

Pace said, "We can create manipulated videos that will appear real. Customized offensive stimuli that will change the beliefs to what we want. It's mind-blowing stuff, and incredibly dangerous. But this is all under government supervision. And to be honest, we have more work to do on those. The images can appear smudgy or low-resolution."

Ava said, "Can you show us this in action?"

Pace sighed and looked up at the screen. "This woman here on the TV screen was a vegan, based on her feelings toward protecting animals. She was one hundred percent against using animals as a food source. And this is her at the end of the test."

"She's eating a steak."

Colt said, "How long did the opinion shift take?"

"Ninety days," Pace said.

"This has to be illegal."

"All five hundred participants signed waivers," Kim said.

"Are the subjects made aware of what the experiment is trying to do?"

"No, it wouldn't work if they were aware," said Pace. "Listen, obviously some of us have qualms about these studies. But we need to understand the technology. Think about what you could do with this type of AI. Technology is changing how people interact. More and more often, human beings are isolated, alone, using their own technological devices to get information. It would be hard to know if one individual's information was being customized and manipulated if you didn't have as much outside contact with others. This would have been impossible a few years ago. But now, with some of our more powerful AI programs, it can be done."

Colt said, "This could swing an election."

Pace said, "Easily. It could also overthrow a government. Destroy a rival company. Think about what you might be able to convince people to do if you had no morals. Think about what a computer program might convince people to do, if it helped it to achieve its goals."

Colt felt a chill go down his spine. "I would like to think that I am strong enough to avoid manipulation by a machine."

"We all would," said Kim. A beep at the door. "Come in."

The door slid open. "Mr. Kim, your helicopter is arriving soon."

Kim looked up. "Time to go."

Kim led them out of The Facility. The building was a collection of hallways and research rooms, data storage and security rooms. The quantum computer and its support systems made up a significant chunk of the building.

As they walked, Colt continued asking questions. "Luke, what are those?"

Pace said, "Battery storage chambers. Power is an issue here. We need to have access to huge amounts of power at the right moments, and we can't run out."

"Is that because of the quantum computer? That must suck a lot of power."

Kim shook his head. "No, actually. One of the benefits of quantum computing is that it *doesn't* take up as much power. Your typical supercomputer takes up around five megawatts of power. Enough electricity to power a town. But our quantum computer uses only about five hundred kilowatts of power. It's very efficient compared to traditional computers."

Colt said, "So why do you need all those solar panels and windmills and batteries?"

"Deep learning uses good old legacy computing. It's the legacy computers that use up so much energy and those servers generate a lot of heat. Did you see that water tower on the way in?"

"Yes."

"It's not for drinking. If we ever ran out of electricity to blow our fans and run cool air across our data storage and servers, we have a backup system of water cooling. The heat generated by all our computers would transform that liquid water into steam. The transfer of energy will cool it down, in the case of an absolute emergency. If you ever see steam shooting up from above The Facility, that means we're about to lose all our data and burn up. We need power to run our computers, but also to cool them. Know how fast that water would be transformed into vapor?"

"How fast?"

"About two minutes."

"No way."

"Seriously."

"It's the size of a city water tower. That's nuts."

"Major data centers use these emergency systems as well. If the shit really hits the fan, it buys us a few extra minutes. We have backup electrical systems, but they can take a few seconds to get online. So the water tower could prevent hundreds of billions of dollars in lost research."

They walked out of the main exit and toward the helicopter landing pad. Once again, Colt was struck by the expansive Pacific Northwest forest. Mountains and evergreen trees as far as he could see. The cool, crisp air. And the quiet, except for a humming drone emanating from The Facility and the occasional cry of eagles echoing throughout the land.

He looked over at Ava. She was unusually quiet.

While they waited for the helicopter, Colt said, "You mentioned that Kozlov was crucial to your AGI progress. What could he do that was so special?"

Kim said, "It's a bit complex, but . . . are you familiar with the control problem?"

Colt said, "Let's pretend I'm not."

Kim turned to Pace, who said, "The control problem. Okay. Our goal is to create a super-intelligent AI system. One that is safe and friendly. One that will help us, and not hurt us. In order to do that, we must make sure that any super-intelligent agent wouldn't just take control of its own programming after birth and prevent us from modifying it."

Colt said, "And Kozlov used this neural interface to solve the control problem?"

Kim shrugged. "More like managed it than solved it."

Colt looked up, hearing the echo of a distant helicopter. "Is that our ride?"

"Yes." Kim checked his watch. "They'll be here any moment."

Colt said, "So how was Kozlov able to manage the control problem?"

Pace said, "There are several theoretical solutions to the control problem. One of our safety protocols in developing a super-intelligent agent is to ensure that certain *tripwires* exist. These tripwires simulate the various probable ways that a super-intelligent agent could . . . go wrong. It includes the most likely ways it would attempt to take control of itself. So . . . we run simulations with our AI systems."

Colt said, "This sounds like you are working on bringing Frankenstein to life."

Pace shifted his stance, laughing nervously. "Kind of. We add different ingredients to our lifeless body and see what happens. We add different algorithms, integrate new capsule neural networks, add more power. Each time we test and see how it behaves. How it solves problems. How it communicates. If it makes certain choices . . ."

"And if the tripwires are set off?"

"Then we know that the super-intelligent agent is trying to do something we don't want it to do."

"But if it is truly super-intelligent, couldn't it just think of a way to go around the tripwires that we mere mortals hadn't thought of?"

The helicopter was in visual range now, flying toward them. A speck of gray and blue getting lower in altitude, its rotors growing louder.

Kim said, "We have several controls in place to make sure that even if the AI *does* bypass our tripwires, it will be limited in its capability."

Pace piped in. "Meaning that it wouldn't be able to harm us . . . easily."

"That doesn't sound very reassuring."

Pace said, "Well, like the first nuclear bombs in the

Manhattan Project. None of the scientists really knew what would happen when they set off Trinity."

Colt noticed Kim twitch at the last word.

"Trinity," Colt said. "Like the AI group."

"Yup," said Pace. "The news article I read on Trinity said that's where the name came from. Their conspiracy theory lore says their founders were scientists in the Manhattan Project or something."

Colt was watching Kim, who remained tense. "Jeff, what's your opinion on Trinity?"

Kim was looking up at the approaching helicopter. "They want to make all AI open, even as we close in on creating a superintelligence. I think the group that calls themselves Trinity is the worst kind of conspiracy theory. The kind that is harmful to society."

Ava said, "I agree. It's ignorant to make such harmful technology available to the masses."

Colt said, "I've read there is a big counter-movement forming. Anti-AI groups."

Pace waved away the idea. "You might as well stop rabbits from breeding. AGI will happen. It's the natural progression of technology. Humanity won't stop advancing. Fire. Wheel. Horse-drawn carriage. Automobile. Plane. Space shuttle. Satellite TV. 5G cellular networks. Voice assistants. Drones."

Kim nodded. "He's right. The cycle time of technological advancement is getting faster. Some people argue we have already achieved a superintelligence, collectively. Because the internet has connected us to each other. Human beings are a sort of hive mind now, with access to all of the world's information."

Colt said, "I think certain politicians might prove wrong your idea that we've reached superintelligence."

Kim smiled. "The point is this: the world is going to invent an AGI superintelligence. Our goal is to beat them there. We need to make sure it has values that align with our own."

The helicopter was flaring into a hover above the pad now. The group turned away to avoid the dirt kicked up by the rotor wash. A security guard waited until the aircraft had touched down and then escorted them into the cabin, shutting the door behind them. They buckled into their seat harnesses, and the aircraft took off.

Colt felt his stomach flutter as the helicopter made a steep bank around a mountain, heading toward the California coast. The ocean reflected orange in the setting sun. They didn't talk much on the flight, and in less than an hour, the helicopter landed on the pad just next to the Pax AI headquarters.

The aircraft shut down and the group got out. Colt could hear the sound of traffic and cable cars. One of those self-driving cars passed by, its LiDAR spinning on the roof.

Kim looked at Ava and Colt. "Both of you have signed nondisclosure agreements. You are not to discuss the details of what you saw today. Colt, I understand you'll need to convey some topline information to your firm. But no details. And I'll need to approve anything that discusses our government programs or AGI progress. Understood?"

They both nodded.

An SUV pulled up to the helipad and a security guard opened the door for Kim to get in. "If you'll excuse me, I have a meeting." He paused, studying Colt's face. "I hope you now see that we are not doing anything nefarious at The Facility. Quite the opposite. We want to ensure AI is used safely and for the benefit of all mankind."

Colt nodded. "I appreciate the tour. It was eye-opening and very helpful. I'll make sure to convey what I can to my superiors, and keep my mouth shut about the confidential parts. They want my judgment on the safety and efficacy of investing in this company. After seeing what I did today, I can better do my job." It wasn't a glowing endorsement, but it was all Colt could think to say in this situation.

Kim nodded and the SUV drove away. Pace headed toward the headquarters building, back to work.

Ava and Colt stood by the helicopter, now silent and tied down.

Colt looked at her. "Are you okay?"

"No. I'm ready to meet with your friend."

26

The next day, Ava and Colt took a self-driving taxi to an office building in North Beach. They climbed the stairs to the second floor, a dark hallway with only one room lit up.

As expected, Wilcox and Rinaldi were waiting inside. Wilcox closed the door behind them and offered Ava a bottle of water, gesturing for them both to take a seat on the old couch.

"Ava, this is Ed Wilcox. The friend I was telling you about."

"And I'm Special Agent Rinaldi." They all shook hands. Ava looked nervous.

"I should begin by saying that I have reservations just being here. I don't know of any coworkers who are doing anything illegal and I think they're all good people."

Rinaldi was gentle. "We understand. No one is in any trouble, Ms. Klein. So what made you want to speak with us?"

She exhaled and looked at Colt, who nodded supportively. Ava said, "I recently saw a lot more detail on some of Pax AI's programs. Projects I hadn't seen before. I won't be able to tell you about them. A lot are government projects. But the nature of these programs made me think about my work differently. I don't think I saw how dangerous it could be, until now. And with Kozlov's death—you know about Kozlov, right?"

Wilcox nodded. "Yes, ma'am, we're familiar with what happened to Mr. Kozlov."

Ava tightened her lips. "I've seen things recently that concern me. And I think it's my responsibility to help ensure no one steals any of Pax AI's technology. Colt said you are looking for help with that."

Wilcox nodded. "Ms. Klein, we want you to know how grateful we are for your help in this matter. Colt is right. When we found out he had been assigned to Pax AI, I let him know about our security concerns. Now unfortunately, this isn't something we can investigate by going directly to Pax AI itself. We need to look at this without stirring the hornet's nest, so to speak. We have reason to believe that someone is actively trying to steal Pax AI technology. And we need help identifying that person before they can succeed."

Ava glanced at Colt uneasily. Wilcox began asking Ava about the upcoming tests, and she recited the details of the Pax AI language-prediction demonstration being held this week.

Wilcox said, "So most of your leadership team will be on the fourth floor during the demonstration, is that right, Ava?"

"That's right."

"Would you be willing to bring a small device up there during the test? This device might be able to detect whether anyone is trying to hack into Pax AI's system."

Ava looked dubious. "But they make us check all electronics and phones at the door by the staircase before we enter. The security is very tight. I can't even bring in my watch." She pointed at an Apple watch on her wrist.

Wilcox looked thoughtful. "Purses, jackets, clothes, shoes? Anything else checked before you enter?"

Ava described the security procedure, including the body scan. "It's a double door that leads into an airlock of sorts. Then the security guard buzzes us in."

Rinaldi said, "Hmm. Okay. I'll relay this to my team. They are very familiar with that type of equipment. We'll figure something out. We'll provide you with something innocuous you can bring in there—maybe something you can wear—that will help us gather the information we need."

Ava frowned at Colt. "You can trust them, Ava," he assured her. "I've worked with them before. It'll be okay."

She bit her lower lip. "Okay. I'll think about it."

The week went by fast. Colt visited Pax AI each day, attending meetings and going over financials, taking time with different project teams to look at their work. The leadership team worked from the fourth floor most of the week, getting ready for their big demonstration.

After hours Colt worked with the counterintelligence unit. Weng had briefed him on her conversation with SANDSTONE, and they had set up another meeting for Wednesday. It was the earliest she could make it. And if she came through, they just might get the name of whoever was inside Pax AI, stealing their data.

Colt didn't see Ava as much over the next few days. She had lunch with him once and coffee at the Starbucks across from the Pax AI headquarters. She agreed to meet with Wilcox and Rinaldi again the morning of the demonstration.

Colt ordered one of the self-driving taxis and picked her up, taking her to meet with Wilcox early in the morning.

Wilcox handed Ava a pair of shoes. "Please change into

these. Check that they fit. We have a few extra sizes in case they don't."

Ava sat on the couch and removed hers, then slipped on the pair that Wilcox had given her.

"The heel of each shoe contains a communications device." Then he ran through the procedures Ava was to follow later that day.

"So you'll go through the fourth-floor security chamber just like normal. If they ask you to take off your shoes, go ahead and do it. Don't be alarmed. Nothing will show up on the scanner. That's it. You don't have to press any buttons or anything."

"What if they pick up the devices in the scan?" Ava said.

"They won't. We're familiar with their equipment."

She looked nervous. "You're sure it won't set off any alarms."

"We're sure," Wilcox said. "Colt will be in the building with you. He'll know when you're up on the fourth floor. He's going to be in his office on the second floor. When Colt is sure you are up there, he'll trigger the device to activate it."

"How will he do that?"

Wilcox shook his head. "Don't worry about that. All you need to know is your shoes won't feel or sound any different. It will be unnoticeable to you. But you'll need to be up on the fourth floor. And Colt, we won't want you to activate the device unless she's there. That could cause issues with Pax AI detecting electronic emissions."

"Understood," said Colt.

"And this is all legal?" asked Ava.

"Yes, of course it is," replied Rinaldi. "We're the FBI, ma'am."

"You'll do fine." Colt gave her a gentle pat on the shoulder.

She looked petrified. "Okay. Well, I guess it's time. What

should I do with these?" She held up her other pair of shoes. Wilcox took them and set them by the door.

Colt said, "Ava, I won't be going to work with you. I have another meeting this morning. But I'll be in by the time the demonstration begins."

"All right."

Wilcox said, "After your meeting is over, come back here and I'll get the device and we'll swap shoes again."

They stood up and she nodded. They thanked her again and she left the room, heading to work.

Colt turned to face Wilcox. "Have we heard from SAND-STONE yet?"

"Weng just texted. Your agent hasn't confirmed she'll be there yet."

Colt cursed. He and Weng had sent SANDSTONE a meeting time and place yesterday. It was unlike Marisha to be this tardy in her responses.

"I'm going to go join up with Weng so if SANDSTONE shows, we'll be ready."

"You need to keep an eye on the clock. I'll appreciate getting a name from SANDSTONE. But if Ava is in there when their Facility servers communicate with their fourth floor, that could get us a lot more."

Colt nodded. "I won't be late."

27

Colt reached the counterintelligence unit safehouse twenty minutes later. Heather Weng and Jennifer Sims were there, set up for the SANDSTONE meet.

"Anything?" Colt asked.

"She just checked in," Weng said. "You ready?"

Colt nodded. Weng walked to the back room and opened the gun safe, removing a 9mm pistol and holster and clipping it to the inside of her jeans. "You want one?"

He shook his head. "No, I need to run to Pax AI afterward."

A few moments later Weng was driving them in a sedan across town. She parked them near the Opera House, a block away from City Hall. They locked the car and began walking, separated by one to two blocks at all times so Weng could help provide counter-surveillance. Both of them wore in-ear headphones, and Sims was monitoring them from the safehouse. A mix of CCTVs provided her with good coverage of the meeting location near the intersection of Market Street and 8th.

After several minutes of doing figure eights around the same few blocks, Weng was sufficiently satisfied Colt was in the clear. "Okay, you're black. Let's go."

Colt turned down Market Street and headed toward the rendezvous.

Now Sims was in his ear. "I think I see SANDSTONE approaching. She's in a purple shirt. Two blocks to your north. You should see her soon."

Colt paused at a traffic light. A crowd of pedestrians gathered around him, waiting. The light changed and the crowd surrounding Colt began moving forward across the street.

That's when he spotted them.

"Gray van, one block to the east. Right across from me," Colt whispered, looking away and running his hand through his hair to shield his face as he crossed the street.

He turned away from the vehicle and held up his phone like he was taking a selfie, careful to keep the van in the frame. He snapped a picture and sent it to Sims and Weng.

"Got it, what's up?" Weng responded in his earpiece.

"Sims, zoom in on the man in the passenger seat, and run him through facial recognition, please."

A beat of silence as Sims digested what he said. Then, "Copy."

"What's wrong, Colt?" Weng asked. "I'm passing them now. The light just changed. They left. What did you see?"

Sims said, "The guy in the passenger seat had the same tattoo as the Kozlov shooter."

"Same location?" Colt asked. That was what he had seen.

"Affirmative."

Weng said, "They kept driving, Colt. They're gone."

Sims said, "Do you want to abort?"

Colt continued walking and could now see Marisha Stepanova only one block away, wearing a travel bag over her shoulder. She had stopped at a newspaper vendor and was looking in Colt's direction. When she saw him, Marisha looked frightened. She held her phone to her chest, signaling him. Did she want him to hold in position and contact her with his phone?

Something sure as hell wasn't right. Colt stopped walking and moved to the edge of the sidewalk, gripping the phone in his pocket and pulling it out.

"Sims, you still got eyes on that van?"

"Standby . . . yes. They're half a mile to the north."

Colt turned back in the direction he'd come from to see if he was being followed. He saw Weng, who had stopped to keep her distance, but he didn't spot any coverage.

Almost every instinct told him he needed to abort. Something was very wrong. If that hit team was there, they might have been waiting to find out who he or SANDSTONE was meeting. And now Marisha was telling him to hold back.

He slid open the encrypted messaging app. Marisha was now sitting down on a bench one block ahead, her face buried in her phone, typing with her thumbs.

Marisha: Don't approach.

Colt: Okay.

Marisha: I have the name.

Colt: Okay.

Marisha: I think I'm being followed.

Colt: What do you want to do?

Marisha: I think it might be time for me to come in.

Colt cursed. He was about to lose his best agent. But if they didn't extract her now, she would be apprehended by Russian counterintelligence and interrogated in a basement somewhere before getting a bullet.

"We're going to need to bring her in," Colt said.

"Are you sure?" Weng asked.

"Yeah."

Colt had grown so accustomed to the whining sound of the autonomous navigation vehicles in San Francisco, with their spinning LiDAR on the roof, that he didn't notice this one at first.

The SUV came whirring down the road, looking just like all the others, but with one major difference.

The rear window had been removed, and the barrel of a fully-automatic weapon now protruded from the opening. Just below and connected to the weapon was an electro-optic scope, attached to a computer. A simple facial recognition and tracking software program had been installed. Finding its target, the weapon locked onto Marisha Stepanova's face and began unloading its magazine.

28

Colt shuddered at the sound. The rapid popping, accompanied by the fiery spray, went on for a full fifteen seconds. Screaming hordes of pedestrians scrambled in every direction away from the carnage.

Marisha's headless body lay on the sidewalk.

Colt, hands on his thighs, caught his breath as the car drove away and then began slowly walking forward. His ears were ringing. He could barely hear Weng's footsteps as she ran up.

"What are you doing?" She grabbed his arm, trying to pull him away. "We need to get out of here."

Colt shrugged her off and kept walking. Sirens in the distance. One, then many. He reached her body. His former agent's torso was a mass of red. Colt knew he was in shock. He knew he needed to heed Weng's pleas to leave.

Her phone.

Colt saw SANDSTONE's phone lying on the ground, where it had fallen from her hand. He looked at the screen, which was still lit up. Her last text, typed and unsent, had a single name.

Ava Klein

"Colt, talk to me. Are you okay?" Heather Weng's voice drifted from the driver's seat. They were headed to the safehouse.

"I'm okay." He knew he didn't sound convincing.

His phone buzzed, but he didn't pick up. "It's Wilcox. Shit. I need to go into Pax AI."

Weng looked at him. "Are you able to do that right now?"

"I can do it."

Wilcox: Where are you? Call me now.

Weng typed in the navigation to get them to the Pax AI headquarters. She took the next exit to get them on course.

Colt dialed Wilcox.

He picked up on the first ring. "Where the hell are you?"

"SANDSTONE is dead."

"I know. Are you guys all right?"

"Listen, I . . ."

"Shut up. Are you good to go? This is important."

Colt forced himself upright. "Yes. What do you need?"

"Where are you?"

Colt glanced at the car's navigation console. "A few minutes from Pax AI. Heading there now. There's something I need to tell you." He filled him in on SANDSTONE's text with Ava's name on it.

Wilcox cursed. "This is what I was going to talk to you about. Colt, we put a tail on Ava this morning, after our meeting. Just as a precaution. She lost them."

Colt said, "What are you talking about, she lost them?"

"I mean she left a pair of experienced FBI counterintelligence agents scratching their heads, wondering where the hell she went." Colt heard Wilcox sigh. "Rinaldi has been doing some digging. Our investigators found inconsistencies in her past living history. A two-year gap where she wasn't where she says she was. You know she had dual Israeli citizenship?"

"Her mother was Israeli," Colt replied. The beginnings of a tingling sensation formed on the back of his neck.

"Ten years ago, her official record places her in New York. We had the FBI's New York field office look into it. She wasn't really there. It's just a dead paper trail. Her age would be right for being recruited into the program, too. And she has worked internationally, which they like."

Colt's mind was racing. "What are you saying, Ed?"

Wilcox said, "We think she is *Mossad*, Colt. Israeli Intelligence."

29

Colt arrived at the Pax AI headquarters building a few minutes later. Nader was at one of the front tables interviewing a prospective new hire. Delivery men were dropping off packages, signing them in at the front desk. The normally busy downstairs was almost empty.

"Where is everyone?" Colt asked the woman at the front desk as she scanned his badge.

"The demonstration, of course. It's an off-site event for everyone but the leadership team . . . and me. Hey, how come you aren't there?"

Colt looked around. "Is Ava Klein in yet?"

"Sure, she's right over there," said the woman, pointing.

Colt turned to see Ava sitting in an open booth, a young woman sitting across from her. He walked up and waved to catch Ava's attention. She nodded back to him, making an awkward face and mouthing the word *interview*. She was interviewing a potential new hire to the company.

Colt said, "I need to speak with you," just loud enough to be heard. She held up five fingers to tell him how many minutes she'd be. "I'll swing by your office after." She didn't hold eye contact for long.

Colt walked up to the second floor, passing Nader on the way. "Big day today," said Nader.

Colt replied, "Good luck."

He entered his office and turned on the computer. He checked his phone for any missed calls or messages but didn't see anything out of the ordinary.

He let out a long, slow breath, allowing his face to collapse in his hands. Marisha's corpse kept flashing through his mind. He was starting to feel guilty. What if he had moved sooner? Pulled her out sooner.

And what was the meaning of SANDSTONE's last text? Had SANDSTONE also learned that Ava was Mossad? Was that even possible?

Colt ran through everything he knew about Ava from the time they'd met. Everything he remembered her telling him about her nationality and family. How she looked at him back then. She was young, innocent. He remembered her minimal interest in politics and government.

Was that an act? Was Colt being recruited from the start of their relationship? Was she Mossad back then? Or would they have recruited her afterward? Mossad wouldn't use one of their own agents to seduce some random US Navy junior officer. Would they? Israel was America's ally. Every smile. Every look. Could she really just have been seducing him that entire time?

It was years ago, he told himself. But his feelings weren't. They were raw and open. Gushing out. He felt so stupid. So blind. But it didn't all fit. He kept coming back to the same conclusion: there was no motive, no logic to it.

"Hey, you wanted to see me?" Ava stood in his doorway.

Colt looked up, removing his elbows from the desktop. Ava

was wearing the CIA-issued shoes. She looked nervous, but there was nothing to suggest she was anything other than what she had portrayed herself to be.

"Hi." He swallowed, his throat dry. Wilcox had instructed Colt to act normal.

"Are you okay? You look upset." Genuine concern in her voice.

Nader was coming up the stairs. "Ava! It's showtime! Let's go."

She turned back to Colt. "Wish me luck. Talk later?" Her eyes locked onto his. Real emotion there, like she was holding back.

Ava turned and walked away, joining Nader as they headed up to the fourth floor.

Wilcox had told him to let her go. They had made the quick decision because there wasn't anything else they could do, given the time. Colt was instructed to let her continue with the operation as planned. Then when she left the building, the FBI would apprehend her. Quietly.

He was to wait for five minutes after she went upstairs, then take out his phone and send a text to Weng, who would activate the NSA cyber weapon built into the heels of Ava's shoes. Wilcox's team would have what they needed from Pax AI, and Ava could be apprehended without hurting the mission.

Colt checked his watch. Four more minutes, then he would send the text.

That was what was supposed to happen, anyway.

Ava was now hurrying down the stairs. She froze on his floor, looking in his direction. She waved frantically for him to follow, her eyes wide with fear. Colt stood, and then Ava resumed rushing down the steps.

30

Ten minutes earlier

Ava looked at the young woman across the table from her and said, "Okay, last question: why do you want to work here?"

The young woman's eyes flickered relief. It was a softball, and the job interview was almost over.

"I want to change the world," the girl said, like she'd practiced this answer a million times in front of the mirror. She probably had.

Ava said, "Go on. Expand."

"AI is the future. It's going to change everything. And this company is at the forefront of that."

"Okay. But everyone is working on AI now. Your resume is flawless for the position you are applying for. Why here? You could work at Google or Microsoft or any other company's top-notch artificial intelligence programs."

The girl tilted her head. "Yeah, but come on. I mean, very few of them are doing what you guys are doing."

Ava raised an eyebrow.

"*Forbes* listed Pax AI as one of the top three companies

most likely to be the first to achieve artificial general intelligence." She shook her head in amazement. "I mean, just think of the possibilities. Hunger, inequality, climate change. All of those problems could be solved."

Ava looked inquisitive. "So, you are one of the optimists?"

The girl's expression went serious. "Well, of course I understand the need for caution."

"Do you?"

"Sure, I mean . . . it will be important to make sure the values programming is early and accurate."

"Tell me. How would you feel if your life's work brings forth the end of all humankind?"

The girl's face drained of color. "Um . . ."

Ava waved away the question, smiling. "Relax. You are applying for an engineering position. Engineers don't need to worry about that stuff, right?"

The girl gave a relieved laugh. "Right . . ."

Ava rose, her tone growing sharp. "Thanks for coming in."

"Oh. We're finished?"

"I'm afraid so." She gestured toward the front desk. "You can turn in your guest ID to the receptionist. It was very nice meeting you."

The girl's smile looked manic. "Thank you so much. I hope to hear from you soon!"

Ava watched as the receptionist took the girl's ID and logged her out. Then she headed toward the stairs.

"Afternoon, Miss Klein," the security guard greeted her.

"Good afternoon."

She pulled on the extendable identification card clipped to one of the belt loops on her jeans. George, the security guard, scanned it, saw the green confirmation symbol with the accompanying ding sound, and nodded for her to proceed up the stairs.

"Still me." She smiled.

"Still you."

"This easier than the San Francisco PD?"

"Oh, just slightly, ma'am." George smiled.

Ava checked her watch again as she made her way up the hardwood staircase. She saw Colt through the clear glass walls of his second-floor office. All the other offices were empty. Everyone was at the company off-site demonstration event, including Jeff.

Ava saw Colt's face in his hands. She hesitated, then walked over and cracked open his door. "Hey . . . you wanted to see me?"

Colt looked up at her, his face red. "Hi." The words came out slow and soft and she knew something was very wrong.

"Are you okay? You look worried," she said.

Nader called out from behind her. "Ava! It's time! Let's go."

She looked at Nader on the stairs and then turned back to Colt, taking the opportunity to move on. "Gotta run. Showtime." Their eyes locked together for a moment and she fought off the emotions welling up inside. *Keep moving*, she told herself.

Ava turned and walked away before Colt could speak, joining Nader walking up to the fourth floor. She forced herself not to look back toward Colt, whose eyes she felt on her.

Nader made small talk as they walked upstairs. "You finish that new-hire interview?"

"Yup. I had three today, back-to-back."

"Any good ones?"

"They all said they want to change the world."

"How original." Nader laughed.

They reached the fourth floor, with Nader almost out of

breath. Ava kept in good shape, and barely registered the climb.

"Afternoon, sir, ma'am. I have you both on the schedule for a ten o'clock lead team meeting. Says here . . . language-prediction demonstration."

"That's right." Ava once again pulled the ID card from her waist and allowed the security guard to scan it. He then tapped a code and the opaque glass door in front of Ava made an unlocking sound.

"Cellphone?"

Ava frowned. "Sorry." She reached in her jeans pocket for her phone and paused before she handed it to the security guard. "Hmm . . . let me just check something."

Nader had already handed his phone to the security guard. "Come on, Ava, you can check your Instagram later," he chided.

Ava didn't respond. She was reading a text.

The message was alphanumeric. It would appear meaningless to anyone else, but she immediately felt a chill.

"Hmm. I actually need to . . ." She stepped backward, down one stair, looking at her phone while gripping the handrail. They would only send her this message if it was a true emergency.

"I'm sorry, Gerry, but I need to go make a phone call really quick. Tell them to start without me."

Nader looked surprised. "You're kidding, right? You are lucky Jeff's not here."

Ava offered an apologetic shrug and then began hustling back down the stairs. She tried to keep a normal pace as she flipped to the Starbucks app on her phone. There were five pre-paid cards stored on the app. One she used frequently. The others had always remained untouched.

Until now. One of the cards had a very recent purchase.

The use of that particular card identified which extraction plan she was to use.

Ava was in immediate danger.

Nader walked down the hallway toward the high-security meeting room. Pax AI's fourth floor was a spartan environment. Part of that was the company's executive culture. The other part was security. Nothing on this floor was ever removed from the premises. No office decorations or family pictures hung from the walls. Computers were regularly scanned by in-house cyber security specialists. Even the cleaning people were put through rigorous background checks.

The Pax AI lead team, sans Jeff Kim and Ava, were all waiting in the glass-walled conference space. He reached the door and placed his right eye to a retinal scanner. The locking display went green, the door latch clicked, and Nader walked inside.

"Where's Ava?"

"She had to make a call. She said to begin without her."

Colt bolted down the stairs, twisting his headphone into his right ear as he went. "Ava! Wait up!"

She was walking fast. Colt yelled loud enough that she must have heard him, but she didn't so much as slow, practically running out the main exit.

Colt plowed past a few delivery men carrying bags and boxes on their way into the building, hearing the receptionist's shrill voice greet them.

Outside the building, Colt squinted in the sunlight, looking in both directions for Ava. Reaching for his phone, he called the tech counterintelligence unit. Weng answered, "She's one block north, and on foot still. She's jogging. Rinaldi wants to know what the hell happened?"

"I don't know yet. I'm having a very bad day," Colt answered, jogging north on the street.

A gray van pulled up along the curb next to him. The driver's window rolled down, revealing Rinaldi behind the wheel. The sliding door opened, and Colt saw Wilcox and Weng inside.

"Hurry up and get in," Wilcox called.

"She just got in a car," said Weng, who was monitoring several screens in the back of the van. The oversized van was a mobile surveillance unit. Colt had seen them before, but had never been inside one. Computers and screens along one wall. A metal shelf with half a dozen types of communications equipment behind the passenger seat. Several swivel seats and little room to maneuver.

"Give me a description," said Rinaldi.

"Black sedan. Tinted windows. Toyota, I think. About three blocks ahead of us. You want me to put anything out to local law enforcement?"

"Negative. Just us for now," Wilcox said. "What the hell happened?"

Colt shook his head. "I don't know. She went up to the fourth floor like she was supposed to, and then one minute later she was running down the stairs. She waved at me to follow her like . . . I don't know, like she was scared about something." He took out his phone. "I'm going to try calling her." It went straight to voicemail. "Her phone is off."

"No one's phone is off. She's not answering you," said Rinaldi from the driver's seat.

Weng said, "If she's Israeli Intelligence, she's not going to . . ."

Colt said, "We don't know that she's Israeli Intelligence."

Heads turned at that. Skeptical looks in their eyes.

Weng said, "Colt . . . come on, dude."

She was still looking at one of the screens. "Here, Colt, take a look. This is CCTV from two minutes ago. Here's Ava coming out of the Pax AI building. What do you see?"

Colt watched as Ava walked out the door, scanning the street in swift, precise motions. Like a professional.

"What's she doing?" Sims asked.

"Looking at her phone."

The screen showed Ava studying her phone and then tossing it into a public waste basket. She did the same with her purse.

Colt had a sinking feeling in his chest.

"Still think she's not Mossad? She's going on the run," Wilcox said.

"Why?" Colt asked.

Wilcox, monitoring the real-time video feed on another screen, called out, "Sedan's making a right turn. Rinaldi, you have visual?"

"Negative."

"Two blocks ahead, they made a right turn."

"Copy."

Colt watched the replay of Ava walking out the Pax AI entrance. Something caught his eye. "Hey, rewind the surveillance feed one minute."

Weng did as he said.

"Who's that?"

On the screen, a delivery truck had pulled up to the curb right outside the Pax AI building, and three men got out, heading in, one carrying large boxes and another a duffle bag. Colt had walked right past them as he was following Ava out of the building. He mentally replayed the image in his head. Three delivery men at once. Why the duffle bag? He cursed himself for not noticing it. He had been distracted.

"Ed, take a look at this," called Weng.

Wilcox looked, frowning. "Do we have video feed from inside Pax AI?"

"Negative. Couldn't get it."

"What about audio?"

Weng was multitasking from the front. "We have a long-range audio from across the street. It's pointed at the fourth floor. It's not great, but it's something."

"Put it on the speakers."

Weng flipped a switch, and they all heard muffled screams.

Two minutes earlier

The receptionist waved to Ava as she walked out the building's main exit. "Have a nice weekend!" Ava didn't look up.

"Hmph. Well that wasn't very polite," the receptionist muttered to herself, and then went back to scrolling through her social media feed. She looked up when the front door slid open.

Two young men wearing backpacks, T-shirts, and khaki pants walked in. Both wore dark blue gaiter-style cloth face masks. She frowned. *Those* types of masks were shown to be ineffective. And besides, there hadn't been a health recommendation to wear them in the Bay Area in quite some time.

Just then one of the other Pax AI personnel rushed down the stairs and out the door. It looked like that nice man from New York.

"Not sure why everyone's in such a hurry." The receptionist smiled at her new arrivals. "Good afternoon, gentlemen, how may I help you?"

The first man said, "I'm here for an interview with Dr. Pace."

The receptionist frowned. "Oh, I'm sorry, I thought the interviews were finished for the day." She looked down at her computer monitor and squinted at the schedule. When she looked up, a delivery man had entered the building. He was wheeling in a large cardboard package. He also wore a face mask, she noticed. She craned her neck to look around the young man in front of her and said, "You need anyone to sign for that?"

The delivery man didn't reply.

The second backpack-wearing man was walking toward the stairway. The receptionist said, "Honey, you need help with something? You looking for a bathroom?"

George, the security guard, had just started to look up from his computer screen as the man raised a silenced pistol. The man standing in front of the receptionist had raised his own. Both men fired into the forehead of their target, the bodies falling to the hard floor.

The delivery guy had opened his package and removed two silenced sub machine-guns, handing one to the man at the reception desk and keeping the other for himself. The team worked quickly, ensuring that all entrances were closed and locked. The man wearing the delivery uniform used the guard's badge to unlock the security room. Then he disabled all the internal cameras and communications, except for the secure satellite link connecting the Mountain Research Facility and the fourth-floor conference room.

The team began making their way up the stairs.

Nader said, "Are we up?"

"Yup. We have a good connection with The Facility. Data only, no voice. How much longer until Jeff's ready?"

Pace said, "They said they'd be set up for the top of the hour. So any minute now." He checked the time on his watch. "Ava should really be here for this. Nader, you said she was with you coming up the stairs, right?"

"She said she needed to make a call. You want me to go look for her?"

Pace shook his head. "No, I'll call down to Mary and see if she's at the front entrance." He tapped the speaker button on the table's center control panel to ring the front desk receptionist, but there was no tone. "Line's dead. I hate not being able to instant message from up here."

"Security. Talk to Miller."

One of them did their best Miller impersonation. "Security is important to our mission."

Pace said, "Nader, would you mind?"

"Sure."

Nader walked out of the secure conference room and through the barren hallway, hearing the conference room's high-security door close with a hiss behind him.

He thought about stopping at one of the desks and trying the receptionist again, but he could use the climb down the stairs. More steps, even if he did have to leave his Apple watch outside with his phone.

Nader nodded to the guard sitting inside the fourth-floor security entry chamber. The guard nodded and buzzed him out, the glass doors sliding open. On the far side of the chamber, bright sunlight was shining through the opaque glass walls.

But there was something odd there. A dripping dark patch of liquid spattered on the glass. Nader heard the guard behind him say, "What the hell?" It almost looked like . . .

The doors slid open in front of him before he pressed the button, and three men wearing masks appeared in the entrance, the dead security guard at their feet.

Nader saw the muzzle flash and flinched at the noise. A clatter of shells hit the ground and fell down the stairs as the men advanced. The other security guard hit the floor behind him.

Pace and the two other members of the leadership team heard the knock at the door to the secure conference room and didn't know what to make of it.

No one knocked on this door.

The door used a biometric scanner for entry. You either had access or you didn't.

"Did Nader lose a finger?"

The other two lead team members snickered.

Pace walked over to the door and was about to open it when he hesitated. Near the intersection of the tall glass panels that made up the wall and the door was the tiniest sliver of clear glass through which he could see the other side.

And what he saw confused him.

Two sets of sneakers. Nader was known for being a well-dressed man. Neither of those looked like Nader's fine leather shoes.

"Something's wrong," Pace said.

The CFO looked confused. "What are you talking about?"

Pace turned to her. "Erika, there are two men standing on the other side of this door."

The COO said, "How'd they get in? This floor is secure."

Erika sounded scared now. "Why do they want to get in here?"

"I'm going to de-polarize the glass so we can see."

The COO held out his hands. "Wait. Hold on. Wait, let's think . . ."

Pace didn't wait. He tapped a few commands on the control panel next to the door and the glass walls and door went from opaque to clear.

Erika let out a scream behind him.

Standing on the other side of the door were three very fit-looking men, each carrying weapons. Nader sat on the floor next to the third man, a gun to his temple.

The lead intruder tapped on the glass with his gun, then gestured down toward the control panel.

"They're trying to get in. Pace, don't . . ."

Pace said, "I *know*."

"Can they shoot through the glass?"

"Somebody check the phones again."

"They don't call outside here."

"Do we have a connection with Kim's team?"

"No. Just data to The Facility. What the hell?"

"Can they shoot through the glass?"

"I don't think so. It's supposed to be bulletproof, that's what Miller always said."

The gunman walked back toward Nader, pointing down at him, then to the door. His eyes were expressionless.

"He's going to shoot Nader. Oh my God, oh my God." Erika's voice was hysterical.

The lead gunman grabbed Nader by the back of the neck and pulled him up, then prodded him over to the door. Two of them held Nader's finger down on the fingerprint reader. Nader thrashed around, but it was no use.

The security panel inside the room glowed green and Nader's identification displayed on the screen.

Now the gunmen were holding his face down to the retinal scanner. Nader was again struggling and closing his eyes. This proved a much more challenging assignment for the armed men. After a moment of resistance, the lead gunman threw Nader back to the floor, raised his weapon, and fired into Nader's chest. Bursts of red spray popped up from his torso.

Pace let out a yell and covered his mouth, his watery eyes wide. Erika screamed and began dry-heaving.

The lead gunman barked more orders, but they could barely hear him through the soundproof walls. It was like watching a horrific silent film.

The men flipped Nader's now-lifeless body onto his back. One of them took off his backpack and removed a small bag, unzipping it.

"What is that? What are they doing?" Erika asked through her tears.

"I think it's a surgical blade."

One of the gunmen walked over to Nader's face and began cutting out his right eye. Erika vomited on the floor. The lead gunman was staring at Pace as his subordinates conducted their gruesome surgery. Pace could feel his heart pounding.

The surgeon removed the eyeball and held it up for all to see. The lead gunman nodded approval and said something. The second man walked the eyeball over to the retinal scanner and held it appropriately for the system to analyze it. A green glow, a beep, and the door unlocked with a hiss.

Pace and the others shuffled back to the far side of the conference room, huddling in the corner.

The lead gunman walked into the room, pulling down his face mask. He had a square jaw. Mid-thirties. An incredibly deadly look in his eyes. The look of a man who killed people for a living.

"What do you want?" asked Pace.

The gunman motioned with his silenced pistol. "Would you each take a seat, please?"

The second gunman walked into the room behind the first. He was holding the surgical knife.

Ava sat in the passenger seat of a small sedan. The car drove as fast as possible without drawing attention, winding through the hilly streets of San Francisco. Ava had never met the driver. One of Mossad's, she was sure. He offered no conversation, but she knew he was a pro. He knew where to take her, and not to speak. And little else about her, in case he was questioned.

Ava kept looking behind them for any sign of a tail, but nothing stuck out. Seventeen minutes after she had fled the Pax AI headquarters, the vehicle pulled into a warehouse, the garage door shutting behind them.

Ava had already changed her clothes in the vehicle and tied her hair in a bun. The man handed her an umbrella and a backpack, which she took. Ava walked two hundred yards through an area of the building devoid of security cameras, then left the building, opening the umbrella to cover her as she transited outside to the next warehouse. She tossed the umbrella once inside that one. No drone footage or satellite imagery would confirm her identity. She ended her walk in the back of another vehicle that waited in a similar small garage, half a mile from the first. A second driver started the new car and drove her to a private airport, where she boarded a jet chartered by a Mossad shell company.

Within minutes, Ava was airborne, headed for Mexico City. Once there, she switched to a new private jet, owned by a different shell company. Again, she was airborne within minutes, this time heading east over the Atlantic.

Ava Klein was gone.

31

Two days later

BREAKING NEWS

Trinity has claimed credit for the break-in and violence at the Pax AI headquarters this week. While they have disavowed being involved in the killing of Russian diplomat Marisha Stepanova, online Trinity message boards have a lot of theories connecting her with the group. The US State Department and the CIA have yet to comment on rumors that Stepanova was part of Russian Intelligence. Nor have US authorities said if there is any connection between Stepanova's murder by an AI-controlled machine gun, fired from an autonomous vehicle, and the break-in and violence at the Pax AI headquarters. San Francisco Police and the FBI have been on high alert in the city and are urging citizens to contact the hotline if they have any information on the three men involved.

When Colt walked into the interrogation room at the FBI's San Francisco field office, his first observation was that Jeff

Kim looked like he'd aged ten years. Some of the news reports were calling the killers AI terrorists. Other news sites claimed there was a connection to Russia, citing the fact that a Russian diplomat was killed in spectacular fashion around the same time.

Kim's leadership position had been called into question by the board of directors. Ava, one of his senior executives and few personal confidants, was missing, with rumors swirling about her being part of an international conspiracy. Nader, three security guards, and the receptionist were dead.

Pace and two of his executives were so psychologically shaken they didn't want to speak with him. But they spoke to the FBI, describing the three men who entered the fourth-floor conference room as cold and brutal. The gunmen had known what to ask for and how to get it, using a window of connectivity between The Facility and the Pax AI headquarters to access some of Kim's most closely guarded intellectual property.

Jeff Kim sat next to his lead attorney. He wrinkled his eyebrows as Colt entered, and then whispered something to his lawyer.

The lawyer nodded slowly and then said, "Who's this?"

"Mr. McShane is working with us," Special Agent Rinaldi answered.

Kim whispered something in the lawyer's ear. "My client informs me that he was working on behalf of Pax AI's investors. Is that right?"

"I'll remind you that the US government was one of those investors. And that your client has signed multiple agreements with the federal government."

"Special Agent Rinaldi, I hope for your sake you have all your paperwork in order, because if not . . ."

"It is."

". . . if not, we're going to have quite the reckoning in court. We will seek damages for violation of Mr. Kim's Fourth Amendment rights and make sure it's plastered on every news show from here to—"

"Mr. Kim's rights were not violated," said Wilcox from a chair in the corner of the room. "And if they were, we'll pay damages. But it is in everyone's best interest to focus on the real perpetrators here. We want to find out who did this. I do not recommend going after the government for trying to catch them."

Kim again whispered to his lawyer, who this time remained quiet. Kim said, "What can I do to help?"

They peppered him with questions. Many were the same ones he'd already been asked.

Rinaldi said, "Let's talk about what they stole."

"Our AI research data from the Mountain Research Facility. We were running several experiments there. That's what they took."

"And were they able to get what they came for?"

"Some of it. Not all."

Wilcox leaned forward. "Including your AGI research?"

Kim said, "They were able to access some of that data. But no one can fully run that program without having access to the equipment in our Mountain Research Facility."

Rinaldi said, "Mr. Kim, why weren't you there?"

Kim nodded. "I was preparing to lead a demonstration of our AI language-prediction algorithm."

Agent Rinaldi said, "Did you know this was going to happen?"

Kim frowned. His lawyer raised his hands. "Come on. We're cooperating. Please don't push it."

Kim flashed anger. "Of course not. I would never want this to happen. This has ruined my life's work. And if the wrong people got hold of our technology, it could be dangerous. I want our work to be an agent of good. Not a weapon."

"Do you think that's what the people who stole it will use it for? To create a weapon?"

"I can only speculate."

Rinaldi said, "If they wanted to, what is the worst that could happen?"

Jeff Kim didn't blink. "They could take over the world."

Rinaldi huffed.

Wilcox said, "Why don't you think Ava was involved?"

Kim turned toward Wilcox. "I worked with Ava for the past two years. I got to know her very well. Her understanding of AI ethics is very good. And her motives have always proven to be altruistic. If she is working for a foreign intelligence organization or a competitor that wished to steal our tech, she could have done this at other times. Or in another, less violent manner. Another thing. She came into work that day. It doesn't make any sense to me that she would do that and then go on the run."

Colt agreed with Kim on that point. The FBI and CIA had been arguing over Ava's potential role for the past two days. Colt's opinion was that she very well could be Israeli Intelligence. But he didn't think they were the ones responsible for the killings.

Rinaldi said, "Maybe she was the scout? Making sure the coast was clear before the muscle came in?"

Kim shook his head. "It's not logical. And it doesn't fit with her opinions of the technology. She knows how important it is. And how powerful it can be. Nothing she's ever said or done would indicate to me she would want anything but the best of outcomes for this moment in our history. She wanted AGI to help mankind."

"You sure it wasn't just an act? Women are good at acting."

"So are men," Kim said, looking at Colt.

Rinaldi took a breath, and Wilcox tapped him on the shoulder. "Can I speak with you for a moment?"

Rinaldi nodded and rose. "Let's take a bathroom break. Anyone need anything? Coffee?"

Kim's lawyer glanced at him. "You okay if I run to the restroom?"

Kim nodded and the lawyer left.

Alone in the room, Kim turned to Colt. "So what are you? Some type of informant for the FBI?"

Colt shrugged. "Something like that." He paused. "Listen, I'm very sorry about all of this."

Kim stared toward the wall. "I guess it's not your fault, is it?" He sighed. "I cared about her. Ava, I mean. I shouldn't say this, but I'm just as upset by her betrayal as I am about the rest of it, I think. That's one of the things I've realized in the past few years. The success and money are only good if you are surrounded by the right people. People that you enjoy. That you love. As the money rolled in and we were approached by the CIA and many others, I began to realize how powerful our organization would become. We're still in our infancy when you think about the lifecycle of a business. But we have what no one else in the world does."

"What's that?"

"Me. I know I sound arrogant, but I'm being realistic. I was given a gift. I'm good at math, and this field comes naturally to me. I'm moderately good at running a company. And together, those things are enough to attract the world's leading talent. So, they gave me billions of dollars and free rein to create. I thought I was going to build an empire. But we barely got started."

"Is that what you want? To create an empire?"

Kim looked at Colt. "This AI revolution won't be like the

industrial jumps that came before. Especially AGI. No one knows what happens when we flip that switch. If things go well, then yes, we'll build an empire. Maybe we'll build a new world order."

"And if things don't go well?"

Kim put his fingers together and then brought them apart. "Poof."

Colt couldn't tell if he felt angry or afraid. Or both. "That's a lot of responsibility."

Kim shrugged. "If not me, someone else. You know what the difference is between the billionaire entrepreneurs and others with similar gifts?"

"Hard work?"

Kim shook his head. "Timing. People like me were in the right place, at the right time, with the right gifts. There are a lot of smart people in the world. Most of them end up old and angry. Maybe that is my path now?"

"You sound like you think it's all over. Didn't you say that the Russians—if that's who it was—wouldn't be able to replicate your AI program without the equipment you have at The Facility?"

"That's correct."

"Then why—"

"Because it won't be me." Kim nodded toward the door. "On the other side of that door, your bosses are speaking with my lawyer. In a moment, they're going to come in and my lawyer is going to say he needs to speak with me. The CIA will have informed him that for national security reasons, they need to place my company in a black box. They'll make it completely classified. Controlled by the US government. It will be my own personal hell. Everything I do will be overseen by them. Innovation and creativity stifled. Speed governed by the pace of bureaucracy. We won't win the AI race like that. And while I will do my part, I won't be at the helm. Not really."

Colt looked through the small glass window. Sure enough, he could see Rinaldi and Wilcox speaking with Jeff Kim's lawyer.

Colt said, "Can I ask you a question?"

"Sure."

"How did Kozlov really die?"

Kim's face went slack, and suddenly he looked afraid.

The door opened and in came the lawyer with Wilcox and Agent Rinaldi, who motioned for Colt to leave the room.

The lawyer said, "Jeff, we need to discuss something in private."

Colt's eyes were on Kim as he left. He never answered the question.

Outside in the hallway, with the door shut behind them, Wilcox and Rinaldi both had funny expressions on their faces.

Colt said, "What is it?"

Wilcox said, "You just got a message from Trinity."

32

The text message went to Colt's phone, which was monitored by the CIA. They noticed it before he did, as his phone was on silent while he had been speaking to Jeff Kim. The contents of the message were immediately flagged and sent up the chain of command.

Colt and the counterintelligence team sat around the main table in their safehouse.

Wilcox said, "Trinity wants the buyers to be ready to travel anywhere in the world within twenty-four hours. They have given each buyer the names of who is to represent them. We expect them to send a travel destination any moment now. Once at the location, Trinity will allow us to evaluate the product and make an offer. Each buyer will have a specific asking price."

"Do we know who the other buyers are?" Colt asked.

Weng said, "No, but we do know that the SVR received an invite. So, there is a pattern."

"I've received information that the MSS and at least one competitor technology firm have also received invites. So . . .

intelligence agencies involved with tech companies, and competitors," said Wilcox.

Colt said, "Ed, are we really going along with this? Isn't this like negotiating with terrorists?"

Wilcox looked at Rinaldi. "We were given approval at the highest level. The reasoning is that if there is a chance Russia and China could get their hands on this tech, we need to know what they have."

The group switched to reviewing the video surveillance of the Pax AI incident.

"Here," said Sims. "This is the best section of video we have. Facial recognition software gives each man a ninety percent match to these two." She pointed to another screen that showed two Russian men. Both former military, now thought to be contractors for a Russian mercenary group. "We don't have an ID on the third assailant."

"Any tattoos?" Colt asked.

"Not in these videos. All their clothing covered their forearms. It could be the same team that did the Kozlov job in Seattle, but we can't be sure. And before you ask, we don't have that level of detail on the two men who got the facial recognition match."

Rinaldi said, "Look, the FBI San Francisco office is a zoo right now. Everyone is working on this, and they've all got Russian assassination theories. The State Department is pressuring Russia to fess up. But before we embarrass ourselves, let's be honest. We just don't know for sure who these guys are, or who they are working for."

Sims sighed. "That's right."

Colt watched the video replay of them leaving the building. Walking right into the delivery van they had used as transportation. Then driving to a large distribution center with hundreds of identical vehicles and parking in a video surveillance blind spot, three cameras disabled the evening prior. Over the next few hours, dozens of similar delivery vans left that warehouse. The lead theory was that the team of gunmen had been on one or more of those trucks, then put on another truck or an aircraft. The drivers had all been interviewed, but no one knew anything. Something would turn up.

"The NSA confirmed what Jeff Kim said. They got some data, but not all. And they can't run the program without Pax AI's equipment," said Weng.

Colt said, "And Ava? Was she working with them?"

"We've dug up enough on her to know she almost certainly wasn't." Rinaldi typed a few keystrokes into his laptop and spun it around.

"Here. She was spotted training with the Israeli military eight years ago."

"Cute haircut," said Weng.

Colt shot her a look.

Wilcox said, "So this picture shows her training at an Israeli military base. This section of the base is where a lot of their special operations forces train. Ava's official records say she was in New York at the time. But we think her first time in the city was actually a year later. She went to business school right after finishing her training with Mossad."

"So, was she Mossad when I met her? Was that a planned meeting?" Colt asked.

"We don't think she was Mossad when you met. It seems more likely she began her training just after."

Colt could feel everyone's eyes on him. "Okay. So she left the Pax AI headquarters in a rush. Right before an assault team hit it. If she's not working with the assault team, how do you explain that?"

Wilcox said, "Maybe it was the Russians and Israeli Intelligence had some damn good intel on what they were planning."

Colt nodded. "Or . . ."

"Or maybe Israel hired that team and she is working with them. But it doesn't make sense that she would show up to work that day. It's not like she was needed for them to conduct that operation. Hell, we gave her a means to take all of that data."

Colt said, "I almost forgot about that. What happened to that? Did she—er, Mossad—get our data collection?"

"She's still got the shoes. But we never activated it. So no, they didn't use our tech to steal Pax AI data. That would really have pissed my boss off," said Wilcox.

Colt said, "I assume Israel is denying she works for them."

"Of course," Wilcox said. "They say they don't know anything about her. They asked for another few days. Trust me, we are applying pressure. But it's not like they did anything unusual."

"You're kidding, right? Industrial espionage? Spying on US citizens and companies?"

"Israel does that all the time. So do we, for that matter. You should know."

Colt shook his head. "But I'm not spying on Canada or Israel or the UK. Israel is our ally. And they broke the rules and got caught—"

"Did they? Ava worked for Pax AI. You and I asked her to spy on Pax AI. Then she left the building in a rush and fled the country. What law did she break, exactly? The industrial espionage evidence looks thin."

Colt fumed.

Weng looked up from her computer. "Another message from Trinity."

Everyone's heads went to their phones and computers.

They were all now part of a small group that was getting forwarded Trinity's messages.

Weng read aloud. "Trinity is pleased to announce the sale of Pax AI's AGI program technology. Each buyer's representative should arrive in Rome, Italy, within twenty-four hours' time of receiving this message. If any buyer sends a representative who is not on our approved list, they will forfeit their right to participate in the sale. We will contact each representative upon arrival in Rome."

"Who's our representative?"

Everyone turned to face Colt. He looked up from his phone, dumbfounded.

"I guess I'm going to Italy."

PART III

"China, Russia, soon all countries with strong computer science. Competition for AI superiority at national level most likely cause of WW3 IMO."

– Elon Musk, 2017

33

Colt's flight landed in Rome before dawn, local time. As soon as he stepped foot on the pavement, he received a text message from Trinity.

St. Regis Hotel

Colt took a taxi to the hotel and walked into the main lobby with its stunning white marble floors and fine rugs. The lobby was spacious and filled with a wealthy-looking international crowd. Twelve-foot-tall trees in large pots were scattered throughout the space. A giant gold and crystal chandelier hung overhead.

The clean-shaven Italian man behind the front desk said, "Mr. McShane? Welcome, your room is ready."

"Thank you," Colt replied, looking around the lobby. Various people eyed him. An Asian couple sipped tea at the nearest table in the hotel restaurant. He noticed a large man with a crew cut who looked like he had trouble fitting into his suit. And a few others who blended in with the tourists and businesspeople coming in and out of the hotel.

"Here is your room key, sir. The bill has been taken care of.

Oh, and I have a message for you here." The man handed Colt a sealed envelope.

Roma Termini. 0630 hours, tomorrow. Further instructions to follow.

"Thank you." Colt felt eyes on his back as he made his way into the elevator. As he rode to the third floor, he put to memory the faces he'd seen in the lobby and tried to ignore the unsettling feeling that Trinity was in such absolute control.

The suite was amazing. Definitely not in his price range. Every piece of furniture looked like it belonged in a palace. The art hanging on the walls was on loan from a museum. The minibar was stocked with high-end Italian brands. A fiery orange set of fresh flowers in several vases were placed throughout the suite. And on the flatscreen TV in the living room, images of the food and drinks from the hotel dining options showed an array of delectable treats and savory dishes.

Colt placed his bag on the bed and took a hot shower, fighting the urge to check in with Wilcox via the CIA phone. Trinity had proven to be extremely capable. The room was surely bugged.

Colt didn't like the decision to participate in Trinity's game. Americans shouldn't pay a ransom for American technology. Maybe they wouldn't. Colt didn't know what Wilcox and his superiors had planned. Rinaldi had said there were many people working on this case now. Colt imagined teams in the FBI and CIA all working to find out who was sending messages under the name Trinity.

He couldn't help wonder why Trinity had chosen him as the US representative. He supposed his cover was burned now, and decided to talk to Weng when he returned about taking a future assignment as an operations officer under an official cover.

Colt got out of the shower, toweled off, and dove into the soft bed. He took a nap to stave off the jet lag he knew would hit him the next day.

He awoke hungry, dressed, and headed down to the hotel's Lumen Garden restaurant. Lush greenery was everywhere. Ivy climbed the walls. Baskets of decorative plants hung overhead. Colt sat on a wicker couch with big blue cushions. A glass coffee table in front of him was prepared with high-end place settings and glassware.

A waiter came over and handed him a menu. More people were arriving for lunch. Colt recognized several familiar faces, including a few from the lobby. He was pretty sure these were surveillance teams, here to assist their respective foreign intelligence servicemen. He wondered if Trinity would follow through with its warning and issue a penalty?

Colt glanced overhead but didn't see any security cameras. Were they being watched? Did Trinity have their own human intelligence capability here? Or was Colt just being paranoid, falling victim to the conspiracy legend?

Trinity. The Bigfoot of the intelligence world.

An Asian man sat in the couch seat to Colt's left. Colt nodded politely to him. The man was in his mid-forties, an expensive Cartier watch on his left wrist.

"First time at this hotel?" the man asked Colt. Fluent, American-accented English.

"It is," Colt replied.

The Asian man said, "It's a very nice place."

"It is."

"San Francisco was nice too." The Asian man was looking at the menu as he said this.

Colt turned and studied the man's face, realizing that he recognized him. *Chinatown*. He was the man sitting across the street at the outdoor café the day he went there with Weng. Colt tried to remember his name.

"Do we know each other?" he asked.

The man put out his hand. "I'm sorry. I don't mean to be rude. My name is Liu." Colt shook his hand. Liu said, "You and I are here for the same reason, I believe."

"What reason is that?"

"We're both on the buyer list."

"I see," Colt said. Not an admission. But not a denial either.

Colt thought about his best play. It made sense to keep the man talking. Gain intelligence on a potential foe.

Across the restaurant garden space, a balding man sat down. Colt recognized him from the FBI images he had studied. Petrov. SVR. The *rezident* in Russia's Houston consulate. He had been Marisha Stepanova's superior. Colt felt his pulse quicken.

Liu said, "So . . . any idea why they chose you?"

Colt shrugged. "Why do you think they chose you?"

"I asked them to," Liu said.

The waiter came over. "Sir, are you ready to order?"

Colt said, "The club sandwich, please. Water is fine."

"I'll take the caprese salad, please," said Liu.

The waiter took their menus and departed.

Colt said, "How long did you work in the US?"

"A long time. Fourteen years, on and off."

Colt said, "You like it?"

Liu smiled. "I did. But in my line of work, in my country, you must be careful not to like it too much. Or your time there will be shorter."

Colt chuckled. "That's very honest of you."

"What about you? How long did you do this type of thing?"

Colt felt uneasy, but said, "A while."

"You were military?"

"I was. You?"

"No. They recruited me right out of school."

Colt said, "Your English is excellent."

"Thank you."

"So, were you mostly on the West Coast, then?"

Liu answered, "Yes. Business consulting. Working with investors in the US and Canada. Helping to forge ties with my clients' companies." Colt translated in his mind. *Economic espionage in North America's tech hotbeds. Helping China to steal secrets and gain intelligence on competitors.*

They spoke for a few minutes like that. Cryptic, guarded sentences. Trading superficial information without sharing anything vital. The food came and they ate in silence. Colt kept stealing glances at Petrov across the restaurant and caught the Russian looking at them a few times.

"Who are you looking at? Petrov? Hmph. Now that he spotted us, he'll probably write up a report that China and America were plotting against him over lunch," Liu said.

Colt snorted.

Liu said, "That might not be the worst thing, however. But it also might not stay secret, if we tried . . ."

Colt placed his club sandwich on the plate and wiped his mouth with his napkin. "What do you mean by that?"

Liu took a sip of water from his glass. "Because someone on your side is working with them." He stuck a forkful of fresh mozzarella and tomato in his mouth and began chewing.

Colt frowned. "Working with the Russians?" he asked softly. "Do you know that for sure?"

Liu said, "Let me ask you something. When they brought you to San Francisco, what did they tell you about Kozlov's death?"

Colt remained silent.

Liu said, "Did they tell you he died in Seattle? In a hotel? Or did they tell you he died at Pax AI's Mountain Research Facility?"

Colt forced himself to breathe in a normal rhythm. He couldn't show how unsettled this line of questioning made him.

Liu raised his eyebrows. "My guess is that they told you Kozlov died in a *hotel* . . . just like they told the newspapers. But he didn't. Kozlov died at The Facility. He was working for the Russians. Something happened to him at The Facility, and there was a coverup. There are some people who want everyone to believe Kozlov died far away from Pax AI. Who misled you, Colt?"

Colt saw the waiter taking the Russian man's order.

Liu continued, "Who knew about your relationship with Ava Klein, all those years ago? It was in your file. Who set up the meeting with Kozlov in Seattle? It had to be someone who also knew about your agent, Marisha Stepanova. And who knew about your meeting with her in San Francisco? Your team has already discovered that these assassins have ties to Russia. But you need to ask yourself . . . how are the Russians getting all this great intelligence? Who is their man on the inside?"

Colt was clenching his jaw, growing angry at Liu's onslaught. Because everything he had mentioned was of sound logic. These were the things that had been bothering Colt.

"Who do you think it was?" he whispered.

Liu said, "I think it could only be one person. Your CIA handler. The head of Vancouver station. Ed Wilcox. I've seen him in action before. He's a very smart man. But he was the only one who had access to all this information. He is the only one who could control who saw various bits of data. Don't you wonder how all this happened right under your nose?"

Colt had to push back. He knew he was being played. The MSS was trying to manipulate him for their own purposes.

"Pax AI showed me a video of Kozlov's last day. He looked fine."

"What did Luke Pace say about it?"

Colt ignored the question. "The FBI investigation showed . . ."

"Tell me about the video."

Colt frowned. "What video?"

"The video of Kozlov's interview. Was there anything unusual about it?"

Colt wasn't willing to go any further. "Look, Mr. Liu, what is your point with all of this? I imagine you aren't just trying to look out for my best interests."

"My point is this: you may not be able to trust those above you. If you run into trouble, I would be happy to find ways to work together. The Russians are nearsighted. They see this technology only as a weapon. We see it as so much more. It is my belief that your superior is aligned with the Russians. Be careful. Think of Kozlov and Stepanova. You don't want to end up like them."

34

Colt awoke early the next morning to the sound of his alarm beeping in the dark. He briefly thanked God that none of the competitor nations had sent anyone to eliminate him while he slept.

Colt forced himself out of bed, showered, dressed, and headed downstairs. His car was waiting, and he saw Liu getting into his own vehicle ahead of him, behind another car with men he didn't recognize. All the buyers were traveling to the same place: the main train station in Rome, *Roma Termini.*

The cars dropped them off under the station's giant white overhang and they headed inside. Colt checked his watch. He was fifteen minutes early. Another buzz on his phone. Instructions on what tickets to pick up, with a warning.

0700 to Naples. Any buyer who brings unauthorized passengers will be eliminated from the sale.

Colt wondered how Trinity would control that. Did they have hired guns? Henchmen who could take on the MSS and SVR? They had planned everything else down to the last detail. Colt was curious how they planned to handle that part.

The tickets were for a high-speed train, red and gray with

an angular nose like a jet. Colt had been on them before in other parts of Europe. These trains could reach speeds in excess of two hundred miles per hour. The one-hundred-and-forty-mile trip would take an hour and ten minutes. Colt, having lived in New York City for the past few years, chuckled to himself. The same journey on the East Coast highway system might take three times that.

He spotted several faces from the hotel while boarding the train. It was obvious that Trinity's warnings weren't being heeded. Some of the competitors were definitely trying to bring extra muscle, and Colt wondered what they might use it for. He wasn't armed. Not smart, Wilcox. Or perhaps that had been by design?

Now inside his compartment, Colt's heart skipped a beat when he saw her sitting in one of the seats.

Ava's hair was now short and blonde. Probably part of her extraction tactics, Colt thought. Their eyes met and he could see the emotion on her face. Colt felt awkward and unsure how to react. The eyes of others in the car were on him. He just sat in his seat, his back now to her, facing forward in the train.

Ava was having none of it. When an older Italian man sat beside Colt a minute later, Ava immediately got up and politely asked him if he would trade seats with her. The man was more than happy to accommodate the pretty young blonde.

A voice in Italian came on the overhead speaker system, preparing everyone for departure. Ava's face was close to Colt's as the train began moving. The scent of her perfume wafted into his nostrils, taking him back to his memories of their time together. A simpler time when they were young, and life wasn't filled with disinformation and confusion. When the only thing that mattered was being with a woman he loved, in the sun and by the water.

"I'm sorry," she said. The sounds of the train masked her soft voice.

"There are others in here, Ava. They're watching us."

"I don't care."

"You should." Colt turned to her. "From one professional to another."

She whispered, "I'm so sorry for deceiving you."

Outside the train window, the station gave way to Roman neighborhoods. Soon they gained speed, the world turning into a blur.

Colt looked into her eyes. "Who do you work for?"

"You must know the answer to that by now."

"I feel like I don't know anything anymore."

She took his hand. "You know you can trust me, right?"

"Can I really?"

"Yes."

Colt said, "Then there's something I need you to tell me."

"Anything."

"What happened to you after I left Haifa?"

She nodded slowly, and then began telling her story.

35

Haifa, Israel
Ten years earlier

At a café ten kilometers to the south of the harbor, Ava was sitting with her mother, checking her phone and wondering why Colt hadn't called her back. They ordered drinks at an outdoor table on the busy sidewalk.

Ava's mother said, "So he is handsome?"

Ava laughed and shot her mother a defiant look. "Yes."

Her mother was gleeful. "It must be serious for you to introduce us both."

Ava frowned. "It was now or never. Colt is leaving on his Navy ship and Father wanted to see me today. Better to rip off the bandage."

Her mother stirred sugar into her iced tea. The sun was beating down on them. Ava reached up and maneuvered the table's umbrella so they were better covered by the shade. The busy marketplace across from the café was filled with people. A dark-featured man was staring at her, eating a piece of fruit. Ava was used to the hungry looks from men. She'd been getting them since she was a teenager. Ava stared back menacingly at the man until he broke off his gaze and walked away.

Ava's mom said, "Colt. A horse is a funny name for a boy."

"Mother."

"Your father will think so, too. Colt. Maybe you can name your first child Mustang?"

Ava fully expected the three of them to share a laugh over the name Colt.

Ava's girlfriends from school marveled at how well her divorced parents got along. She used to wonder why they ever separated. But as Ava matured, she knew it was her father's fault. His work was all there was room for. He was obsessed with his secretive business. Ava and her mother weren't a part of that world. Eventually, his emotional distance became too much for her mother.

At least he kept up a healthy relationship with them both. He paid for Ava's boarding school in the US and sent a stipend to her mother. He was a good man, Ava thought. Even if he hadn't approved of her desire to pursue music. She knew he cared for her. Although she was never really close enough to know him beyond his walled exterior.

"Are you nervous?" her mother asked.

Ava realized she had been bouncing her knee under the table. She stopped. "I'm fine."

Her mother said, "Relax. If you are serious about him, your father would have to meet him eventually anyway."

"I know . . ."

"Although I can't see you being serious with a *Goy*." Her mother's eyes glimmered.

Ava cast her mother a warning look. "Please don't keep calling him that."

"Why not? He won't know what it means."

Ava shook her head, sighing.

An SUV pulled up to the curb and a pair of security guards wearing suits and sunglasses got out. One of the men opened the rear door and her father stepped out.

Heinrich Klein was of average height, lean, and tanned. He had intelligent eyes. His hair was thinning and brown, and he wore expensive business-casual attire appropriate for the warm weather of Israel's coast.

Ava stood, as did her mother. He embraced both women, kissing his daughter on the cheek. His manner was always tense. The relationship was cordial, one of kindness, loyalty, and respect, but not overly close. Ava knew only a little of what her father did for a living. He was financially successful enough to travel by personal jet and always had at least two security guards with him. His work dealt with both technology and investments.

She was much more familiar with his demanding attitude toward her studies. He was not happy with her decision to take a year off between college and her next phase, whatever that turned out to be. He saw her love of performing music as a childish pursuit. And she was worried he wouldn't want her to follow around some American sailor, throwing away her talents for silly young love.

So, she wouldn't tell him all of that. Instead, she would merely introduce him to her new American friend. It was the minimum requirement, she told herself. Whether he would recognize it for what it was remained to be seen.

The three of them sat at the table, catching up. One of her father's security men positioned himself just out of earshot, standing by the nearest street corner. The other security guard was somewhere in the market across the street.

A waiter came over and Ava's father ordered a mineral water. When he left, Ava's father said, "So I understand I have arrived at an opportune moment."

Ava reddened. "Please be kind to him."

Heinrich said, "A quick, merciful judgment."

"See, Ava? He promises to make the slaughter quick," her mother said.

They ordered a plate of olives and hummus, then spoke about the usual things: Ava's future plans, her mother's relatives, their shared local friends, and her father's travel. The minutes went by, but still no Colt.

"When will he be here?" her father asked, checking his watch.

"Soon, I think," Ava replied. She checked her phone again. No messages or calls. He was a few minutes late. Perhaps he had trouble getting off the ship again? If that was the case, she wished he would call.

A van was honking its horn down the block. Ava saw her father's security man snap his head in that direction and begin speaking into his earpiece. They were always overly cautious. Ava had gotten used to it over the years. Once her father had taken her to a play in New York City and one of his security men had actually slammed a bothersome street peddler up against a brick wall for getting too close to her.

"Would you like some more drinks? Or are you ready to order?" the waiter asked.

"I'll take another water," Ava said. "We'll wait to order."

Ava checked her watch again. Colt should have arrived by now. She could see the impatience on her father's face. The tardiness made her second-guess her optimism. Was she being ridiculous about the whole relationship? Moving too quickly with a man she had met only a few months earlier? Maybe Colt wasn't as perfect as she had hoped and it was just young desire, projecting the image she wanted to see.

More honking from down the block. Her father looked up, frowning.

Her new sense of doubt grew as she kept up conversation with her parents, avoiding any talk of her singing. She tried to keep noncommittal on her master's degree plans. As the minutes went by, Ava knew this first meeting would forever paint Colt as undependable in their minds. They would never approve. She cursed herself. She should have made it more clear how important this was. Or maybe she shouldn't have pushed it so soon. Or realized he wasn't what she was pining for.

"Where is your horse?" asked her mother.

Ava stood, annoyed. "Let me give him a call."

She rose from the table and walked inside the café. Behind her a diesel motor grumbled. Brakes screeched. She walked deeper into the café, turning at the noise. A food delivery truck had just stopped in front of the restaurant.

The interior was dark and she just barely missed running into a waitress carrying a food tray. Ava squinted as she typed a text message to Colt and pressed send, but she got an error message. No signal. So annoying. Ava looked up when she heard shouting in the street outside. Her father's security guard was arguing with the truck driver. Ava and everyone else in the café were staring at the commotion.

Then the passenger in the truck opened his door and ran away, morbid fear in his eyes.

The café went dead silent.

Ava's survival instincts pricked up.

A patron stood from the table beside Ava, knocking over his glass while frantically pulling his wife along with him.

She realized her father's security guard was kneeling on the ground, clutching his stomach.

Blood on his hands as he looked up.

The second security guard was now hunched over him,

looking at Ava's father, shouting. Then the rattle of gunfire in the distance, followed by screams.

"Get out!" someone in the café shouted, and then people were scrambling, bumping into each other.

Ava's first thought was to rush to her parents. She could see her mother's long dark hair, streaked with gray. Her father standing up. The restaurant's guests raced past Ava and out the back door of the café. Someone placed an arm around her and threw her into the kitchen behind a steel refrigerator.

Then a booming explosion sucked all the air from the room.

Shrapnel tore through fleeing civilians, smoke and flesh and fire.

Everything went to shreds.

And everything went dark.

Ava awoke in a hospital bed a day later. A nurse informed her that both of her parents were dead. The nurse cried, but Ava didn't. The doctor told her she was in shock. She was bruised and concussed, but she would recover soon. Physically.

Two of her college friends came to see her. They flew from the US as soon as they found out she was in the hospital. They were both a bawling mess before long, but Ava barely spoke to them and they went home two days later. She didn't want to see them. She was still numb.

A day before she was to be released from the hospital, a woman came to visit her. Ava recognized the face but had trouble placing a name to it.

"Good morning, Ava. May I come in?"

"Aunt Samantha. Yes, of course."

Samantha Klein was her father's sister. Ava had met her

fewer than five times in her entire life, most recently at her father's home in the Hamptons two Christmases ago. Aunt Samantha was, like her father, of dual US-Israeli citizenship.

She pulled a chair close to Ava's bed and spoke softly in Hebrew. "I am so sorry that this happened." Her aunt's face looked worn and tired.

"Thank you."

"I have made funeral arrangements for your father, and I have been in contact with your mother's sister. She is doing the same for your mother. I will make sure you are taken care of, Ava."

She nodded. "Thank you."

They sat in silence for a while. Aunt Samantha seemed comfortable just sitting there. The hum of hospital equipment and an old air-conditioning unit sputtered along.

Ava almost forgot she was there, until her aunt whispered, "Did you see the men who did this?"

She felt a wave of anger. Shaking her head, Ava said, "I was in the back of the café. I couldn't—"

"It's okay, dear. It's okay."

"I only know what they said on the news. A terrorist group."

Her aunt patted the white hospital sheets covering her legs. "Yes."

"Why would they go after my father?"

Aunt Samantha glanced at the empty doorway and then turned back to look at Ava. She cocked her head, the same way Ava's all-knowing boarding school instructors did when they were explaining something they felt was too adult for the children.

"Your father was a powerful man."

Ava said, "On the radio, one of the news reports implied he had ties to Mossad."

Her aunt didn't answer.

"Is that true?" asked Ava.

Aunt Samantha looked down at the ground. "Let us speak of this another time."

Ava sighed, resting her head back on the pillow.

"They say you are free to leave tomorrow. Do you have anyone to take you home?"

"I believe my mother's sister—"

"I will take you."

The next morning, Aunt Samantha walked Ava out of the hospital and drove her to Tel Aviv. Ava cracked the window open when they got off the main road, relishing the fresh air, the scent of the sea. This was her home, even if she'd spent most of her formative years in America. But now she had no mother to live with. And she felt lost.

Aunt Samantha said, "What will you do when you are rested and healthy?"

"I don't know." There were boys playing in the street. Without thinking, Ava put the window back up.

Aunt Samantha's voice was gentle but firm. "You are afraid. And angry."

"Of course I am."

"May I ask you something? Are you angry at the men who did this?"

Ava turned toward her aunt.

Aunt Samantha glanced at her, and then continued looking forward while she drove.

"What do you mean?"

Her aunt said, "You asked about a news story concerning your father. It mentioned our country's intelligence service."

"Our country?" Ava was born in the US.

"Israel." Aunt Samantha's eyes darkened. "You are an Israeli citizen. Is this not your country?"

"I . . ." Ava paused. "I've always considered myself an American. I haven't spent much time here." In truth, she had made sure to spend less than one month per year in Israel to make sure she maintained her exemption from military service.

"Well, you are also a citizen of Israel."

"What does this have to do with my father?"

"What if it were true? About him being involved with the Institute for Intelligence and Special Operations? That is the official name, you know."

"Is it true?"

"If it were, would that make you any more interested in serving your country in the same fashion?"

Ava blinked. "Why are you asking me this?"

Her aunt shrugged, turning the wheel as they made their way into a neighborhood. "Just a thought."

Ava stared at her aunt's face, which didn't reveal much.

"I am interested."

Her aunt said, "You will never get your parents back, Ava. And no matter what you do, nothing will solve the way you feel. This wouldn't be about revenge."

Ava said, "I understand."

"Would you still like to hear more?"

"Yes." The spark of purposefulness formed inside her.

They pulled up to the curb outside her dead mother's house. Her mother's sister was waiting by the door. Aunt Samantha said, "I can't promise anything. Very few are selected. But if they choose you . . . it is a very noble calling."

"How do you know?" Ava asked.

Her aunt waved away the question. "Don't tell anyone what we spoke of here."

The phone call came two weeks later.

"Is this Ava Klein?"

"It is, who is this?"

"Your name was provided for a possible job opening with the Prime Minister's Office. Are you available to come in for some tests and fill out questionnaires?"

At first Ava had no idea what the person was talking about. She was about to tell them they had made a mistake when the conversation with her aunt came back to her.

"Yes. Yes, I am available."

Two days later she found herself in a government office answering computer questionnaires about her life and psychological makeup.

Ava was always a good test taker. And this was just another test. She figured that Mossad wanted their operatives to fit a certain psychological profile. Someone who was open to taking risks, but was also a very good decision maker. She figured Mossad would want them to be brave, patriotic, loyal, and intelligent. That last part couldn't be faked, but Ava had it in spades. Part of the test involved reasoning: solving puzzles of shapes and patterns. Mathematical problems. The second part of the test was a psychological questionnaire. But for Ava, they were both reasoning tests. In both instances, she identified the answer they would want her to choose. As the test went on, she became more and more confident she would receive a job offer.

The tests were just the beginning, however.

Two days later she was asked to come in for more questions, these ones not on a computer. Ava was hooked up to a polygraph and a man wearing unfashionable eyeglasses proceeded to ask her questions for the next two hours. He asked her everything. Drug use. Sexual habits. Any crimes she hadn't been caught for yet?

By the end of it, she was red-faced and decidedly less confident in her decision to apply to the Institute. The man questioning her thanked her with an impassive face and told her she would hear from them if they needed anything else. A full week went by and she hadn't heard a thing.

Then an email came.

It was from Colt.

Ava's heart skipped a beat when she read it.

She hadn't responded to any of the previous three emails. She hadn't been ready. She had been so downtrodden and consumed by her parents' deaths she couldn't bring herself to write him back.

Colt's explanation for why he had missed the meal that day was reasonable. The loss of her parents had numbed any sense of young love she felt prior to the incident. Ava didn't harbor any anger toward him. She wasn't sure what she felt anymore. It was easier to be alone with her despair and anger.

But reading this email now—and with the knowledge she likely hadn't gotten the job with Mossad—she warmed to the idea of seeing Colt again. She learned he had just arrived home in the United States. His deployment was finished, and she was surprised to learn he would be getting out of the Navy within a few months. He had some type of terminal leave vacation he could take, and he wanted to know if he could fly out to visit her.

The idea was enthralling. Maybe that was exactly what she needed. She began typing a response but stopped as the phone rang.

"Hello?"

"Is this Ava Klein?"

"Yes."

"Congratulations. You have been selected for our next class of recruits."

She listened as the man informed her she had been selected for Mossad, although he never said the name of the organization. He also told her she wasn't to discuss her new job with anyone. A bus would leave from Tel Aviv on Friday. They would have paperwork waiting.

She thanked him and hung up.

Ava looked at the email she had drafted to Colt, her cursor hanging over the send button.

It had been eight weeks since her parents had been killed. Her training to become a Mossad officer would last for the next two years.

She moved her cursor and clicked to delete the email. Then she shut down her computer, staring at the blank screen.

That part of her life was over.

36

Present Day

The train came to a halt in Naples. Colt felt his phone buzz. Another Trinity message. He turned to look at the other passengers in his car. Several had heads down in their phones as well. So far, he knew three buyer identities. Ava for Israel. Liu for China. Petrov for Russia.

There were a few others he thought he'd seen in the hotel. They were either corporate buyers or part of the Russian "extras," testing Trinity's security.

Colt looked at his phone and read the message. Ava was already done reading. "One night in Naples. Then an early wakeup. No hotel listed this time."

"Wonder why?"

"They probably knew some of us were going to get competitive. It isn't a good idea to put us too close. Well, some of us." She stared at him, a provocative look in her eyes.

For all the anger and frustration Colt felt, those eyes still caused a stirring in him. A glimmer of hope for what might lie ahead.

But a part of his mind called out a warning. He couldn't help thinking she may be trying to use him still. At least she had told him the truth about Haifa. He didn't have to always wonder if it was his fault. He felt relieved and realized he had been angry at himself about that for a very long time. When he was young, he told himself there would be others like her. But there weren't.

They decided to catch a cab together and stay at the same hotel. "We'll work better as a team," she said.

"You're probably right."

The cab ride was a death-defying trip through roundabouts and busy streets in downtown Naples. The cabdrivers all drove like they were trying out for Formula One, if the competition gave additional points for shouting and hand gestures. Ava found a boutique hotel that looked safe and had good visibility and exit routes if there was any trouble. They walked inside and she said, "Let's just get one room." Colt didn't argue.

They got their key and walked upstairs without saying much, and Colt saw that the "two beds" were really two single mattresses pressed up against each other.

He felt her hand tug on his as she drew him close. Tension welled up inside him. A decade of daydreaming about her, lusting after her memory, and wishing back the days. The door was barely closed when Ava was pressed up against him. Open-mouth kisses were exchanged as they shuffled toward the bed. Then her arms were up as he helped her squirm out of her shirt, a black bra underneath tantalizingly full. Colt felt adrenaline coursing through him, and she slipped her arms tight around his torso as they continued to kiss. Her bra was unstrapped and fell to the ground. More clothes came off and soon they were in bed, gliding and sliding, sweating and moaning.

Mount Vesuvius loomed in the distance, silently approving of the new seismic activity.

They rose afterward, showering before venturing out for an early dinner. The instructions from Trinity would have them up well before dawn the next day. They walked along the crowded Naples street, horns honking and scooters zipping along. Arriving at a pizzeria, they sat outdoors and split a bottle of red wine. The pizzas arrived steaming hot. Fresh basil atop a simple sauce and fresh mozzarella, the crust charred from the brick oven. Ava ate with a fork, Colt with his hands. They got some gelato in cones afterward and ate while walking along the *Via Caracciolo*, with nice views of the Mediterranean Sea. Colt wondered if the CIA was getting pissed at his vacation as they monitored his purchases from Langley.

Ava said, "There's something we should discuss."

"I'm not seeing anyone right now, if you were concerned."

"Stop joking."

"Okay. But I'm not."

"We need to discuss what to do tomorrow."

"What about it?"

"Trinity will try to sell us Pax AI's AGI technology. All of us, at the same time. We don't know what to expect. We may be forced to bid against each other. Other buyers may coordinate and form factions. They may move against us."

"They're all competitors. And they don't trust each other."

Ava said, "They trust you and me less, I think."

"Given our recent history, do you think we can trust each other?"

Ava looked hurt. "You didn't seem to have a problem with that a little while ago."

"You mean when you were eating your pizza with a fork? It was a challenge for me."

She punched his arm. "I trust you now. And don't forget, you were lying to me in San Francisco too. But I understand why that is. I understand what you were fighting for. This AI revolution . . . it's going to change everything. I'm not sure you even know how dangerous a weapon this thing is."

"Everyone keeps saying that. Talking about this thing like it's a doomsday machine."

"It might be."

"It's hard to fear. Not like a nuclear bomb, which you can see vaporize whole landscapes on a slow-motion reel."

"It could do that, just like in the movies. Not yet, but someday. And that day can approach rapidly, if we don't monitor the technology's use carefully."

Colt had stopped walking. He stood at a corner in the cobblestone walkway, taking the opportunity to scan the streets in either direction.

"You see that man with the white short-sleeve shirt two blocks down?" Colt turned away so they wouldn't both be looking at the same time.

"Yes."

"I recognize him from the hotel in Rome. He was in the lobby when I came in."

Ava said, "Let's keep walking."

They began heading up *Via Carducci*, picking up their pace. The man in the white shirt stayed with them, two blocks back.

"We can't let him know where we are staying. We might be his mission. If he finds out where we are sleeping, they'll come there at night and take us off the buyer list."

Ava motioned to a small church off to their right. "Let's go in here."

Colt could see several doors that appeared unlocked. They went in the main entrance and waited. Inside, a few people sat in the pews up front, praying silently. One held rosary beads. It was deathly still, and Colt could feel his heart pounding as they stood near the entrance.

"Now what? Exit out to the other street?"

"No. Let's wait here." She pointed to the confessional booth, a small wooden space about the size of a broom closet.

"Are you crazy? What if he comes in?"

"I want him to."

Colt frowned. "No, that's nuts. Come on, we need to move. Let's go out—"

Commotion outside. Someone was talking in Russian.

Ava placed her finger over her lips, signaling Colt to be quiet. Her movement was quick and graceful as she maneuvered behind the main entrance door, her footsteps silent and steady as a ballerina's. Colt's every instinct told him to flee, and that he shouldn't put himself in this vulnerable position.

The towering main church door creaked open. Ava was still behind it, out of view.

Through a crack in the confessional, Colt saw the man who had been following them appear in the doorway, his eyes bloodshot and wild. The eyes of a predator who had just seen dinner. He stepped forward, a glimmer flashing from a blade in his hand.

One step.

Another.

And then he paused. Looked confused.

His left hand held his neck.

"Shh. Shh. Down you go," Ava whispered behind him, helping him down. "Colt!" she whispered. He came out of the confessional and glanced toward the front of the church. One of the people saying the rosary turned toward them but didn't make eye contact, and was soon back to praying.

Ava, Colt, and the Russian body were hidden from view on the floor behind the rear row of pews. Ava was nodding to get the man's collapsing body into the confessional booth. They heaved him inside and sat him in the corner of the dark room, then stepped outside and shut the door.

"What did you do?" Colt whispered, still not understanding what he had just seen.

Ava held up a small, pen-like object.

"What is that?"

She placed the object back in her purse and then nodded for them to head out the side door. Colt agreed, and they started moving in that direction. The Russian might have one or more conspirators out on the street.

As they walked out the side door, Ava put on sunglasses and Colt a ball cap. They walked apart for two blocks, away from the scene of the crime, before meeting up again and heading toward their hotel. When they got back to their room, Colt again asked, "What was that back there? What did you do to him?"

Ava again took out the pen-like object. "It's made to look like an e-cigarette. But when you press this button here, it will inject a pressurized burst of chemical solution into the bloodstream. Enough to do the job."

"Is he dead?"

"No. He's probably already up. But he'll be suffering from some unpleasant side effects for the next few hours. Bad headache. Still, we should probably sleep lightly tonight, in case any of his friends followed us."

Colt nodded. "Sounds smart." He took out his phone. "I need to check in."

"Me too."

Colt felt sheepish as he moved to a chair in the corner of the hotel room. Ava sat on the bed. Both were on their phones typing away, updating their handlers through encrypted satellite comms.

Colt sent his update to Wilcox, trying not to think too hard about the suspicion Liu had cast on him. He finished typing and then sat waiting for a response.

He looked over at Ava on the bed and found himself wondering what she was typing and reading. Had she accomplished part of her mission earlier that day by sleeping with him? It went back to the fundamental question . . . could he trust her? Was she telling him the truth? Did Ava really plan to collaborate during Trinity's deal tomorrow? Colt wasn't sure what to believe.

He felt his phone vibrate and looked down to see a response from Wilcox.

COPY ALL. KIM IS MISSING AND PRESUMED OUTCONUS. POSSIBLE ENEMY KIDNAPPING. WATCH YOUR BACK.

"What is it?" Ava asked. She'd been watching his face.

Colt looked at her, sitting cross-legged on the bed, her back to the headboard. She'd placed her phone on the nightstand and was applying moisturizer to her legs, the smooth skin glistening under the strokes of her fingers. Her cleavage was accentuated due to the way she was leaning, and he again found himself wondering if he was being manipulated.

"Nothing. Just a warning we should be careful."

"A little late for that."

37

The next message from Trinity came at 0400 local time.

Sorrento docks. 0530

With admirable foresight, Ava had arranged for a car to pick them up at dawn. The drive from Naples to the coastal city of Sorrento was a little more than an hour. They arrived only a few minutes early.

As they stepped out of the car near the ferry docks, dawn began to creep over the horizon, and Colt marveled at the old city. Its walls of dark gray stone rose up from the coast like the boundaries of a giant castle. Colorful multistory Italian city homes lined the cobblestone streets, which were wet and empty at this time of morning. The docks, however, were alive with the sound of diesel motors rumbling and seafarers preparing for their day.

"Excuse me, Mr. McShane? Ms. Klein?"

They turned to see a woman in a stylish white business suit, her blonde hair wound back into a tight bun.

"Yes?" Colt said.

"You may call me Irina."

Irina was flanked by two bodyguards. They were Caucasian, but Colt couldn't tell their nationality.

Irina said, "I've been hired to serve as the broker for the Trinity transaction."

"Who are you with?" Ava asked.

"My organization prefers not to have its name involved."

Colt noticed the Chinese and Russian buyers twenty yards down the dock. A man Colt recognized from the hotel in Rome stood next to them, as well as a tall brunette he'd never seen before.

"Are those the other buyers?"

"That's right," Irina said, and she began leading them in that direction.

"Some of them have more than one buyer from the same nation?" Colt asked, noticing that the Russians had two representatives. One of them was the man Ava had jabbed in the neck. She glanced at Colt. The look on her face said, "Oh shit."

Irina said, "Correct. Some of our buyers asked for certain conditions, and they were approved." She spoke in short, terse sentences. She was all business.

They boarded a hydrofoil ferry boat, and Irina gathered them in the aft section. There were sixteen buyer representatives in all. Colt counted seven armed guards who were working for Irina the broker. Each had on Kevlar vests and wore earpieces. That likely meant more security men were stationed in the vicinity, ready to provide support.

Irina said, "A few days ago, my firm was contacted by the organization you each know as Trinity. They hired us to facilitate this meeting. Before you ask, the answer is no. I don't know who Trinity is. So please don't ruin your chance at participating in this sale by attempting anything . . . *impolite* . . . toward me. You'll notice my bodyguards. They are the best.

And there are many more that you won't see. Rest assured, we've taken all the proper precautions, knowing the size and capability of each of your organizations. I hate risk. I'm a lawyer, by trade, and somehow ended up in finance." She smiled. No one smiled back. "I've received specific instructions on how we are to conduct this event. From here we are to travel to Capri. We've made special arrangements that will ensure no other ferries will leave this port for the next six hours. By that time, the lines will be so long it will be very challenging for any of your support teams to travel that way. Not that any of you have support teams here. The airspace around the island has also been reserved for military training today. So, any attempt to send in a helicopter with members of your team will face resistance from the authorities." She sighed. "But I really hope it doesn't come to that. Let us all agree to provide mutual respect to each other, and we'll be all right. When we arrive on the island, we'll walk to a small hotel that we've rented out for the day. My agency will confiscate all unauthorized items, including weapons and communication devices. We will then provide a briefing, which I've yet to see. After the briefing is over, we will return your communication devices, which you may use to contact your superiors. My firm will help facilitate payment and communications, should you need assistance. Each party will have a three-hour time period to decide whether they want to participate in the purchase of the technology. When it's all over, we'll return your personal items and be on our way. I'm sorry, but I'm not able to answer any further questions at this time. Now, if you'll please have a seat and put on your safety harnesses. This boat travels fast, and sometimes the waves get bumpy. My assistants will be going around with a bag to collect all weapons and electronic devices."

They each sat down, and the vessel departed the pier, slowly at first, motoring at just above idle in the marina's no-wake zone. The sea was a bit choppy, and they were rocking as they strapped into the seats.

After they were two hundred yards from the pier, one of the Russians began arguing with the security guard trying to collect his belongings. He was the same man Ava had subdued yesterday, and he was sitting next to Petrov.

"What's he saying?" Ava asked.

Colt's Russian wasn't great, but he got the gist of it. "He doesn't want to give up his phone." Colt found this amusing since he'd handed over a pistol without complaint. That was what spy craft had come to, nowadays.

The guard looked up at Irina, who said something to the two SVR men in perfect Russian. Petrov frowned, but said something to his subordinate, who relented, handing over the phone.

The guard moved on. But two seats later, he encountered another resister. This one was a man in a business suit.

"Who's he?"

"Tech company out of Germany. One of Pax AI's main competitors in machine learning." This man spat on the floor, irate at the guard. Irina nodded to one of the guards standing at the bulkhead fifteen feet away. Colt saw that guard flip a switch and heard a snapping sound echo throughout the seating area, then felt a jolt in his seat harness.

Irina said, "We don't want anyone standing up when the boat gets moving fast, so we've taken the liberty of locking your harnesses in place for the duration of the journey." She nodded to the guard standing in front of the resisting businessman. Two other guards had joined him. One reached out and grabbed the metal handles near the top of the seat, depressing a latch.

"What the . . ."

The guards had picked up the man's seat with him in it. He

was locked in place by the fastening straps. They walked over to the aft end of the ship and heaved him into the ocean. Several of the passengers let out cries of alarm.

Petrov looked at his Russian colleague and made a face.

Colt felt sick as he watched the poor man go underwater, strapped in and weighed down by the heavy metal seat. Irina's eyes were staring coldly at her passengers as she sat in a seat herself and strapped in.

Ava whispered, "Well I guess we now know what type of people we're dealing with."

Soon they were speeding to the south, the sun coming up over the horizon, illuminating the island of Capri.

As the boat motored toward the island, Colt realized the logic of Trinity's meeting location. They had sequestered the buyer representatives for the next few hours. There were only a few ways onto Capri. Choke points that could easily be monitored by Trinity's security. If the SVR or CIA or anyone else wanted to send a team onto the island, they would immediately be spotted. The meeting could be called off and attendees dispersed. And as far as he knew, no one from Trinity was actually here. Irina and the guards were hired guns.

The peril of the situation was contrasted by the beauty of Capri.

Multimillion-dollar yachts were anchored off the coast. Beautiful homes and hotels were scattered throughout the island's greenery and surrounded by deep blue water. Stone cliffs rose one thousand feet over the sea.

"The cliffs of Tiberius," Ava said.

They pulled into the island's pier and began walking up steep stone steps. No one spoke. The competitive tension was palpable, each player sizing up the others.

After several minutes of climbing, they reached the top of the stairs, now several hundred feet above the water and out of breath. A courtyard with restaurants and shops awaited them, the beginning of a maze of winding city paths.

As they walked, they passed countless ocean-view homes and boutique hotels tucked between stone and cypress trees. Ancient ruins and luxury shops and five-star restaurants. The old mixed with the new. Crisp mountain air, colorful flowers, sunlight, and expansive, incredible views of the Mediterranean now lit up in a full golden sunrise, illuminating the *faraglioni,* the one-hundred-foot-tall rock stacks that jutted out of the sea at the foot of the island. Yachts and tourists on small rentals sailed around the island's rocky shore. Everywhere Colt looked, the island was serene and beautiful.

After walking for twenty minutes, the group was shown through an arched gateway of a private hotel. Tables and chairs were set up for them under the shade of towering cypress trees and a scattering of Mastics. A dark blue swimming pool, thin and rectangular, lay off to the side.

Irina stood on the patio, the sea to her back. "Ladies and gentlemen, if you'll have a seat. We have coffee and a light breakfast for you. We will begin soon."

One of the guards came around with a metal detector, zipping it around each buyer's body and limbs. Another security check, just to be sure. Everyone was in compliance. Colt noticed that Ava's e-cigarette hadn't set off the warning. It made him wonder what other deadly weapons might be hidden among this crew.

Irina sat down while one of her guards rolled out a large monitor connected to a laptop. The screen lit up, and a single man stared at them.

Jeff Kim.

38

On screen, Kim said, "When I began Pax AI, I did it with the best of intentions. I was young and perhaps naive. I thought that the best and brightest minds of our generation would want to work on this project, bringing superintelligence to life. I was right. They did."

His face darkened.

"But just because you have a great mind doesn't mean you aren't susceptible to temptation." He sighed. "I was contacted by the Trinity organization for the first time one month ago. Right after one of our scientists, a man by the name of Kozlov, died. The FBI had just informed me that Kozlov died while attending a tech conference in Seattle. Trinity told me he was stealing secrets for national intelligence services. For more than one country, if you can believe it. Allowing one nation dominance over another is the exact opposite of what I wanted to happen. After an investigation, we at Pax AI realized we were infected with agents trying to commit economic espionage. I was lost."

Kim raised his chin. "But Trinity gave me a way out. A way we can all share the technology and its benefits."

"What is he saying?" said the Russian.

"The big dilemma was how to ensure all of us will behave appropriately. Trinity suggested a solution."

Some of the others were getting visibly upset now too.

Ava turned to Colt. She whispered, "I think he's saying we must use a blockchain contract."

"I'm offering a licensing deal to each party here. We have a payment request from each of you. The price is individualized based on what I thought you could afford. But there are two additional requirements. One is that each of you will recall any person you have actively employed in an industrial espionage operation against Pax AI. The other requirement is that you vow never to use this AGI in a way that violates our ethical standards. That includes using it to develop or implement weapons. Neither can you use this technology to engage in any criminal activities such as the creation of deepfakes, propaganda, or psychological manipulation. Any party that signs this contract will have access to our AGI, when it becomes ready. But you'll have access only remotely, not in our lab. You'll have access to its capabilities. You'll be able to use its powers for *good*. To research medicines and energy innovations. To solve problems that will benefit society. If anyone is in violation of these rules, the blockchain contract you sign will lock you out from further use of our AGI system. You will be forever relegated to a non-AGI status. This is my offer. Take a share of the technology. Pay the price and play by our rules. Or get left out of the game."

The screen went black. Irina stood and motioned her men to begin handing out standard laptops.

Colt received his and opened it. Inside he saw biometric scanners. He allowed his fingerprints and eyes to be scanned. Then he viewed a screen with a timer and a price, and a text box where he was to enter information.

Ten billion US dollars, in crypto, with a ten percent down payment due today. And a promise to halt all undercover federal investigations into the company. That was the price for the US delegation.

There was some contract boilerplate detail around how disputes would be handled and how the contract obligations were to be interwoven among the participants. But the payment terms were rather simple, if steep.

Colt figured the powers that be in Washington, DC were going to piss themselves. Not to mention their reaction when they learned that a US citizen was essentially betraying his country to sell classified technology to foreign governments.

Petrov, cursing in his native tongue, turned to Irina. "This is extortion! This is not what was indicated to us. Sharing the technology was never discussed."

"Does that mean you won't participate?" Irina asked, one eyebrow raised. Her tone was a challenge to the Russian man's machismo. The second Russian man eyed her, and then looked for the guards standing nearby.

Petrov stood. "We must have more time."

"Three hours is all you have. We've arranged private rooms for you in this hotel. Communications equipment has been tested and is ready for your use. And you may have your phones back if you need them."

"Why would I trust your communications equipment? Give me my phone. I will be back in a few hours."

"Don't be late," Irina said, the hint of a smile on her face.

The Russian cursed under his breath and left.

Irina said, "Okay, everyone. Thank you for sitting down with us. You can sign your blockchain contract via the computers we gave you. Once we confirm that the money has moved, your part of the contract will execute. You'll have until the timer runs out. Let me know if you need any help. I'll be here."

People moved quickly, with a few using the rooms on site to call superiors.

Colt saw Ava standing at the hotel exit. She nodded for him to come over.

"I need to speak with you," she said.

"Okay. But I need to call my superiors."

"You should talk to me first."

Colt shook his head. "I'm sorry, but I can't."

"Okay. Let's talk after. But not here."

Colt bit his lip. "Ava."

She whispered into his ear, "Trust me. This is important. I don't think everything we just heard was accurate."

"Which part?"

She nodded. "Trinity."

39

Colt got his phone back from Irina's guard and left the hotel, walking along Capri's winding stone paths until he found a private bench overlooking one of the island's many scenic cliffs. He called Wilcox, who picked up on the second ring. Colt did his best to summarize everything he had just learned, knowing that others were very likely listening in on their conversation.

Wilcox said, "Ten *billion*? The guarantees on how the technology will be used will be laughed at over here. And the idea of guaranteeing an American-based company that we won't investigate them when they're crawling with foreign spies is ludicrous. There are factions in our leadership that have echoed your 'America doesn't pay ransoms' argument."

Colt said, "Wasn't that the whole reason I was sent here?"

"One of the reasons."

Colt wondered what that meant. He said, "What do they want me to do, Ed? If we're going to pull the trigger on this, the clock is ticking. Two hours and forty-five minutes."

"Be ready to close the deal. I'll work on my end to present all options to the decision makers."

"Will do. What about afterward? Where do you want me to meet you when this is over?"

"You stay put."

One of the reasons. Colt realized Wilcox intended on coming to him. He should have expected something like that. Colt decided to hold back on relaying what Ava had said about Trinity.

The US government wouldn't sit back and wait for a cyber-criminal organization to dictate terms. There were probably half a dozen American operatives on the Amalfi Coast now waiting for the go-order. Wilcox had been using Colt to gather intelligence.

But this realization also made Colt nervous. "Ed, you heard the description of the blockchain contract, right? Taking any action contradictory to their terms might lock us out from ever getting access . . ."

"Yeah, we got it. That's all for now." The phone call ended. Colt let out a long, slow breath. He hoped Wilcox wasn't making a mistake.

A text notification on his phone.

Ava: Talk now?

A few minutes later Colt met Ava a half-kilometer north. She led him inside a small, unremarkable building hidden on a street of countless others. The old stairway creaked as they traversed the steps to the rooftop. The roof had a table and chairs, and walls on three sides gave them some privacy. Two people stood in wait, their backs turned as Colt and Ava approached. A man and an older woman, speaking to each other in a language Colt couldn't understand. Hebrew, he was pretty sure.

"Who are they?" Colt asked, still out of earshot.

"My colleagues," replied Ava, looking at him. "People we can trust."

Colt wondered if Wilcox's team was watching him right now. Would they think he was conspiring with the Israelis?

Colt stepped further onto the roof terrace and the two people turned. He recognized both of them. The first was the curly-haired man who had been watching him in Banff. The second was Ava's Aunt Samantha.

"Hello, Colt." Samantha held out her hand. "It's good to see you again."

He shook her hand and then turned to Ava, who was watching him closely.

Samantha smiled and turned to her male colleague. "Moshe, could you excuse us, please?" The man nodded and left the rooftop, walking down the stairway. She turned back to Colt. "We don't have much time, so I'll be very brief. Ava told you that Jeff Kim was not providing accurate information."

"That's right," Colt said. "How did she know that?"

"We have been monitoring Jeff Kim and Pax AI for some time. We have also been monitoring members of other intelligence services, and the group known as Trinity. We would know if Jeff Kim was in contact with Trinity. He is not."

Ava said, "We are looking at one of three scenarios. One, Jeff Kim is being forced to do this. Two, he's trying to deceive everyone for his own gain."

"And three?"

"That wasn't Jeff Kim on the video."

Colt frowned at Ava. She looked back at him, serious and concerned. Then it dawned on him what Samantha meant. "A deepfake?"

Samantha looked at Ava, and then back at Colt. "We can't be sure without sending the video to our tech team."

"What are you asking from me?"

"Nothing yet. We don't know who is behind this, or what their end game is. But we wanted to warn you. One friend to another."

Colt said, "Your agency's activity with respect to Pax AI hasn't exactly been friendly."

Samantha tilted her head. "I would argue to the contrary. That is certainly a discussion we may have. But this isn't the time for it."

Colt felt his phone buzz in his pocket. He looked at the screen and said, "I need to take this." The two women nodded.

Colt walked over to the corner of the terrace, answering the phone in a low voice.

Wilcox's voice was in his ear. "Where are you?"

"Five minutes from the meeting site, why?"

"Get back there and sign. The money's being transferred."

"It was approved?" Colt was shocked. He hadn't expected the US government to go along with the criminal sale of the technology.

"Yes. Go sign. Text me when it's done."

"Ed, wait. I've met with Ava and her handler. The Israelis—"

"You *what*?"

"Listen . . . they don't think we should believe Jeff Kim's video. They don't think Trinity really reached out to him."

A pause on the line.

"So what does Mossad think?" A trace of cynicism in his voice.

"The video could be a fake," Colt said.

He heard Wilcox let out a sigh of frustration.

Colt said, "Do you still want me to sign?"

"Wait one." The phone went mute. When Wilcox came back on, he said, "Yes. You have the same instructions."

"Understood."

Colt saw Ava and Samantha watching him from across the rooftop, whispering to each other. What were they discussing, Colt wondered?

Wilcox said, "Colt, I'm en route to your location. I won't show up on the island until tonight. I don't want to spook the deal. When you are done, plan to stay on Capri and meet me. I'll send you the exact site after the transaction goes through."

"Will do." Colt hung up and walked back over to Ava and her aunt.

"Who was on the phone?" Samantha asked.

"The man I report to. I need to head back."

"Is the US going through with this?" Samantha asked.

Colt hesitated, then nodded. "They want me to sign. We're going to do it."

Samantha turned to her niece. A wordless communication transpired between them.

"I'll go with you," said Ava.

Moments later the two of them were walking through the backstreets of Capri. They passed carts of tourists' luggage and restaurant food supplies being dragged up stone walkways by the island's laborers.

Ava was unusually silent on their walk, which fed into Colt's growing wariness. Something about Samantha's meeting just now bothered him. As an intelligence officer, Colt had an objective every time he met with one of his agents. If there wasn't an objective, he wouldn't hold a meeting. It wasn't worth the risk. The objective could be large, like convincing someone to betray their country for the first time. Or it could be small. Give them a gift and develop trust.

Mossad was an excellent intelligence agency. They would

operate under the same principles of agent handling. So what was Ava and Samantha's purpose just now? To warn him that Jeff Kim's video wasn't legitimate?

No.

It would be something else. Some more important call to action. Had they aborted that part of the meeting?

Colt slowed, moving to the side of the stone path. Ava frowned. "What's wrong?" Colt brought her further off to seclusion, under the shade of an overhanging tree. The cliffs just beyond the path plummeted down to the ocean a few hundred feet below.

"Why do I get the feeling you two decided not to tell me something?" Colt asked.

Ava averted her gaze.

"Ava, what is it?"

"I am not supposed to—"

"*Ava*. You've got something to say. Say it." He couldn't believe she was talking like this. "After everything you said, are you still keeping secrets from me?"

Ava faced him, determination in her eyes. "We think one of your superiors is working with the Russians."

Colt felt the air rush from his lungs.

He looked at her, wondering if this was all part of a Mossad operation. Were Samantha and the curly-haired brute listening to this conversation? Had they decided it would pack more punch coming from Ava when they were alone?

Colt threw away that hypothesis. This was twice in the past twenty-four hours he had heard a similar rumor. From two agencies that weren't known for their close ties. What had Liu said?

I think it could only be one person. Your CIA handler. The head of Vancouver station. Ed Wilcox . . . he was the only one who had access to all this information . . .

Colt's palms grew sweaty as he stood there looking at Ava. Her deep brown eyes stared back at him.

"What do you know, Ava?"

Ava said, "Sheryl Hawkinson. You remember me pointing her out to you at the party . . ."

"I know who she is."

"Did you know that her brother's company recently got the security contract for Pax AI's Mountain Research Facility?"

"No." Colt found that hard to believe.

"It's through a subsidiary, but it's his. Guy Hawkinson. And the likely reason you haven't heard about that is because it's been kept from you. Has anyone in your organization steered you away from investigating the Hawkinsons?"

Colt didn't reply. He thought of what Ed had told him when he first arrived in San Francisco. *Steer clear of her for now. It's not worth the political flames.*

Ava said, "The Hawkinsons have connections all over. Including Petrov, the SVR officer who is here in Capri. Petrov and his SVR team were running Kozlov before he died."

Colt nodded. "I was aware."

Ava said, "The Russians wanted Kozlov to pull data from the Pax AI fourth floor and The Facility. Just like everyone else, the Russians want to win the AI race. But instead of building their own facility, which would have been cost-prohibitive, they decided to place agents on the inside of Pax AI and do all of their research there."

"Using other people's money," Colt said. "Smart, if you can make it work."

Ava said, "They recruited Kozlov a few months ago. He began stealing data and providing the information in drips to his handler. But then something happened. Do you know how The Facility shifts work? Kozlov was there for a few weeks at a time. At some point, just before his most recent shift, Kozlov discovered something. Someone else was stealing data too."

So far everything she was telling Colt matched what he already knew. He nodded patiently. "Okay."

Ava said, "Two nights before Kozlov's supposed death in Seattle, our intelligence personnel intercepted a series of messages. Sheryl Hawkinson met with an American working counterintelligence on the West Coast of the United States. Her brother was present at that meeting."

Colt said, "That's unusual but not incriminating. My understanding is that Guy Hawkinson's security company has done work for US intelligence before."

Ava frowned. "Petrov was also present."

Colt raised his eyebrow, pausing for a moment to take that in. "Do you know what they discussed?"

Ava shook her head. "We only know that they met. We have the locations of their phones when they went black. And our satellites were able to track their vehicles to Sheryl Hawkinson's mansion after their phones went offline. Our surveillance systems are set to raise a flag whenever suspected intelligence operatives turn their phones off." Colt knew American agencies like the NSA did the same thing. No one turned their phone off unless they didn't want to be tracked.

Colt's eyes narrowed. "Wait, if you could track the phones, wouldn't you have the identity of the American?"

Ava smiled. "Your scrambler security program obscures the exact identity."

"So how did you know it was an American intelligence official?"

"Our cyber team has a way to track batches of phones. We could only tell what batch the phone came from. It was the same group that all of your intelligence officers use."

Colt said, "That sounds like a security threat."

"Definitely."

Colt mentally stored that fact for a debrief with the crypto geeks later, and said, "So an American counterintelligence officer met with Sheryl, her brother, and Petrov, and then two days later, Kozlov shows up dead."

Ava nodded.

A thought occurred to him. "Ava, who killed Kozlov?"

She looked at him, ice in her eyes. "We don't know."

Colt said, "Why didn't Samantha say any of this? Why are you telling me this now, seconds before we go back in there?"

"Samantha wasn't convinced you were trustworthy. For all she knows, you were that American in the meeting with Sheryl."

Colt let out a breath, rubbing his chin and looking over the water. "How do you know she isn't right?"

Ava gave him a look. "She's not. I know your heart, Colt. You are honest and true."

He sighed, turning away. "I am not sure what to believe right now. I've worked with Wilcox for years."

"Ed Wilcox?"

"Yes."

"He's high on our list of possibilities."

"He's coming here to meet with me."

Ava's eyes widened. "When?"

"Afterward."

"You need to be careful."

Colt swore to himself. "So what is all of this, then? This Trinity meeting in Capri? Transferring cash in cryptocurrency. The video about Jeff Kim trying to spread out the technology in a safe way? Why would Wilcox tell me to facilitate the US purchase if he's part of the conspiracy?"

Ava said, "We don't know for sure who has set up this Capri meeting. But if it is Wilcox and the Russians, he'll stand to benefit. Think about it. One of the demands was to identify and recall all the spies within the Pax AI organization. If the Russians have organized this meeting, it would be an elegant way to eliminate their competition."

"But they'll be giving away the code? Sharing the technology?"

"Do you really think the US government will allow this deal to be honored?"

"But the smart contracts?"

Ava said, "We aren't convinced they'll work unless Jeff Kim is really involved. If this is a deception, it could just be a way for whoever is behind it to steal money and unmask their competitors' spies. And with all that's happened, Jeff Kim's access would be limited at best. Wilcox will have more than enough evidence to suggest Kim is corrupt. Hell, that video we just watched proves it. He's trying to sell classified technology to the enemies of your country . . ."

"Of our country, I thought."

Ava gave him a disapproving look. "We can discuss that later. I need you to get on board with this. You have to understand the urgency of the situation, and where everyone's loyalty lies. I don't think you should trust Wilcox. It is very likely he is in bed with the Russians."

"This is crazy, Ava—"

"All conspiracies are crazy until proven true."

"But Jeff Kim's video . . ."

"Pax AI can easily generate a deepfake of that quality now. Our competitors can too."

"You're saying I can't believe my eyes and ears."

She gave him a look. "You never could. You have to follow your internal compass. And yours is as strong as they come."

She gripped his arm and they stared at each other for a moment, a tug of war in Colt's mind. The pull of decades of training and service to country against the allure of a woman he trusted and cared for deeply.

"Ava, why are you telling me this?"

"Because I don't know when I'm going to see you next. After this meeting, we will go our separate ways. I don't know what will happen, but I think we can work together. I think you want to do what's right to protect humanity from disaster. To protect us from ourselves."

Colt looked at his watch. "We need to get back to the meeting and sign."

"You still don't believe me. Fine. I don't blame you. But you should believe me, Colt." Ava's eyes were dark as she turned away. She stormed around the corner, her footfalls echoing along the cobblestone walkway.

Colt thought of calling after her but felt the buzzing in his pocket once again. He looked down at his phone and saw another text from Wilcox.

Status update?

A group of nearby birds began squawking and fluttered by. In the distance, the off-key sound of an Italian ambulance or police siren began to wail.

Colt started to type a response to Wilcox but was distracted by a group of tourists running along the path, casting frightened looks over their shoulders.

The sirens in the distance grew louder.

Wilcox: Call me ASAP.

Colt dialed and Wilcox picked up.

"Where are you? Don't go to your meeting. There's been an incident."

40

Wilcox spoke on the phone. "Italian police are responding to some type of chemical attack on the island of Capri. NSA just picked it up on the Italian police scanner. We think it's at your meeting spot."

Ava.

Colt ended the phone call and began running around the corner, in view of the hotel.

Several bodies were spread about the cobblestone court outside the hotel entrance. They looked to be catering and hotel staff. One middle-aged woman lay on her back, her eyes bulging, spittle and vomit dripping from her mouth.

An intense fear gripped Colt as he saw the dead victims. If this was some type of nerve toxin, how close could he get before he was in danger of breathing it in? He stepped sideways, desperately trying to look inside the hotel without coming any closer.

"Psst. Colt! Up here." Ava was standing twenty feet up the stone path, waving for his attention. She was climbing up onto a rock wall that rose around the hotel grounds.

"Is it safe?" Colt said, jogging over.

"I think so, based on the winds. We can stay away from the east building. From the looks of it, that's where the attack happened."

He hustled up to stand with her, ignoring the chilling thought he was even now inhaling some toxic gas. Climbing over the stone wall, Colt followed her into the hotel's ivy-covered archway and onto the roof of the westernmost building. The location seemed safe, with a good one hundred feet of distance from their meeting location.

A moment later they stood overlooking the back garden area where their meeting had occurred. More than a dozen bodies were strewn about the lawn.

Irina and several of her guards. Several men and women Colt had identified as intelligence officers from other nations, a few competitor business representatives, and more hotel staff. None of them were moving. Each had the same foam dripping from their mouth and nasal cavities.

Colt and Ava easily could have been among them, if they had arrived a few moments earlier.

"No sign of the SVR men," Ava said.

"Or the MSS," Colt noted. He nudged Ava, motioning for her to follow him out of there.

They left together and began walking away from the crime scene just as the Italian emergency services pulled up. Colt walked up to the Italian police officer and told him in English they shouldn't go in there. Toxic gas. The man nodded, apparently already aware. He kept emergency services at bay and began setting up a perimeter, which allowed Colt and Ava to depart without interruption.

After a few minutes, Ava said, "What kind of toxin do you think they used? Will we be affected?"

Colt said, "I don't know."

Ava took out her phone and made a call to Samantha.

They arrived at the Mossad safehouse, and Samantha showed them to separate bathrooms where they showered and changed into spare sets of clothes. The Mossad man wore latex gloves as he placed their original clothing into a trash bag and disposed of it.

When they were finished, Ava and Colt sat at a kitchen table. Colt's clothes felt a size too tight. He was texting and calling Wilcox, who had yet to respond.

"Wilcox is not picking up."

Samantha and Ava shared a look at that.

Soon Samantha was on her own phone, speaking in Hebrew. After a moment, she hung up.

Looking at Colt, she said, "Your CIA handler is not on your side."

"Please don't start with that. I appreciate you providing me shelter right now, but—"

She shook her head. "You don't understand. This is new information. We just received a joint intelligence message warning of a possible Russian operation. The information came from the Americans. *One hour ago*."

Colt frowned. "What are you saying?"

Samantha sighed. "If the Americans knew something like this was about to happen, why didn't Wilcox warn you?"

Colt shook his head. He looked down at his phone screen, displaying all the calls to Wilcox that had gone unanswered. "I don't know."

The curly-haired Israeli man called from the other room. Samantha walked out of the kitchen, leaving Colt alone with Ava.

"She is telling you the truth, you know," Ava said. She looked worried about him more than anything.

Colt nodded. "Okay."

"You don't believe her?"

"Would you, if you were in my shoes?"

Ava didn't answer.

Samantha called from the other room for them to come in. "You need to see this."

Ava and Colt walked into the room. A small couch sat in front of a TV. Skynews was on, showing a police bulletin with an image of a man's face. It was a partial picture from CCTV, probably taken this morning as Colt walked through the Capri town square.

Colt was wanted for questioning in relation to the Capri chemical attack.

"What the hell?" he said.

Colt's phone began vibrating. He picked up to hear Wilcox's voice. "I'm on the island. Have you seen the news?"

"Yes."

Wilcox said, "Someone is framing you."

Colt said, "I'm aware." *Is it you?*

"We need to get you off the island quietly. The docks are a madhouse right now. Between the ferry backup this morning and the hazmat emergency, the whole island is trying to leave at once. Where are you? I'll come meet you."

Colt looked at Ava and Samantha. Samantha's expression was very serious. She had written out a note and was holding it up for him to see. *Meet somewhere public.* She had known what Wilcox would say.

Colt said, "How about we meet somewhere public?"

A pause on the other end. "We need to take some precautions, given the situation. Keep you out of sight."

"Ed, I have security concerns of my own."

Wilcox paused. Either he now understood and was sympathetic, or he was trying to think of a way to outmaneuver his agent. "Give me some time and I'll text you a location to be at." The phone went dead.

Samantha tilted her head. "You still think he's on your side?"

Colt rubbed his chin. "I need to make another call."

Colt borrowed a burner phone from Samantha and dialed a number by memory.

"This is Heather."

"Hey, it's me."

A pause as she placed his voice. Then, "Holy shitballs, man. What the hell happened? And why are you calling me?"

"Are we all ears?" *Is anyone else listening to this call?*

"No, the line is private."

"Promise?"

"Colt, say what you need to say. I shouldn't even be talking to you."

"I'm worried Wilcox is compromised."

Weng sounded shocked. "Are you kidding right now? Your face is on international news. Our operation is tits up."

"Exactly. Why do you think that is?"

"Why do *you* think that is?"

"I've had some interesting conversations with other members of my cohort."

"You mean other nations' intelligence officers? That's what you mean when you say that, right? Let me guess, a female Israeli agent? Colt . . . don't fall for it, dude—"

"I've heard evidence—"

"You've heard what they *want* you to hear. Come on. You know how this works."

"I believe there may be a Russian mole inside US counter-intelligence on the West Coast."

Weng paused. "Well shit, if that's true, then you shouldn't be telling me this either."

"I have to trust someone. Time's too short to do it any other way. Wilcox wants to meet with me in another hour. I'm worried something bad might happen."

"I've worked with Ed Wilcox for a long time—"

"So have I . . . Will you just do me a favor? I want you to look into something, okay?"

"Fine, what is it?"

"Two nights before Kozlov died, Petrov and the Hawkinsons met with someone at Sheryl Hawkinson's home in California. I think they met with our traitor. Can you look up where Ed was on that night?"

"That should be easy, hold on."

Colt heard a pause and some typing.

Weng said, "He flew from Vancouver to San Francisco that morning. Then flew back the next day."

"Any record of what he was doing?"

"No. But it could have been him, Colt. He didn't travel here that often before you came to town. So, I gotta be honest. This doesn't look good for Ed. Shit. Can you explain to me—"

"Not now."

"Colt, we need to get you out of there. Should I start calling people to grab Wilcox?"

"Not yet. There's one more thing I need you to look up."

41

An hour later, Colt received Ed Wilcox's text message.

"*Villa Jovis*, sunset," he read aloud. "Where's that?"

Ava said, "That's the ruins. The first Roman Imperial Palace on the east end of the island."

Samantha said, "Not a good meeting spot. Well, not if you are worried about an escape route. It's surrounded by cliffs. You should let us help cover you."

Colt shook his head. "If he's going to arrest me, he's going to arrest me. That's just how it will have to happen."

"What if he's going to kill you?" Ava said.

Colt didn't respond.

"At least take this." Samantha handed him a firearm.

"Since we're in Italy, I suppose I should make a joke about taking a cannoli," Colt said.

Samantha said, "I get it. That's funny." She didn't sound convinced.

"Here, give me that." He took the gun. A Glock 17 pistol.

"Have you ever fired one of these?" asked Samantha.

"Well, not at a person."

"If you have to do it, keep shooting until they go down,"

said the curly-haired Israeli man. This was the first thing Colt had heard him say in English.

"Thanks for the advice."

He held up a finger for Colt to wait, then handed him a holster. "Use the holster. Don't stuff it in your pants like a cowboy." He turned to Samantha and said something in Hebrew. She chuckled.

"What did he say?"

"He said maybe the American wants to get a cheap circumcision."

Colt took the holster and clipped it in place. He walked out the door and Ava followed. They were alone in a small courtyard. The sun was setting but the air was still warm. The distant sirens were still present, hazmat teams cleaning up the attack site.

"Please, this is stupid," Ava said. "You shouldn't go."

"I have to."

"Be very careful."

He nodded and began walking along the city streets, sunglasses on and a white ball cap pulled down low over his brow. He wasn't carrying a phone, to ensure he couldn't be electronically tracked. The CIA-issued phones were supposed to have location tracking disabled when he used the security app, but he couldn't be too careful.

The streets were filled with tourists who either couldn't get off the island or didn't want to. He didn't blame them. It seemed like the danger had passed and the place was magnificent. A paradise of great food and luxurious hotels surrounded by lush gardens and lofty views of the Mediterranean.

His own view was getting better by the step. The path had thinned to a paved walkway lined by decorative orange bricks. A stone wall rose up on one side of the path and tall green shrubs on the other.

The ruins of *Villa Jovis* sat atop a one-thousand-foot mountain on the east end of the island. An impressive array of stone walls and rooms, tunnels and doorways. The remnants of a once-great empire.

Colt was sweating and breathing heavily after the uphill walk. The sun had just set over the horizon, and he didn't yet see anyone else. Tours had stopped more than an hour before. He continued past the ruins and walked up to a promenade, on which a small church was built. A statue of the Madonna was in the center of the promenade. A guardrail surrounded the area, the sea and sky beyond it.

Now he saw Ed, who stood alone by the handrail, carefully studying Colt's approach. As he walked, Wilcox nodded to someone to Colt's left. Colt felt a rush of fear as three people appeared. Two men with H&K submachine guns, one of them prodding a frightened guest along.

Colt knew the guest well.

Jeff Kim.

It was late morning in San Francisco, and Weng was typing furiously at her computer.

"Are you going to tell me what you're going so crazy about over there? You've been at it all morning," said Sims. "You know this whole project is going to get shut down, right? There isn't anything your computer can find that's—"

Weng spun around in her chair. "If I tell you something, will you promise not to scream at me?"

Sims saw the look in her younger colleague's eye and said, "Tell me what's wrong, honey."

"I spoke to Colt."

Sims's pupils dilated, but she kept cool. "When?"

"A few hours ago. Colt thinks he has evidence that Wilcox is working with the Russians."

Sims's chin rose ever so slightly, and a grim look came over her. When she spoke, her voice was low and dead serious. "Why didn't you immediately report this?"

Sims walked over to the landline phone, picked it up, and began dialing.

"Who are you calling?" Weng asked.

"Rinaldi."

Weng's head hung low. Rinaldi was working out of the FBI's San Francisco field office a lot more after the attack on Pax AI's headquarters. And with the situation in Capri, it was looking like their tech counterintelligence unit would probably get shut down.

"Hey, it's Jennifer. I'm calling you on the secure line because we have a situation. Weng's going to fill you in. Here you go."

Sims held out the receiver and Weng took it, preparing herself to get an ass-chewing when she was done. Rinaldi had a lot of questions. He wanted to know everything. The more he spoke, the more Weng realized she had screwed up by not telling them straightaway. The moment Colt called her, she should have reported it.

Sims could hear the pain and embarrassment in Weng's voice. Mercifully, she left the room.

Rinaldi and Sims were seasoned counterintelligence pros with the FBI. Together, they had decades of experience catching criminals and uncovering moles. For all of Weng's knowledge about running agents and intelligence operations, she hadn't worked in a situation where her teammates' loyalty might be in question. She'd cut her teeth in Iraq and spent years in Southeast Asia. Maybe this

Silicon Valley economic espionage stuff just wasn't her forte.

Weng hung up the phone and Sims brought her a fresh cup of coffee. "Thanks," Weng said, taking a sip.

Sims sat next to her. "You done screwed up, girl. But don't worry. We're going to fix it. He coming downtown?"

"Rinaldi? Yeah, he should be here in twenty minutes or so. Said he was going to bring some agents with him to go through the video files. Forensic specialists, or something."

"Video files?"

"Yeah, from the hotel the night that Kozlov was killed."

Sims frowned. "That's what you've been looking for all morning? What does Colt want with those records?"

"I don't know, he wouldn't tell me. But I couldn't find them anyway. The folders were deleted."

"Let me see."

Weng stepped aside and Sims sat at the keyboard, clicking with her mouse and typing in her password. "Hmm."

"What is it?"

"Someone's deleted them."

"That's what I said."

"Yes, but that shouldn't be possible. We have a two-person rule, to prevent . . ." Sims looked at Weng, pouting.

"How's that work? The two-person rule?"

"Any codeword-level surveillance files in our system need authorization from two of us before they can be deleted. It's a safeguard against human error, for one, and prevents a mole in our midst from having free rein. Because a mole inside our office could cover his tracks, or protect other moles, in theory."

"So, if you need two people to delete files, how . . ."

"How did someone do it? I don't know. Maybe it's not deleted? Maybe it's just archived."

"Where would the archived file be?"

"Probably in the server in the back room."

"Is there a username that would show who archived it? Can they do it remotely?"

"No. There is no identity in the system. And we're a closed system. So they would have to be in this building, connected to our server."

"What about a timestamp? Can we tell when they did it?"

Sims squirmed. "I don't know, actually."

Weng said, "Do you mind if I try something? I think if I go into the system memory, I can tell when the files were archived." Sims moved aside and Weng clicked the mouse until she found what she was looking for. "Here. 5:02 a.m. This was the morning after Kozlov was killed. Whoever archived those files, this would lead to the evidence Colt is looking for."

Sims was massaging her temples. "Or you may find video of Colt archiving those files."

"Colt wasn't here then."

Sims nodded. "Touché."

Weng rose and headed to the back room. "I'm going to see if I can dig it up."

"You want some help?"

"Nah, this room's smaller than a closet, I'll do it."

Weng reached the classified server main computer and began searching for video files archived the day after Kozlov's death.

Nothing.

"Jennifer!"

"What?"

"Are those archive times in local?"

"How should I know?"

What if 5:02 a.m. wasn't local time? What if it was UTC? Weng clicked on the previous day's archived files and found what she was looking for. She was even able to un-archive the files and watch the video footage.

She was looking at the raw surveillance video of Kozlov in his hotel room. It showed them carrying the body out after his killing.

Poor bastard.

She paused the video, confused by something she had noticed.

The hotel walls were clean.

Weng distinctly remembered seeing a lot of blood on the walls when she had watched the footage. That had been one of the more disturbing parts of the surveillance video. Watching the man's flesh and blood painted on the hotel wall by a fifty-caliber round was something you didn't forget.

But these walls were clean.

She unpaused the video.

And went pale.

"Holy fucking shit . . ."

Weng wasn't watching surveillance footage of Kozlov's body being carried *out* of the hotel.

Kozlov's body was being carried *in*.

"He was dead before he got there."

But then that meant . . .

"Rinaldi's here!" Sims called from the other room. "And he brought his agents."

42

Two weeks earlier

"Would you like anything to drink?" Sheryl asked.

"Nothing for me," Rinaldi said.

Guy Hawkinson sat next to his sister, studying him. Rinaldi admired the man for his contributions to the cause. And his contributions to Rinaldi's cryptocurrency accounts. But Guy Hawkinson was still creepy, as were his two human attack dogs observing from twenty-five yards away, by the mansion.

The Hawkinsons were always lean and hungry-looking, both seemingly ready to devour whoever lay in front of them. And that was what Rinaldi sensed they expected here.

"What do you got?" Rinaldi asked, trying to project strength.

Sheryl said, "This is going to be a very delicate matter. But if we're going to continue on with our relationship, it's something we need your help with."

"Don't keep me in suspense, Sheryl."

She said, "A scientist will go missing at Pax AI. I need to

make sure that any investigation into this person's whereabouts doesn't lead to anyone inside the company."

Rinaldi raised his eyebrows. "I'm almost afraid to ask more questions about this."

Guy leaned forward, his voice stern. "Ask them."

Rinaldi said, "Is a body going to turn up?"

"Not if we don't want it to," Guy said.

Rinaldi closed his eyes in pain, and then opened them. "Fuck, Sheryl. What are you asking here? You've got a dead scientist that you need to hide?"

"*We* need to hide him."

"Why *we*? How am I involved in this?"

"Because of our relationship. The person in question may have significant value to Pax AI. And my understanding is that Pax AI has significant value to the US government."

Rinaldi frowned. "What's the guy's name?"

"Kozlov."

Rinaldi let the air escape his lips. "You've got to be kidding me."

"You know the name?"

"I do," Rinaldi said. "Do you know how I know his name?"

Sheryl and Guy looked at each other in confusion, which Rinaldi enjoyed. "No," the sister said.

"Because we plan to speak with him in Seattle in a few days. Let's keep that here within our circle, if you please."

Guy let out a snort. "That's not going to happen."

Rinaldi narrowed his eyes, and then realization struck. "So when you say that he's going to go missing, can I assume he already is missing?"

"You may."

Rinaldi sighed. "I'd appreciate a little more lead time to prepare in the future. Look, I really value this partnership. You guys have helped eliminate a lot of Chinese espionage operations. Some that the government knows about, and some they frankly don't need to know about. But I can sleep well at night knowing I'm helping our country and getting properly compensated for my services. I'm fully on board with our arrangement. Lord knows the FBI doesn't pay me as well as Mr. Hawkinson's outfit pays me, and I feel like we're a good team. I've always tried to do right by you. But this is a big ask. And it's on short notice. And it seems our paths have coincidentally crossed on this one. I am going to have a hard time explaining to my team why we shouldn't be worried about one of our new informants going missing."

Sheryl and Guy exchanged a look of alarm. Sheryl said, "Your new informant? So . . . you have Kozlov on your payroll?"

"Not yet. But that was the plan."

Guy began laughing. When he calmed down, he said, "Seriously. How do we make sure there is no concern about an investigation leading back to the company?"

"I'm not sure it's in my best interests to help."

Guy started to get upset, but Sheryl held out her hand to calm him. "I'm afraid this is crucially important, Mr. Rinaldi. You see, we suspect a Chinese agent has penetrated Pax AI, very high up. We've almost got that person identified. But if this investigation turns Pax AI upside down, I'm afraid our private anti-Chinese espionage operation will have to be shut down. We can't risk keeping it open, due to the proximity of our own operations inside the company. And if that happens, our payments to you will come to a stop. And God forbid, if we were ever investigated carefully, a trained special agent like yourself might be able to find a trail back to you."

Rinaldi frowned at that. "I've always been very careful. And I hope you would never say anything."

"Oh God, no. That's not something you need to worry

about. Not really. But you just never know with that type of thing."

Rinaldi sulked. "Well it would have been a lot better if we could have confirmed that Kozlov was in an area unrelated to the company. Can we do that?"

"Sure. We can have the body wherever you need it."

Rinaldi said, "But anybody can move a body. Forensics will be a problem. They'll be able to tell when and how he died. For this to work, you need to leave no question that he actually died somewhere else. Construct solid evidence. Video, if possible. Can you do that?"

Sheryl said, "When and where was your meeting supposed to be? I may have an idea. An AI program I just observed might come in handy. But we'll need help from some friends. You won't want to know them."

Rinaldi shrugged. "Long as it doesn't come back to bite me."

After Rinaldi left the home, Petrov came down from the second floor where he had been observing with surveillance equipment.

"Quite an asset you have developed," said Petrov, taking the glass of scotch that Guy Hawkinson offered.

"He's been extremely productive," said Sheryl.

Guy said, "And now you know it wasn't the Americans who killed Kozlov. Well, it wasn't the FBI anyway."

Petrov said, "I should tell my subordinate not to travel to Seattle. She was planning to meet with Kozlov there on the same day the FBI planned to meet with him."

Sheryl could see Petrov's mind spinning at that thought. Rinaldi hadn't revealed how the FBI knew to recruit Kozlov.

But Kozlov's handler, whoever she was, would surely become the target of a counterintelligence operation now. Poor girl.

Guy said, "I don't recommend that. We need the Americans to think everything is normal. If there is even a remote possibility your subordinate may be the leak there, then I suggest you say nothing. Let her find out on her own. You may learn whether or not she is loyal by how she reacts. Besides, do you have enough resources to run two operations at once in Seattle?"

"What operations am I running?"

Guy said, "I'll need some of your contractors. They're going to make it look like Kozlov is shot through his hotel window, right after the FBI interrogates him."

Petrov's expression slowly transformed into one of amusement. "This does not sound like a good idea. There are many potential problems, I think."

Guy held up his hand. "Hear out our plan first. This could solve a lot of issues. And when we're done, you'll have extremely good *kompromat* on Special Agent Rinaldi. He'll have to begin feeding you names just to save his own skin."

Petrov sipped his drink and nodded. "Okay. Let me hear your idea."

Present day

Weng heard a loud crack that caused her to jump in her seat. She rose slowly, peeking around the corner at the main room of the safehouse.

Sims's body lay on the floor, blood pooled around her.

Weng felt the area around her hip where she used to carry a sidearm, back when she was stationed overseas. Nothing there now but her cellphone.

Footsteps in the other room. She had an immediate urge to pee. The long fingers of death approaching. She took out her cellphone and found the number of Colt's last call. She typed in a text. Weng had just pressed send when she saw the gunman, tattoo on his arm, raising a suppressed submachine gun. He emptied several rounds into her body as Rinaldi stood behind him, averting his eyes.

43

Colt stood on the stone promenade next to the *Villa Jovis* ruins. He and Wilcox were near the guardrails, far enough away from the others that they could speak privately, the thousand-foot cliff just beyond. A serene blue sea was sprinkled with the white wakes of multimillion-dollar yachts and the dark shore of mainland Italy on the horizon.

"What is Kim doing here?" Colt said. Two men he hoped were CIA special operations group were keeping Jeff Kim very close.

Wilcox said, "That's what we're going to find out. We picked him up from a villa on the other side of the island, on Annacapri, about an hour ago."

"How'd you know to look there?"

"The NSA picked up communication between the Trinity broker and the house he was being held at. We traced it to that location and found him. He was tied up on a bed with no one else in the house."

"Ed, the Israelis got a warning from US intelligence about a Russian operation here on Capri. They got the warning one hour before the chemical attack. Why didn't you tell me that?"

Wilcox shook his head. "Colt, I never received that information. To be honest, I've heard very little from the operations guys since I left."

"Is Rinaldi on the team?"

Wilcox saw where he was going, and his face darkened. "Yes."

"Ed, I asked Heather Weng to look into something for me. But I want to ask you. The day Kozlov died. Did you ever see him alive with your own eyes?"

Wilcox frowned. "I saw him on the surveillance cam."

"Not what I mean."

"Then no, I didn't." His voice was low.

Colt took out the burner phone the Israelis had loaned him to contact Heather Weng. He held up the screen for Wilcox to see.

Weng: Rinaldi installed Kozlov's surveillance video day of interview. No one else allowed in room by his order, according to FBI records. I just watched unedited video that was archived. They brought Kozlov's dead body into the room. The surveillance videos were faked. SOS

Colt turned to look at Wilcox, whose eyes were wide. "Oh my God . . ."

"Yeah."

"What's with the SOS?"

Colt frowned. "I don't know for sure, but I haven't heard from her since."

Wilcox cursed.

Colt turned to look at Jeff Kim, who was staring back at them from thirty feet away. "Why is Kim here, Ed? Who brought him here, and why would they have left him unattended?"

Wilcox said, "Let's go ask him."

"In a minute. I need to ask you a few more questions." Colt

felt his face growing hot. "You brought me to San Francisco to identify traitors within Pax AI, and to learn about the intentions of their inner circle. But you purposely steered me away from investigating Sheryl Hawkinson."

"Now that was different. She's a minefield for us. Her uncle is a senator on the Intel Committee. One wrong move and we'd be on the chopping block—"

"You weren't trying to protect her?"

Wilcox looked hurt. "No. Of course not."

"The Israelis told me that Sheryl Hawkinson and her brother met with someone who works as an American counterintelligence officer. They don't know which one. And that the SVR's Houston *rezident*, Petrov, was also present."

Colt watched Wilcox's reaction carefully.

Wilcox looked genuinely shocked. "When did this happen?"

"Two days before Kozlov was killed."

"Rinaldi."

Colt said, "That's my guess too. How did he do this under our noses, Ed?"

Wilcox shook his head. "We have known there was a leak somewhere in our West Coast tech spy network for a while now. The Russians were learning a lot of our operational details in the area. We had a statistician go through all our data. The numbers were eye-popping. We haven't been able to catch anyone of importance in their network for more than three years. At the same time, we were having a ton of success at identifying and curtailing Chinese operations. The numbers discrepancy was more than just an issue of the Russians using good tradecraft or having fewer spies. We determined the Russians had someone on the inside."

"And the reason you didn't tell me . . . is because you thought it could have been me?"

"We couldn't count anyone out, Colt."

"Except yourselves."

Wilcox nodded. "Me and Rinaldi. We were the two senior members of the counterintelligence team for that area."

Colt let out a huff of disbelief. "But you still used me for this Pax AI operation."

"After Kozlov's murder, we were desperate. We needed someone to see behind the curtain at Pax AI. You had your connection to Ava Klein, who was an insider. We needed to use that. I knew by the time you were in San Francisco, we could verify whether you had reported blue dye details to your Russian handler, if you had one."

"What do you mean?"

"It was a calculated risk," he said. "Rinaldi and I decided to run a blue dye experiment. We would speak to Kozlov, and then tell you what he said. But we would add a few details. Bit of intel that, if you were working with the Russians, you would have to tell them."

They both stood in silence for a moment. Colt felt betrayed, but also knew it was far less likely that Wilcox was a traitor himself.

"The smudges on the video," Colt said. "That night with Kozlov. I remember asking you about the surveillance video and saying the resolution was poor. But it was probably just an AI-created video, made to look and sound real. A deepfake." Colt looked toward Kim, standing next to the two CIA guards. "I think it's time for us to speak with him."

"We probably should have picked a better meeting spot. This is a little secluded, and the egress will suck," Wilcox replied.

Colt looked at him, confused. "Your choice, man."

Wilcox furrowed his brow. "What the hell are you talking about?"

"What?"

Wilcox's voice took on a wary tone. "You wanted to meet here . . . you texted me to meet here, at this location."

Colt looked around, realizing they were standing out in the open, with a cliff to their back. Samantha's words ran through his mind. *Not a good meeting spot if you are worried about an escape route.*

The first crack of gunfire rang out.

One of the CIA guards was flung backward and over the guard rail, a spray of crimson surrounding him as he disappeared over the cliff.

Then Colt's world erupted into a haze of blood and shattered stone.

The two-man assault team moved with swift precision. Both mercenaries had years of experience operating in Syria and parts of Africa. They were hardened ex-Spetsnaz soldiers, and had been more than happy to take what they thought would be a cushy assignment on the shores of the Mediterranean.

Their orders were clear. They were a support element for an SVR officer who needed non-SVR operators who could handle weapons. Both men knew what that meant. They were expendable, and likely to be witness to—or partake in—something criminal in nature. Both men also understood they would be well compensated for the risk. And while they no longer fought under the banner of their motherland, they did share a sense of sentimental patriotism upon learning the client's identity.

The two mercenaries were expecting to conduct surveillance operations. Possibly conduct an assault on a soft target. Maybe a kidnapping or interrogation. These were the types of jobs similar clients had hired them for before.

They had *not* expected this epic mess.

This job was a nightmare that grew progressively worse with each passing minute, every step pulling them further toward catastrophe. It would be a miracle if they weren't arrested by the Italian police, who were now crawling over most of the island.

The toxic gas at the hotel wasn't something either man was proud of. Both wanted nothing more than to get off this damn island and go underground.

But first, they needed to eliminate the Americans.

Their SVR client had just increased their payment by double if they did. He had also informed them the Americans were the only ones who could connect them to the crime scene. So this extension was about more than money. It was about self-preservation.

Just before the gunfire began, the first mercenary lay in the prone position, hidden among a line of cypress trees adjacent to the ruins of *Villa Jovis*. He was looking through his scope at the Americans in the courtyard, just where the SVR client had said they would be.

Two targets stood by themselves, talking and looking agitated. Two of the other Americans looked like they were holding a third—an Asian man—prisoner against his will.

The commencement of gunfire was earlier than expected. One of the guards took a round in the chest. He flew backward and over the rails, falling down the cliffs. The first mercenary called to his partner on his headset, trying to find out why he had begun shooting. No response. The courtyard was exploding with stone shrapnel and bullets. The Americans scattered for cover.

Then the gunfire stopped as abruptly as it had begun.

The mercenary looked through his scope again. He could see three of them hiding behind a section of the ruins. Easy targets. He thought about calling to his partner again but decided against it. The Americans might try to move in on him and his opportunity would be lost.

He lined up his reticle, controlled his breathing, and curled his pointer finger around the trigger.

"Uh-hum."

The mercenary froze at the man's voice. It sounded impossibly close. Right on top of him. If the man was armed, there was no way he could access a weapon or turn his gun quicker than the owner of the voice could fire back. If he wasn't armed, it wouldn't matter. He turned to see a curly-haired man with a dark complexion and cruel eyes aiming a suppressed pistol at the mercenary's forehead.

"*Buona notte*," said Moshe, before firing two rounds into the Russian's head.

When the gunfire stopped, Colt heard Ava calling his name. She was jogging over to him, Samantha walking quickly behind her. "Are you hurt?"

Colt shook his head. "No, but they need medical attention. We need to call an ambulance."

Samantha said, "We have help on the way."

Colt looked around him. Wilcox clutched his arm, which was bleeding from the bicep. Jeff Kim and the CIA man were looking over the guard rail. Colt did the same. The body of the other CIA man was several hundred feet below, battered and bloody.

The curly-haired Israeli man walked down from a nearby

hillside and the CIA guard went to reach for his sidearm. Samantha said, "He's on your side."

Wilcox grimaced. "What the hell just happened?"

Samantha said, "We believe the SVR sent these two contractors to kill you. We caught word of it as you were about to have your meeting."

"How did you catch word of it?" Wilcox asked.

Samantha looked insulted. "You don't need to know that. But you are welcome for saving your life."

Colt said, "Thank you."

The curly-haired man pointed up at the dusk sky and said something in Hebrew.

"Here is our ride," said Samantha. She looked at Wilcox. "We should probably discuss some things. I think it is best for you—for all of us—if we leave together now. It would be best if the Russians are not aware of the result of this attack."

Colt and Wilcox both understood. Samantha was saying they should let the Russians think they might be dead. That gave them more options, and the benefit of surprise when they made their next move. Colt could hear the low, thick echo of helicopter rotors in the distance. Looking to the south, he could now make out the aircraft silhouette approaching their cliff.

Wilcox looked at Colt and the other CIA man, who said, "I'm staying here. I need to see to him." He nodded to the corpse on the rocks below.

Samantha turned to face Wilcox and Colt. "I have a team coming here. They will dispose of the bodies and clean up most evidence. They will be gone before the police arrive."

The three CIA men traded looks. Wilcox said, "Okay." He turned to the CIA guard. "Try to keep as low a profile as possible. Don't admit you were here, if you can help it. You know what to do."

The CIA man nodded and left them.

The helicopter arrived, landing in the courtyard just next to the cliff. Ava, Colt, Samantha, Wilcox, and Jeff Kim were escorted inside the aircraft. The cabin door slid shut, and it took off, flying toward the mainland.

44

The helicopter cabin was cramped and noisy. The engine and rotors made it difficult to hear conversation. A single pilot sat up front. A medical technician in the back was patching up Wilcox's wounded arm.

Samantha handed each of them a pair of headphones and the noise died down. Through the headphone intercom system, Samantha said, "The aircrew are ours. We may speak freely. You need to read this." She handed Wilcox her phone. It was a news story. Both Wilcox's and Colt's faces were above the fold.

AMERICANS WANTED FOR QUESTIONING OVER TRINITY TERRORIST PLOT

Colt read the article over Wilcox's shoulder. It described a fire in a small shop in San Francisco. The picture showed the tech counterintelligence unit's operations center.

Two dead at the scene.

"Does it say the names?" Colt asked, his insides turning to mush.

Wilcox said, "No. But we can assume the worst."

"Rinaldi is setting us up."

Colt turned to Kim. "Jeff, it's time for you to tell us everything."

Kim looked ill, but nodded agreement. "What do you want to know?"

"Did you set up this meeting in Capri?"

Kim stared back. "No."

"Do you know who did?"

"I have a guess. Sheryl Hawkinson."

The intelligence officers in the cabin shared a look.

Samantha said, "We can discuss that later. Right now we need to know where to tell our plane to fly. We'll be at the airport in five minutes. I would like to be off the ground shortly after that."

Wilcox said, "Where do you think we should go?"

Samantha turned to Kim. "I think Sheryl Hawkinson helped arrange this so-called Trinity sale. And it allowed the Russians to eliminate all their competition for Pax AI's intellectual property. I think they had help from a member of the US government. Someone high up in their counterintelligence operation. Now, is it possible they could access your Mountain Research Facility and steal your AGI technology?"

Kim shook his head. "It would be nearly impossible."

"Why?"

"Because they would need me to approve access to the site."

"What if you were killed or kicked out of the company by your board of directors? Are you saying that no one in your company could access the technology?"

"They would need at least one lead team member to go along with it. And they would need some way to get by government security. We have multiple classified projects at the site. There are US Air Force security personnel who actively patrol our perimeter. If someone tried to access The Facility without authorization, they would stop them."

Samantha looked unconvinced. "I would assume they have a plan to gain access. Otherwise they would not have moved on you. Now please answer the question. If they got into that research facility, what could they do?"

Kim's face was solemn. "Then they could win the war."

The Israeli helicopter landed at the airport and the group shuffled into a charter jet, which began taxiing as soon as they were in their seats. The jet headed west on a journey across the Atlantic, courtesy of the Israeli government. Everyone was exhausted, pushing through days of intense stress, a gunfight, and the ominous words that Jeff Kim had left them with on the helicopter.

After takeoff the group came together in the jet's central lounge area. Colt asked Kim to expand on what he meant by *win the war.* "What is so valuable about your technology that the SVR is willing to behave this way?"

"You already know," Kim said to Colt, sounding annoyed and shaken from his recent near-death experiences. "I showed you."

Wilcox said, "For the rest of us, could you please elaborate? What is so important that people are publicly killing each other to steal it?"

Kim said, "All of us are in a technology race. And whoever wins will control everything." He looked around the aircraft cabin. "Can't you people see it? Colt, I showed you AI programs that could influence, with precision, how people *think*. My God, don't you understand the power in that? We have AI programs that can predict what people will do and say. Do you understand the implications? Do you know what a language-prediction program will become in a few more generations?"

Colt shook his head. "I don't know, what?"

"It becomes a program that can see into the *future*. It will be able to predict everything. No business can compete with that. No army can either. Therefore, businesses and armies will become *obsolete*."

Wilcox looked skeptical.

Kim said, "Our AI programs are getting better and better at writing their own code. But the real advancement is in the creativity space. Soon the bots won't need us to tell them what to think or write next. Our AGI breakthroughs, made possible from our neural AI-human augmentation interface, will allow the technology to take off like a rocket ship. Whoever is in control when that happens will control the rest of us. It boggles my mind how few people are aware of this. We are on the precipice of a massive industrial revolution. A massive societal shift. The power my company holds is greater than all of America's nuclear weapons combined."

The group looked unconvinced. Colt could understand why. Kim sounded desperate and exasperated, as if explaining things to children incapable of understanding something crucially important.

Kim said, "The history of technology parallels the history of war and empires. When one army gains technological superiority, it almost always wins. Steel blades. Gunpowder. Smart bombs. There are programs in my facility that would give a decade leap in AI superiority to whoever holds them. If this person or organization or nation state doesn't have a benevolent purpose, the results could be very bad. Imagine all the world's electronic money suddenly transferred into the account of one man. Stock markets and banks stop functioning. Imagine electricity and internet grids suddenly held captive by a far-off master. We can bargain with our ruler, but he may not want to bargain. He may just want to dictate terms. Or maybe let us starve, in mind or body. This is the kind of future that could await us if we lose the AI race." Kim sighed, his hands clasped together. "But there is an even worse scenario, if someone doesn't control the AGI explosion properly."

"How could it be worse?" Wilcox said.

Kim replied, "If we screw up the control problem, it will be worse. Think of a super-intelligent machine as you would think of a God. But creating a God, as it turns out, is a tricky and dangerous thing. Particularly when it comes to proper values programming. The famous example is Bostrom's paper-clip apocalypse. An AI program is developed with the prime directive of creating paperclips. The AI is at some point made super-intelligent. It is magnitudes smarter than any human being. Soon the world is flooded with paperclips. Even if we program it to value human life and happiness, its primary objective is to make paperclips, and that takes precedence. It begins transforming every visible surface of the earth into a paperclip factory. Clouds cover the sky from paperclip factories, which now dominate the landscape. Humans are ground up and transformed into paperclip parts or fuel for the factories. The machine, predicting that humans will have a problem with this future, creates swarms of nanobots that envelop cities and destroy every bit of non-paperclip-useful flesh, leaving a massacre in their wake. That is the danger of creating an AGI before we are ready."

Colt looked around the group. Now they were worried.

Wilcox cleared his throat. "Jeff, would you be so kind as to take us through everything you know about Sheryl Hawkinson and Trinity."

"This is off the record?" Kim straightened in his seat.

Wilcox said, "Correct. This conversation won't be used against you in court. This is for national security. We need to know what we're dealing with."

Kim said, "I'm ashamed to say I first learned of Kozlov's death three days before his supposed killing in Seattle."

The group was deathly quiet. The truth was coming out, finally.

"I received a call from our security contractors at The Facility. Kozlov's body had been found in one of our secure research labs. There was no apparent cause of death. And when we checked, the security cameras had erased everything from the previous twenty-four hours. My chief scientist, Luke Pace, discovered his body during the shift change. There were double the usual number of people inside The Facility, but none of them were made aware. The suspect list is long, however."

Wilcox said, "Does the FBI know . . .?"

Kim said, "No one knows what I'm telling you except myself, and three other members of my leadership team. Nader, our CTO, now deceased. Miller, my head of security. And Pace, who has struggled with the ethical compromise we made thereafter."

Colt's and Ava's eyes met, but neither betrayed their emotions.

Colt said, "You contacted Sheryl Hawkinson?"

Kim looked up at him. "Yes, I did."

"Why?"

"I needed a solution. I was afraid of what would happen if Kozlov's death was announced. Our next round of funding was coming up, but it wasn't approved yet, and Pax AI has huge debts coming due. The competition in our industry is monumentally fierce. We don't just compete with other companies. We compete with nation states. And the classified government programs in our Mountain Research Facility mean that when Kozlov's death was uncovered, we would be subject to intense scrutiny from the CIA and DOD. We would have been destroyed from every direction. The best-case scenario would be we were turned into a black box. A classified government-controlled company where I would be little more than a glorified researcher. The worst case would be that we would be completely shut down. Either way, Pace and I agreed we would lose the AI race if we went public with Kozlov's death on the premises. I told you the consequences of losing the AI race. To me, that wasn't acceptable."

Wilcox spoke in a quiet voice. "Who killed him? Do you have any idea?"

Kim shook his head. "No."

"Did you ever find out how he died?"

"We did not. It wasn't possible to conduct a thorough investigation, obviously."

Colt said, "Why Sheryl?"

Kim said, "I had dealings with her in the past. She has powerful connections and helped me with some very important competitor problems. She has, over the years, pressed me to let her buy a small equity stake in the company. Until now I resisted, satiating her instead by awarding her brother with one of our lucrative private security contracts. But it was her connection to less traditional resources that I knew would come in handy here."

Wilcox said, "Her brother's private security affiliates?"

Kim said, "Correct. And others."

Colt thought he already knew the answer, but he wanted Kim to say it. "Like who?"

Kim took a deep breath. "Foreign spies who work in the American tech sector. If you work there long enough, you start to see signs of it. But rumor has it that Sheryl maintains backchannel connections among them. This is one way she gains advantage over her rivals."

Wilcox said, "What did Sheryl say when you called her?"

"We made an arrangement. A gentlemen's agreement—do you still call it that when one party is female—that I would sell her a percentage of the company if she could make this problem go away."

"Did she tell you how she was going to make it go away?" Colt asked.

"No. And I told her I didn't want to know. I was truly shocked when I read about the sniper shot that killed Kozlov . . ."

"But it didn't kill him," Colt said.

"Yes, well. I was still surprised."

"And everything you told the FBI?" Wilcox said.

"I'll deny ever saying this, but I told them only what my lawyer told me I should say in order to protect my company."

Samantha said, "What about Trinity? Do you have any connection to them?"

Kim shook his head. "No. Miller showed me reports of Trinity followers attempting to penetrate our company ranks. But these were low-level programmers and engineers who had somewhat radical social media habits, that is all. We never hired any of those types. My belief is that Trinity is more of a cult or a conspiracy theory than anything. A group of people who want to unleash a superintelligence on the world and let it become our ruler? I have trouble believing that people who believe such lunacy have formed into an ultra-secretive, ultra-powerful organization."

"So was Sheryl Hawkinson the one who made it look like Trinity killed Kozlov?"

"I assume so, yes. I never had that conversation with her.

Like I said, I didn't want to know. All I know is Kozlov's body was gone from The Facility within hours of our agreement being made."

"What about the attack on your headquarters the day of your AI language demonstration? The one that killed Nader and others. Was that Sheryl's gunmen?" Wilcox asked.

"I don't think so," Kim said. "It doesn't make sense to me that she would try to harm Pax AI after she secured shares in the company."

Samantha said, "I would tend to agree."

Colt said, "Stepanova was also killed then. That one feels like the Russians were trying to take advantage of an opportunity."

Wilcox said, "What about Capri? This whole Trinity sale. Who organized that? Who took you to Capri, and why?"

Kim said, "I'm not sure. I was taken from my home shortly after speaking to you gentlemen two days ago. They blindfolded me and placed earplugs in my ears. I never saw their faces."

Wilcox narrowed his eyes. "So what you're saying is that Sheryl Hawkinson framed Trinity for committing the Kozlov killing, but he was actually already dead. He died at The Facility several days earlier. You don't know who killed him."

"Correct."

"And then, Trinity begins contacting all the intelligence agencies and business competitors who are trying to get their hands on your AI programs . . . Trinity then steals these AI programs and holds a supposed Pax AI sale in Capri."

"I never saw evidence anyone actually stole any of my data. Except for a weather-prediction algorithm."

"So the Trinity sale was a ruse?" Wilcox asked.

"Possibly." Kim shrugged.

Colt said, "When did they take the weather-prediction program?"

"My head of security discovered that breach just after Kozlov's death."

"Who took it?"

"We don't know."

"Could that have been the Hawkinsons as well? Maybe they weren't satisfied with your arrangement?"

Kim frowned. "I don't think that is likely. The actual data theft occurred before Kozlov's death. Kozlov's user history was in that file. It would be very difficult to steal that information. That is more likely the work of a state-sponsored offensive cyber unit. Miller believed Kozlov was working with the Russians, and that he took the files. His involvement with such men might also explain his death."

Colt said, "Considering that Sheryl used Trinity as the scapegoat, don't you think it's possible that she organized Capri?"

Kim didn't look convinced. "This seems unnecessarily risky. The Kozlov job was not typical for her. She must have made every effort to cover her tracks. There won't be any proof. She swims in very powerful circles. People like that don't get caught. And this Capri scenario . . . this is much too precarious for someone of her stature. Chemical weapons? I don't believe she would ever consider such a thing."

Wilcox said, "The SVR has been known to use nerve agents in some of its operations. Although this seems unusually sloppy for them."

Samantha nodded. "The Capri attack smells like SVR to me."

Wilcox turned to Kim. "Is there any chance Sheryl actually could be working with the Trinity organization? You did say she has questionable contacts."

Kim shook his head. "I am not convinced Trinity has much of an organization. I think Trinity was a convenient mirage. One of Pax AI's largest government contracts is to study disinformation on the internet. Trinity has all the hallmarks of a conspiracy theory. It functions just like an alternate-reality game, allowing its participants to follow a trail of clues, both online and in real life. People's brains are hardwired to make order out of chaos. We naturally see connections, when in fact there are none. It's satisfying to solve puzzles. It is in our nature to form groups that will defeat a common enemy. In the case of Trinity, the AI superintelligence is their savior that will solve all problems. And people like me are the enemy. But in actuality, Trinity is just nonsense. There was no group of scientists and spies from the Manhattan Project whose descendants have come together to save mankind by unleashing an AI overlord onto the world. Think of how ridiculous that sounds. *But* . . . there are many who believe it, which creates an opportunity for people like Sheryl. She took Trinity and dressed it up as the villain, because there were believable connections to Pax AI. But it does not make sense that she continued on with this tack and extended it to Capri. She wouldn't have anything to gain from giving away Pax AI's information now that I promised her equity."

"She could have gained billions of dollars if the buyers paid those ransoms."

Kim scoffed. "Still nothing compared to what Pax AI can earn, frankly."

Colt wasn't sure what to make of Jeff Kim anymore. Where he once saw an inspiring genius, he now saw a half-crazed man of dubious morality. But if the danger of his technology was real . . . then Colt could almost understand the decisions Kim made. Almost.

Samantha said, "I think the SVR is most likely responsible

for Capri. If that is so, perhaps the Hawkinsons made a deal with them? Playing both sides, so to speak?"

Wilcox said, "It's certainly possible."

Samantha said, "We should assume that our bad actors will also move on the Mountain Research Facility, doing what they can to extract its technology and destroy whatever is left."

Kim said, "Even if that is remotely possible, we can't allow it. Can't we just contact the FBI and warn them?"

Samantha shook her head, then pointed to Colt and Wilcox. "Each of your names are being put out by the FBI as persons of interest. My superiors have been contacted by American authorities. The FBI has asked anyone with information on your whereabouts to turn you in at once." She smiled. "Just so you know, we won't be doing that."

Colt looked at Wilcox. "Rinaldi."

Wilcox swore. "We have to assume he's covered all of his bases."

"What does that mean?" Colt said.

"It means we can't just call home and report in. We have to assume he's planted information that compromises us. We won't be believed anymore."

Colt said, "Why would Rinaldi do this?"

"I don't know. I've worked with him for the past year and he's never drawn any scrutiny. But then again, he was often the one leading most of the counterintelligence inquiries . . ."

Colt thought of the tales he'd heard of Robert Hanssen, the FBI agent who had worked in counterintelligence and spied for the Russians for more than twenty years. There were advantages to being inside the counterintelligence division. It made it easier to hide.

Colt said, "If you and I are unable to go through official channels, how do we stop the Russians from going into The Facility and firing up Pax AI's computers and cleaning house?"

Kim said, "They won't be able to get access."

Ava gave him a look. "Jeff, who did you say your security team was run by?"

Kim frowned, then looked nauseous. "The Hawkinsons wouldn't. She's going to get equity."

Ava said, "Maybe a piece of the pie isn't enough. Or maybe she made a deal with the Russians and the SVR double-crossed her."

Kim said, "But whoever tries to get into The Facility . . . even if they could turn the guards away, they would be caught. It would be impossible. US military security personnel are there, for crying out loud."

Colt said, "I do keep wondering about that. How would they get past security without triggering a big blowback? They can't buy off the US military guarding the perimeter. And Kim's right. If Hawkinson security folds, that would look pretty bad for them."

Ava nodded. "Seems like a flaw."

Colt scratched his head. "I think we just need to figure out their plan. They must have one."

Samantha stood. "I have the pilots taking us to a small airport outside of Vancouver. We have more than eight hours of flight time left. I suggest everyone get some food and rest. I need to contact my superiors and go over our options after we land. Mr. Wilcox, I plan on recommending that we forcibly stop whoever is trying to steal Pax AI's technology. Do you agree?"

Wilcox said, "Even during the Cold War, the Soviets never would have tried to break into an American company in the middle of broad daylight. We need to take drastic measures. Yes, I agree."

45

Ava and Samantha ate near the back of the plane. Jeff Kim sat in the middle while an Israeli guard kept an unwavering eye on him. Wilcox and Colt sat near the front, speaking softly while they ate. A satellite TV was on in front of them. Colt saw a news show and turned up the volume.

The headline read TRINITY – TERRORISTS OR FREEDOM FIGHTERS?

One of the nightly opinion show hosts was interviewing a US senator with bright gray hair.

"This organization is better organized and better funded than anybody knew," said the host. "But who is funding them? Who is funding them, Senator Hawkinson?"

Senator Hawkinson.

Colt wondered how much *he* knew about his niece's activities.

"That's a very interesting question," the senator answered. "You can bet that we'll be looking into that during my next senate intelligence briefing."

The interview ended and the host continued to discuss conspiracy theories about Trinity.

Colt turned to Wilcox. "Do you really think Rinaldi is working with Russian intelligence?"

Wilcox was chewing his food. "I deal in probabilities. To me, it's more probable that he is working with them, based on the information we have."

Colt said, "He would have to be desperate. By now, Rinaldi knows you and I weren't killed in Capri."

"That's why we're persona non grata."

"But he must know that can't last. Eventually, someone will verify enough of the facts of our story and check up on his activities."

"Correct. We just need to stay out of his way until then."

"My point is, Rinaldi is going to want to move fast. That's what I would do. My guess is they are planning to get into The Facility right now."

Colt saw Ava looking at her laptop while speaking to her aunt. She looked up, catching Colt's eye and waving him over. When he got there, Ava said, "I am still getting company-wide emails from Pax AI. This one jumped out at me. An alert from Pax AI security is telling all personnel to be prepared to evacuate the Pax AI Mountain Research Facility."

"Why?"

"Read. There is a forest fire in the vicinity. Right now, they are saying they don't know if it will be a problem, but to prepare . . ."

They gathered everyone together in the center of the plane cabin again to discuss it.

Colt said, "Jeff, who would evacuate if there was a forest fire at The Facility?"

Kim shrugged. "Everyone, I suppose. That's what the security procedure calls for."

"All of the guards?"

"Well . . . yes. But the place would be locked down. And on fire . . ."

There was a thought tugging at Colt's mind. *Fire. Quantum computer. Stability. AI. Weather prediction.*

Colt looked at Kim. "Your quantum computer's security system requires environmental stability. This includes natural disasters, such as large-scale forest fires."

Kim said, "That's right."

"Didn't you say your weather-prediction algorithm could be used to predict where a fire was going to spread?"

Kim nodded. "Yes, we think we can save thousands of lives—"

Colt held up his hand. "Not now. Hypothetically, could someone use that same AI program to plan an arson? To set a forest fire at just the right time and location that you could control where the fire was going to spread."

Kim's eyes shifted as he thought it through. "You could certainly reverse engineer the travel pattern . . . if you had enough wind and topographical data, and the forestry . . . the further out in time you get, the harder it becomes, but . . . yes. It's possible."

Colt looked up at the group. "This is them. The Facility's security systems will shut down and require evacuation for a forest fire like this. Whoever stole the weather algorithm is involved and is going to use this wildfire to leave The Facility free of security when they arrive."

Wilcox said, "But . . . won't that mean they'll have to go steal everything during a *wildfire*? I understand they can get pretty hot."

Ava nodded. "Over one thousand degrees Fahrenheit. If it's a big one, it could melt a lot of those topside structures."

Kim said, "Which they'll need to use if they're trying to send data. And for someone to successfully steal the data, they'll need an expert who knows our Facility network procedures, too."

Colt said, "We need a plan to get access to The Facility and stop them."

Ava said, "But if Sheryl's men control security, and they have access to The Facility, I don't know how we would get in. Once The Facility external doors lock, it is built like a nuclear bomb shelter. You won't be able to access it."

"Could we blow it up?" Samantha asked.

Kim looked horrified.

Colt said, "We would need some serious military hardware to do that."

Wilcox turned to Samantha. "Neither Colt nor I will be able to get the US government to move fast enough on this. Are you able to—"

Samantha shook her head. "Ava is under suspicion as a Mossad agent. And that has caused consternation between our two governments. Unfortunately, I think the best course of action is a covert operation."

Wilcox nodded. "I concur."

Colt said, "I'll go."

Samantha said, "I recommend we use a minimum number of personnel and equipment. We can support the operation. Just tell us what you need."

Colt rubbed his chin. "If the fire progresses enough that they clear out security, we'll still need a way to get into The Facility."

Moshe said, "We could blow up the doors."

Colt said, "I like where your head is at, but I worry about the negative consequences. Jeff, will you still have access to those buildings?"

Kim shook his head. "No. Security access is highly restricted and issued on a per-entry basis. It is managed from a security desk on the fourth floor of our headquarters. Even I must make an appointment through this system when I travel there."

Colt said, "So who do we have that can access the fourth floor?"

"Me and Ava," Kim said. "Unless they changed it."

Wilcox shook his head. "Kim is too well known. Probably Ava, too. And the police will be guarding it. It's a crime scene. Hell, the FBI might be in there. What are you going to do, sneak them in wearing janitor outfits?"

Colt ignored the question, saying to Kim, "If we can get access to the Pax AI fourth floor, could we then grant one of us access to The Facility?"

"Yes. As long as it is Ava or me. And as long as they haven't changed our security status."

Colt paused. "What about the weather-prediction program? Could we get access to that?"

"If I was there, maybe."

"No. I need you with me. You're going into The Facility," Colt replied.

"I might be able to write something you could use to manipulate the weather algo," Kim said.

"Can we trust you to do the right thing here?" Wilcox said to Kim.

"I swear that you can. I apologize that I was not truthful with you before. Please allow me to help fix this." Kim looked at Colt. "But I don't understand. Why do you need access to the weather program?"

Colt said, "If their operation is based on when the wildfire arrives at Pax AI, we need to know when the clock runs out."

46

Pax AI HQ
24 hours later

Special Agent Joe Smith was checking work emails on his phone inside the Pax AI lobby. The forensics folks were all over the building. San Francisco police outside had secured traffic in the street.

A steady stream of agents and tech specialists had been in and out all day, so it wasn't unusual when the revolving door spun and a pretty blonde woman wearing a suit walked in.

"Good morning," she said.

"Morning, can I help you?" Smith replied, standing up from his stool.

She said, "I'm Special Agent LaVassiere. I don't believe we've met, what office are you from?"

Smith blinked, his instincts of treating a fellow agent appropriately competing with the security procedures in place for this assignment. The female agent smiled and removed her sunglasses. Whew. She was really a knockout, Smith thought.

He cleared his throat. "I'm local. San Francisco field office. You from DC?"

"How'd you know? Any of my friends from Cyber Division here?"

"Nah, they're out for lunch. Just left."

"Shoot. I just flew in today, so I haven't connected with them yet. Beautiful weather here, by the way. Hey, do I need a badge or anything to go upstairs?"

Smith, feeling more comfortable now, said, "Only the fourth floor, but that's off limits right now. We need a company escort to go up there anyway, and they aren't coming in today."

"Oh, okay. Well, I'll stop at the third floor, I guess. That's where my boss told me to go."

"Sure thing. Let me know if you need any help."

Ava smiled, feeling his eyes on her as she walked up the stairs. Probably not out of security concern. She was out of view soon enough and made her way up to the fourth-floor security door. This was the moment of truth. Had they changed the access restrictions?

Ava scanned her fingerprints, then tapped her personal code into the display.

The double doors glowed green and slid open, and she exhaled.

One hundred and twenty miles northeast, Colt was in the back of a Cessna Caravan, a single-prop plane that had taken off from a small airport in the mountains. Jeff Kim and Moshe were also on board. All three wore parachutes, which Colt was trying not to think about. Kim looked equally nervous, his brow covered in sweat. His eyes darted from the plane's windows to Colt's face. Moshe looked amused.

The pilot craned his neck and said, "We're about five minutes out from the jump spot."

Moshe smiled. "Time to go on our hike in the woods."

47

Ava sat down at the fourth-floor computer terminal that controlled the weather-prediction AI program and checked her watch. They should be almost at the jump spot. It would take them about thirty minutes to get in position from there. She needed to accomplish her mission before then.

She typed in her username and password and removed the electronic device that stored Jeff Kim's modification code from her purse. Ironically, this never would have made its way past security if the Pax AI guard were still at the fourth-floor entrance.

She accessed the appropriate program and began making inputs. She could now see the fire's progress, and an estimate of how long before the Mountain Research Facility was consumed.

Two hours and forty minutes. She held her breath, shocked. Had she done something wrong? She reran the data, and then looked again.

No, it was right. The winds had picked up from the worst possible direction. She needed to hurry and warn her team.

But first, Ava needed to get Kim's access to The Facility installations updated with today's date.

Ava was about to head over to the security desk when she froze.

The fourth-floor sliding door whirred behind her.

"Excuse me, who are you?" said a voice.

"I don't think I can do it." Kim was breathing heavily. The wind whipped through the airplane cabin from the open jump door.

"Doesn't matter. I can," Moshe said.

Moshe was attached to him. Kim's eyes were wide.

Moshe looked back at Colt. "You ready?"

Colt gritted his teeth and nodded. Shit shit shit shit shit. He had only done this once before, and not in terrain like this. They had chosen the best landing spot they could find, a grassy hill about two miles from their destination. The plane would come in low, masked by the nearest mountain. Security guards, if any remained, would probably hear the noise but wouldn't see the chutes. But Ava had sent them the latest company email a few hours ago. The fires were getting closer, and all employees and government security personnel had been ordered to evacuate.

"Go," Moshe said, and pushed Colt out the door. Colt flexed every muscle in his body, feeling the terror of falling from one thousand feet above the ground for what seemed like an eternity, pulling his cord the moment he was away from the plane. The pine-covered mountains swirling around him. A bright blue sky. A grassy landing site below. And his stomach, somewhere back in the aircraft cabin.

The chute opened and Colt lurched to a halt, then felt the

sensation of slowly floating downward. They landed in a flat field. Moshe had quick-released himself and Kim from their gear, then came over to check on Colt.

"Are you good?"

Colt nodded. "Thanks for the push."

Moshe grunted.

Colt unstrapped from the chute and checked his watch. "We better get a move on."

Moshe looked in the direction of the gray smoke coming from the nearest mountainside. "It looks close."

Colt could smell the fire. And above them, the sky was filling with ash. "It does. Any word from Ava yet?"

Moshe looked at the phone-like device strapped to his wrist. "No. Come this way. We should run." They began jogging through the grass, Colt doing his best to keep up with the incredibly fit Mossad operative who ran like a gazelle. Jeff Kim awkwardly followed them both. They reached the nearest tree line a few minutes later and transitioned to a quick hike, the pace still brutal over uneven terrain. Thank God for the boots and gear the Israeli support team had provided in Vancouver yesterday.

After a while, Moshe came to a halt.

"Are we there?" Kim asked, out of breath. Colt was peering into the dark forest ahead of them.

Moshe said, "Almost. The fence is ahead. About fifty meters. If we keep moving, we will trip the security cameras. We need to hear from Ava first."

Colt looked behind them. The fire seemed to take up the entire skyline.

48

Ava spun around in her seat to see a man wearing a blue FBI windbreaker jacket holding a clipboard. He was frowning at her.

"I'm sorry, who are you?"

Ava stood, smiling. "Oh hi, are you with Cyber?"

The agent turned his head, like he sensed something was off. Ava knew she needed to defuse the situation.

"I'm sorry, I just flew in from DC. They told me to get started on this floor."

"No one is supposed to have access to this floor. I just got a custom key made for us and was testing it out. How did you get in?"

Ava estimated the man was ten feet away. A little over two meters tall, ninety kilos by the look of him. She began walking toward him, casually looking in her purse. "Sorry, I should have shown you my ID. Here you go." She purposely dropped the ID card on the floor, watching as the man's eyes followed it.

Ava's hand moved quickly, jabbing the pressurized injection pen into the man's neck.

Pfft.

He looked shocked as he placed his hand to his neck. Then his eyes glazed over, his knees grew weak, and soon he was on the floor in a heap.

Ava raced back to the computer, flipping her wrist to check her watch. Colt and the others would be approaching The Facility's security perimeter soon. She needed to get Jeff Kim's access approved.

And she was late.

"I'm not getting any signal," Moshe said, looking at his wrist-mounted communication device.

"Satellite?" Colt asked.

"Yes. But this model is always crashing."

Kim said, "This area is awful for communications. Has to do with the proximity to the mountains. That was one of the reasons we chose it. Lousy connections, no cell signal for miles. Makes security easier."

Moshe said, "We need to go."

Colt said, "If the security system is still up . . ."

"Then they will come," said the Israeli. "And they will find us."

The three men stopped about twenty feet ahead of a towering spiral of barbed wire. Moshe then handed the two other men barbed wire clippers.

"Let's begin." They spent the next five minutes clipping out a man-sized section of the razor wire barrier and dragging it out of the way. Moshe then reached the tall chain-link fence behind the razor wire and clipped a hole they could fit through. He said, "Wait. Ava just sent a message."

Colt halted, looking at Moshe as he read the text on his wrist. "What's the time?"

Moshe looked up. "One hour, fifty-eight minutes."

"That's a lot less time than we had expected." Colt looked back in the direction they had come from.

"Winds," Moshe said.

Far in the distance, a thirty-foot wall of bright yellow flame had erupted along the forest floor of sticks, pine straw, and bark, now visible over the closest ridgeline.

"Let's go through." Moshe was sweating as he made his way through the hole in the fence, and Colt and Kim followed.

Kim said, "Did she say anything about the security clearance?"

Moshe said, "No."

Colt looked back again through the fence. About two miles away, the forest was now alive with fire. Crackling wood and grayish smoke rose up. Ava had better succeed in her mission.

The three men began walking down the slope on the inside of the fence.

"Shh." Moshe held out his hand. "Over here. Get down."

Colt hid behind a thick evergreen on the ridge line. He looked down the path, in the direction Moshe was staring.

An all-terrain security vehicle was rumbling toward them, about two football fields away and closing fast.

"Place your hands up," yelled a heavily accented voice from nearby. Colt spun around to see two security men aiming rifles at them.

Moshe cursed and placed his hands in the air. The others followed suit.

49

Ava watched the bar slide all the way to one hundred percent and turn green. The security clearance was active. She looked at her watch again. Fifteen minutes behind schedule. She heard a groan behind her. The FBI agent was going to wake up soon. She thought about giving him another dose of the drug but decided against it. She was about to shut off the monitor when she saw a red blinking warning icon on the bottom of her screen. She clicked on it and saw The Facility's security program. Several fire alerts had illuminated. That was expected.

And a security perimeter breach warning. The status read *security team en route.*

Shit. She hoped Moshe saw them coming.

Ava was about to shut down the computer when she saw another red label on her dashboard.

Evacuation in progress. Security clearance not transmitted.

"You just approved the security clearance, why won't you send it?" she whispered to herself.

Ava looked at the digital timer on her watch, which she had synced with the fire's approach. One hour and forty-five minutes.

The man behind her groaned again. Ava looked back at him. He was still immobile, on the floor.

His newly printed keycard around his neck.

Ava ran over and snatched the keycard, then brought it back to the security station, sticking it into the card slot. Her fingers danced over the keys, transferring Jeff Kim's newly approved Facility security access to the card. After twenty excruciating seconds, the screen turned green and she pulled the card, tucking it in her purse.

She exited through the security chamber, doors sliding open and closing behind her. Then she walked down the stairs, passing the third-floor window.

Her eyes were drawn to movement outside the window. The company helicopter was sitting on the landing pad next to the building. The aircrew was washing the exterior with soap and water. As Ava raced down the stairway, she sent a text from her phone.

Need air transport now.

Moshe had left them.

He disappeared just before the private security guards arrived.

The Israeli had been about to open fire on the first vehicle when a second appeared over the ridge, changing his calculation. His split-second decision was to Colt both unexpected and disconcerting.

"You stay here. Don't tell them anything," Moshe had said, then vanished behind a set of boulders. At first, Colt had expected him to jump out to rescue them as the guards were restraining them. But when that didn't happen, Colt began to second-guess how expendable Moshe considered his new American partners to be.

"This was a bad idea," Kim whispered.

He and Colt sat in the back seat of the lead off-road security vehicle now bouncing its way toward The Facility. The forest around them was a weird reddish color, sunlight fighting its way through the smoke now covering the sky. The smell of firewood was thick in the air.

A young guard with Slavic features had his eyes on them from the passenger seat. Moments ago, the same man had placed zip ties around their wrists while two other guards held them at gunpoint. As they were being tied up, a third security vehicle appeared, this one with a man in a silver reflective fire suit. They parked their vehicle near the fence, and he began spraying a chemical fire retardant into the area.

"How much longer until the fire gets here?" Kim asked, keeping his voice to a hush.

"Not really sure. Ninety minutes, tops," said Colt.

"Was this what you expected to happen?"

The guard narrowed his eyes.

Colt said, "Which part? Ending up prisoners of a private security team, heading toward a secretive AI research facility now ostensibly hijacked by a rogue FBI agent and a Russian spymaster while our Israeli protector ditched us in the woods at the first sign of trouble?"

Kim blinked.

Colt said, "No, that was not part of my plan."

The driver shouted back at them to be quiet, his knuckles white on the steering wheel. His comrade in the passenger seat began speaking over the radio in Russian or Ukrainian, his words too fast for Colt to pick up.

Their vehicle pulled up to the security shack next to the helipad. The Facility entrance was fifty yards away, tucked into the side of the mountain. The above-ground laboratories were closer, enclosed platforms tucked in the woods under the water tower. Near the security shack, three guards headed toward them, long guns visible.

"The light above The Facility entrance is red," Kim said.

Colt looked and saw what he meant. The large, futuristic-looking metal door in the side of the mountain had a rectangular LED strip atop it, illuminating the shaded area in red underneath.

"What's that mean?" Colt asked.

"It means they've started one of the AI programs. The security protocols in place have locked all the doors."

50

Ava sat in the front seat of the Pax AI helicopter as the aircraft began spinning up. The pilot's nametag read "Carl," but that was not his name. Samantha had acquired uniforms and IDs for a Mossad pilot trained in hundreds of different types of aircraft. He had been flown in from Vancouver the previous night. The Pax AI mechanic had been paid three thousand US dollars to make sure the helicopter was fueled and ready. The Mossad pilot then locked the mechanic in the aviation shed next to the landing pad, providing him with plausible evidence he wasn't involved.

After walking out of the Pax AI headquarters and over to the helicopter landing pad next door, the Israeli pilot had given Ava a headset, helped her strap in, and politely asked her not to touch anything.

Within minutes, they were flying north over the San Francisco Bay.

Colt and Jeff Kim were made to sit on the ground outside the security shack for what seemed like an eternity. The guards were content to leave them there. They didn't even try to contact anyone. Colt figured they must have had orders not to disturb what was going on inside the buildings.

"Where the hell is Moshe?" Kim asked.

Colt didn't answer. Behind his back, he held a small rock in one hand and was trying unsuccessfully to cut the plastic zip tie binding his wrists. Even if he did manage to do that, Colt wasn't sure what his next step would be. The guards were heavily armed and looked very capable as they patrolled the area with military vigilance.

At this point, Moshe was their best hope.

The main door suddenly let out a loud beep and opened. Half a dozen men appeared and exited The Facility, including Rinaldi and three men Colt recognized from surveillance videos—the gunmen thought to have killed Kozlov. One wore the infamous wrist tattoo. Then came the SVR. Petrov and his thick henchman, the one Ava had stabbed in the neck. The last man was a surprise.

"Luke?" Kim blurted out. Luke Pace, Pax AI's chief scientist, was being prodded along at gunpoint, his face red and puffy.

Pace turned to see Kim and Colt tied up outside the security shack.

Rinaldi met Colt's eyes. Colt shook his head, disgusted. Rinaldi looked like he was about to say something, but Petrov whispered to him, and he turned and kept walking. Petrov studied the two men, gazed up at the sky, and then checked his watch.

He frowned, then turned to head into the tree line. The group split in two, with half going into one platform research lab, and the second half going into another.

The men entered the labs through the tree trunk-like doorways, which shut behind them.

"He probably wants the fires to kill us. Cleaner that way. He can deny ever being here," Colt whispered.

"Those forest fires are definitely getting closer."

"I know," Colt said. "I'm surprised they aren't hurrying more."

The sky was covered in a reddish-brown haze, the sun just barely visible. Kim had begun to cough every so often. And the campfire smell was pervasive.

Kim said, "If they are topside, it won't take them much longer now. That means Pace has helped them move whatever data they are trying to steal into one of the external lab segmented data servers. It will allow them to transmit via satellite."

"How long do we have to stop them?"

Kim shrugged. "Depends what they took."

"Assume the worst."

"Maybe thirty minutes."

"They'll beat the fires, I think," Colt said, checking his watch. "Not by much, though. Don't they have your weather-prediction program? Why weren't they in a bigger hurry? They must know they're cutting it close."

Kim shook his head. "I don't know."

They sat in silence for a while as the distant sound of the wildfire reverberated throughout the smoky sky. Branches falling. Bark burning. Large tree trunks snapping and bursting amidst raging flames.

Still far away. But getting closer.

Then a new sound.

The nearest guard heard it first, his eyes turning to the ridgeline.

Then Colt heard it too. The faint echo of helicopter rotors beating in the distance.

One of the guards began shouting, pointing toward the direction from which Colt and Kim had been captured.

"I can't see anything through the smoke," Colt said.

The security shack door slammed open. Some of the guards began yelling and running to a nearby pickup truck.

The dark silhouette of a Bell helicopter appeared through the smoke.

51

Ava's heart raced as she craned her neck to look out the right-side helicopter window. Flying just above the treetops, they were circling the Mountain Research Facility, desperately looking through the haze for somewhere to land while avoiding obstacles: mountains, the approaching wildfire, and potentially, hostile gunmen.

"Looks like some vehicles are approaching," Carl said into his headset microphone.

Ava looked in the direction he was pointing. Two small off-road security vehicles followed a large pickup truck. She recognized the Pax AI logo on the former.

The helicopter lurched left as a stream of yellow tracer rounds shot out from the bed of the pickup truck.

Ava was pressed into her seat as Gs came on the aircraft. They rolled out of the turn and dove low over a hilltop, hugging the trees even closer and speeding away from The Facility.

Ava heard Carl curse over the microphone.

"What's wrong?"

She looked at the master caution panel in the center of the

dashboard. A bunch of lights had illuminated, including one that flashed WARNING. Another said HYDRAULICS in bright red letters.

"Are we okay?"

Carl gripped the cyclic control stick like he was wrestling an alligator. He quickly flipped a metal switch and Ava felt a shudder. His face turned red, his hands jamming the controls.

"Brace for impact," he said through gritted teeth.

Ava's eyes went wide. The aircraft was getting lower and slower, headed into the short grass field inside the fence. They sliced through the top of a pine tree and the crash followed in what felt like slow motion.

The skids of the helicopter slid through the grass.

Carl used his body weight to push the left lever downward, his right hand racing to pull the engines off.

And then Ava gripped her seat as she felt them about to roll over.

Carl swore loudly, and just as the helicopter was about to tip, the momentum ceased, and it rolled hard to the other side, flattening out.

Carl said, "We should get away from here."

Ava looked out the window. The pickup truck was already in sight, racing toward them. "It may be too late."

Colt heard a crunching sound echo through the mountains from where the tracers had fired. The security men had fired a fifty-caliber machine gun mounted in the back of that pickup truck.

A few minutes later, the truck was barreling back down the mountain road. Colt continued to scrape at his zip tie, feeling the plastic fray, but not enough to make a difference. He looked at the two remaining security men near the shack. This might be his best chance to escape. Now, before the other security men returned. Colt knew he had little chance of succeeding, but he had to try. A wall of smoke and flames loomed in the distance.

The nearest security man stood over him, pointing a rifle at Colt's chest and saying something in Russian. He repeated it, louder this time, moving the rifle and his head. *Turn around.* The guard wanted to see Colt's wrists.

Colt dropped the rock. He got on one knee, making it look like he was going to turn, and then barreled toward the security guard with all his might.

It was a bad choice.

The guard easily side-stepped him, and Colt received a face full of dirt and the guard's steel-toed boot to the rib cage.

The guard was shouting now, rifle raised. Through the ringing in his ears, Colt heard Kim yelling something unintelligible.

The guard trained his weapon at Colt's head and lined up his eyes behind the sight, finger over the trigger. Colt tensed his body involuntarily.

Crack.

He shuddered at the sound of the rifle.

And then looked up.

The guard dropped to his knees, falling on his face.

Crack. Crack.

Two more guards fell to the gravel, blood spouting from their bodies.

The pickup truck was twenty-five yards away. Moshe was in the driver's seat, aiming a rifle in their direction. He got out and jogged over, weapon still held up, scanning the area for more targets. Then he removed a knife from his belt and sliced through Colt's and Kim's restraints.

Colt stood slowly, still dizzy and wheezing from the guard's beating, an odd ringing in his ears.

Kim kept yelling, "It's yellow! It's yellow!"

Moshe still held the rifle at the ready, scanning their surroundings. Ava and a man in a pilot's uniform got out of the truck behind him.

"Colt, are you all right?" Soon she was at his side, crouched over him. Her hand gripped his shoulder.

Colt nodded, finally catching his breath enough to ask, "How are you here?"

"The security clearance wouldn't transfer because of the fire. I had to bring it myself."

Colt's sense of awareness had returned now. He said, "What's yellow?"

Ava frowned. "I'm sorry?"

Kim pointed toward The Facility door. The LED rectangle above had changed colors to yellow. "It's yellow!"

"What's that mean?" Colt asked.

"The safety protocol has been triggered. The fire must have set off enough sensors. They will have a mandatory thirty-minute break from any AI programs. They won't be able to transmit."

Moshe said, "Can we go inside?"

Ava held up the security card. "Yes."

Kim nodded. "But we must hurry. They can manually override the system."

Colt said, "We need a way out of here; that fire is getting really close." He could see the flames less than a mile away now, hear the sounds of tree bursts cracking loudly in the air.

Moshe nodded toward the pickup truck. "We will take the truck. But we must ensure they do not transmit the data. Yes?" He picked up the rifle from one of the guards he had shot and tossed it to Colt. "Here. Let's go."

Kim used Ava's security card and his handprint to get them into the first treehouse-looking research lab. They entered through the trunk-like base, with Moshe leading the way, weapon pointing forward. Then they walked up a spiral staircase ending at a closed door.

Colt whispered, "What's inside?"

"Just a small lab with monitors and communications equipment. We use these labs to transmit and receive research data remotely."

"Are there any closed rooms inside?" Moshe asked.

"There's a bathroom, but otherwise it is an open floor plan," Kim said.

Moshe removed a canister from his vest and pulled the pin, nodding to Colt to open the door as he did. As Colt turned the handle and pulled the door open, Moshe threw the cannister inside the room and then slammed the door.

BOOM.

Moshe immediately opened the door and rushed inside, firing controlled bursts of gunfire from his rifle. Seconds later, smoke clearing, Colt counted three lifeless men on the ground.

"These are the guys we thought killed Kozlov," Colt said.

"Where are the others? Pace and that FBI guy?" Kim asked quietly, looking unsettled as he scanned the dead bodies.

Moshe's eyes remained emotionless. "Next building. Let's go."

Colt said, "Wait. Jeff, can you use any of the computers in here to stop them from transmitting in the other building?"

Kim made a face. "I can try."

Colt checked his watch. "That fire's going to be here soon. We need to be sure."

Kim said, "I think we should just leave. If the fire comes, they'll be dead anyway—"

"No," Moshe said. "We must be sure."

"If we don't hurry, we'll get cooked alive," Ava said. "Come on."

They raced down the stairs and were about to exit when Moshe held up his hand, halting them.

"What is it?" Ava asked. For the first time Colt saw she was carrying a pistol, holding it toward the floor as she stood.

Moshe said, "Someone just left the other building."

"Who?" Ava asked.

Colt narrowed his eyes, looking over Moshe's shoulder. "Petrov. He's going for the truck. We have to stop him. That's the only way out of here."

Moshe moved out the door and took a knee, aiming his rifle and firing. The shot echoed through the woods, and Colt saw Petrov spin around. He was looking their way, apparently uninjured.

Moshe cursed and fired again, but a hollow click announced his empty magazine. Colt took aim with his rifle as Petrov got in the truck. He fired as the truck drove away, a spiderweb crack in the rear glass forming. He continued firing as the truck sped down the road and disappeared in the smoky haze.

Moshe cursed. "No one took the keys?"

Ava said, "I did." She reached in her pocket and held out a key fob. "He must have had another set."

Kim said, "We need to take shelter."

Colt said, "Can we go in the main building and wait it out? Or will we be cooked alive?"

Kim shrugged. "I honestly don't know. Our protocol is to evacuate. But the bunker is very sturdy. There is a good chance—"

"Good enough for me," said Colt. "You go to the bunker and open the door. Stay there and make sure we can get in. We'll go into the—"

A rattle of gunfire, and then tiny explosions of dirt kicking up around them.

Moshe pulled a pistol from his waist holster and fired two shots in the direction of the gunfire, hitting the shooter center mass and knocking him backward. Then a second man fired and hit Moshe, whipping him around. His gun clattered on the stone floor outside their lab entrance. Moshe was on the ground nearby, writhing in pain, blood spurting from his leg.

52

The remaining shooter was Petrov's SVR subordinate, the man Ava had stuck in the neck in Italy. The Russian had opened the door of the second external lab and seen them firing at Petrov's escaping truck. He had opened fire from behind a pine tree, hitting Moshe in the leg and wounding Carl.

Ava was now firing back with her pistol, pinning him down. Colt raced to the left, using the thick pines for cover while trying to flank him.

More rifle fire, and then silence. Colt was breathing heavily, sweating from the run and also from the increase in air temperature as the fire drew near. He looked back toward Ava. She was in the prone position, aiming her pistol, waiting.

Colt decided to move, braving a peek around the tree, searching.

Nothing there. The door was shut. The Russian man had either gone back inside or disappeared into the woods. The fire crackled and howled in the distance, and Colt felt the intense survival instinct grow inside him.

Shit.

He rose and began walking toward the second external lab,

slowly at first, and then at a trot. In his peripheral vision, he saw Ava doing the same, Jeff Kim in tow, looking unhappy.

"He went inside," Ava said as they met at the doorway of the second lab.

Kim placed his hand on the biometric scanner and Ava held up the security card. The light went green, and she opened the door, pistol forward.

Ava fired without hesitation.

Then fired twice more at a moving target. Soon she was through the door, Colt behind her. Ava had just dropped the Russian on the spiral staircase, and he was now draped over the lower rung.

They looked up the staircase to see an open door. Pace's head was poking through the doorway, with a 9mm Beretta at his temple.

"He made me do it," Pace said. "The transmission is about to start. I didn't know."

Rinaldi called from behind the wall, "Where's Petrov?"

Colt and Ava crouched as they crept up the staircase, aiming their weapons at the doorway.

Colt fought his disgust and answered, "He's gone, Rinaldi."

"Bullshit, this was almost done. Why would he leave now? How are you even here?"

"Rinaldi, we can discuss that later. There's a forest fire about to burn us alive."

"It's still hours away . . ."

"It's minutes away. We need to get out of here and get to safety. Petrov took the only vehicle. Now can you please put the gun down and . . ."

The gun lowered from Pace's head, and Colt saw Rinaldi's

hand push the scientist forward. Pace, stunned, turned to look back and then began walking down the stairway.

Colt kept his weapon trained on the door. When Pace reached them, he whispered to Colt without looking at him, "I didn't really start the transmission. He just thinks I did."

Colt nodded and turned to Ava. "Can you take Pace back? Make sure Kim and the others are in the bunker. I'll be there soon."

Ava hesitated, but then nodded and escorted Pace down the stairs and out the door.

"Rinaldi, it's just us now," Colt said.

Rinaldi stepped into the doorway. He was looking at something in his hand. A phone. "I don't believe you about the fire."

"Believe me. I saw it with my own eyes. We need to get back to the main building. It's underground. We think it will protect us."

"We used their weather-prediction algorithm. It's live-updating based on where the fire is." He looked down at the phone. "It says the fire is still more than two hours away. We—"

"Rinaldi. Come with me." Colt held out his hand from fifteen feet down the steps. He didn't know why Rinaldi's phone said that, but it was wrong.

"I had good intentions," Rinaldi said. "A lot of what I did was good . . ."

Colt thought about Heather Weng and Jennifer Sims. "Okay."

"You're lying about the fire, aren't you?" Rinaldi suddenly looked like a completely different man. "Trying to make me leave before this data transmits?"

"It's not going to transmit."

Rinaldi narrowed his eyes. "Sure it is."

"Last chance. We need to go. I'm telling you the truth, Rinaldi."

"Hard to know anymore," Rinaldi said, sounding defeated. Then he stepped back and shut the door.

Colt took a breath and then looked at his watch. He was out of time.

Once they were inside the Mountain Research Facility's underground building, Colt and the others could hardly tell the fire was blazing outside. Air quality was controlled by an internal system that could last days if necessary. The fire only lasted an hour or so.

Kim monitored the external security cameras until the lenses melted. The last ones to go were the cameras mounted on the water tower.

Those cameras showed the forest fire in all its horrific glory. Melting the external research buildings to liquid metal and stone and ash. Decimating the forest, the off-road vehicles, and the security shack.

The electricity went out and The Facility shifted to backup power. When that happened, the water tower spewed steam as the internal tanks drained into the coolant chamber of the underground server farms. The water was used up within seconds. Shortly after, without a main power source available, the servers overheated, and years of research and AI technology were wiped out.

Kim seemed like he was in shock when they exited The Facility hours later to an otherworldly landscape. Charred earth and wisps of smoke were all that remained.

53

One week later

Colt sat in Wilcox's office in the Vancouver CIA station. The couch was worn and the room dark. Through the blinds Colt could make out some of the city's taller buildings and the water beyond.

"You feeling better?" Colt asked. Wilcox had just returned from a few days of convalescent leave.

"I am. Thanks for asking. Will you attend the funeral this weekend?"

"Weng's? Yes."

"She'll be missed."

Colt nodded. "Any word on Russian repercussions?"

"There will be payback. Both official and unofficial. Petrov will never travel again to a country with a US extradition treaty. We've kicked out half of their Houston spies. They'll return the favor, but probably let us keep a few extra to even the scorecard."

"Please don't talk like that. Like it's a sport."

Wilcox shrugged. "Whether or not I want it to be true, that's how the system works."

Colt said, "Is there any progress on Kozlov's death?"

"The FBI's official investigation will take several more months. But I spoke to the SAC and I have a guess on where it'll end up. The lead theory is that a rival intelligence service is responsible. Either Kozlov stumbled onto them, or they stumbled onto him. Whatever happened, they decided killing him was their best course of action."

"Who?"

"China, probably. Although we also know of another intelligence service that had an operative inside Pax AI. Have you heard from Ava lately?" Wilcox asked.

"Not since last week. Something tells me Israel isn't going to want her speaking to any Americans for a while."

"I would have to agree with that. There are those in Washington who are downright livid that Israel was running this operation without giving us a heads up."

"Well, they were also quite helpful."

"I tend to agree. And I've argued on their behalf. The White House is going to overlook it. They asked the prime minister to slap Mossad on the wrist."

"That's laughable, considering they work for him."

Wilcox nodded. "Yes, well."

"So now that my non-official cover days are over, I guess I'm going to have to start filing papers if I want to go on vacation overseas?"

"Yes. And since you'll be working for me, I'll be double-checking that paperwork to make sure Tel Aviv is not a destination."

Colt chuckled.

Wilcox said, "Funny thing about the Israelis, though."

"What's that?"

"They said nothing officially. Unofficially, they said all the right things. Their director of Mossad came to visit Langley and briefed the directors of the CIA and the DNI personally. And the Israeli prime minister called our president. Things are smoothed over, but . . ."

"But what?"

"Well, we asked them to confirm all the members of that operation. Unofficially."

"And?"

"They gave us a list."

"So what's unusual?"

"Ava wasn't on the list."

"What's that mean?" Colt asked.

Wilcox shrugged again. "Probably just that they plan to keep using her as a covert operative."

Colt said, "Did you speak to the FBI about Rinaldi?"

"Oh yes. I had a lot of discussions about him. Many under polygraph."

"What happened to that guy, Ed? Why would he turn?"

Wilcox shook his head. "I wish I could explain it."

"Who was his Russian handler?"

"FBI counterintelligence thinks it was Petrov."

"You don't?"

"Too little evidence. Any potential contact between Petrov and Rinaldi was very recent."

"Who do you think recruited him?"

"If I had to guess, I would say Sheryl Hawkinson."

Colt said, "And she's gotten off scot-free from all of this."

"It makes me sick to say it . . . but there is no evidence tying any of this to her or her family."

"And she still owns a piece of Pax AI."

"Yes, but that company is a shell of itself. The government

contracts were shut down, and as you know, investors have walked for the most part."

Colt frowned. "I am not so sure. I wouldn't count Jeff Kim out. There's something about that guy. I think he's playing the long game."

54

San Francisco

Jeff Kim sat in his soundproof meditation room, watching the sunset through the window. The clock reached the top of the hour, and the incoming call lit up his phone screen. On time, as usual.

"Hello," Kim answered.

"That was quite a risk you took," Liu said. The Chinese intelligence officer did not sound happy.

"A necessary risk," said Kim. He stood and walked over to his computer, making sure that the scrambling software he used to keep his communications anonymous was active.

"My superiors do not agree."

Kim said, "I'm sorry to hear that."

The line was quiet, and he imagined Liu was restraining his anger. "We saw the greatness in you before anyone else. Years ago, when no one believed in you, who helped get your seed funding? I did. I have always been your champion. For all the bravado and confidence my nation shows in its scientists and engineers . . . I know that if given the chance, you would beat us all. You will win the race. You have a once-in-a-generation intellect. And our goals are aligned."

Kim heard the talk, knowing what it was. The same sweet song as always. But he knew his Chinese support came with a price.

Liu said, "You have destroyed your research facility."

"I will rebuild it," Kim said.

"Your investors have fled."

"Not all of them," Kim said.

"You shouldn't place your trust in Sheryl Hawkinson."

"I don't trust her."

"Then why did you do what you did? In Capri?"

The words hung in the air, and Kim wondered whether Liu was fishing, or whether he really knew everything.

Kim made his choice, guessing that Liu only knew a part of it. "I used Ms. Hawkinson to flush out my spies and mislead my competition. She helped me to gather the players together. It forced everyone to show their hands."

"Including us?" Liu meant the Chinese. He was clearly angered at being lumped in with the others. "Did you order the gas attack?"

"Of course not. The Russians didn't want to share, I assume."

"You were never going to let them."

"They didn't know that."

"Don't be naïve," said Liu. "You could have been killed. Did you think about that?"

Kim said, "How did you know I arranged the Capri meeting with Sheryl? There should have been nothing leading you to us."

Liu snorted. "Pax AI? Your company was named after the Roman Peace. The assassins used the Roman emperor's palace on the cliffs of Tiberius as their ambush location. A palace that Tiberius went to because he was afraid of assassination in Rome. Poetic. But obvious, to someone who knows you well."

"I will admit to you that I suggested the meeting be held on Capri. But I didn't have anything to do with the planning or execution of violent acts committed there. Again, I would point you to the Russians."

"Or perhaps Sheryl Hawkinson?"

"I wouldn't know. We are no longer on speaking terms."

"Why?"

"Because things didn't go like she said they would."

"You should never have trusted her."

Kim closed his eyes, sighing. "She promised me a way out."

Liu said, "The Hawkinsons are untrustworthy. They care only for themselves."

"It was a lapse in judgment."

"Please don't ever have a lapse like that again. We are partners. Together, we will find a way forward."

Kim could feel the chains. Governments and investors would always try to control him. He wanted to be free. To control his own destiny. But he had to be delicate. "There will be a lot of eyes on me now. More than before. Perhaps it is best if we break off contact for a while."

"We will adapt our communication methods to avoid discovery. But the work you do continues. We will make plans to protect your future well-being."

"Thank you." Kim sighed.

"And please, if you ever make plans with Sheryl or anyone else to *find a way out*—I hope you know enough not to include us on your list of people to escape from. That could harm my ability to protect what I know is truly important to you. Your company."

"Liu."

"Please, let me speak. There are those in my organization who have less faith in you than I do. They think you would betray us and forsake all that we have invested in you. It is hard for me to stand up to people like that if you give them ammunition. They would punish you, if given the opportunity, and make our long collaboration known. If the Americans find out you are beholden to the Chinese government, everything will end. I don't want to see your precious creation taken from you, or see the Americans lock you up in a high-security prison. Please, keep me informed and be honest with me. Let's work together to make sure you are protected."

Kim clenched his jaw. "I understand. Goodbye for now."

"Goodbye, Jeff."

The call ended and Kim walked to his computer on a standing desk near the window. He entered his password and scanned his fingerprint while uttering a passphrase. The screen came to life and a box that had been fixed to the desk opened, revealing a small, thin helmet with wires leading out the back and to his computer.

Kim placed the helmet on his head and pressed down, moving it just right until the magnets took hold. Then a short electronic buzz as the electrode needles protruded downward, followed by the tingling, slightly painful feeling on his scalp.

The feeling that told him the connection was made.

Kim typed a few commands and watched the screens around his desk come to life as the AI system began connecting with the synapses in his brain. He began accessing data from his secure servers buried several levels beneath him. His own private research facility, here in his home, where no one could interfere.

He began running experiments, conducting math problems. Writing code. Solving puzzles and testing the AI system now connected to his mind. It wasn't a great system, and it was far from ready. But he was improving it every day. And it was something only he knew about. A way for him to control his technology. A way for him to expand his capability, and rise to power, without the help of others.

Moving the most valuable research data and AI programs from his secure facility and headquarters had been challenging. It had taken months to get here. Only one hiccup, when Kozlov discovered his illicit activity.

Killing Kozlov had been distasteful. As had reprogramming the weather-prediction algorithm so that the wildfire appeared to Rinaldi to be advancing much slower than it actually was. But whether eliminating a scientist for seeing something he wasn't supposed to—or leading an FBI agent to his death by showing him a false reality—Kim would do whatever it took. If he had to burn someone alive to attain his goal, so be it.

Great men had to do such things, if they wanted to change the world.

Agent of Influence
Book 2 of The Firewall Spies

In a world where artificial intelligence offers unlimited power, government spies and tech giants fight a ruthless battle to come out on top.

When an undercover Mossad agent is killed on a private Caribbean island, the death sets off alarm bells in Washington, Tel Aviv, and Moscow. The island is owned by Guy Hawkinson, the controversial CEO of Hawk Enterprises, and member of one of America's most powerful family dynasties.

Within hours of the agent's death, multiple agencies set new plans in motion.

Israeli Intelligence Officer Ava Klein is ordered to Washington, D.C. Tasked with salvaging their operation, she'll need to infiltrate the Hawkinson's inner circle.

To beat Mossad to the punch, CIA officer Colt McShane must steer clear of Ava—a former love interest—and recruit a fresh face with no former ties to the intelligence community: a young female veteran who is just finishing up a masters degree in machine learning.

And a Russian SVR chief has agreed to provide counterintelligence support for the Hawkinsons—at a price.

Each side is playing the world's most dangerous game of espionage, attempting to win the ultimate technological victory.

But with foreign agents and Hawkinson private security violently eliminating threats, any false move will be deadly.

Get your copy today at
severnriverbooks.com/series/the-firewall-spies

ABOUT THE AUTHOR

Andrew Watts graduated from the US Naval Academy in 2003 and served as a naval officer and helicopter pilot until 2013. During that time, he flew counter-narcotic missions in the Eastern Pacific and counter-piracy missions off the Horn of Africa. He was a flight instructor in Pensacola, FL, and helped to run ship and flight operations while embarked on a nuclear aircraft carrier deployed in the Middle East. Today, he lives with his family in Virginia.

Sign up for Andrew Watts' reader list at
severnriverbooks.com/authors/andrew-watts